A prolific author of more than one hundred books, **Diana Palmer** got her start as a newspaper reporter. A *New York Times* bestselling author and voted one of the top ten romance writers in America, she has a gift for telling the most sensual tales with charm and humor. Diana lives with her family in Cornelia, Georgia. Visit her website at dianapalmer.com.

Brenda Jackson is a *New York Times* bestselling author of contemporary multicultural romance novels. Her books have earned awards from *RT Book Reviews* in 2010, 2011 and 2012, and she is a recipient of an RWA Lifetime Achievement Award. There are more than three million of her books currently in print. She is the first African American author to appear on the bestseller lists for the series romance genre and has won a number of awards for her work throughout her career. Her book *A Silken Thread* was a 2012 NAACP Image Award nominee. Visit her website at brendajackson.net.

New York Times **Bestselling Author**

DIANA PALMER

TEXAS TYCOON

Previously published as *Matt Caldwell: Texas Tycoon*

**HARLEQUIN
BESTSELLING
AUTHOR
COLLECTION**

**HARLEQUIN®
BESTSELLING
AUTHOR
COLLECTION**

Recycling programs
for this product may
not exist in your area.

ISBN-13: 978-1-335-00748-3

Texas Tycoon
First published as Matt Caldwell: Texas Tycoon in 2000.
This edition published in 2023.
Copyright © 2000 by Diana Palmer

Hidden Pleasures
First published in 2010. This edition published in 2023.
Copyright © 2010 by Brenda Streater Jackson

For questions and comments about the quality of this book, please contact us at CustomerService@Harlequin.com.

Harlequin Enterprises ULC
22 Adelaide St. West, 41st Floor
Toronto, Ontario M5H 4E3, Canada
www.Harlequin.com

Printed in U.S.A.

CONTENTS

Visit her Author Profile page at Harlequin.com,
or dianapalmer.com, for more titles!

TEXAS TYCOON

Diana Palmer

To Eldarador and W.G. with love

Chapter 1

The man on the hill sat on his horse with elegance and grace, and the young woman found herself staring at him. He was obviously overseeing the roundup, which the man at her side had brought her to view. This ranch was small by Texas standards, but around Jacobsville, it was big enough to put its owner in the top ten in size.

"Dusty, isn't it?" Ed Caldwell asked with a chuckle, oblivious to the distant mounted rider, who was behind him and out of his line of sight. "I'm glad I work for the corporation and not here. I like my air cool and unpolluted."

Leslie Murry smiled. She wasn't pretty. She had a plain, rather ordinary sort of face with blond hair that had a natural wave, and gray eyes. Her one good feature besides her slender figure was a pretty bow mouth. She had a quiet, almost reclusive demeanor these days. But she hadn't always been like that. In her early teens, Leslie had been flamboyant and outgoing, a live wire of a girl whose friends had laughed at her exploits. Now, at twenty-three, she was as sedate as a matron. The change in her was shocking to people who'd once known her. She knew Ed Caldwell from college in Houston. He'd graduated in her sophomore year, and she'd quit the following semester to go to work as a paralegal for his father's law firm in Houston. Things had gotten too complicated there, and Ed had come to the rescue once again. In fact, Ed was the reason she'd just been hired as an executive assistant by the mammoth Caldwell firm. His cousin owned it.

She'd never met Mather Gilbert Caldwell, or Matt as he was known locally. People said he was a nice, easygoing man who loved an underdog. In fact, Ed said it frequently himself. They were down here for roundup so that Ed could introduce Leslie to the head of the corporation. But so far, all they'd seen was dust and cattle and hardworking cowboys.

"Wait here," Ed said. "I'm going to ride over and find Matt. Be right back." He urged his horse into a trot and held on for dear life. Leslie had to bite her lip to conceal a smile at the way he rode. It was painfully obvious that he was much more at home behind the wheel of a car. But she wouldn't have been so rude as to have mentioned it, because Ed was the only friend she had these days. He was, in fact, the only person around who knew about her past.

While she was watching him, the man on horseback on the hill behind them was watching her. She sat on a horse with style, and she had a figure that would have attracted a connoisseur of women—which the man on horseback was. Impulsively he spurred his horse into a gallop and came down the rise behind her. She didn't hear him until he reined in and the harsh sound of the horse snorting had her whirling in the saddle.

The man was wearing working clothes, like the other cowboys, but all comparisons ended there. He wasn't ragged or missing a tooth or unshaven. He was oddly intimidating, even in the way he sat the horse, with one hand on the reins and the other on his powerful denim-clad thigh.

Matt Caldwell met her gray eyes with his dark ones and noted that she wasn't the beauty he'd expected, despite her elegance of carriage and that perfect figure. "Ed brought you, I gather," he said curtly.

She'd almost guessed from his appearance that his voice would be deep and gravelly, but not that it would cut like a knife. Her hands tightened on the reins. "I... yes, he...he brought me."

The stammer was unexpected. Ed's usual sort of girl was brash and brassy, much more sophisticated than this shrinking violet here. He liked to show off Matt's ranch and impress the girls. Usually it didn't bother Matt, but he'd had a frustrating day and he was out of humor. He scowled. "Interested in cattle ranching, are you?" he drawled with ice dripping from every syllable. "We could always get you a rope and let you try your hand, if you'd like."

She felt as if every muscle in her body had gone taut. "I...came to meet Ed's cousin," she managed. "He's rich." The man's dark eyes flashed and she flushed. She couldn't believe she'd made such a remark to a stranger. "I mean," she corrected, "he owns the company where Ed works. Where I work," she added. She could have bitten her tongue for her artless mangling of a straight-forward subject, but the man rattled her.

Something kindled in the man's dark eyes under the jutting brow; something not very nice at all. He leaned forward and his eyes narrowed. "Why are you really out here with Ed?" he asked.

She swallowed. He had her hypnotized, like a cobra with a rabbit. Those eyes…those very dark, unyielding eyes…!

"It's not your business, is it?" she asked finally, furious at her lack of cohesive thought and this man's assumption that he had the right to interrogate her.

He didn't say a word. Instead, he just looked at her.

"Please," she bit off, hunching her shoulders uncomfortably. "You're making me nervous!"

"You came to meet the boss, didn't you?" he asked in a velvety smooth tone. "Didn't anyone tell you that he's no marshmallow?"

She swallowed. "They say he's a very nice, pleasant man," she returned a little belligerently. "Something I'll bet nobody in his right mind would dream of saying about you!" she added with her first burst of spirit in years.

His eyebrows lifted. "How do you know I'm not nice and pleasant?" he asked, chuckling suddenly.

"You're like a cobra," she said uneasily.

He studied her for a few seconds before he nudged his horse in the side with a huge dusty boot and eased so close to her that she actually shivered. He hadn't been impressed with the young woman who stammered and stuttered with nerves, but a spirited woman was a totally new proposition. He liked a woman who wasn't intimidated by his bad mood.

His hand went across her hip to catch the back of her saddle and he looked into her eyes from an unnervingly close distance. "If I'm a cobra, then what does that make you, cupcake?" he drawled with deliberate sensuality, so close that she caught the faint smoky scent of his breath, the hint of spicy cologne that clung to his lean, tanned face. "A soft, furry little bunny?"

She was so shaken by the proximity of him that she tried desperately to get away, pulling so hard on the reins that her mount unexpectedly reared and she went down on the ground, hard, hitting her injured left hip and her shoulder as she fell into the thick grass.

A shocked sound came from the man, who vaulted out of the saddle and was beside her as she tried to sit up. He reached for her a little roughly, shaken by her panic. Women didn't usually try to back away from him; especially ordinary ones like this. She fell far short of his usual companions.

She fought his hands, her eyes huge and overly bright, panic in the very air around her. "No…!" she cried out helplessly.

He froze in place, withdrawing his lean hand from her arm, and stared at her with scowling curiosity.

"Leslie!" came a shout from a few yards away. Ed bounced up as quickly as he could manage it without being unseated. He fumbled his way off the horse and knelt beside her, holding out his arm so that she could catch it and pull herself up.

"I'm sorry," she said, refusing to look at the man who was responsible for her tumble. "I jerked the reins. I didn't mean to."

"Are you all right?" Ed asked, concerned.

She nodded. "Sure." But she was shaking, and both men could see it.

Ed glanced over her head at the taller, darker, leaner man who stood with his horse's reins in his hand, staring at the girl.

"Uh, have you two introduced yourselves?" he asked awkwardly.

Matt was torn by conflicting emotions, the strongest of which was bridled fury at the woman's panicky attitude. She acted as if he had plans to assault her, when he'd only been trying to help her up. He was angry and it cost him his temper. "The next time you bring a certifiable lunatic to my ranch, give me some advance warning," the tall man sniped at Ed. He moved as curtly as he spoke, swinging abruptly into the saddle to glare down at them. "You'd better take her home," he told Ed. "She's a damned walking liability around animals."

"But she rides very well, usually," Ed protested. "Okay, then," he added when the other man glowered at him. He forced a smile. "I'll see you later."

The tall man jerked his hat down over his eyes, wheeled the horse without another word and rode back up on the rise where he'd been sitting earlier.

"Whew!" Ed laughed, sweeping back his light brown hair uneasily. "I haven't seen him in a mood like that for years. I can't imagine what set him off. He's usually the soul of courtesy, especially when someone's hurt."

Leslie brushed off her jeans and looked up at her

friend morosely. "He rode right up to me," she said unsteadily, "and leaned across me to talk with a hand on the saddle. I just…panicked. I'm sorry. I guess he's some sort of foreman here. I hope you don't get in trouble with your cousin because of it."

"That *was* my cousin, Leslie," he said heavily.

She stared at him vacantly. "That was Matt Caldwell?"

He nodded.

She let out a long breath. "Oh, boy. What a nice way to start a new job, by alienating the man at the head of the whole food chain."

"He doesn't know about you," he began.

Her eyes flashed. "And you're not to tell him," she returned firmly. "I mean it! I will not have my past paraded out again. I came down here to get away from reporters and movie producers, and that's what I'm going to do. I've had my hair cut, bought new clothes, gotten contact lenses. I've done everything I can think of so I won't be recognized. I'm not going to have it all dragged up again. It's been six years," she added miserably. "Why can't people just leave it alone?"

"The newsman was just following a lead," he said gently. "One of the men who attacked you was arrested for drunk driving and someone connected the name to your mother's case. His father is some high city official in Houston. It was inevitable that the press would dig up his son's involvement in your mother's case in an election year."

"Yes, I know, and that's what prompted the producer to think it would make a great TV movie of the week." She ground her teeth together. "That's just what we all need. And I thought it was all over. How silly of me," she said in a defeated tone. "I wish I were rich and famous," she added. "Then maybe I could buy myself some peace and privacy." She glanced up where the tall man sat silently watching the herding below. "I made some stupid remarks to your cousin, too, not knowing who he really was. I guess he'll be down in personnel first thing Monday to have me fired."

"Over my dead body," he said. "I may be only a lowly cousin, but I do own stock in the corporation. If he fires you, I'll fight for you."

"Would you really, for me?" she asked solemnly.

He ruffled her short blond hair. "You're my pal," he said. "I've had a pretty bad blow of my own. I don't want to get serious about anybody ever again. But I like having you around."

She smiled sadly. "I'm glad you can act that way about me. I can't really bear to be…" She swallowed. "I don't like men close to me, in any physical way. The therapist said I might be able to change that someday, with the right man. I don't know. It's been so long…"

"Don't sit and worry," he said. "Come on. I'll take you back to town and buy you a nice vanilla ice-cream cone. How's that?"

She smiled at him. "Thanks, Ed."

He shrugged. "Just another example of my sterling character." He glanced up toward the rise and away again. "He's just not himself today," he said. "Let's go."

Matt Caldwell watched his visitors bounce away on their respective horses with a resentment and fury he hadn't experienced in years. The little blond icicle had made him feel like a lecher. As if she could have appealed to him, a man who had movie stars chasing after him! He let out a rough sigh and pulled a much-used cigar from his pocket and stuck it in his teeth. He didn't light it. He was trying to give up the bad habit, but it was slow going. This cigar had been just recently the target of his secretary's newest weapon in her campaign to save him from nicotine. The end was still damp, in fact, despite the fact that he'd only arrived here from his office in town about an hour ago. He took it out of his mouth with a sigh, eyed it sadly and put it away. He'd threatened to fire her and she'd threatened to quit. She was a nice woman, married with two cute little kids. He couldn't let her leave him. Better the cigar than good help, he decided.

He let his eyes turn again toward the couple growing smaller in the distance. What an odd girlfriend Ed had latched onto this time. Of course, she'd let Ed touch her. She'd flinched away from Matt as if he was contagious. The more he thought about it, the madder he got. He turned his horse toward the bawling cattle in the distance. Working might take the edge off his temper.

Ed took Leslie to her small apartment at a local boardinghouse and left her at the front door with an apology.

"You don't think he'll fire me?" she asked in a plaintive tone.

He shook his head. "No," he assured her. "I've already told you that I won't let him. Now stop worrying. Okay?"

She managed a smile. "Thanks again, Ed."

He shrugged. "No problem. See you Monday."

She watched him get into his sports car and roar away before she went inside to her lonely room at the top corner of the house, facing the street. She'd made an enemy today, without meaning to. She hoped it wasn't going to adversely affect her life. There was no going back now.

Monday morning, Leslie was at her desk five minutes early in an attempt to make a good impression. She liked Connie and Jackie, the other two women who shared administrative duties for the vice president of marketing and research. Leslie's job was more routine. She kept up with the various shipments of cattle from one location to another, and maintained the herd records. It was exacting, but she had a head for figures and she enjoyed it.

Her immediate boss was Ed, so it was really a peachy job. They had an entire building in downtown Jacobsville, a beautiful old Victorian mansion, which Matt had painstakingly renovated to use as his corporation's headquarters. There were two floors of offices, and a canteen for coffee breaks where the kitchen and dining room once had been.

Matt wasn't in his office much of the time. He did a lot of traveling, because aside from his business interests, he sat on boards of directors of other businesses and even on the board of trustees of at least one college. He had business meetings in all sorts of places. Once he'd even gone to South America to see about investing in a growing cattle market there, but he'd come home angry and disillusioned when he saw the slash and burn method of pasture creation that had already killed a substantial portion of rain forest. He wanted no part of that, so he turned to Australia instead and bought another huge ranching tract in the Northern Territory there.

Ed told her about these fascinating exploits, and Leslie listened with her eyes wide. It was a world she'd never known. She and her mother, at the best of times, had been poor before the tragedy that separated them. Now, even with Leslie's job and the good salary she made, it still meant budgeting to the bone so that she could afford even a taxi to work and pay rent on the small apartment where she lived. There wasn't much left over for travel. She envied Matt being able to get on a plane—his own private jet, in fact—and go anywhere in the world he liked. It was a glimpse inside a world she'd never know.

"I guess he goes out a lot," she murmured once when Ed had told her that his cousin was away in New York for a cattlemen's banquet.

"With women?" Ed chuckled. "He beats them off with a stick. Matt's one of the most hunted bachelors in south Texas, but he never seems to get serious about any one woman. They're just accessories to him, pretty things to take on the town. You know," he added with a faint smile, "I don't think he really likes women very much. He was kind to a couple of local girls who needed a shoulder to cry on, but that was as far as it went, and they weren't the sort of women to chase him. He's like this because he had a rough time as a child."

"How?" she asked.

"His mother gave him away when he was six."

Her intake of breath was audible. "Why?"

"She had a new boyfriend who didn't like kids," he

said bluntly. "He wouldn't take Matt, so she gave him to my dad. He was raised with me. That's why we're so close."

"What about his father?" she asked.

"We…don't talk about his father."

"Ed!"

He grimaced. "This can't go any further," he said.

"Okay."

"We don't think his mother knew who his father was," he confided. "There were so many men in her life around that time."

"But her husband…"

"What husband?" he asked.

She averted her eyes. "Sorry. I assumed that she was married."

"Not Beth," he mused. "She didn't want ties. She didn't want Matt, but her parents had a screaming fit when she mentioned an abortion. They wanted him terribly, planned for him, made room for him in their house, took Beth and him in the minute he was born."

"But you said your father raised him."

"Matt has had a pretty bad break all around. Our grandparents were killed in a car wreck, and then just a few months later, their house burned down," he added. "There was some gossip that it was intentional to collect on insurance, but nothing was ever proven. Matt was outside with Beth, in the yard, early that morning when it happened. She'd taken him out to see the roses, a pretty strange and unusual thing for her. Lucky for Matt, though, because he'd have been in the house, and would have died. The insurance settlement was enough for Beth to treat herself to some new clothes and a car.

She left Matt with my dad and took off with the first man who came along." His eyes were full of remembered outrage on Matt's behalf. "Grandfather left a few shares of stock in a ranch to him, along with a small trust that couldn't be touched until Matt was twenty-one. That's the only thing that kept Beth from getting her hands on it. When he inherited it, he seemed to have an instinct for making money. He never looked back."

"What happened to his mother?" she asked.

"We heard that she died a few years ago. Matt never speaks of her."

"Poor little boy," she said aloud.

"Don't make that mistake," he said at once. "Matt doesn't need pity."

"I guess not. But it's a shame that he had to grow up so alone."

"You'd know about that."

She smiled sadly. "I guess so. My dad died years ago. Mama supported us the best way she could. She wasn't very intelligent, but she was pretty. She used what she had." Her eyes were briefly haunted. "I haven't gotten over what she did. Isn't it horrible, that in a few seconds you can destroy your own life and several other peoples' like that? And what was it all for? Jealousy, when there wasn't even a reason for it. He didn't care about me—he just wanted to have a good time with an innocent girl, him and his drunk friends." She shivered at the memory. "Mama thought she loved him. But that jealous rage didn't get him back. He died."

"I agree that she shouldn't have shot him, but it's hard to defend what he and his friends were doing to you at the time, Leslie."

She nodded. "I know," she said simply. "Sometimes kids get the short end of the stick, and it's up to them to do better with their future."

All the same, she wished that she'd had a normal upbringing, like so many other kids had.

After their conversation, she felt sorry for Matt Caldwell and wished that they'd started off better. She shouldn't have overreacted. But it was curious that he'd been so offensive to her, when Ed said that he was the soul of courtesy around women. Perhaps he'd just had a bad day.

Later in the week, Matt was back, and Leslie began to realize how much trouble she'd landed herself in from their first encounter.

He walked into Ed's office while Ed was out at a meeting, and the ice in his eyes didn't begin to melt as he watched Leslie typing away at the computer. She hadn't seen him, and he studied her with profound, if prejudiced, curiosity. She was thin and not much above average height, with short blond hair that curled toward her face. Nice skin, but she was much too pale. He remembered her eyes most of all, wide and full of distaste as he came close. It amazed him that there was a woman on the planet who could find his money repulsive, even if he didn't appeal to her himself. It was new and unpleasant to discover a woman who didn't want him. He'd never been repulsed by a woman in his life. It left him feeling inadequate. Worse, it brought back memories of the woman who'd rejected him, who'd given him away at the age of six because she didn't want him.

She felt his eyes on her and lifted her head. Gray eyes

widened and stared as her hands remained suspended just over the black keyboard.

He was wearing a vested gray suit. It looked very expensive, and his eyes were dark and cutting. He had a cigar in his hand, but it wasn't lit. She hoped he wasn't going to try to smoke it in the confined space, because she was allergic to tobacco smoke.

"So you're Ed's," he murmured in that deep, cutting tone.

"Ed's assistant," she agreed. "Mr. Caldwell…"

"What did you do to land the job?" he continued with a faintly mocking smile. "And how often?"

She wasn't getting what he implied. She blinked, still staring. "I beg your pardon?"

"Why did Ed bring you in here above ten other more qualified applicants?" he persisted.

"Oh, that." She hesitated. She couldn't tell him the real reason, so she told him enough of the truth to distract him. "I have the equivalent of an associate in arts degree in business and I worked as a paralegal for his father for four years in a law office," she said. "I might not have the bachelor's degree that was preferred, but I have experience. Or so Ed assured me," she added, looking worried.

"Why didn't you finish college?" he persisted.

She swallowed. "I had…some personal problems at the time."

"You still have some personal problems, Miss Murry," he replied lazily, but his eyes were cold and alert in a lean, hard face. "You can put me at the top of the list. I had other plans for the position you're holding. So you'd better be as good as Ed says you are."

"I'll give value for money, Mr. Caldwell," she assured him. "I work for my living. I don't expect free rides."

"Don't you?"

"No, I don't."

He lifted the cigar to his mouth, looked at the wet tip, sighed and slipped it back down to dangle, unlit in his fingers.

"Do you smoke?" she asked, having noted the action.

"I try to," he murmured.

Just as he spoke, a handsome woman in her forties with blond hair in a neat bun and wearing a navy-and-white suit, walked down the hall toward him.

He glared at her as she paused in the open door of Ed's office. "I need you to sign these, Mr. Caldwell. And Mr. Bailey is waiting in your office to speak to you about that committee you want him on."

"Thanks, Edna."

Edna Jones smiled. "Good day, Miss Murry. Keeping busy, are you?"

"Yes, ma'am, thank you," Leslie replied with a genuine smile.

"Don't let him light that thing," Edna continued, gesturing toward the cigar dangling in Matt's fingers. "If you need one of these—" she held up a small water pistol "—I'll see that you get one." She smiled at a fuming Matt. "You'll be glad to know that I've already passed them out to the girls in the other executive offices, Mr. Caldwell. You can count on all of us to help you quit smoking."

Matt glared at her. She chuckled like a woman twenty years younger, waved to Leslie, and stalked off back to the office. Matt actually started to make a comical lunge after her, but caught himself in time. It wouldn't do to show weakness to the enemy.

He gave Leslie a cool glance, ignoring the faint amusement in her gray eyes. With a curt nod, he followed Edna down the hall, the damp, expensive cigar still dangling from his lean fingers.

Chapter 2

From her first day on the job, Leslie was aware of Matt's dislike and disapproval of her. He piled the work on Ed, so that it would inevitably drift down to Leslie. A lot of it was really unnecessary, like having her type up old herd records from ten years ago, which had never been converted to computer files. He said it was so that he could check progress on the progeny of his earlier herd sires, but even Ed muttered when Leslie showed him what she was expected to do.

"We have secretaries to do this sort of thing," Ed grumbled as he stared at the yellowed pages on her desk. "I need you for other projects."

"Tell him," Leslie suggested.

He shook his head. "Not in the mood he's been in lately," he said with a rueful smile. "He isn't himself."

"Did you know that his secretary is armed?" she asked suddenly. "She carries a water pistol around with her."

Ed chuckled. "Matt asked her to help him stop smoking cigars. Not that he usually did it inside the building," he was quick to add. "But Mrs. Jones feels that if you can't light a cigar, you can't smoke it. She bought a water pistol for herself and armed the other secretaries, too. If Matt even lifts a cigar to his mouth in the executive offices, they shoot him."

"Dangerous ladies," she commented.

"You bet. I've seen…"

"Nothing to do?" purred a soft, deep voice from behind Ed. The piercing dark eyes didn't match the bantering tone.

"Sorry, Matt," Ed said immediately. "I was just passing the time of day with Leslie. Can I do anything for you?"

"I need an update on that lot of cattle we placed with Ballenger," he said. He stared at Leslie with narrowed eyes. "Your job, I believe?"

She swallowed and nodded, jerking her fingers on the keyboard so that she opened the wrong file and had to push the right buttons to close it again. Normally she wasn't a nervous person, but he made her ill at ease, standing over her without speaking. Ed seemed to be a little twitchy, himself, because he moved back to his own office the minute the phone rang, placing himself out of the line of fire with an apologetic look that Leslie didn't see.

"I thought you were experienced with computers,"

Matt drawled mockingly as he paused beside her to look over her shoulder.

The feel of his powerful body so close behind her made every muscle tense. Her fingers froze on the keyboard, and she was barely breathing.

With a murmured curse, Matt stepped back to the side of the desk, fighting the most intense emotions he'd ever felt. He stuck his hands deep into the pockets of his slacks and glared at her.

She relaxed, but only enough to be able to pull up the file he wanted and print it for him.

He took it out of the printer tray when it was finished and gave it a slow perusal. He muttered something, and tossed the first page down on Leslie's desk.

"Half these words are misspelled," he said curtly.

She looked at it on the computer screen and nodded. "Yes, they are, Mr. Caldwell. I'm sorry, but I didn't type it."

Of course she hadn't typed it, it was ten years old, but something inside him wanted to hold her accountable for it.

He moved away from the desk as he read the rest of the pages. "You can do this file—and the others—over," he murmured as he skimmed. "The whole damned thing's illiterate."

She knew that there were hundreds of records in this particular batch of files, and that it would take days, not minutes or hours, to complete the work. But he owned the place, so he could set the rules. She pursed her lips and glanced at him speculatively. Now that he was physically out of range, she felt safe again. "Your wish is my command, boss," she murmured dryly, surprising a quick glance from him. "Shall I just put aside all of Ed's typing and devote the next few months to this?"

Her change of attitude from nervous kid to sassy woman caught him off guard. "I didn't put a time limit on it," Matt said curtly. "I only said, do it!"

"Oh, yes, sir," she agreed at once, and smiled vacantly.

He drew in a short breath and glared down at her. "You're remarkably eager to please, Miss Murry. Or is it just because I'm the boss?"

"I always try to do what I'm asked to do, Mr. Caldwell," she assured him. "Well, almost always," she amended. "Within reason."

He moved back toward the desk. As he leaned over to put down the papers she'd printed for him, he saw her visibly tense. She was the most confounding woman he'd ever known, a total mystery.

"What would you define as 'within reason'?" he drawled, holding her eyes.

She looked hunted. Amazing, that she'd been jovial and uninhibited just seconds before. Her stiff expression made him feel oddly guilty. He turned away. "Ed! Have you got my Angus file?" he called to his cousin through the open door to Ed's private office.

Ed was off the phone and he had a file folder in his hands. "Yes, sorry. I wanted to check the latest growth figures and projected weight gain ratios. I meant to put it back on your desk and I got busy."

Matt studied the figures quietly and then nodded. "That's acceptable. The Ballenger brothers do a good job."

"They're expanding, did you know?" Ed chuckled. "Nice to see them prospering."

"Yes, it is. They've worked hard enough in their lives to warrant a little prosperity."

While he spoke, Leslie was watching him covertly. She thought about the six-year-old boy whose mother had given him away, and it wrung her heart. Her own childhood had been no picnic, but Matt's upbringing had been so much worse.

He felt those soft gray eyes on his face, and his own gaze jerked down to meet them. She flushed and looked away.

He wondered what she'd been thinking to produce such a reaction. She couldn't have possibly made it plainer that she felt no physical attraction to him, so why the wide-eyed stare? It puzzled him. So many things about her puzzled him. She was neat and attractively dressed, but those clothes would have suited a dowager far better than a young woman. While he didn't encourage short skirts and low-cut blouses, Leslie was covered from head to toe; long dress, long sleeves, high neck buttoned right up to her throat.

"Need anything else?" Ed asked abruptly, hoping to ward off more trouble.

Matt's powerful shoulders shrugged. "Not for the moment." He glanced once more at Leslie. "Don't forget those files I want updated."

After he walked out, Ed stared after him for a minute, frowning. "What files?"

She explained it to him.

"But those are outdated," Ed murmured thoughtfully. "And he never looks at them. I don't understand why he has to have them corrected at all."

She leaned forward. "Because it will irritate me and make me work harder!" she said in a stage whisper. "God forbid that I should have time to twiddle my thumbs."

His eyebrows arched. "He isn't vindictive."

"That's what you think." She picked up the file Matt had left and grimaced as she put it back in the filing cabinet. "I'll start on those when I've finished answering your mail. Do you suppose he wants me to stay over after work to do them? He'd have to pay me overtime." She grinned impishly, a reminder of the woman she'd once been. "Wouldn't that make his day?"

"Let me ask him," Ed volunteered. "Just do your usual job for now."

"Okay. Thanks, Ed."

He shrugged. "What are friends for?" he murmured with a smile.

The office was a great place to work. Leslie had a ball watching the other women in the executive offices lie in wait for Matt. His secretary caught him trying to light a cigar out on the balcony, and she let him have it from behind a potted tree with the water pistol. He laid the cigar down on Bessie David's desk and she "accidentally" dropped it into his half-full coffee cup that he'd set down next to it. He held it up, dripping, with an accusing look at Bessie.

"You told me to do it, sir," Bessie reminded him.

He dropped the sodden cigar back in the coffee and left it behind. Leslie, having seen the whole thing, ducked into the rest room to laugh. It amazed her that Matt was so easygoing and friendly to his other employees. To Leslie, he was all bristle and venom. She wondered what he'd do if she let loose with a water pistol. She chuckled, imagining herself tearing up Main Street in Jacobsville ahead of a cursing Matt Caldwell. It was such a pity that she'd changed so much. Before tragedy had touched her young life, she would have been very attracted to the tall, lean cattleman.

A few days later, he came into Ed's office dangling a cigar from his fingers. Leslie, despite her amusement at the antics of the other secretaries, didn't say a word at the sight of the unlit cigar.

"I want to see the proposal the Cattlemen's Association drafted about brucellosis testing."

She stared at him. "Sir?"

He stared back. She was getting easier on his eyes, and he didn't like his reactions to her. She was repulsed by him. He couldn't get past that because it destroyed his pride. "Ed told me he had a copy of it," he elaborated. "It came in the mail yesterday."

"Okay." She knew where the mail was kept. Ed tried to ignore it, leaving it in the In box until Leslie dumped it on his desk in front of him and refused to leave until he dealt with it. This usually happened at the end of the week, when it had piled up and overflowed into the out-box.

She rummaged through the box and produced a thick letter from the Cattlemen's Association, unopened. She carried it back through and handed it to Matt.

He'd been watching her walk with curious intensity. She was limping. He couldn't see her legs, because she was wearing loose knit slacks with a tunic that flowed to her thighs as she walked. Very obviously, she wasn't going to do anything to call attention to her figure.

"You're limping," he said. "Did you see a doctor after that fall you took at my ranch?"

"No need to," she said at once. "It was only a bruise. I'm sore, that's all."

He picked up the receiver of the phone on her desk and pressed the intercom button. "Edna," he said abruptly, "set Miss Murry up with Lou Coltrain as soon as possible. She took a spill from a horse at my place a few days ago and she's still limping. I want her x-rayed."

"No!" Leslie protested.

"Let her know when you've made the appointment. Thanks," he told his secretary and hung up. His dark eyes met Leslie's pale ones squarely. "You're going," he said flatly.

She hated doctors. Oh, how she hated them! The doctor at the emergency room in Houston, an older man retired from regular practice, had made her feel cheap and dirty as he examined her and made cold remarks about tramps who got men killed. She'd never gotten over the double trauma of her experience and that harsh lecture, despite the therapists' attempts to soften the memory.

She clenched her teeth and glared at Matt. "I said I'm not hurt!"

"You work here. I'm the boss. You get examined. Period."

She wanted to quit. She wished she could. She had no place else to go. Houston was out of the question. She was too afraid that she'd be up to her ears in reporters, despite her physical camouflage, the minute she set foot in the city.

She drew a sharp, angry breath.

Her attitude puzzled him. "Don't you want to make sure the injury won't make that limp permanent?" he asked suddenly.

She lifted her chin proudly. "Mr. Caldwell, I had an…accident…when I was seventeen and that leg suffered some bone damage." She refused to think about how it had happened. "I'll always have a slight limp, and it's not from the horse throwing me."

He didn't seem to breathe for several seconds. "All the more reason for an examination," he replied. "You like to live dangerously, I gather. You've got no business on a horse."

"Ed said the horse was gentle. It was my fault I got thrown. I jerked the reins."

His eyes narrowed. "Yes, I remember. You were trying to get away from me. Apparently you think I have something contagious."

She could see the pride in his eyes that made him resent her. "It wasn't that," she said. She averted her gaze to the wall. "It's just that I don't like to be touched."

"Ed touches you."

She didn't know how to tell him without telling him everything. She couldn't bear having him know about her sordid past. She raised turbulent gray eyes to his dark ones. "I don't like to be touched by strangers," she amended quickly. "Ed and I have known each other for years," she said finally. "It's…different with him."

His eyes narrowed. He searched over her thin face. "It must be," he said flatly.

His mocking smile touched a nerve. "You're like a steamroller, aren't you?" she asked abruptly. "You assume that because you're wealthy and powerful, there isn't a woman alive who can resist you!"

He didn't like that assumption. His eyes began to glitter. "You shouldn't listen to gossip," he said, his voice deadly quiet. "She was a spoiled little debutante who thought Daddy should be able to buy her any man she wanted. When she discovered that he couldn't, she came to work for a friend of mine and spent a couple of weeks pursuing me around Jacobsville. I went home one night and found her piled up in my bed wearing a sheet and nothing else. I threw her out, but then she told everyone that I'd assaulted her. She had a field day with me in court until my housekeeper, Tolbert, was called to tell the truth about what happened. The fact that she lost the case should tell you what the jury thought of her accusations."

"The jury?" she asked huskily. Besides his problems with his mother, she hadn't known about any incident in his past that might predispose him even further to distrusting women.

His thin lips drew up in a travesty of a smile. "She had me arrested and prosecuted for criminal assault," he returned. "I became famous locally—the one black mark in an otherwise unremarkable past. She had the misfortune to try the same trick later on an oilman up in Houston. He called me to testify in his behalf. When he won the case, he had her prosecuted for fraud and extortion, and won. She went to jail."

She felt sick. He'd had his own dealings with the press. She was sorry for him. It must have been a real ordeal after what he'd already suffered in his young life. It also explained why he wasn't married. Marriage involved trust. She doubted he was capable of it any longer. Certainly it explained the hostility he showed toward Leslie. He might think she was pretending to be repulsed by him because she was playing some deep game for profit, perhaps with some public embarrassment in mind. He might even think she was setting him up for another assault charge.

"Maybe you think that I'm like that," she said after a minute, studying him quietly. "But I'm not."

"Then why act like I'm going to attack you whenever I come within five feet of you?" he asked coldly.

She studied her fingers on the desk before her, their short fingernails neatly trimmed, with a coat of colorless sheen. Nothing flashy, she thought, and that was true of her life lately. She didn't have an answer for him.

"Is Ed your lover?" he persisted coldly.

She didn't flinch. "Ask him."

He rolled the unlit cigar in his long fingers as he watched her. "You are one enormous puzzle," he mused.

"Not really. I'm very ordinary." She looked up. "I don't like doctors, especially male ones…"

"Lou's a woman," he replied. "She and her husband are both physicians. They have a little boy."

"Oh." A woman. That would make things easier. But she didn't want to be examined. They could probably tell from X-rays how breaks occurred, and she didn't know if she could trust a local doctor not to talk about it.

"It isn't up to you," he said suddenly. "You work for me. You had an accident on my ranch." He smiled mirthlessly. "I have to cover my bets. You might decide later on to file suit for medical benefits."

She searched his eyes. She couldn't really blame him for feeling like that. "Okay," she said. "I'll let her examine me."

"No comment?"

She shrugged. "Mr. Caldwell, I work hard for my paycheck. I always have. You don't know me, so I don't blame you for expecting the worst. But I don't want a free ride through life."

One of his eyebrows jerked. "I've heard that one before."

She smiled sadly. "I suppose you have." She touched her keyboard absently. "This Dr. Coltrain, is she the company doctor?"

"Yes."

She gnawed on her lower lip. "What she finds out, it is confidential, isn't it?" she added worriedly, looking up at him.

He didn't reply for a minute. The hand dangling the cigar twirled it around. "Yes," he said. "It's confidential. You're making me curious, Miss Murry. Do you have secrets?"

"We all have secrets," she said solemnly. "Some are darker than others."

He flicked a thumbnail against the cigar. "What's yours? Did you shoot your lover?"

She didn't dare show a reaction to that. Her face felt as if it would crack if she moved.

He stuck the cigar in his pocket. "Edna will let you know when you're to go see Lou," he said abruptly, with a glance at his watch. He held up the letter. "Tell Ed I've got this. I'll talk to him about it later."

"Yes, sir."

He resisted the impulse to look back at her. The more he discovered about his newest employee, the more intrigued he became. She made him restless. He wished he knew why.

There was no way to get out of the doctor's appointment. Leslie spoke briefly with Dr. Coltrain before she was sent to the hospital for a set of X-rays. An hour later, she was back in Lou's office, watching the older woman pore somberly over the films against a lighted board on the wall.

Lou looked worried when she examined the X-ray of the leg. "There's no damage from the fall, except for some bruising," she concluded. Her dark eyes met Leslie's squarely. "These old breaks aren't consistent with a fall, however."

Leslie ground her teeth together. She didn't say anything.

Lou moved back around her desk and sat down, indicating that Leslie should sit in the chair in front of the desk after she got off the examining table.

"You don't want to talk about it," Lou said gently. "I won't press you. You do know that the bones weren't properly set at the time, don't you? The improper alignment is unfortunate, because that limp isn't going to go away. I really should send you to an orthopedic surgeon."

"You can send me," Leslie replied, "but I won't go."

Lou rested her folded hands on her desk over the

calendar blotter with its scribbled surface. "You don't know me well enough to confide in me. You'll learn, after you've been in Jacobsville a while, that I can be trusted. I don't talk about my patients to anyone, not even my husband. Matt won't hear anything from me."

Leslie remained silent. It was impossible to go over it again with a stranger. It had been hard enough to elaborate on her past to the therapist, who'd been shocked, to put it mildly.

The older woman sighed. "All right, I won't pressure you. But if you ever need anyone to talk to, I'll be here."

Leslie looked up. "Thank you," she said sincerely.

"You're not Matt's favorite person, are you?" Lou asked abruptly.

Leslie laughed without mirth. "No, I'm not. I think he'll find a way to fire me eventually. He doesn't like women much."

"Matt likes everybody as a rule," Lou said. "And he's always being pursued by women. They love him. He's kind to people he likes. He offered to marry Kitty Carson when she quit working for Dr. Drew Morris. She didn't do it, of course, she was crazy for Drew and vice versa. They're happily married now." She hesitated, but Leslie didn't speak. "He's a dish—rich, handsome, sexy, and usually the easiest man on earth to get along with."

"He's a bulldozer," Leslie said flatly. "He can't seem to talk to people unless he's standing on them." She folded her arms over her chest and looked uncomfortable.

So that's it, Lou thought, wondering if the young woman realized what her body language was giving away. Lou knew instantly that someone had caused those breaks in the younger woman's leg; very probably a man. She had reason to know.

"You don't like people to touch you," Lou said.

Leslie shifted in the chair. "No."

Lou's perceptive eyes went over the concealing garments Leslie wore, but she didn't say another word. She stood up, smiling gently. "There's no damage from the recent fall," she said gently. "But come back if the pain gets any worse."

Leslie frowned. "How did you know I was in pain?"

"Matt said you winced every time you got out of your chair."

Leslie's heart skipped. "I didn't realize he noticed."

"He's perceptive."

Lou prescribed an over-the-counter medication to take for the pain and advised her to come back if she didn't improve. Leslie agreed and went out of the office in an absentminded stupor, wondering what else Matt Caldwell had learned from her just by observation. It was a little unnerving.

When she went back to the office, it wasn't ten minutes before Matt was standing in the doorway.

"Well?" he asked.

"I'm fine," she assured him. "Just a few bruises. And believe me, I have no intention of suing you."

He didn't react visibly. "Plenty have." He was irritated. Lou wouldn't tell him anything, except that his new employee was as closemouthed as a clam. He knew that already.

"Tell Ed I'll be out of the office for a couple of days," he said.

"Yes, sir."

He gave her a last look, turned and walked back out. It wasn't until Matt was out of sight that Leslie began to relax.

Chapter 3

The nightmares came back that night. Leslie had even expected them, because of the visit to Dr. Lou Coltrain and the hospital's X-ray department. Having to wear high heeled shoes to work hadn't done her damaged leg any good, either. Along with the nightmare that left her sweating and panting, her leg was killing her. She went to the bathroom and downed two aspirin, hoping they were going to do the trick. She decided that she was going to have to give up fashion and wear flats again.

Matt noticed, of course, when he returned to the office three days later. His eyes narrowed as he watched her walk across the floor of her small office.

"Lou could give you something to take for the pain," he said abruptly.

She glanced at him as she pulled a file out of the

metal cabinet. "Yes, she could, Mr. Caldwell, but do you really want a comatose secretary in Ed's office? Painkillers put me to sleep."

"Pain makes for inefficiency."

She nodded. "I know that. I have a bottle of aspirin in my purse," she assured him. "And the pain isn't so bad that I can't remember how to spell. It's just a few bruises. They'll heal. Dr. Coltrain said so."

He stared at her through narrowed, cold eyes. "You shouldn't be limping after a week. I want you to see Lou again…"

"I've limped for six years, Mr. Caldwell," she said serenely. Her eyes kindled. "If you don't like the limp, perhaps you shouldn't stand and watch me walk."

His eyebrows arched. "Can't the doctors do anything to correct it?"

She glared at him. "I hate doctors!"

The vehemence of her statement took him aback. She meant it, too. Her face flushed, her eyes sparkled with temper. It was such a difference from her usual expression that he found himself captivated. When she was animated, she was pretty.

"They're not all bad," he replied finally.

"There's only so much you can do with a shattered bone," she said and then bit her lip. She hadn't meant to tell him that.

The question was in his eyes, on his lips, but it never made it past them. Just as he started to ask, Ed came out of his office and spotted him.

"Matt! Welcome back," he said, extending a hand. "I just had a call from Bill Payton. He wanted to know if you were coming to the banquet Saturday night. They've got a live band scheduled."

"Sure," Matt said absently. "Tell him to reserve two tickets for me. Are you going?"

"I thought I would. I'll bring Leslie along." He smiled at her. "It's the annual Jacobsville Cattlemen's Association banquet. We have speeches, but if you survive them, and the rubber chicken, you get to dance."

"Her leg isn't going to let her do much dancing," Matt said solemnly.

Ed's eyebrows lifted. "You'd be surprised," he said. "She loves Latin dances." He grinned at Leslie. "So does Matt here. You wouldn't believe what he can do with a mambo or a rhumba, to say nothing of the tango. He dated a dance instructor for several months, and he's a natural anyway."

Matt didn't reply. He was watching the play of expressions on Leslie's face and wondering about that leg. Maybe Ed knew the truth of it, and he could worm it out of him.

"You can ride in with us," Matt said absently. "I'll hire Jack Bailey's stretch limo and give your secretary a thrill."

"It'll give me a thrill, too," Ed assured him. "Thanks, Matt. I hate trying to find a parking space at the country club when there's a party."

"That makes two of us."

One of the secretaries motioned to Matt that he had a phone call. He left and Ed departed right behind him for a meeting. Leslie wondered how she was going to endure an evening of dancing without ending up close to Matt Caldwell, who already resented her standoffish attitude. It would be an ordeal, she supposed, and wondered if she could develop a convenient headache on Saturday afternoon.

Leslie only had one really nice dress that was appropriate to wear to the function at the country club. The gown was a long sheath of shimmery silver fabric, suspended from her creamy shoulders by two little spaghetti straps. With it, she wore a silver-and-rhinestone clip in her short blond hair and neat little silver slippers with only a hint of a heel.

Ed sighed at the picture she made when the limousine pulled up in front of the boardinghouse where she was staying. She met him on the porch, a small purse clenched in damp hands, all aflutter at the thought of her first evening out since she was seventeen. She was terribly nervous.

"Is the dress okay?" she asked at once.

Ed smiled, taking in her soft oval face with its faint blush of lipstick and rouge, which was the only makeup she ever wore. Her gray eyes had naturally thick black lashes, which never needed mascara.

"You look fine," he assured her.

"You're not bad in a tux yourself," she murmured with a grin.

"Don't let Matt see how nervous you are," he said as they approached the car. "Somebody phoned and set him off just as we left my house. Carolyn was almost in tears."

"Carolyn?" she asked.

"His latest trophy girlfriend," he murmured. "She's from one of the best families in Houston, staying with her aunt so she'd be on hand for tonight's festivities. She's been relentlessly pursuing Matt for months. Some of us think she's gaining ground."

"She's beautiful, I guess?" she asked.

"Absolutely. In a way, she reminds me of Franny."

Franny had been Ed's fiancée, shot to death in a foiled bank robbery about the time Leslie had been catapulted into sordid fame. It had given them something in common that drew them together as friends.

"That must be rough," Leslie said sympathetically.

He glanced at her curiously as they approached the car. "Haven't you ever been in love?"

She shrugged, tugging the small faux fur cape closer around her shoulders. "I was a late bloomer." She swallowed hard. "What happened to me turned me right off men."

"I'm not surprised."

He waited while the chauffeur, also wearing a tuxedo, opened the door of the black super-stretch limousine for them. Leslie climbed in, followed by Ed, and the door closed them in with Matt and the most beautiful blond woman Leslie had ever seen. The other woman was wearing a simple black sheath dress with a short skirt and enough diamonds to open a jewelry store. No point in asking if they were real, Leslie thought, considering the look of that dress and the very real sable coat wrapped around it.

"You remember my cousin, Ed," Matt drawled, lounging back in the leather seat across from Ed and Leslie. Small yellow lights made it possible for them to see each other in the incredibly spacious interior. "This is his secretary, Miss Murry. Carolyn Engles," he added, nodding toward the woman at his side.

Murmured acknowledgments followed his introduction. Leslie's fascinated eyes went from the bar to the phones to the individual controls on the air-conditioning and heating systems. It was like a luxury apartment on wheels, she thought, and tried not to let her amusement show.

"Haven't you ever been in a limousine before?" Matt asked with a mocking smile.

"Actually, no," she replied with deliberate courtesy. "It's quite a treat. Thank you."

He seemed disconcerted by her reply. He averted his head and studied Ed. His next words showed he'd forgotten her. "Tomorrow morning, first thing, I want you to pull back every penny of support we're giving Marcus Boles. Nobody, and I mean nobody, involves me in a shady land deal like that!"

"It amazes me that we didn't see through him from the start," Ed agreed. "The whole campaign was just a diversion, to give the real candidate someone to shoot down. He'll look like a hero, and Boles will take the fall manfully. I understand he's being handsomely paid for his disgrace. Presumably the cash is worth his reputation and social standing."

"He's got land in South America. I hear he's going over there to live. Just as well," Matt added coldly. "If he's lucky, he might make it to the airport tomorrow before I catch up with him."

The threat of violence lay over him like an invisible mantle. Leslie shivered. Of the four people in that car, she knew firsthand how vicious and brutal physical violence could be. Her memories were hazy, confused, but in the nightmares she had constantly, they were all too vivid.

"Do calm down, darling," Carolyn told Matt gently. "You're upsetting Ms. Marley."

"Murry," Ed corrected before Leslie could. "Strange, Carolyn, I don't remember your memory being so poor."

Carolyn cleared her throat. "It's a lovely night, at least," she said, changing the subject. "No rain and a beautiful moon."

"So it is," Ed drawled.

Matt gave him a cool look, which Ed met with a vacant smile. Leslie was amused by the way Ed could look so innocent. She knew him far too well to be fooled.

Matt, meanwhile, was drinking in the sight of Leslie in that formfitting dress that just matched her eyes. She had skin like marble, and he wondered if it was as soft to the touch as it seemed. She wasn't conventionally pretty, but there was a quality about her that made him weak in the knees. He was driven to protect her, without knowing why he felt that way about a stranger. It irritated him as much as the phone call he'd fielded earlier.

"Where are you from, Ms. Murbery?" Carolyn asked.

"Miss Murry," Leslie corrected, beating Ed to the punch. "I'm from a little town north of Houston."

"A true Texan," Ed agreed with a grin in her direction.

"What town?" Matt asked.

"I'm sure you won't have heard of it," Leslie said confidently. "Our only claim to fame was a radio station in a building shaped like a ten-gallon hat. Very much off the beaten path."

"Did your parents own a ranch?" he persisted.

She shook her head. "My father was a crop duster."

"A what?" Carolyn asked with a blank face.

"A pilot who sprays pesticides from the air in a small airplane," Leslie replied. "He was killed…on the job."

"Pesticides," Matt muttered darkly. "Just what the groundwater table needs to—"

"Matt, can we forget politics for just one night?" Ed asked. "I'd like to enjoy my evening."

Matt gave him a measured glare with one eye narrowed menacingly. But he relaxed all at once and leaned back in his seat, to put a lazy arm around Carolyn and let her snuggle close to him. His dark eyes seemed to mock Leslie as if comparing her revulsion to Carolyn's frank delight in his physical presence.

She let him win this round with an amused smile. Once, she might have enjoyed his presence just as much as his date was reveling in now. But she had more reason than most to fear men.

The country club, in its sprawling clubhouse on a man-made lake, was a beautiful building with graceful arches and fountains. It did Jacobsville proud. But, as Ed had intimated, there wasn't a single parking spot available. Matt had the pager number of the driver and could summon the limousine whenever it was needed. He herded his charges out of the car and into the building, where the reception committee made them welcome.

There was a live band, a very good one, playing

assorted tunes, most of which resembled bossa nova
rhythms. The only time that Leslie really felt alive was
when she could close her eyes and listen to music; any
sort of music—classical, opera, country-western or gos-
pel. Music had been her escape as a child from a world
too bitter sometimes to stomach. She couldn't play an
instrument, but she could dance. That was the one thing
she and her mother had shared, a love of dancing. In
fact, Marie had taught her every dance step she knew,
and she knew a lot. Marie had taught dancing for a year
or so and had shared her expertise with her daughter.
How ironic it was that Leslie's love of dance had been
stifled forever by the events of her seventeenth year.

"Fill a plate," Ed coaxed, motioning her to the small
china dishes on the buffet table. "You could use a little
more meat on those bird bones."

She grinned at him. "I'm not skinny."

"Yes, you are," he replied, and he wasn't kidding.
"Come on, forget your troubles and enjoy yourself. Tonight, there is no tomorrow. Eat, drink and be merry."

For tomorrow, you die, came the finish to that ad-
monishing verse, she recalled darkly. But she didn't say
it. She put some cheese straws and finger sandwiches
on a plate and opted for soda water instead of a drink.

Ed found them two chairs on the rim of the dance
floor, where they could hear the band and watch the
dancing.

The band had a lovely dark-haired singer with a
hauntingly beautiful voice. She was playing a guitar
and singing songs from the sixties, with a rhythm that
made Leslie's heart jump. The smile on her face, the

sparkle in her gray eyes as she listened to the talented performer, made her come alive.

From across the room, Matt noted the abrupt change in Leslie. She loved music. She loved dancing, too, he could tell. His strong fingers contracted around his own plate.

"Shall we sit with the Devores, darling?" Carolyn asked, indicating a well-dressed couple on the opposite side of the ballroom.

"I thought we'd stick with my cousin," he said carelessly. "He's not used to this sort of thing."

"He seems very much at home," Carolyn corrected, reluctantly following in Matt's wake. "It's his date who looks out of place. Good heavens, she's tapping her toe! How gauche!"

"Weren't you ever twenty-three?" he asked with a bite in his voice. "Or were you born so damned sophisticated that nothing touched you?"

She actually gasped. Matt had never spoken to her that way.

"Excuse me," he said gruffly, having realized his mistake. "I'm still upset by Boles."

"So...so I noticed," she stammered, and almost dropped her plate. This was a Matt Caldwell she'd never seen before. His usual smile and easygoing attitude were conspicuous for their absence tonight. Boles must really have upset him!

Matt sat down on the other side of Leslie, his eyes darkening as he saw the life abruptly drain out of her. Her body tensed. Her fingers on her plate went white.

"Here, Carolyn, trade places with me," Matt said

suddenly, and with a forced smile. "This chair's too low for me."

"I don't think mine's much higher, darling, but I'll do it," Carolyn said in a docile tone.

Leslie relaxed. She smiled shyly at the other woman and then turned her attention back to the woman on the stage.

"Isn't she marvelous?" Carolyn asked. "She's from the Yucatán."

"Not only talented, but pretty, as well," Ed agreed. "I love that beat."

"Oh, so do I," Leslie said breathlessly, nibbling a finger sandwich but with her whole attention on the band and the singer.

Matt found himself watching her, amused and touched by her uninhibited joy in the music. It had occurred to him that not much affected her in the office. Here, she was unsure of herself and nervous. Perhaps she even felt out of place. But when the band was playing and the vocalist was singing, she was a different person. He got a glimpse of the way she had been, perhaps, before whatever blows of fate had made her so uneasy around him. He was intrigued by her, and not solely because she wounded his ego. She was a complex person.

Ed noticed Matt's steady gaze on Leslie, and he wanted to drag his cousin aside and tell him the whole miserable story. Matt was curious about Leslie, and he was a bulldozer when he wanted something. He'd run roughshod right over her to get his answers, and Leslie would retreat into the shell her experiences had built around her. She was just coming into the sunlight, and here was Matt driving her back into shadow. Why couldn't Matt be content with Carolyn's adoration? Most women flocked around him; Leslie didn't. He was sure that was the main attraction she held for his cousin. But Matt, pursuing her interest, could set her back years. He had no idea what sort of damage he could do to her fragile emotions.

The singer finished her song, and the audience applauded. She introduced the members of the band and the next number, a beautiful, rhythmic feast called "Brazil." It was Leslie's very favorite piece of music, and she could dance to it, despite her leg. She longed, ached, for someone to take her on the dance floor and let her show those stiff, inhibited people how to fly to that poignant rhythm!

Watching her, Matt saw the hunger in her eyes. Ed couldn't do those steps, but he could. Without a word, he handed Carolyn his empty plate and got to his feet.

Before Leslie had a chance to hesitate or refuse outright, he pulled her gently out of her seat and onto the dance floor.

His dark eyes met her shocked pale ones as he caught her waist in one lean, strong hand and took her left hand quite reverently into his right one.

"I won't make any sudden turns," he assured her. He nodded once, curtly, to mark the rhythm.

And then he did something remarkable.

Leslie caught her breath as she recognized his ability. She forgot to be afraid of him. She forgot that she was nervous to be held by a man. She was caught up in the rhythm and the delight of having a partner who knew how to dance to perfection the intricate steps that accompanied the Latin beat.

"You're good," Matt mused, smiling with genuine pleasure as they measured their quick steps to the rhythm.

"So are you." She smiled back.

"If your leg gives you trouble, let me know and I'll get you off the floor. Okay?"

"Okay."

"Then let's go!"

He moved her across the floor with the skill of a professional dancer and she followed him with such perfection that other dancers stopped and got out of the way, moving to the sidelines to watch what had become pure entertainment.

Matt and Leslie, enjoying the music and their own interpretation of it, were blind to the other guests, to the smiling members of the band, to everything except the glittering excitement of the dance. They moved as if they were bound by invisible strings, each to the other, with perfectly matching steps.

As the music finally wound down, Matt drew her in close against his lean frame and tilted her down in an elegant, but painful, finish.

The applause was thunderous. Matt drew Leslie upright again and noticed how pale and drawn her face was.

"Too much too soon," he murmured. "Come on. Off you go."

He didn't move closer. Instead, he held out his arm and let her come to him, let her catch hold of it where the muscle was thickest. She clung with both hands, hating herself for doing something so incredibly stupid. But, oh, it had been fun! It was worth the pain.

She didn't realize she'd spoken aloud until Matt eased her down into her chair again.

"Do you have any aspirin in that tiny thing?" Matt asked, indicating the small string purse on her arm.

She grimaced.

"Of course not." He turned, scanning the audience. "Back in a jiffy."

He moved off in the general direction of the punch bowl while Ed caught Leslie's hand in his. "That was great," he enthused. "Just great! I didn't know you could dance like that."

"Neither did I," she murmured shyly.

"Quite an exhibition," Carolyn agreed coolly. "But silly to do something so obviously painful. Now Matt will spend the rest of the night blaming himself and trying to find aspirin, I suppose." She got up and marched off with her barely touched plate and Matt's empty one.

"Well, she's in a snit," Ed observed. "She can't dance like that."

"I shouldn't have done it," Leslie murmured. "But it was so much fun, Ed! I felt alive, really alive!"

"You looked it. Nice to see your eyes light up again."

She made a face at him. "I've spoiled Carolyn's evening."

"Fair trade," he murmured dryly, "she spoiled mine the minute she got into the limousine and complained that I smelled like a sweets shop."

"You smell very nice," she replied.

He smiled. "Thanks."

Matt was suddenly coming back toward them, with Lou Coltrain by the arm. It looked as if she were being forcibly escorted across the floor and Ed had to hide the grin he couldn't help.

"Well," Lou huffed, staring at Matt before she lowered her gaze to Leslie. "I thought you were dying, considering the way he appropriated me and dragged me over here!"

"I don't have any aspirin," Leslie said uneasily. "I'm sorry…"

"There's nothing to be sorry about," Lou said instantly. She patted Leslie's hand gently. "But you've had some pretty bad bruising and this isn't the sort of exercise I'd recommend. Shattered bones are never as strong, even when they're set properly—and yours were not."

Embarrassed, Leslie bit her lower lip.

"You'll be okay," Lou promised with a gentle smile. "In fact, exercise is good for the muscles that support that bone—it makes it stronger. But don't do this again for a couple of weeks, at least. Here. I always carry aspirin!"

She handed Leslie a small metal container of aspirin and Matt produced another cup of soda water and stood over her, unsmiling, while she took two of the aspirins and swallowed them.

"Thanks," she told Lou. "I really appreciate it."

"You come and see me Monday," Lou instructed, her dark eyes full of authority. "I'll write you a prescription for something that will make your life easier. Not narcotics," she added with a smile. "Anti-inflammatories. They'll make a big difference in the way you get around."

"You're a nice doctor," she told Lou solemnly.

Lou's eyes narrowed. "I gather that you've known some who weren't."

"One, at least," she said in a cold tone. She smiled at Lou. "You've changed my mind about doctors."

"That's one point for me. I'll rush right over and tell Copper," she added, smiling as she caught her red-headed husband's eyes across the room. "He'll be impressed!"

"Not much impresses the other Dr. Coltrain," Matt told her after Lou was out of earshot. "Lou did."

"Not until he knew she had a whole closetful of Lionel electric trains," Ed commented with a chuckle.

"Their son has a lot to look forward to when he grows up," Matt mused. He glanced beside Leslie. "Where's Carolyn?"

"She left in a huff," Ed said.

"I'll go find her. Sure you'll be okay?" he asked Leslie with quiet concern.

She nodded. "Thanks for the aspirin. They really help."

He nodded. His dark eyes slid over her drawn face and then away as he went in search of his date.

"I've spoiled his evening, too, I guess," she said wistfully.

"You can't take credit for that," Ed told her. "I've hardly ever seen Matt having so much fun as he was when he was dancing with you. Most of the women around here can only do a two-step. You're a miracle on the dance floor."

"I love to dance," she sighed. "I always did. Mama was so light on her feet." Her eyes twinkled with fond memories. "I used to love to watch her when I was little and she danced with Daddy. She was so pretty, so full of life." The light went out of her eyes. "She thought I'd encouraged Mike, and the others, too," she said dully. "She…shot him and the bullet went through him, into my leg…"

"So that's how your leg got in that shape."

She glanced at him, hardly aware of what she'd been saying. She nodded. "The doctor in the emergency room was sure it was all my fault. That's why my leg wasn't properly set. He removed the bullet and not much else. It wasn't until afterward that another doctor put a cast on. Later, I began to limp. But there was no money for any other doctor visits by then. Mama was in jail and I was all alone. If it hadn't been for my best friend Jessica's family, I wouldn't even have had a home. They took me in despite the gossip and I got to finish school."

"I'll never know how you managed that," Ed said. "Going to school every day with the trial making headlines week by week."

"It was tough," she agreed. "But it made me tough, too. Fire tempers steel, don't they say? I'm tempered."

"Yes, you are."

She smiled at him. "Thanks for bringing me. It was wonderful."

"Tell Matt that. It might change him."

"Oh, he's not so bad, I think," she replied. "He dances like an angel."

He stared toward the punch bowl, where Matt was glancing toward him and Leslie. The dark face was harder than stone and Ed felt a tingle of apprehension when Matt left Carolyn and started walking toward them. He didn't like that easygoing stride of Matt's. The only time Matt moved that slowly was when he was homicidally angry.

Chapter 4

Leslie knew by the look in Matt's eyes that he was furious. She thought his anger must be directed toward her, although she couldn't remember anything she'd done to deserve it. As he approached them, he had his cellular phone out and was pushing a number into it. He said something, then closed it and put it back in his pocket.

"I'm sorry, but we have to leave," he said, every syllable dripping ice. "It seems that Carolyn has developed a vicious headache."

"It's all right," Leslie said, and even smiled as relief swept over her that she hadn't put that expression on his handsome face. "I wouldn't have been able to dance again." Her eyes met Matt's shyly. "I really enjoyed it."

He didn't reply. His eyes were narrow and not very

friendly. "Ed, will you go out front and watch for the car? I've just phoned the driver."

"Sure." He hesitated noticeably for a moment before he left.

Matt stood looking down at Leslie with an intensity that made her uncomfortable. "You make yourself out to be a broken stick," he said quietly. "But you're not what you appear to be, are you? I get the feeling that you used to be quite a dancer before that leg slowed you down."

She was puzzled. "I learned how from my mother," she said honestly. "I used to dance with her."

He laughed curtly. "Pull the other one," he said. He was thinking about her pretended revulsion, the way she constantly backed off when he came near her. Then, tonight, the carefully planned capitulation. It was an old trick that had been used on him before—backing away so that he'd give chase. He was surprised that he hadn't realized it sooner. He wondered how far she'd let him go. He was going to find out.

She blinked and frowned. "I beg your pardon?" she asked, genuinely puzzled.

"Never mind," he said with a parody of a smile. "Ed should be outside with the driver by now. Shall we go?"

He reached out a lean hand and pulled her to her feet abruptly. Her face was very pale at the hint of domination not only in his eyes, but the hold he had on her. It was hard not to panic. It reminded her of another man who had used domination; only that time she had no knowledge of how to get away. Now she did. She turned her arm quickly and pushed it down against his thumb, the weakest spot in his hold, freeing herself instantly as the self-defense instructor had taught her.

Matt was surprised. "Where did you learn that? From your mother?" he drawled.

"No. From my Tae Kwon Do instructor in Houston," she returned. "Despite my bad leg, I can take care of myself."

"Oh, I'd bet on that." His dark eyes narrowed and glittered faintly. "You're not what you seem, Miss Murry. I'm going to make it my business to find out the truth about you."

She blanched. She didn't want him digging into her past. She'd run from it, hidden from it, for years. Would she have to run some more, just when she felt secure?

He saw her frightened expression and felt even more certain that he'd almost been taken for the ride of his life. Hadn't his experience with women taught him how to recognize deceit? He thought of his mother and his heart went cold. Leslie even had a look of her, with that blond hair. He took her by the upper arm and pulled her along with him, noticing that she moved uncomfortably and tugged at his hold.

"Please," she said tightly. "Slow down. It hurts."

He stopped at once, realizing that he was forcing her to a pace that made walking painful. He'd forgotten about her disability, as if it were part of her act. He let out an angry breath.

"The damaged leg is real," he said, almost to himself. "But what else is?"

She met his angry eyes. "Mr. Caldwell, whatever I am, I'm no threat to you," she said quietly. "I really don't like being touched, but I enjoyed dancing with you. I haven't danced…in years."

He studied her wan face, oblivious to the music of

the band, and the murmur of movement around them. "Sometimes," he murmured, "you seem very familiar to me, as if I've seen you before." He was thinking about his mother, and how she'd betrayed him and hurt him all those years ago.

Leslie didn't know that, though. Her teeth clenched as she tried not to let her fear show. Probably he had seen her before, just like the whole country had, her face in the tabloid papers as it had appeared the night they took her out of her mother's bloodstained apartment on a stretcher, her leg bleeding profusely, her sobs audible. But then her hair had been dark, and she'd been wearing glasses. Could he really recognize her?

"Maybe I just have that kind of face." She grimaced and shifted her weight. "Could we go, please?" she asked on a moan. "My leg really is killing me."

He didn't move for an instant. Then he bent suddenly and lifted her in his strong arms and carried her through the amused crowd toward the door.

"Mr...Mr. Caldwell," she protested, stiffening. She'd never been picked up and carried by a man in her entire life. She studied his strong profile with fascinated curiosity, too entranced to feel the usual fear. Having danced with him, she was able to accept his physical closeness. He felt very strong and he smelled of some spicy, very exotic cologne. She had the oddest urge to touch his wavy black hair just over his broad forehead, where it looked thickest.

He glanced down into her fascinated eyes and one of his dark eyebrows rose in a silent question.

"You're...very strong, aren't you?" she asked hesitantly.

The tone of her voice touched something deep inside him. He searched her eyes and the tension was suddenly thick as his gaze fell to her soft bow of a mouth and lingered there, even as his pace slowed slightly.

Her hand clutched the lapel of his tuxedo as her own gaze fell to his mouth. She'd never wanted to be kissed like this before. When she'd been kissed during that horrible encounter, it had been repulsive—a wet, invading, lustful kiss that made her want to throw up.

It wouldn't be like that with Matt. She knew instinctively that he was well versed in the art of lovemaking, and that he would be gentle with a woman. His mouth was sensual, wide and chiseled. Her own mouth tingled as she wondered visibly what it would feel like to let him kiss her.

He read that curiosity with pinpoint accuracy and his sharp intake of breath brought her curious eyes up to meet his.

"Careful," he cautioned, his voice deeper than usual. "Curiosity killed the cat."

Her eyes asked a question she couldn't form with her lips.

"You fell off a horse avoiding any contact with me," he reminded her quietly. "Now you look as if you'd do anything to have my mouth on yours. Why?"

"I don't know," she whispered, her hand contracting on the lapel of his jacket. "I like being close to you," she confessed, surprised. "It's funny. I haven't wanted to be close to a man like this before."

He stopped dead in his tracks. There was a faint vibration in the hard arms holding her. His eyes lanced into hers. His breath became audible. The arm under her back contracted, bringing her breasts hard against him as he stood there on the steps of the building, totally oblivious to everything except the ache that was consuming him.

Leslie's body shivered with its first real taste of desire. She laughed shakily at the new and wonderful sensations she was feeling. Her breasts felt suddenly heavy. They ached.

"Is this what it feels like?" she murmured.

"What?" he asked huskily.

She met his gaze. "Desire."

He actually shuddered. His arms contracted. His lips parted as he looked at her mouth and knew that he couldn't help taking it. She smelled of roses, like the tiny pink fairy roses that grew in masses around the front door of his ranch house. She wanted him. His head began to spin. He bent his dark head and bit at her lower lip with a sensuous whisper.

"Open your mouth, Leslie," he whispered, and his hard mouth suddenly went down insistently on hers.

But before he could even savor the feel of her soft lips, the sound of high heels approaching jerked his head up. Leslie was trembling against him, shocked and a little frightened, and completely entranced by the unexpected contact with his beautiful mouth.

Matt's dark eyes blazed down into hers. "No more games. I'm taking you home with me," he said huskily.

She started to speak, to protest, when Carolyn came striding angrily out the door.

"Does she have to be carried?" the older woman asked Matt with dripping sarcasm. "Funny, she was dancing eagerly enough a few minutes ago!"

"She has a bad leg," Matt said, regaining his control. "Here's the car."

The limousine drew up at the curb and Ed got out, frowning when he saw Leslie in Matt's arms.

"Are you all right?" he asked as he approached them.

"She shouldn't have danced," Matt said stiffly as he moved the rest of the way down the steps to deposit her inside the car on the leather-covered seat. "She made her leg worse."

Carolyn was livid. She slid in and moved to the other side of Leslie with a gaze that could have curdled milk. "One dance and we have to leave," she said furiously.

Matt moved into the car beside Ed and slammed the door. "I thought we were leaving because you had a headache," he snapped at Carolyn, his usual control quite evidently gone. He was in a foul mood. Desire was frustrating him. He glanced at Leslie and thought how good she was at manipulation. She had him almost doubled over with need. She was probably laughing her head off silently. Well, she was going to pay for that.

Carolyn, watching his eyes on Leslie, made an angry sound in her throat and stared out the window.

To Ed's surprise and dismay, they dropped him off at his home first. He tried to argue, but Matt wasn't having that. He told Ed he'd see him at the office Monday and closed the door on his protests.

Carolyn was deposited next. Matt walked her to her door, but he moved back before she could claim a good-night kiss. The way she slammed her door was audible even inside the closed limousine.

Leslie bit her lower lip as Matt climbed back into the car with her. In the lighted interior, she could see the expression on his face as he studied her slender body covetously.

"This isn't the way to my apartment," she ventured nervously a few minutes later, hoping he hadn't meant what he said just before they got into the limousine.

"No, it isn't, is it?" he replied dangerously.

Even as he spoke, the limousine pulled up at the door to his ranch house. He helped Leslie out and spoke briefly to the driver before dismissing him. Then he swung a frightened Leslie up into his arms and carried her toward the front door.

"Mr. Caldwell..." she began.

"Matt," he corrected, not looking at her.

"I want to go home," she tried again.

"You will. Eventually."

"But you sent the car away."

"I have six cars," he informed her as he shifted his light burden to produce his keys from the pocket of his slacks and insert one in the lock. The door swung open. "I'll drive you home when the time comes."

"I'm very tired." Her voice sounded breathless and high-pitched.

"Then I know just the place for you." He closed the door and carried her down a long, dimly lit hallway to a room near the back of the house. He leaned down to open the door and once they were through it, he kicked it shut with his foot.

Seconds later, Leslie was in the middle of a huge king-size bed, sprawled on the beige-brown-and-black comforter that covered it and Matt was removing her wrap.

It went flying onto a chair, along with his jacket and

tie. He unbuttoned his shirt and slid down onto the bed beside her, his hands on either side of her face as he poised just above her.

The position brought back terrible, nightmarish memories. She stiffened all over. Her face went pale. Her eyes dilated so much that the gray of them was eclipsed by black.

Matt ignored her expression. He looked down the length of her in the clinging silver dress, his eyes lingering on the thrust of her small breasts. One of his big hands came up to trace around the prominent hard nipple that pointed through the fabric.

The touch shocked Leslie, because she didn't find it revolting or unpleasant. She shivered a little. Her eyes, wide and frightened, and a little curious, met his.

His strong fingers brushed lazily over the nipple and around the contours of her breast as if the feel of her fascinated him.

"Do you mind?" he asked with faint insolence, and slipped one of the spaghetti straps down her arm, moving her just enough that he could pull the bodice away from her perfect little breast.

Leslie couldn't believe what was happening. Men were repulsive to her. She hated the thought of intimacy. But Matt Caldwell was looking at her bare breast and she was letting him, with no thought of resistance. She hadn't even had anything to drink.

He searched her face as his warm fingers traced her breast. He read the pleasure she was feeling in her soft eyes. "You feel like sun-touched marble to my hand," he said quietly. "Your skin is beautiful." His gaze traveled down her body. "Your breasts are perfect."

She was shivering again. Her hands clenched beside her head as she watched him touch her, like an observer, like in a dream.

He smiled with faint mockery when he saw her expression. "Haven't you done this before?"

"No," she said, and she actually sounded serious.

He discounted that at once. She was far too calm and submissive for an inexperienced woman.

One dark eyebrow lifted. "Twenty-three and still a virgin?"

How had he known that? "Well…yes." Technically she certainly was. Emotionally, too. Despite what had been done to her, she'd been spared rape, if only by seconds, when her mother came home unexpectedly.

Matt was absorbed in touching her body. His forefinger traced around the hard nipple, and he watched her body lift to follow it when he lifted his hand.

"Do you like it?" he asked softly.

She was watching him intensely. "Yes." She sounded as if it surprised her that she liked what he was doing.

With easy self-confidence, he pulled her up just a little and pushed the other strap down her arm, baring her completely to his eyes. She was perfect, like a warm statue in beautifully smooth marble. He'd never seen breasts like hers. She aroused him profoundly.

He held her by the upper part of her rib cage, his thumbs edging onto her breasts to caress them tenderly while he watched the expressions chase each other across her face. The silence in the bedroom was broken only by the sound of cars far in the distance and the sound of some mournful night bird outside the window. Closer was the rasp of her own breathing and her heart beating in her ears. She should be fighting for her life, screaming, running, escaping. She'd avoided this sort of situation successfully for six years. Why didn't she want to avoid Matt's hands?

Matt touched her almost reverently, his eyes on her hard nipples. With a faint groan, he bent his dark head and his mouth touched the soft curve of her breast.

She gasped and stiffened. His head lifted immediately. He looked at her and realized that she wasn't trying to get away. Her eyes were full of shocked pleasure and curiosity.

"Another first?" he asked with faint arrogance and a calculating smile that didn't really register in her whirling mind.

She nodded, swallowing. Her body, as if it was ignoring her brain, moved sensuously on the bed. She'd never dreamed that she could let a man touch her like this, that she could enjoy letting him touch her, after her one horrible experience with intimacy.

He put his mouth over her nipple and suckled her so insistently that she cried out, drowning in a veritable flood of shocked pleasure.

The little cry aroused Matt unexpectedly, and he was rougher with her than he meant to be, his mouth suddenly demanding on her soft flesh. He tasted her hungrily for several long seconds until he forced his mind to remember why he shouldn't let himself go in headfirst. He wanted her almost beyond bearing, but he wasn't going to let her make a fool of him.

He lifted his head and studied her flushed face clinically. She was enjoying it, but she needn't think he was going to let her take possession of him with that pretty body. He knew now that he could have her. She was willing to give in. For a price, he added.

She opened her eyes and lay there watching him with wide, soft, curious eyes. She thought she had him in her pocket, he mused. But she was all too acquiescent. That, he thought amusedly, was a gross miscalculation on her part. It was her nervous retreat that challenged him, not the sort of easy conquest with which he was already too familiar.

Abruptly he sat up, pulling her with him, and slid the straps of her evening dress back up onto her shoulders. She watched him silently, still shocked by his ardor and puzzled at her unexpected response to it.

He got to his feet and rebuttoned his shirt, reaching for his snap-on tie and then his jacket. He studied her there, sitting dazed on the edge of his bed, and his dark eyes narrowed. He smiled, but it wasn't a pleasant smile.

"You're not bad," he murmured lazily. "But the fascinated virgin bit turns me right off. I like experience."

She blinked. She was still trying to make her mind work again.

"I assume that your other would-be lovers liked that wide-eyed, first-time look?"

Other lovers. Had he guessed about her past? Her eyes registered the fear.

He saw it. He was vaguely sorry that she wasn't what she pretended to be. He was all but jaded when it came to pursuing women. He hated the coy behavior, the teasing, the manipulation that eventually ended in his bedroom. He was considered a great catch by single women, rich and handsome and experienced in sensual techniques. But he always made his position clear at the outset. He didn't want marriage. That didn't really matter to most of the women in his life. A diamond here, an exotic vacation there, and they seemed satisfied for as long as it lasted. Not that there were many affairs. He was tired of the game. In fact, he'd never been more tired of it than he was right now. His whole expression was one of disgust.

Leslie saw it in his eyes and wished she could curl up into a ball and hide under the bed. His cold scrutiny made her feel cheap, just as that doctor had, just as the media had, just as her mother had…

He couldn't have explained why that expression on her face made him feel guilty. But it did.

He turned away from her. "Come on," he said, picking up her wrap and purse and tossing them to her. "I'll run you home."

She didn't look at him as she followed him down the length of the hall. It was longer than she realized, and even before they got to the front door, her leg was throbbing. Dancing had been damaging enough, without the jerk of his hand as they left the ballroom. But she ground her teeth together and didn't let her growing discomfort show in her face. He wasn't going to make her feel any worse than she already did by accusing her of putting on an act for sympathy. She went past him out the door he was holding open, avoiding his eyes. She wondered how things could have gone so terribly wrong.

The spacious garage was full of cars. He got out the silver Mercedes and opened the door to let her climb inside, onto the leather-covered passenger seat. He closed her door with something of a snap. Her fingers fumbled the seat belt into its catch and she hoped he wouldn't want to elaborate on what he'd already said.

She stared out the window at the dark silhouettes of buildings and trees as he drove along the back roads that eventually led into Jacobsville. She was sick about the way she'd acted. He probably thought she was the easiest woman alive. The only thing she didn't understand was why he didn't take advantage of it. The obvious reason made her even more uncomfortable. Didn't they say that some men didn't want what came easily? It was probably true. He'd been in pursuit as long as she was backing away from him. What irony, to spend years being afraid of men, running crazily from even the most platonic involvement, to find herself capable of torrid desire with the one man in the world who didn't want her!

He felt her tension. It was all too apparent that she was disappointed that he hadn't played the game to its finish.

"Is that what Ed gets when he takes you home?" he drawled.

Her nails bit into her small evening bag. Her teeth clenched. She wasn't going to dignify that remark with a reply.

He shrugged and paused to turn onto the main highway. "Don't take it so hard," he said lazily. "I'm a little too sophisticated to fall for it, but there are a few rich single ranchers around Jacobsville. Cy Parks comes to mind. He's hell on the nerves, but he is a widower." He glanced at her averted face. "On second thought, he's had enough tragedy in his life. I wouldn't wish you on him."

She couldn't even manage to speak, she was so choked up with hurt. Why, she wondered, did everything she wanted in life turn on her and tear her to pieces? It was like tracking cougars with a toy gun. Just when she seemed to find peace and purpose, her life became nothing but torment. As if her tattered pride wasn't enough, she was in terrible pain. She shifted in the seat, hoping that a change of position would help. It didn't.

"How did that bone get shattered?" he asked conversationally.

"Don't you know?" she asked on a harsh laugh. If he'd seen the story about her, as she suspected, he was only playing a cruel game—the sort of game he'd already accused her of playing!

He glanced at her with a scowl. "And how would I know?" he wondered aloud.

She frowned. Maybe he hadn't read anything at all! He might be fishing for answers.

She swallowed, gripping her purse tightly.

He swung the Mercedes into the driveway of her boardinghouse and pulled up at the steps, with the engine still running. He turned to her. "How *would* I know?" he asked again, his voice determined.

"You seem to think you're an expert on everything else about me," she replied evasively.

His chin lifted as he studied her through narrowed eyes. "There are several ways a bone can be shattered," he said quietly. "One way is from a bullet."

She didn't feel as if she were still breathing. She sat like a statue, watching him deliberate.

"What do you know about bullets?" she asked shortly.

"My unit was called up during Operation Desert Storm," he told her. "I served with an infantry unit. I know quite a lot about bullets. And what they do to bone," he added. "Which brings me to the obvious question. Who shot you?"

"I didn't say...I was shot," she managed.

His intense gaze held her like invisible ropes. "But you were, weren't you?" he asked with shrewd scrutiny. His lips tugged into a cold smile. "As to who did it, I'd bet on one of your former lovers. Did he catch you with somebody else, or did you tease him the way you teased me tonight and then refuse him?" He gave her another contemptuous look. "Not that you refused. You didn't exactly play hard to get."

Her ego went right down to her shoes. He was painting her over with evil colors. She bit her lower lip. It was unpleasant enough to have her memories, but to have this man making her out to be some sort of nymphomaniac was painful beyond words. Her first real taste of tender intimacy had been with him, tonight, and he made it sound dirty and cheap.

She unfastened her seat belt and got out of the car with as much dignity as she could muster. Her leg was incredibly painful. All she wanted was her bed, her heating pad and some more aspirins. And to get away from her tormenter.

Matt switched off the engine and moved around the car, irritated by the way she limped.

"I'll take you to the door…!"

She flinched when he came close. She backed away from him, actually shivering when she remembered shamefully what she'd let him do to her. Her eyes clouded with unshed angry tears, with outraged virtue.

"More games?" he asked tersely. He hadn't liked having her back away again after the way she'd been in his bedroom.

"I don't…play games," she replied, hating the hiccup of a sob that revealed how upset she really was. She clutched her wrap and her purse to her chest, accusing eyes glaring at him. "And you can go to hell!"

He scowled at the way she looked, barely hearing the words. She was white in the face and her whole body seemed rigid, as if she really was upset.

She turned and walked away, wincing inwardly with every excruciating step, to the front porch. But her face didn't show one trace of her discomfort. She held her head high. She still had her pride, she thought through a wave of pain.

Matt watched her go into the boardinghouse with more mixed, confused emotions than he'd ever felt. He remembered vividly that curious "Don't you know?" when he'd asked who shot her.

He got back into the Mercedes and sat staring through the windshield for a long moment before he started it. Miss Murry was one puzzle he intended to solve, and if it cost him a fortune in detective fees, he was going to do it.

Chapter 5

Leslie cried for what seemed hours. The aspirin didn't help the leg pain at all. There was no medicine known to man that she could take for her wounded ego. Matt had swept the floor with her, played with her, laughed at her naiveté and made her out to be little better than a prostitute. He was like that emergency room doctor so long ago who'd made her ashamed of her body. It was a pity that her first real desire for a man's touch had made her an object of contempt to the man himself.

Well, she told herself as she wiped angrily at the tears, she'd never make that mistake again. Matt Caldwell could go right where she'd told him to!

The phone rang and she hesitated to answer it. But it might be Ed. She picked up the receiver.

"We had a good laugh about you," Carolyn told her

outright. "I guess you'll think twice before you throw yourself at him again! He said you were so easy that you disgusted him…!"

Almost shaking with humiliation, she put the receiver down with a slam and then unplugged the phone. It was so close to what Matt had already said that there was no reason not to believe her. Carolyn's harsh arrogance was just what she needed to make the miserable evening complete.

The pain, combined with the humiliation, kept her awake until almost daylight. She missed breakfast, not to mention church, and when she did finally open her eyes, it was to a kind of pain she hadn't experienced since the night she was shot.

She shifted, wincing, and then moaned as the movement caused another searing wave of discomfort up her leg. The knock on her door barely got through to her. "Come in," she said in a husky, exhausted tone.

The door opened and there was Matt Caldwell, unshaven and with dark circles under his eyes.

Carolyn's words came back to haunt her. She grabbed the first thing that came to hand, a plastic bottle of spring water she kept by the bed, and flung it furiously across the room at him. It missed his head, and Ed's, by a quarter of an inch.

"No, thanks," Ed said, moving in front of Matt. "I don't want any water."

Her face was lined with pain, white with it. She glared at Matt's hard, angry face with eyes that would have looked perfectly natural over a cocked pistol.

"I couldn't get you on the phone, and I was worried,"

Ed said gently, approaching her side of the double bed she occupied. He noticed the unplugged telephone on her bedside table. "Now I know why I couldn't get you on the phone." He studied her drawn face. "How bad is it?"

She could barely breathe. "Bad," she said huskily, thinking what an understatement that word was.

He took her thick white chenille bathrobe from the chair beside the bed. "Come on. We're going to drive you to the emergency room. Matt can phone Lou Coltrain and have her meet us there."

It was an indication of the pain that she didn't argue. She got out of bed, aware of the picture she must make in the thick flannel pajamas that covered every inch of her up to her chin. Matt was probably shocked, she thought as she let Ed stuff her into the robe. He probably expected her to be naked under the covers, conforming to the image he had of her nymphomania!

He hadn't said a word. He just stood there, by the door, grimly watching Ed get her ready—until she tried to walk, and folded up.

Ed swung her up in his arms, stopping Matt's instinctive quick movement toward her. Ed knew for a fact that she'd scream the house down if his cousin so much as touched her. He didn't know what had gone on the night before, but judging by the way Matt and Leslie looked, it had been both humiliating and embarrassing.

"I can carry her," he told Matt. "Let's go."

Matt glimpsed her contorted features and didn't hesitate. He led the way down the hall and right out the front door.

"My purse," she said huskily. "My insurance card…"

"That can be taken care of later," Matt said stiffly. He opened the back door of the Mercedes and waited while Ed slid her onto the seat.

She leaned back with her eyes closed, almost sick from the pain.

"She should never have gotten on the dance floor," Matt said through his teeth as they started toward town. "And then I jerked her up out of her chair. It's my fault."

Ed didn't reply. He glanced over the seat at Leslie with concern in his whole expression. He hoped she hadn't done any major damage to herself with that exhibition the night before.

Lou Coltrain was waiting in the emergency room as Ed carried Leslie inside the building. She motioned him down the hall to a room and closed the door behind Matt as soon as he entered.

She examined the leg carefully, asking questions that Leslie was barely able to answer. "I want X-rays," she said. "But I'll give you something for pain first."

"Thank you," Leslie choked, fighting tears.

Lou smoothed her wild hair. "You poor little thing," she said softly. "Cry if you want to. It must hurt like hell."

She went out to get the injection, and tears poured down Leslie's face because of that tender concern. She hardly ever cried. She was tough. She could take anything—near-rape, bullet wounds, notoriety, her mother's trial, the refusal of her parent to even speak to her...

"There, there," Ed said. He produced a handkerchief and blotted the tears, smiling down at her. "Dr. Lou is going to make it all better."

"For God's sake…!" Matt bit off angry words and walked out of the room. It was unbearable that he'd hurt her like that. Unbearable! And then to have to watch Ed comforting her…!

"I hate him," Leslie choked when he was gone. She actually shivered. "He laughed about it," she whispered, blind to Ed's curious scowl. "She said they both laughed about it, that he was disgusted."

"She?"

"Carolyn." The tears were hot in her eyes, cold on her cheeks. "I hate him!"

Lou came back with the injection and gave it, waiting for it to take effect. She glanced at Ed. "You might want to wait outside. I'm taking her down to X-ray myself. I'll come and get you when we've done some tests."

"Okay."

He went out and joined Matt in the waiting room. The older man's face was drawn, tormented. He barely glanced at Ed before he turned his attention to the trees outside the window. It was a dismal gray day, with rain threatening. It matched his mood.

Ed leaned against the wall beside him with a frown. "She said Carolyn phoned her last night," he began. "I suppose that's why the phone was unplugged."

It was Matt's turn to look puzzled. "What?"

"Leslie said Carolyn told her the two of you were laughing at her," he murmured. "She didn't say what about."

Matt's face hardened visibly. He rammed his hands into his pockets and his eyes were terrible to look into.

"Don't hurt Leslie," Ed said suddenly, his voice quiet

but full of venom. "She hasn't had an easy life. Don't make things hard on her. She has no place else to go."

Matt glanced at him, disliking the implied threat as much as the fact that Ed knew far more about Leslie than he did. Were they lovers? Old lovers, perhaps?

"She keeps secrets," he said. "She was shot. Who did it?"

Ed lifted both eyebrows. "Who said she was shot?" he asked innocently, doing it so well that he actually fooled his cousin.

Matt hesitated. "Nobody. I assumed...well, how else does a bone get shattered?"

"By a blow, by a bad fall, in a car wreck..." Ed trailed off, leaving Matt with something to think about.

"Yes. Of course." The older man sighed. "Dancing put her in this shape. I didn't realize just how fragile she was. She doesn't exactly shout her problems to the world."

"She was always like that," Ed replied.

Matt turned to face him. "How did you meet her?"

"She and I were in college together," Ed told him. "We used to date occasionally. She trusts me," he added.

Matt was turning what he knew about Leslie over in his mind. If the pieces had been part of a puzzle, none of them would fit. When they first met, she avoided his touch like the plague. Last night, she'd enjoyed his advances. She'd been nervous and shy at their first meeting. Later, at the office, she'd been gregarious, almost playful. Last night, she'd been a completely different woman on the dance floor. Then, when he'd taken her home with him, she'd been hungry, sensuous, tender. Nothing about her made any sense.

"Don't trust her too far," Matt advised the other man. "She's too secretive to suit me. I thinks she's hiding something…maybe something pretty bad."

Ed didn't dare react. He pursed his lips and smiled. "Leslie's never hurt anyone in her life," he remarked. "And before you get the wrong idea about her, you'd better know that she has a real fear of men."

Matt laughed. "Oh, that's a good one," he said mockingly. "You should have seen her last night when we were alone."

Ed's eyes narrowed. "What do you mean?"

"I mean she's easy," Matt said with a contemptuous smile.

Ed's eyes began to glitter. He called his cousin a name that made Matt's eyebrows arch.

"Easy. My God!" Ed ground out.

Matt was puzzled by the other man's inexplicable behavior. Probably he was jealous. His cell phone began to trill, diverting him. He answered it. He recognized Carolyn's voice immediately and moved away, so that Ed couldn't hear what he said. Ed was certainly acting strange lately.

"I thought you were coming over to ride with me this afternoon," Carolyn said cheerfully. "Where are you?"

"At the hospital," he said absently, his eyes on Ed's retreating back going through the emergency room doors. "What did you say to Leslie last night?"

"What do you mean?"

"When you phoned her!" Matt prompted.

Carolyn sounded vague. "Well, I wanted to see if she was better," she replied. "She seemed to be in a lot of pain after the dance."

"What else did you say?"

Carolyn laughed. "Oh, I see. I'm being accused of something underhanded, is that it? Really, Matt, I thought you could see through that phony vulnerability of hers. What did she tell you I said?"

He shrugged. "Never mind. I must have misunderstood."

"You certainly did," she assured him firmly. "I wouldn't call someone in pain to upset them. I thought you knew me better than that."

"I do." He was seething. So now it seemed that Miss Murry was making up lies about Carolyn. Had it been to get even with him, for not giving in to her wiles? Or was she trying to turn his cousin against him?

"What about that horseback ride? And what are you doing at the hospital?" she added suddenly.

"I'm with Ed, visiting one of his friends," he said. "Better put the horseback ride off until next weekend. I'll phone you."

He hung up. His eyes darkened with anger. He wanted the Murry woman out of his company, out of his life. She was going to be nothing but trouble.

He repocketed the phone and went outside to wait for Ed and Leslie.

A good half hour later, Ed came out of the emergency room with his hands in his pockets, looking worried.

"They're keeping her overnight," he said curtly.

"For a sore leg?" Matt asked with mild sarcasm.

Ed scowled. "One of the bones shifted and it's pressing on a nerve," he replied. "Lou says it won't get any better until it's fixed. They're sending for an orthopedic man from Houston. He'll be in this afternoon."

"Who's going to pay for that?" Matt asked coldly.

"Since you ask, I am," Ed returned, not intimidated even by those glittery eyes.

"It's your money," the older man replied. He let out a breath. "What caused the bone to separate?"

"Why ask a question when you already know the answer?" Ed wanted to know. "I'm going to stay with her. She's frightened."

He was fairly certain that even if Leslie could fake pain, she couldn't fake an X-ray. Somewhere in the back of his mind he found guilt lurking. If he hadn't pulled her onto the dance floor, and if he hadn't jerked her to her feet...

He turned away and walked out of the building without another word. Leslie was Ed's business. He kept telling himself that. But all the way home, his conscience stabbed at him. She couldn't help being what she was. Even so, he hadn't meant to hurt her. He remembered the tears, genuine tears, boiling out of her eyes when Lou had touched her hair so gently. She acted as if she'd never had tenderness in her life.

He drove himself home and tried to concentrate on briefing himself for a director's meeting the next day. But long before bedtime, he gave it up and drank himself into uneasy sleep.

The orthopedic man examined the X-rays and seconded Lou's opinion that immediate surgery was required. But Leslie didn't want the surgery. She refused to talk about it. The minute the doctors and Ed left the room, she struggled out of bed and hobbled to the closet to pull her pajamas and robe and shoes out of it.

In the hall, Matt came upon Ed and Lou and a tall, distinguished stranger in an expensive suit.

"You two look like stormy weather," he mused. "What's wrong?"

"Leslie won't have the operation," Ed muttered worriedly. "Dr. Santos flew all the way from Houston to do the surgery, and she won't hear of it."

"Maybe she doesn't think she needs it," Matt said.

Lou glanced at him. "You have no idea what sort of pain she's in," she said, impatient with him. "One of the bone fragments, the one that shifted, is pressing right on a nerve."

"The bones should have been properly aligned at the time the accident occurred," the visiting orthopedic surgeon agreed. "It was criminally irresponsible of the attending physician to do nothing more than bandage the leg. A cast wasn't even used until afterward!"

That sounded negligent to Matt, too. He frowned. "Did she say why not?"

Lou sighed angrily. "She won't talk about it. She won't listen to any of us. Eventually she'll have to. But in the meantime, the pain is going to drive her insane."

Matt glanced from one set face to the other and walked past them to Leslie's room.

She was wearing her flannel pajamas and reaching for the robe when Matt walked in. She gave him a glare hot enough to boil water.

"Well, at least you won't be trying to talk me into an operation I don't want," she muttered as she struggled to get from the closet to the bed.

"Why won't I?"

She arched both eyebrows expressively. "I'm the enemy."

He stood at the foot of the bed, watching her get into the robe. Her leg was at an awkward angle, and her face was pinched. He could imagine the sort of pain she was already experiencing.

"Suit yourself about the operation," he replied with forced indifference, folding his arms across his chest. "But don't expect me to have someone carry you back and forth around the office. If you want to make a martyr of yourself, be my guest."

She stopped fiddling with the belt of the robe and stared at him quietly, puzzled.

"Some people enjoy making themselves objects of pity to people around them," he continued deliberately.

"I don't want pity!" she snapped.

"Really?"

She wrapped the belt around her fingers and stared at it. "I'll have to be in a cast."

"No doubt."

"My insurance hasn't taken effect yet, either," she said with averted eyes. "Once it's in force, I can have the operation." She looked back at him coldly. "I'm not going to let Ed pay for it, in case you wondered, and I don't care if he can afford it!"

He had to fight back a stirring of admiration for her independent stance. It could be part of the pose, he realized, but it sounded pretty genuine. His blue eyes narrowed. "I'll pay for it," he said, surprising both of them. "It can come out of your weekly check."

Her teeth clenched. "I know how much this sort of

thing costs. That's why I've never had it done before. I'd never be able to pay it back in my lifetime."

His eyes fell to her body. "We could work something out," he murmured.

She flushed. "No, we couldn't!"

She stood up, barely able to stand the pain, despite the painkillers they'd given her. She hobbled over to the chair, where her shoes were placed, and eased her feet into them.

"Where are you going?" he asked conversationally.

"Home," she said, and started past him.

He caught her up in his arms like a fallen package and carried her right back to the bed, dumping her on it gently. His arms made a cage as he looked down at her flushed face. "Don't be stupid," he said in a voice that went right through her. "You're no good to yourself or anyone else in this condition. You have no choice."

Her lips trembled as she fought to control the tears. She would be helpless, vulnerable. Besides, that surgeon reminded her of the man at the emergency room in Houston. He brought back unbearable shame.

The unshed tears fascinated Matt. She fascinated him. He didn't want to care about what happened to her, but he did.

He reached down and smoothed a long forefinger over her wet lashes. "Do you have family?" he asked unexpectedly.

She thought of her mother, in prison, and felt sick to her very soul. "No," she whispered starkly.

"Are both your parents dead?"

"Yes," she said at once.

"No brothers, sisters?"

She shook her head.

He frowned, as if her situation disturbed him. In fact, it did. She looked vulnerable and fragile and completely lost. He didn't understand why he cared so much for her well-being. Perhaps it was guilt because he'd lured her into a kind of dancing she wasn't really able to do anymore.

"I want to go home," she said harshly.

"Afterward," he replied.

She remembered him saying that before, in almost the same way, and she averted her face in shame.

He could have bitten his tongue for that. He shouldn't bait her when she was in such a condition. It was hitting below the belt.

He drew in a long breath. "Leave it to Ed to pick up strays, and make me responsible for them!" he muttered, angry because of her vulnerability and his unwanted response to it.

She didn't say a word, but her lower lip trembled and she turned her face away from him. Beside her hip, her hand was clenched so tightly that the knuckles were white.

He shot away from the bed, his eyes furious. "You're having the damned operation," he informed her flatly. "Once you're healthy and whole again, you won't need Ed to prop you up. You can work for your living like every other woman."

She didn't answer him. She didn't look at him. She wanted to get better so that she could kick the hell out of him.

"Did you hear me?" he asked in a dangerously soft tone.

She jerked her head to acknowledge the question but she didn't speak.

He let out an angry breath. "I'll tell the others."

He left her lying there and announced her decision to the three people in the hall.

"How did you manage that?" Ed asked when Lou and Dr. Santos went back in to talk to Leslie.

"I made her mad," Matt replied. "Sympathy doesn't work."

"No, it doesn't," Ed replied quietly. "I don't think she's had much of it in her whole life."

"What happened to her parents?" he wanted to know.

Ed was careful about the reply. "Her father misjudged the position of some electrical wires and flew right into them. He was electrocuted."

He frowned darkly. "And her mother?"

"They were both in love with the same man," Ed said evasively. "He died, and Leslie and her mother still aren't on speaking terms."

Matt turned away, jingling the change in his pocket restlessly. "How did he die?"

"Violently," Ed told him. "It was a long time ago. But I don't think Leslie will ever get over it."

Which was true, but it sounded as if Leslie was still in love with the dead man—which was exactly what Ed wanted. He was going to save her from Matt, whatever it took. She was a good friend. He didn't want her life destroyed because Matt was on the prowl for a new conquest. Leslie deserved something better than to be one of Matt's ex-girlfriends.

Matt glanced at his cousin with a puzzling expression. "When will they operate?"

"Tomorrow morning," Ed said. "I'll be late getting to work. I'm going to be here while it's going on."

Matt nodded. He glanced down the hall toward the door of Leslie's room. He hesitated for a moment before he turned and went out of the building without another comment.

Later, Ed questioned her about what Matt had said to her.

"He said that I was finding excuses because I wanted people to feel sorry for me," she said angrily. "And I do not have a martyr complex!"

Ed chuckled. "I know that."

"I can't believe you're related to someone like that," she said furiously. "He's horrible!"

"He's had a rough life. Something you can identify with," he added gently.

"I think he and his latest girlfriend deserve each other," she murmured.

"Carolyn phoned while he was here. I don't know what was said, but I'd bet my bottom dollar she denied saying anything to upset you."

"Would you expect her to admit it?" she asked. She lay back against the pillow, glad that the injection they'd given her was taking effect. "I guess I'll be clumping around your office in a cast for weeks, if he doesn't find some excuse to fire me in the meantime."

"There is company policy in such matters," he said easily. "He'd have to have my permission to fire you, and he won't get it."

"I'm impressed," she said, and managed a wan smile.

"So you should be," he chuckled. He searched her

eyes. "Leslie, why didn't the doctor set those bones when it happened?"

She studied the ceiling. "He said the whole thing was my fault and that I deserved all my wounds. He called me a vicious little tramp who caused decent men to be murdered." Her eyes closed. "Nothing ever hurt so much."

"I can imagine!"

"I never went to a doctor again," she continued. "It wasn't just the things he said to me, you know. There was the expense, too. I had no insurance and no money. Mama had to have a public defender and I worked while I finished high school to help pay my way at my friend's house. The pain was bad, but eventually I got used to it, and the limp." She turned quiet eyes to Ed's face. "It would be sort of nice to be able to walk normally again. And I will pay back whatever it costs, if you and your cousin will be patient."

He winced. "Nobody's worried about the cost."

"He is," she informed him evenly. "And he's right. I don't want to be a financial burden on anyone, not even him."

"We'll talk about all this later," he said gently. "Right now, I just want you to get better."

She sighed. "Will I? I wonder."

"Miracles happen all the time," he told her. "You're overdue for one."

"I'd settle gladly for the ability to walk normally," she said at once, and she smiled.

Chapter 6

The operation was over by lunchtime the following day. Ed stayed until Leslie was out of the recovery room and out of danger, lying still and pale in the bed in the private room with the private nurse he'd hired to stay with her for the first couple of days. He'd spoken to both Lou Coltrain and the visiting orthopedic surgeon, who assured him that Miss Murry would find life much less painful from now on. Modern surgery had progressed to the point that procedures once considered impossible were now routine.

He went back to work feeling light and cheerful. Matt stopped him in the hall.

"Well?" he asked abruptly.

Ed grinned from ear to ear. "She's going to be fine.

Dr. Santos said that in six weeks, when she comes out of that cast, she'll be able to dance in a contest."

Matt nodded. "Good."

Ed answered a question Matt had about one of their accounts and then, assuming that Matt didn't want anything else at the moment, he went back to his office. He had a temporary secretary, a pretty little redhead who had a bright personality and good dictation skills.

Surprisingly, Matt followed him into his office and closed the door. "Tell me how that bone was shattered," he said abruptly.

Ed sat down and leaned forward with his forearms on his cluttered desk. "That's Leslie's business, Matt," he replied. "I wouldn't tell you, even if I knew," he added, lying through his teeth with deliberate calm.

He sighed irritably. "She's a puzzle. A real puzzle."

"She's a sweet girl who's had a lot of hard knocks," Ed told him. "But regardless of what you think you know about her, she isn't 'easy.' Don't make the mistake of classing her with your usual sort of woman. You'll regret it."

Matt studied the younger man curiously and his eyes narrowed. "What do you mean, I think she's 'easy'?" he asked, bristling.

"Forgotten already? That's what you said about her."

Matt felt uncomfortable at the words that he'd spoken with such assurance to Leslie. He glanced at Ed irritably. "Miss Murry obviously means something to you. If you're so fond of her, why haven't you married her?"

Ed smoothed back his hair. "She kept me from blowing my brains out when my fiancée was gunned down in a bank robbery in Houston," he said. "I actually had the pistol loaded. She took it away from me."

Matt's eyes narrowed. "You never told me you were that despondent."

"You wouldn't have understood," came the reply. "Women were always a dime a dozen to you, Matt. You've never really been in love."

Matt's face, for once, didn't conceal his bitterness. "I wouldn't give any woman that sort of power over me," he said in clipped tones. "Women are devious, Ed. They'll smile at you until they get what they want, then they'll walk right over you to the next sucker. I've seen too many good men brought down by women they loved."

"There are bad men, too," Ed pointed out.

Matt shrugged. "I'm not arguing with that." He smiled. "I would have done what I could for you, though," he added. "We have our disagreements, but we're closer than most cousins are."

Ed nodded. "Yes, we are."

"You really are fond of Miss Murry, aren't you?"

"In a big brotherly sort of way," Ed affirmed. "She trusts me. If you knew her, you'd understand how difficult it is for her to trust a man."

"I think she's pulling the wool over your eyes," Matt told him. "You be careful. She's down on her luck, and you're rich."

Ed's face contorted briefly. "Good God, Matt, you haven't got a clue what she's really like."

"Neither have you," Matt commented with a cold smile. "But I know things about her that you don't. Let's leave it at that."

Ed hated his own impotence. "I want to keep her in my office."

"How do you expect her to come to work in a cast?" he asked frankly.

Ed leaned back in his chair and grinned. "The same way I did five years ago, when I had that skiing accident and broke my ankle. People work with broken bones all the time. And she doesn't type with her feet."

Matt shrugged. Miss Murry had him completely confused. "Suit yourself," he said finally. "Just keep her out of my way."

That shouldn't be difficult, Ed thought ruefully. Matt certainly wasn't on Leslie's list of favorite people. He wondered what the days ahead would bring. It would be like storing dynamite with lighted candles.

Leslie was out of the hospital in three days and back at work in a week. The company had paid for her surgery, to her surprise and Ed's. She knew that Matt had only done that out of guilt. Well, he needn't flay himself over what happened. She didn't really blame him. She had loved dancing with him. She refused to think of how that evening had ended. Some memories were best forgotten.

She hobbled into Ed's office with the use of crutches and plopped herself down behind her desk on her first day back on the job.

"How did you get here?" Ed asked with a surprised smile. "You can't drive, can you?"

"No, but one of the girls in my rooming house works in downtown Jacobsville and we're going to become a carpool three days a week. I'm paying my share of the gas and on her days off, I'll get a taxi to work," she added.

"I'm glad you're back," he said with genuine fondness.

"Oh, sure you are," she said with a teasing glance. "I heard all about Karla Smith when the girls from Mr. Caldwell's office came to see me. I understand she has a flaming crush on you."

Ed chuckled. "So they say. Poor girl."

She made a face. "You can't live in the past."

"Tell yourself that."

She put her crutches on the floor beside the desk, and swiveled back in her desk chair. "It's going to be a little difficult for me to get back and forth to your office," she said. "Can you dictate letters in here?"

"Of course."

She looked around the office with pleasure. "I'm glad I got to come back," she murmured. "I thought Mr. Caldwell might find an excuse to let me go."

"I'm Mr. Caldwell, too," he pointed out. "Matt's bark is worse than his bite. He won't fire you."

She grimaced. "Don't let me cause trouble between you," she said with genuine concern. "I'd rather quit…"

"No, you won't," he interrupted. He ruffled her short hair with a playful grin. "I like having you around. Besides, you spell better than the other women."

Her eyes lit up as she looked at him. She smiled back. "Thanks, boss."

Matt opened the door in time to encounter the affectionate looks they exchanged and his face hardened as he slammed it behind him.

They both jumped.

"Jehosophat, Matt!" Ed burst out, catching his breath. "Don't do that!"

"Don't play games with your secretary on my time," Matt returned. His cold dark eyes went to Leslie, whose own eyes went cold at sight of him. "Back at work, I see, Miss Murry."

"All the better to pay you back for my hospital stay, sir," she returned with a smile that bordered on insolence.

He bit back a sharp reply and turned to Ed, ignoring her. "I want you to take Nell Hobbs out to lunch and find out how she's going to vote on the zoning proposal. If they zone that land adjoining my ranch as recreational, I'm going to spend my life in court."

"If she votes for it, she'll be the only one," Ed assured him. "I spoke to the other commissioners myself."

He seemed to relax a little. "Okay. In that case, you can run over to Houlihan's dealership and drive my new Jaguar over here. It came in this morning."

Ed's eyes widened. "You're going to let me drive it?"

"Why not?" Matt asked with a warm smile, the sort Leslie knew she'd never see on that handsome face.

Ed chuckled. "Then, thanks. I'll be back shortly!" He started down the hall at a dead run. "Leslie, we'll do those letters after lunch!"

"Sure," she said. "I can spend the day updating those old herd records." She glanced at Matt to let him know she hadn't forgotten his instructions from before her operation.

He put his hands in the pockets of his slacks and his blue eyes searched her gray ones intently. Deliberately he let his gaze fall to her soft mouth. He remembered the feel of it clinging to his parted lips, hungry and moaning…

His teeth clenched. He couldn't think about that. "The herd records can wait," he said tersely. "My secretary is home with a sick child, so you can work for me for the rest of the day. Ed can let Miss Smith handle his urgent stuff today."

She hesitated visibly. "Yes, sir," she said in a wooden voice.

"I have to talk to Henderson about one of the new accounts. I'll meet you in my office in thirty minutes."

"Yes, sir."

They were watching each other like opponents in a match when Matt made an angry sound under his breath and walked out.

Leslie spent a few minutes sorting the mail and looking over it. A little over a half hour went by before she realized it. A sound caught her attention and she looked up to find an impatient Matt Caldwell standing in the doorway.

"Sorry. I lost track of the time," she said quickly, putting the opened mail aside. She reached for her crutches and got up out of her chair, reaching for her pad and pen when she was ready to go. She looked up at Matt, who seemed taller than ever. "I'm ready when you are, boss," she said courteously.

"Don't call me boss," he said flatly.

"Okay, Mr. Caldwell," she returned.

He glared at her, but she gave him a bland look and even managed a smile. He wanted to throw things.

He turned, leaving her to follow him down the long hall to his executive office, which had a bay window

overlooking downtown Jacobsville. His desk was solid
oak, huge, covered with equipment and papers of all
sorts. There was a kid leather–covered chair behind
the desk and two equally impressive wing chairs, and a
sofa, all done in burgundy. The carpet was a deep, rich
beige. The curtains were plaid, picking up the burgundy
in the furniture and adding it to autumn hues. There
was a framed portrait of someone who looked vaguely
like Matt over the mantel of the fireplace, in which gas
logs rested. There were two chairs and a table near the
fireplace, probably where Matt and some visitor would
share a pot of coffee or a drink. There was a bar against
one wall with a mirror behind it, giving an added air
of spacious comfort to the high-ceilinged room. The
windows were tall ones, unused because the Victorian
house that contained the offices had central heating.

Matt watched her studying her surroundings covertly. He closed the door behind them and motioned
her into a chair facing the desk. She eased down into
it and put her crutches beside her. She was still a little
uncomfortable, but aspirin was enough to contain the
pain these days. She looked forward to having the cast
off, to walking normally again.

She put the pad on her lap and maneuvered the leg in
the cast so that it was as comfortable as she could get it.

Matt was leaning back in his chair with his booted
feet on the desk and his eyes narrow and watchful as he
sketched her slender body in the flowing beige pantsuit
she was wearing with a patterned scarf tucked in the
neck of the jacket. The outside seam in the left leg of
her slacks had been snipped to allow for the cast. Otherwise, she was covered from head to toe, just as she had

been from the first time he saw her. Odd, that he hadn't really noticed that before. It wasn't a new habit dating from the night he'd touched her so intimately, either.

"How's the leg?" he asked curtly.

"Healing, thank you," she replied. "I've already spoken to the bookkeeper about pulling out a quarter of my check weekly…"

He leaned forward so abruptly that it sounded like a gunshot when his booted feet hit the floor.

"I'll take that up with bookkeeping," he said sharply. "You've overstepped your authority, Miss Murry. Don't do it again."

She shifted in the chair, moving the ungainly cast, and assumed a calm expression. "I'm sorry, Mr. Caldwell."

Her voice was serene but her hands were shaking on the pad and pen. He averted his eyes and got to his feet, glaring out the window.

She waited patiently with her eyes on the blank pad, wondering when he was going to start dictation.

"You told Ed that Carolyn phoned you the night before we took you to the emergency room and made some cruel remarks." He remembered what Ed had related about that conversation and it made him unusually thoughtful. He turned and caught her surprised expression. "Carolyn denies saying anything to upset you."

Her expression didn't change. She didn't care what he thought of her anymore. She didn't say a word in her defense.

His dark eyebrows met over the bridge of his nose. "Well?"

"What would you like me to say?"

"You might try apologizing," he told her coldly, trying to smoke her out. "Carolyn was very upset to have such a charge made against her. I don't like having her upset," he added deliberately and stood looking down his nose at her, waiting for her to react to the challenge.

Her fingers tightened around the pen. It was going to be worse than she ever dreamed, trying to work with him. He couldn't fire her, Ed had said, but that didn't mean he couldn't make her quit. If he made things difficult enough for her, she wouldn't be able to stay.

All at once, it didn't seem worth the effort. She was tired, worn-out, and Carolyn had hurt her, not the reverse. She was sick to death of trying to live from one day to the next with the weight of the past bearing down on her more each day. Being tormented by Matt Caldwell on top of all that was the last straw.

She reached for her crutches and stood up, pad and all.

"Where do you think you're going?" Matt demanded, surprised that she was giving up without an argument.

She went toward the door. He got in front of her, an easy enough task when every step she took required extreme effort.

She looked up at him with the eyes of a trapped animal, resigned and resentful and without life. "Ed said you couldn't fire me without his consent," she said quietly. "But you can hound me until I quit, can't you?"

He didn't speak. His face was rigid. "Would you give up so easily?" he asked, baiting her. "Where will you go?"

Her gaze dropped to the floor. Idly she noticed that

one of her flat-heeled shoes had a smudge of mud on it. She should clean it off.

"I said, where will you go?" Matt persisted.

She met his cold eyes. "Surely in all of Texas, there's more than one secretarial position available," she said. "Please move. You're blocking the door."

He did move, but not in the way she'd expected. He took the crutches away from her and propped them against the bookshelf by the door. His hands went on either side of her head, trapping her in front of him. His dark eyes held a faint glitter as he studied her wan face, her soft mouth.

"Don't," she managed tightly.

He moved closer. He smelled of spice and aftershave and coffee. His breath was warm where it brushed her forehead. She could feel the warmth of his tall, fit body, and she remembered reluctantly how it had felt to let him hold her and touch her in his bedroom.

He was remembering those same things, but not with pleasure. He hated the attraction he felt for this woman, whom he didn't, couldn't trust.

"You don't like being touched, you said," he reminded her with deliberate sarcasm as his lean hand suddenly smoothed over her breast and settled there provocatively.

Her indrawn breath was audible. She looked up at him with all her hidden vulnerabilities exposed. "Please don't do this," she whispered. "I'm no threat to Ed, or to you, either. Just…let me go. I'll vanish."

She probably would, and that wounded him. He was making her life miserable. Why did this woman arouse such bitter feelings in him, when he was the soul of kindness to most people with problems—especially physical problems, like hers.

"Ed won't like it," he said tersely.

"Ed doesn't have to know anything," she said dully. "You can tell him whatever you like."

"Is he your lover?"

"No."

"Why not? You don't mind if he touches you."

"He doesn't. Not...the way you do."

Her strained voice made him question his own cruelty. He lifted his hand away from her body and tilted her chin up so that he could see her eyes. They were turbulent, misty.

"How many poor fools have you played the innocent with, Miss Murry?" he asked coldly.

She saw the lines in his face, many more than his age should have caused. She saw the coldness in his eyes, the bitterness of too many betrayals, too many loveless years.

Unexpectedly she reached up and touched his hair, smoothing it back as Lou had smoothed hers back in an act of silent compassion.

It made him furious. His body pressed down completely against hers, holding her prisoner. His hips twisted in a crude, rough motion that was instantly arousing.

She tried to twist away and he groaned huskily, giving her a worldly smile when she realized that her attempt at escape had failed and made the situation even worse.

Her face colored. It was like that night. It was the way Mike had behaved, twisting his body against her innocent one and laughing at her embarrassment. He'd said things, done things to her in front of his friends that still made her want to gag.

Matt's hand fell to her hip and contracted as he used one of his long legs to nudge hers apart. She was stiff against him, frozen with painful memories of another man, another encounter, that had begun just this way. She'd thought she loved Mike until he made her an object of lustful ridicule, making fun of her innocence as he anticipated its delights for the enjoyment of his laughing friends, grouped around them as he forcibly stripped the clothes away from her body. He laughed at her small breasts, at her slender figure, and all the while he touched her insolently and made jokes about her most intimate places.

She was years in the past, reliving the torment, the shame, that had seen her spread-eagled on the wood floor with Mike's drug-crazed friends each holding one of her shaking limbs still while Mike lowered his nude body onto hers and roughly parted her legs...

Matt realized belatedly that Leslie was frozen in place like a statue with a white face and eyes that didn't even see him. He could hear her heartbeat, quick and frantic. Her whole body shook, but not with pleasure or anticipation.

Frowning, he let her go and stepped back. She shivered again, convulsively. Mike had backed away, too, to the sound of a firecracker popping loudly. But it hadn't been a firecracker. It had been a bullet. It went right through him, into Leslie's leg. He looked surprised. Leslie remembered his blue eyes as the life visibly went out of them, leaving them fixed and blank just before he fell heavily on her. There had been such a tiny hole in his back, compared to the one in his chest. Her mother was screaming, trying to fire again, trying to kill her. Leslie had seduced her own lover, she wanted to kill them both, and she was glad Mike was dead. Leslie would be dead, too!

Leslie remembered lying there naked on the floor, with a shattered leg and blood pouring from it so rapidly that she knew she was going to bleed to death before help arrived...

"Leslie?" Matt asked sharply.

He became a white blur as she slid down the wall into oblivion.

When she came to, Ed was bending over her with a look of anguished concern. He had a damp towel pressed to her forehead. She looked at him dizzily.

"Ed?" she murmured.

"Yes. How are you?"

She blinked and looked around. She was lying on the big burgundy leather couch in Matt's office. "What happened?" she asked numbly. "Did I faint?"

"Apparently," Ed said heavily. "You came back to work too soon. I shouldn't have agreed."

"But I'm all right," she insisted, pulling herself up. She felt nauseous. She had to swallow repeatedly before she was able to move again.

She took a slow breath and smiled at him. "I'm still a little weak, I guess, and I didn't have any breakfast."

"Idiot," he said, smiling.

She smiled back. "I'm okay. Hand me my crutches, will you?"

He got them from where they were propped against the wall, and she had a glimpse of Matt standing there as if he'd been carved from stone. She took the crutches from Ed and got them under her arms.

"Would you drive me home?" she asked Ed. "I think maybe I will take one more day off, if that's all right?"

"That's all right," Ed assured her. He looked across the room. "Right, Matt?"

Matt nodded, a curt jerk of his head. He gave her one last look and went out the door.

The relief Leslie felt almost knocked her legs from under her. She remembered what had happened, but she wasn't about to tell Ed. She wasn't going to cause a breach between him and the older cousin he adored. She, who had no family left in the world except the mother who hated her, had more respect for family than most people.

She let Ed take her home, and she didn't think about what had happened in Matt's office. She knew that every time she saw him from now on, she'd relive those last few horrible minutes in her mother's apartment when she was seventeen. If she'd had anyplace else to go, she'd leave. But she was trapped, for the moment, at the mercy of a man who had none, a victim of a past she couldn't even talk about.

Ed went back to the office determined to have it out with Matt. He knew instinctively that Leslie's collapse was caused by something the other man did or said, and he was going to stop the treatment Matt was giving her before it was too late.

It was anticlimactic when he got into Matt's office,

with his speech rehearsed and ready, only to find it empty.

"He said he was going up to Victoria to see a man about some property, Mr. Caldwell," one of the secretaries commented. "Left in a hurry, too, in that brand-new red Jaguar. We hear you got to drive it over from Houlihan's."

"Yes, I did," he replied, forcing a cheerful smile. "It goes like the wind."

"We noticed," she murmured dryly. "He was flying when he turned the corner. I hope he slows down. It would be a pity if he wrecked it when he'd only just gotten it."

"So it would," Ed replied. He went back to his own office, curious about Matt's odd behavior but rather relieved that the showdown wouldn't have to be faced right away.

Chapter 7

Matt was doing almost a hundred miles an hour on the long highway that led to Victoria. He couldn't get Leslie's face out of his mind. That hadn't been anger or even fear in her gray eyes. It went beyond those emotions. She had been terrified; not of him, but of something she could see that he couldn't. Her tortured gaze had hurt him in a vulnerable spot he didn't know he had. When she fainted, he hated himself. He'd never thought of himself as a particularly cruel man, but he was with Leslie. He couldn't understand the hostility she roused in him. She was fragile, for all her independence and strength of will. Fragile. Vulnerable. Tender.

He remembered the touch of her soft fingers smoothing back his hair and he groaned out loud with self-hatred. He'd been tormenting her, and she'd seen right through the harsh words to the pain that lay underneath them. In return for his insensitivity, she'd reached up and touched him with genuine compassion. He'd rewarded that exquisite tenderness with treatment he wouldn't have offered to a hardened prostitute.

He realized that the speed he was going exceeded the limit by a factor of two and took his foot off the pedal. He didn't even know where the hell he was going. He was running for cover, he supposed, and laughed coldly at his own reaction to Leslie's fainting spell. All his life he'd been kind to stray animals and people down on their luck. He'd followed up that record by torturing a crippled young woman who felt sorry for him. Next, he supposed, he'd be kicking lame dogs down steps.

He pulled off on the side of the highway, into a lay-by, and stopped the car, resting his head on the steering wheel. He didn't recognize himself since Leslie Murry had walked into his life. She brought out monstrous qualities in him. He was ashamed of the way he'd treated her. She was a sweet woman who always seemed surprised when people did kind things for her. On the other hand, Matt's antagonism and hostility didn't seem to surprise her. Was that what she'd had the most of in her life? Had people been so cruel to her that now she expected and accepted cruelty as her lot in life?

He leaned back in the seat and stared at the flat horizon. His mother's desertion and his recent notoriety had soured him on the whole female sex. His mother was an old wound. The assault suit had made him bitter, yet again, despite the fact that he'd avenged himself on the perpetrator. But he remembered her coy, sweet personality very well. She'd pretended innocence and helplessness and when the disguise had come off, he'd found himself the object of vicious public humiliation. His name had been cleared, but the anger and resentment had remained.

But none of that excused his recent behavior. He'd overreacted with Leslie. He was sorry and ashamed for making her suffer for something that wasn't her fault. He took a long breath and put the car in gear. Well, he couldn't run away. He might as well go back to work. Ed would probably be waiting with blood in his eye, and he wouldn't blame him. He deserved a little discomfort.

Ed did read him the riot act, and he took it. He couldn't deny that he'd been unfair to Leslie. He wished he could understand what it was about her that raised the devil in him.

"If you genuinely don't like her," Ed concluded, "can't you just ignore her?"

"Probably," Matt said without meeting his cousin's accusing eyes.

"Then would you? Matt, she needs this job," he continued solemnly.

Matt studied him sharply. "Why does she need it?" he asked. "And why doesn't she have anyplace to go?"

"I can't tell you. I gave my word."

"Is she in some sort of trouble with the law?"

Ed laughed softly. "Leslie?"

"Never mind." He moved back toward the door. He stopped and turned as he reached it. "When she fainted, she said something."

"What?" Ed asked curiously.

"She said, 'Mike, don't.'" He didn't blink. "Who's Mike?"

"A dead man," Ed replied. "Years dead."

"The man she and her mother competed for."

"That's right," Ed said. "If you mention his name in front of her, I'll walk out the door with her, and I won't come back. Ever."

That was serious business to Ed, he realized. He frowned thoughtfully. "Did she love him?"

"She thought she did," Ed replied. His eyes went cold. "He destroyed her life."

"How?"

Ed didn't reply. He folded his hands on the desk and just stared at Matt.

The older man let out an irritated breath. "Has it occurred to you that all this secrecy is only complicating matters?"

"It's occurred. But if you want answers, you'll have to ask Leslie. I don't break promises."

Matt muttered to himself as he opened the door and went out. Ed stared after him worriedly. He hoped he'd done the right thing. He was trying to protect Leslie, but for all he knew, he might just have made matters worse. Matt didn't like mysteries. God forbid that he should try to force Leslie to talk about something she only wanted to forget. He was also worried about Matt's potential reaction to the old scandal. How would he feel if he knew how notorious Leslie really was, if he knew that her mother was serving a sentence for murder?

Ed was worried enough to talk to Leslie about it that evening when he stopped by to see how she was.

"I don't want him to know," she said when Ed questioned her. "Ever."

"What if he starts digging and finds out by himself?" Ed asked bluntly. "He'll read everyone's point of view except yours, and even if he reads every tabloid that ran the story, he still won't know the truth of what happened."

"I don't care what he thinks," she lied. "Anyway, it doesn't matter now."

"Why not?"

"Because I'm not coming back to work," she said evenly, avoiding his shocked gaze. "They need a typist at the Jacobsville sewing plant. I applied this afternoon and they accepted me."

"How did you get there?" he asked.

"Cabs run even in Jacobsville, Ed, and I'm not totally penniless." She lifted her head proudly. "I'll pay your cousin back the price of my operation, however long it takes. But I won't take one more day of the sort of treatment I've been getting from him. I'm sorry if he hates women, but I'm not going to become a scapegoat. I've had enough misery."

"I'll agree there," he said. "But I wish you'd reconsider. I had a long talk with him..."

"You didn't tell him?" she exclaimed, horrified.

"No, I didn't tell him," he replied. "But I think you should."

"It's none of his business," she said through her teeth. "I don't owe him an explanation."

"I know it doesn't seem like it, Leslie," he began, "but he's not a bad man." He frowned, searching for a way to explain it to her. "I don't pretend to understand why you set him off, but I'm sure he realizes that he's being unfair."

"He can be unfair as long as he likes, but I'm not giving him any more free shots at me. I mean it, Ed. I'm not coming back."

He leaned forward, feeling defeated. "Well, I'll be around if you need me. You're still my best friend."

She reached out and touched his hand where it rested on his knee. "You're mine, too. I don't know how I'd have managed if it hadn't been for you and your father."

He smiled. "You'd have found a way. Whatever you're lacking, it isn't courage."

She sighed, looking down at her hand resting on his. "I don't know if that's true anymore," she confessed. "I'm so tired of fighting. I thought I could come to Jacobsville and get my life in order, get some peace. And the first man I run headlong into is a male chauvinist with a grudge against the whole female sex. I feel like I've been through the wringer backward."

"What did he say to you today?" he asked.

She blotted out the physical insult. "The usual things, most vividly the way I'd upset Carolyn by lying about her phone call."

"Some lie!" he muttered.

"He believes her."

"I can't imagine why. I used to think he was intelligent."

"He is, or he wouldn't be a millionaire." She got up. "Now go home, Ed. I've got to get some rest so I can be bright and cheerful my first day at my new job."

He winced. "I wanted things to be better than this for you."

She laughed gently. "And just think what a terrible world we'd have if we always got what we think we want."

He had to admit that she had a point. "That sewing plant isn't a very good place to work," he added worriedly.

"It's only temporary," she assured him.

He grimaced. "Well, if you need me, you know where I am."

She smiled. "Thanks."

He went home and ate supper and was watching the news when Matt knocked at the door just before opening it and walking in. And why not, Ed thought, when Matt had been raised here, just as he had. He grinned at his cousin as he came into the living room and sprawled over an easy chair.

"How does the Jag drive?" he asked.

"Like an airplane on the ground," he chuckled. He stared at the television screen for a minute. "How's Leslie?"

He grimaced. "She's got a new job."

Matt went very still. "What?"

"She said she doesn't want to work for me anymore. She got a job at the sewing plant, typing. I tried to talk her out of it. She won't budge." He glanced at Matt apologetically. "She knew I wouldn't let you fire her. She said you'd made sure she wanted to quit." He shrugged. "I guess you did. I've known Leslie for six years. I've never known her to faint."

Matt's dark eyes slid to the television screen and seemed to be glued there for a time. The garment company paid minimum wage. He doubted she'd have enough left over after her rent and grocery bill to pay for the medicine she had to take for pain. He couldn't remember a time in his life when he'd been so ashamed of himself. She wasn't going to like working in that plant. He knew the manager, a penny-pinching social climber who didn't believe in holidays, sick days, or paid vacation. He'd work her to death for her pittance and complain because she couldn't do more.

Matt's mouth thinned. He'd landed Leslie in hell with his bad temper and unreasonable prejudice.

Matt got up from the chair and walked out the door without a goodbye. Ed went back to the news without much real enthusiasm. Matt had what he wanted. He didn't look very pleased with it, though.

After a long night fraught with even more night-mares, Leslie got up early and took a cab to the man-ufacturing company, hobbling in on her crutches to the personnel office where Judy Blakely, the person-nel manager, was waiting with her usual kind smile.

"Nice to see you, Miss Murry!"

"Nice to see you, too," she replied. "I'm looking for-ward to my new job."

Mrs. Blakely looked worried and reticent. She folded her hands in a tight clasp on her desk. "Oh, I don't know how to tell you this," she wailed. She grimaced. "Miss Murry, the girl you were hired to replace just came back a few minutes ago and begged me to let her keep her job. It seems she has serious family problems and can't do without her salary. I'm so sorry. If we had anything else open, even on the floor, I'd offer it to you temporarily. But we just don't."

The poor woman looked as if the situation tormented her. Leslie smiled gently. "Don't worry, Mrs. Blakely, I'll find something else," she assured the older woman. "It's not the end of the world."

"I'd be furious," she said, her eyes wrinkled up with worry. "And you're being so nice… I feel like a dog!"

"You can't help it that things worked out like this." Leslie got to her feet a little heavily, still smiling. "Could you call me a cab?"

"Certainly! And we'll pay for it, too," she said firmly. "Honestly, I feel so awful!"

"It's all right. Sometimes we have setbacks that really turn into opportunities, you know."

Mrs. Blakely studied her intently. "You're such a positive person. I wish I was. I always seem to dwell on the negative."

"You might as well be optimistic, I always think," Leslie told her. "It doesn't cost extra."

Mrs. Blakely chuckled. "No, it doesn't, does it?" She phoned the cab and apologized again as Leslie went outside to wait for it.

She felt desolate, but she wasn't going to make that poor woman feel worse than she already did.

She was tired and sleepy. She wished the cab would come. She eased down onto the bench the company had placed out front for its employees, so they'd have a place to sit during their breaks. It was hard and uncomfortable, but much better than standing.

She wondered what she would do now. She had no prospects, no place to go. The only alternative was to look for something else or go back to Ed, and the latter choice wasn't a choice at all. She could never look Matt Caldwell in the face again without remembering how he'd treated her.

The sun glinted off the windshield of an approaching car, and she recognized Matt's new red Jaguar at once. She stood up, clutching her purse, stiff and defensive as he parked the car and got out to approach her.

He stopped an arm's length away. He looked as tired and worn-out as she did. His eyes were heavily lined. His black, wavy hair was disheveled. He put his hands on his hips and looked at her with pure malice.

She stared back with something approaching hatred.

"Oh, what the hell," he muttered, adding something about being hanged for sheep, as well as lambs.

He bent and swooped her up in his arms and started walking toward the Jaguar. She hit him with her purse.

"Stop that," he muttered. "You'll make me drop you. Considering the weight of that damned cast, you'd probably sink halfway through the planet."

"You put me down!" she raged, and hit him again. "I won't go as far as the street with you!"

He paused beside the passenger door of the Jag and searched her hostile eyes. "I hate secrets," he said.

"I can't imagine you have any, with Carolyn shouting them to all and sundry!"

His eyes fell to her mouth. "I didn't tell Carolyn that you were easy," he said in a voice so tender that it made her want to cry.

Her lips trembled as she tried valiantly not to.

He made a husky sound and his mouth settled right on her misty eyes, closing them with soft, tender kisses.

She bawled.

He took a long breath and opened the passenger door, shifting her as he slid her into the low-slung vehicle. "I've noticed that about you," he murmured as he fastened her seat belt.

"Noticed...what?" she sobbed, sniffling.

He pulled a handkerchief out of his dress slacks and put it in her hands. "You react very oddly to tenderness."

He closed the door on her surprised expression and fetched her crutches before he went around to get in behind the wheel. He paused to fasten his own seat belt and give her a quick scrutiny before he started the powerful engine and pulled out into the road.

"How did you know I was here?" she asked when the tears stopped.

"Ed told me."

"Why?"

He shrugged. "Beats me. I guess he thought I might be interested."

"Fat chance!"

He chuckled. It was the first time she'd heard him laugh naturally, without mockery or sarcasm. He shifted gears. "You don't know the guy who owns that little enterprise," he said conversationally, "but the plant is a sweatshop."

"That isn't funny."

"Do you think I'm joking?" he replied. "He likes to lure illegal immigrants in here with promises of big salaries and health benefits, and then when he's got them where he wants them, he threatens them with the immigration service if they don't work hard and accept the pittance he pays. We've all tried to get his operation closed down, but he's slippery as an eel." He glanced at her with narrowed dark eyes. "I'm not going to let you sell yourself into that just to get away from me."

"Let me?" She rose immediately to the challenge, eyes flashing. "You don't tell me what to do!"

He grinned. "That's better."

She hit her hand against the cast, furious. "Where are you taking me?"

"Home."

"You're going the wrong way."

"My home."

"No," she said icily. "Not again. Not ever again!"

He shifted gears, accelerated, and shifted again. He loved the smoothness of the engine, the ride. He loved the speed. He wondered if Leslie had loved fast cars before her disillusionment.

He glanced at her set features. "When your leg heals, I'll let you drive it."

"No, thanks," she almost choked.

"Don't you like cars?"

She pushed back her hair. "I can't drive," she said absently.

"What?"

"Look out, you're going to run us off the road!" she squealed.

He righted the car with a muffled curse and downshifted. "Everybody drives, for God's sake!"

"Not me," she said flatly.

"Why?"

She folded her arms over her breasts. "I just never wanted to."

More secrets. He was becoming accustomed to the

idea that she never shared anything about her private life except, possibly, with Ed. He wanted her to open up, to trust him, to tell him what had happened to her. Then he laughed to himself at his own presumption. He'd been her mortal enemy since the first time he'd laid eyes on her, and he expected her to trust him?

"What are you laughing at?" she demanded.

He glanced at her as he slowed to turn into the ranch driveway. "I'll tell you one day. Are you hungry?"

"I'm sleepy."

He grimaced. "Let me see if I can guess why."

She glared at him. His own eyes had dark circles. "You haven't slept, either."

"Misery loves company."

"You started it!"

"Yes, I did!" he flashed back at her, eyes blazing. "Every time I look at you, I want to throw you down on the most convenient flat surface and ravish you! How's that for blunt honesty?"

She stiffened, wide-eyed, and gaped at him. He pulled up at his front door and cut off the engine. He turned in his seat and looked at her as if he resented her intensely. At the moment, he did.

His dark eyes narrowed. They were steady, intimidating. She glared into them.

But after a minute, the anger went out of him. He looked at her, really looked, and he saw things he hadn't noticed before. Her hair was dark just at her scalp. She was far too thin. Her eyes had dark circles so prominent that it looked as if she had two black eyes. There were harsh lines beside her mouth. She might pretend to be cheerful around Ed, but she wasn't. It was an act.

"Take a picture," she choked.

He sighed. "You really are fragile," he remarked quietly. "You give as good as you get, but all your vulnerabilities come out when you've got your back to the wall."

"I don't need psychoanalysis, but thanks for the thought," she said shortly.

He reached out, noticing how she shrank from his touch. It didn't bother him now. He knew that it was tenderness that frightened her with him, not ardor. He touched her hair at her temple and brushed it back gently, staring curiously at the darkness that was more prevalent then.

"You're a brunette," he remarked. "Why do you color your hair?"

"I wanted to be a blonde," she replied instantly, trying to withdraw further against the door.

"You keep secrets, Leslie," he said, and for once he was serious, not sarcastic. "At your age, it's unusual. You're young and until that leg started to act up, you were even relatively healthy. You should be carefree. Your life is an adventure that's only just beginning."

She laughed hollowly. "I wouldn't wish my life even on you," she said.

He raised an eyebrow. "Your worst enemy," he concluded for her.

"That's right."

"Why?"

She averted her eyes to the windshield. She was tired, so tired. The day that had begun with such promise had ended in disappointment and more misery.

"I want to go home," she said heavily.

"Not until I get some answers out of you…!"

"You have no right!" she exploded, her voice breaking on the words. "You have no right, no right…!"

"Leslie!"

He caught her by the nape of the neck and pulled her face into his throat, holding her there even as she struggled. He smoothed her hair, her back, whispering to her, his voice tender, coaxing.

"What did I ever do to deserve you?" she sobbed. "I've never willingly hurt another human being in my life, and look where it got me! Years of running and hiding and never feeling safe…!"

He heard the words without understanding them, soothing her while she cried brokenly. It hurt him to hear her cry. Nothing had ever hurt so much.

He dried the tears and kissed her swollen, red eyes tenderly, moving to her temples, her nose, her cheeks, her chin and, finally, her soft mouth. But it wasn't passion that drove him now. It was concern.

"Hush, sweetheart," he whispered. "It's all right. It's all right!"

She must be dotty, she thought, if she was hearing endearments from Attila the Hun here. She sniffed and wiped her eyes again, finally getting control of herself. She sat up and he let her, his arm over the back of her seat, his eyes watchful and quiet.

She took a steadying breath and slumped in the seat, exhausted.

"Please take me home," she asked wearily.

He hesitated, but only for a minute. "If that's what you really want."

She nodded. He started the car and turned it around.

* * *

He helped her to the front door of the boardinghouse, visibly reluctant to leave her.

"You shouldn't be alone in this condition," he said flatly. "I'll phone Ed and have him come over to see you."

"I don't need…" she protested.

His eyes flared. "The hell you don't! You need someone you can talk to. Obviously it isn't going to be your worst enemy, but then Ed knows all about you, doesn't he? You don't have secrets from him!"

He seemed to mind. She searched his angry face and wondered what he'd say if he knew those secrets. She gave him a lackluster smile.

"Some secrets are better kept," she said heavily. "Thanks for the ride."

"Leslie."

She hesitated, looking back at him.

His face looked harder than ever. "Were you raped?"

Chapter 8

The words cut like a knife. She actually felt them. Her sad eyes met his dark, searching ones.

"Not quite," she replied tersely.

As understatements went, it was a master stroke. She watched the blood drain out of his face, and knew he was remembering, as she was, their last encounter, in his office, when she'd fainted.

He couldn't speak. He tried to, but the words choked him. He winced and turned away, striding back to the sports car. Leslie watched him go with a curious emptiness, as if she had no more feelings to bruise. Perhaps this kind detachment would last for a while, and she could have one day without the mental anguish that usually accompanied her, waking and sleeping.

She turned mechanically and went slowly into the

house on her crutches, and down the hall to her small apartment. She had a feeling that she wouldn't see much of Matt Caldwell from now on. At last she knew how to deflect his pursuit. All it took was the truth—or as much of it as she felt comfortable letting him know.

Ed phoned to check on her later in the day and promised to come and see her the next evening. He did, arriving with a bag full of the Chinese take-out dishes she loved. While they were eating it, he mentioned that her job was still open.

"Miss Smith wouldn't enjoy hearing that," she teased lightly.

"Oh, Karla's working for Matt now."

She stared down at the wooden chopsticks in her hand. "Is she?"

"For some reason, he doesn't feel comfortable asking you to come back, so he sent me to do it," he replied. "He realizes that he's made your working environment miserable, and he's sorry. He wants you to come back and work for me."

She stared at him hard. "What did you tell him?"

"What I always tell him, that if he wants to know anything about you, he can ask you." He ate a forkful of soft noodles and took a sip of the strong coffee she'd brewed before he continued. "I gather he's realized that something pretty drastic happened to you."

"Did he say anything about it to you?"

"No." He lifted his gaze to meet hers. "He did go to the roadhouse out on the Victoria highway last night and wreck the bar."

"Why would he do something like that?" she asked,

stunned by the thought of the straitlaced Mather Caldwell throwing things around.

"He was pretty drunk at the time," Ed confessed. "I had to bail him out of jail this morning. That was one for the books, let me tell you. The whole damned police department was standing around staring at him openmouthed when we left. He was only ever in trouble once, a woman accused him of assault—and he was cleared. His housekeeper testified that she'd been there the whole time and she and Matt had sent the baggage packing. But he's never treed a bar before."

She remembered the stark question he'd asked her and how she'd responded. She didn't understand why her past should matter to Matt. In fact, she didn't want to understand. He still didn't know the whole of it, and she was frightened of how he'd react if he knew. That wonderful tenderness he'd given her in the Jaguar had been actually painful, a bitter taste of what a man's love would be like. It was something she'd never experienced, and she'd better remember that Matt was the enemy. He'd felt sorry for her. He certainly wasn't in love with her. He wanted her, that was all. But despite her surprising response to his light caresses, complete physical intimacy was something she wasn't sure she was capable of responding to. The memories of Mike's vicious fondling made her sick. She couldn't live with them.

"Stop doing that to yourself," Ed muttered, dragging her back to the present. "You can't change the past. You have to walk straight into the future without flinching. It's the only way, to meet things head-on."

"Where did you learn that?" she asked.

"Actually I heard a televised sermon that caught my attention. That's what the minister said, that you have to go boldly forward and meet trouble head-on, not try to run away from it or hide." He pursed his lips. "I'd never heard it put quite that way before. It really made me think."

She sipped coffee with a sad face. "I've always tried to run. I've had to run." She lifted her eyes to his. "You know what they would have done to me if I'd stayed in Houston."

"Yes, I do, and I don't blame you for getting out while you could," Ed assured her. "But there's something I have to tell you now. And you're not going to like it."

"Don't tell me," she said with black humor, "someone from the local newspaper recognized me and wants an interview."

"Worse," he returned. "A reporter from Houston is down here asking questions. I think he's traced you."

She put her head in her hands. "Wonderful. Well, at least I'm no longer an employee of the Caldwell group, so it won't embarrass your cousin when I'm exposed."

"I haven't finished. Nobody will talk to him," he added with a grin. "In fact, he actually got into Matt's office yesterday when his secretary wasn't looking. He was only in there for a few minutes, and nobody knows what was said. But he came back out headfirst and, from what I hear, he ran out the door so fast that he left his briefcase behind with Matt cursing like a wounded sailor all the way down the hall. They said Matt had only just caught up with him at the curb when he ran across traffic and got away."

She hesitated. "When was this?"

"Yesterday." He smiled wryly. "It was a bad time to catch Matt. He'd already been into it with one of the county commissioners over a rezoning proposal we're trying to get passed, and his secretary had hidden in the bathroom to avoid him. That was how the reporter got in."

"You don't think he...told Matt?" she asked worriedly.

"No. I don't know what was said, of course, but he wasn't in there very long."

"But, the briefcase..."

"...was returned to him unopened," Ed said. "I know because I had to take it down to the front desk." He smiled, amused. "I understand he paid someone to pick it up for him."

"Thank God."

"It was apparently the last straw for Matt, though," he continued, "because it wasn't long after that when he said he was leaving for the day."

"How did you know he was in jail?"

He grimaced. "Carolyn phoned me. He'd come by her place first and apparently made inroads into a bottle of Scotch. She hid the rest, after which he decided to go and get his own bottle." He shook his head. "That isn't like Matt. He may have a drink or two occasionally, but he isn't a drinker. This has shocked everybody in town."

"I guess so." She couldn't help but wonder if it had anything to do with the way he'd treated her. But if he'd gone to Carolyn, perhaps they'd had an argument and it was just one last problem on top of too many. "Was Carolyn mad at him?" she asked.

"Furious," he returned. "Absolutely seething. It

seems they'd had a disagreement of major proportions, along with all the other conflicts of the day." He shook his head. "Matt didn't even come in to work today. I'll bet his head is splitting."

She didn't reply. She stared into her coffee with dead eyes. Everywhere she went, she caused trouble. Hiding, running—nothing seemed to help. She was only involving innocent people in her problems.

Ed hesitated when he saw her face. He didn't want to make things even worse for her, but there was more news that he had to give her.

She saw that expression. "Go ahead," she invited. "One more thing is all I need right now, on top of being crippled and jobless."

"Your job is waiting," he assured her. "Whenever you want to come in."

"I won't do that to him," she said absently. "He's had enough."

His eyes became strangely watchful. "Feeling sorry for the enemy?" he asked gently.

"You can't help not liking people," she replied. "He likes most everybody except me. He's basically a kind person. I just rub him the wrong way."

He wasn't going to touch that line. "The same reporter who came here had gone to the prison to talk to your mother," he continued. "I was concerned, so I called the warden. It seems…she's had a heart attack."

Her heart jumped unpleasantly. "Will she live?"

"Yes," he assured her. "She's changed a lot in six years, Leslie," he added solemnly. "She's reconciled to serving her time. The warden says that she wanted to ask for you, but that she was too ashamed to let them contact you. She thinks you can't ever forgive what she said and did to you."

Her eyes misted, but she fought tears. Her mother had been eloquent at the time, with words and the pistol. She stared at her empty coffee cup. "I can forgive her. I just don't want to see her."

"She knows that," Ed replied.

She glanced at him. "Have you been to see her?"

He hesitated. Then he nodded. "She was doing very well until this reporter started digging up the past. He was the one who suggested the movie deal and got that bit started." He sighed angrily. "He's young and ambitious and he wants to make a name for himself. The world's full of people like that, who don't care what damage they do to other peoples' lives as long as they get what they want."

She was only vaguely listening. "My mother...did she ask you about me?"

"Yes."

"What did you tell her?" she wanted to know.

He put down his cup. "The truth. There really wasn't any way to dress it up." His eyes lifted. "She wanted you to know that she's sorry for what happened, especially for the way she treated you before and after the trial. She understands that you don't want to see her. She says she deserves it for destroying your life."

She stared into space with the pain of memory eating at her. "She was never satisfied with my father," she said quietly. "She wanted things he couldn't give her, pretty clothes and jewelry and nights on the town. All he knew how to do was fly a crop-dusting plane, and it didn't pay much..." Her eyes closed. "I saw him fly

into the electrical wires, and go down," she whispered
gruffly. "I saw him go down!" Her eyes began to glitter
with feeling. "I knew he was dead before they ever got
to him. I ran home. She was in the living room, playing music, dancing. She didn't care. I broke the record
player and threw myself at her, screaming."

Ed grimaced as she choked, paused, and fought for
control. "We were never close, especially after the fu-
neral," she continued, "but we were stuck with each
other. Things went along fairly well. She got a job waiting tables and made good tips when she was working.
She had trouble holding down a job because she slept so
much. I got a part-time job typing when I was sixteen,
to help out. Then when I'd just turned seventeen, Mike
came into the restaurant and started flirting with her. He
was so handsome, well-bred and had nice manners. In
no time, he'd moved in with us. I was crazy about him,
you know the way a young girl has crushes on older
men. He teased me, too. But he had a drug habit that
we didn't know about. She didn't like him teasing me,
anyway, and she had a fight with him about it. The next
day, he had some friends over and they all got high."
She shivered. "The rest you know."

"Yes." He sighed, studying her wan face.

"All I wanted was for her to love me," she said dully.
"But she never did."

"She said that," he replied. "She's had a lot of time to
live with her regrets." He leaned forward to search her
eyes. "Leslie, did you know that she had a drug habit?"

"She what?" she exclaimed, startled.

"Had a drug habit," he repeated. "That's what she
told me. It was an expensive habit, and your father got

tired of trying to support it. He loved her, but he couldn't make the sort of money it took to keep her high. It wasn't clothes and jewelry and parties. It was drugs."

She felt as if she'd been slammed to the floor. She moved her hands over her face and pushed back her hair. "Oh, Lord!"

"She was still using when she walked in on Mike and his friends holding you down," he continued.

"How long had she been using drugs?" she asked.

"A good five years," he replied. "Starting with marijuana and working her way up to the hard stuff."

"I had no idea."

"And you didn't know that Mike was her dealer, either, apparently."

She gasped

He nodded grimly. "She told me that when I went to see her, too. She still can't talk about it easily. Now that she has a good grip on reality, she sees what her lifestyle did to you. She had hoped that you might be married and happy by now. It hurt her deeply to realize that you don't even date."

"She'll know why, of course," she said bitterly.

"You sound so empty, Leslie."

"I am." She leaned back. "I don't care if the reporter finds me. It doesn't matter anymore. I'm so tired of running."

"Then stand and deliver," he replied, getting to his feet. "Come back to work. Let your leg heal. Let your hair grow out and go back to its natural color. Start living."

"Can I, after so long?"

"Yes," he assured her. "We all go through periods of

anguish, times when we think we can't face what lies ahead. But the only way to get past it is to go through it, straight through it. No detours, no camouflage, no running. You have to meet problems head-on, despite the pain."

She cocked her head and smiled at him with real affection. "Were you ever a football coach?"

He chuckled. "I hate contact sports."

"Me, too." She brushed her short hair back with her hands. "Okay. I'll give it a shot. But if your cousin gives me any more trouble…"

"I don't think Matt is going to cause you any more problems," he replied.

"Then, I'll see you on Thursday morning."

"Thursday? Tomorrow is just Wednesday…"

"Thursday," she said firmly. "I have plans for tomorrow."

And she did. She had the color taken out of her hair at a local beauty salon. She took her contact lenses to the local optometrist and got big-lensed, wire-framed glasses to wear. She bought clothes that looked professional without being explicit.

Then, Thursday morning, cast and crutches notwithstanding, she went back to work.

She'd been at her desk in Ed's office for half an hour when Matt came in. He barely glanced at her, obviously not recognizing the new secretary, and tapped on Ed's door, which was standing open.

"I'm going to fly to Houston for the sale," he told Ed. He sounded different. His deep voice held its usual authority, but there was an odd note in it. "I don't suppose you were able to convince her to come back…why are you shaking your head?"

Ed stood up with an exasperated sigh and pointed toward Leslie.

Matt scowled, turning on his heel. He looked at her, scowled harder, moved closer, peering into her upturned face.

She saw him matching his memory of her with the new reality. She wondered how she came off, but it was far too soon to get personal.

His eyes went over her short dark hair, over the feminine but professional beige suit she was wearing with a tidy patterned blouse, lingering on the glasses that she'd never worn before in his presence. His own face was heavily lined and he looked as if he'd had his own share of turmoil since she'd seen him last. Presumably he was still having problems with Carolyn.

"Good morning, Miss Murry," he murmured. His eyes didn't smile at her. He looked as if his face was painted on.

That was odd. No sarcasm, no mockery. No insolent sizing up. He was polite and courteous to a fault.

If that was the way he intended to play it…

"Good morning, Mr. Caldwell," she replied with equal courtesy.

He studied her for one long moment before he turned back to Ed. "I should be back by tonight. If I'm not, you'll have to meet with the county commission and the zoning committee."

"Oh, no," Ed groaned.

"Just tell them we're putting up a two-story brick office building on our own damned land, whether they like it or not," Matt told him, "and that we can accommodate them in court for as many years as it takes to get our way. I'm tired of trying to do business in a hundred-year-old house with frozen pipes that burst every winter."

"It won't sound as intimidating if I say it."

"Stand in front of a mirror and practice looking angry."

"Is that how you did it?" Ed murmured dryly.

"Only at first," he assured the other man, deadpan. "Just until I got the hang of it."

"I remember," Ed chuckled. "Even Dad wouldn't argue with you unless he felt he had a good case."

Matt shoved his hands into his pockets. "If you need me, you know the cell phone number."

"Sure."

Still he hesitated. He turned and glanced at Leslie, who was opening mail. The expression on his face fascinated Ed, who'd known him most of his life. It wasn't a look he recognized.

Matt started out the door and then paused to look back at Leslie, staring at her until she lifted her eyes.

He searched them slowly, intently. He didn't smile. He didn't speak. Her cheeks became flushed and she looked away. He made an awkward movement with his shoulders and went out the door.

Ed joined her at her desk when Matt was out of sight. "So far, so good," he remarked.

"I guess he really doesn't mind letting me stay," she murmured. Her hands were shaking because of that long, searching look of Matt's. She clasped them together so that Ed wouldn't notice and lifted her face. "But what if that reporter comes back?"

He pursed his lips. "Odd, that. He left town yesterday. In a real hurry, too. The police escorted him to the city limits and the sheriff drove behind him to the county line."

She gaped at him.

He shrugged. "Jacobsville is a small, close-knit community and you just became part of it. That means," he added, looking almost as imposing as his cousin, "that we don't let outsiders barge in and start harassing our citizens. I understand there's an old city law still on the books that makes it a crime for anyone to stay in a local place of lodging unless he or she is accompanied by at least two pieces of luggage or a trunk." He grinned. "Seems the reporter only had a briefcase. Tough."

"He might come back with a trunk and two suitcases," she pointed out.

He shook his head. "It seems that they found another old law which makes it illegal for a man driving a rental car to park it anywhere inside the city limits. Strange, isn't it, that we'd have such an unusual ordinance."

Leslie felt the first ripple of humor that she'd experienced for weeks. She smiled. "My, my."

"Our police chief is related to the Caldwells," he explained. "So is the sheriff, one of the county commissioners, two volunteer firemen, a sheriff's deputy and a Texas Ranger who was born here and works out of Fort Worth." He chuckled. "The governor is our second cousin."

Her eyes widened. "No Washington connections?" she asked.

"Nothing major. The vice president is married to my aunt."

"Nothing major." She nodded. She let out her breath. "Well, I'm beginning to feel very safe."

"Good. You can stay as long as you like. Permanently, as far as I'm concerned."

She couldn't quite contain the pleasure it gave her to feel as if she belonged somewhere, a place where she was protected and nurtured and had friends. It was a first for her. Her eyes stung with moisture.

"Don't start crying," Ed said abruptly. "I can't stand it."

She swallowed and forced a watery smile to her lips. "I wasn't going to," she assured him. She moved her shoulders. "Thanks," she said gruffly.

"Don't thank me," he told her. "Matt rounded up the law enforcement people and had them going through dusty volumes of ordinances to find a way to get that reporter out of here."

"Matt did?"

He held up a hand as she started to parade her misgivings about what he might have learned of her past. "He doesn't know why the man was here. It was enough that he was asking questions about you. You're an employee. We don't permit harassment."

"I see."

She didn't, but that was just as well. The look Ed had accidentally seen on Matt's face had him turning mental cartwheels. No need to forewarn Leslie. She wasn't ever going to have to worry about being hounded again, not if he knew Matt. And he didn't believe for one minute that his cousin was flying all the way to Houston for a cattle sale that he usually wouldn't be caught dead at. The foreman at his ranch handled that sort of thing, although Leslie didn't know. Ed was betting that Matt had another reason for going to Houston, and it was to find out who hired that reporter and sent him looking for Leslie. He felt sorry for the source of that problem. Matt in a temper was the most menacing human being he'd ever known. He didn't rage or shout and he usually didn't hit, but he had wealth and power and he knew how to use them.

He went back into his office, suddenly worried despite the reassurances he'd given Leslie. Matt didn't know why the reporter was digging around, but what if he found out? He would only be told what the public had been told, that Leslie's mother had shot her daughter and her live-in lover in a fit of jealous rage and that she was in prison. He might think, as others had, that Leslie had brought the whole sordid business on herself by having a wild party with Mike and his friends, and he wouldn't be sympathetic. More than likely, he'd come raging back home and throw Leslie out in the street. Furthermore, he'd have her escorted to the county line like the reporter who'd been following her.

He worried himself sick over the next few hours. He couldn't tell Leslie, when he might only be worrying for nothing. But the thought haunted him that Matt was every bit as dogged as a reporter when it came to ferreting out facts.

In the end, he phoned a hotel that Matt frequented when he was in Houston overnight and asked for his room. But when he was connected, it wasn't Matt who answered the phone.

"Carolyn?" Ed asked, puzzled. "Is Matt there?"

"Not right now," came the soft reply. "He had an appointment to see someone. I suppose he's forgotten that I'm waiting for him with this trolley full of food. I suppose it will be cold as ice by the time he turns up."

"Everything's all right, isn't it?"

"Why wouldn't it be?" she teased.

"Matt's been acting funny."

"Yes, I know. That Murry girl!" Her indrawn breath was audible. "Well, she's caused quite enough trouble. When Matt comes back, she'll be right out of that office, let me tell you! Do you have any idea what that reporter told Matt about her...?"

Ed hung up, sick. So not only did Matt know, but Carolyn knew, too. She'd savage Leslie, given the least opportunity. He had to do something. What?

Ed didn't expect Matt that evening, and he was right. Matt didn't come back in time for the county commission meeting, and Ed was forced to go in his place. He held his own, as Matt had instructed him to, and got what he wanted. Then he went home, sitting on pins and needles as he waited for someone to call him—either Leslie, in tears, or Matt, in a temper.

But the phone didn't ring. And when he went into work the next morning, Leslie was sitting calmly at her desk typing the letters he'd dictated to her just before they closed the day before.

"How did the meeting go?" she asked at once.

"Great," he replied. "Matt will be proud of me." He hesitated. "He, uh, isn't in yet, is he?"

"No. He hasn't phoned, either." She frowned. "You

don't suppose anything went wrong with the plane, do you?"

She sounded worried. Come to think of it, she looked worried, too. He frowned. "He's been flying for a long time," he pointed out.

"Yes, but there was a bad storm last night." She hesitated. She didn't want to worry, but she couldn't help it. Despite the hard time he'd given her, Matt had been kind to her once or twice. He wasn't a bad person; he just didn't like her.

"If anything had happened, I'd have heard by now," he assured her. His lips pursed as he searched for the words. "He didn't go alone."

Her heart stopped in her chest. "Carolyn?"

He nodded curtly. He ran a hand through his hair. "He knows, Leslie. They both do."

She felt the life ebb out of her. But what had she expected, that Matt would wait to hear her side of the story? He was the enemy. He wouldn't for one second believe that she was the victim of the whole sick business. How could she blame him?

She turned off the word processor and moved her chair back, reaching for her purse. She felt more defeated than she ever had in her life. One bad break after another, she was thinking, as she got to her feet a little clumsily.

"Hand me my crutches, Ed, there's a dear," she said steadily.

"Oh, Leslie," he groaned.

She held her hand out and, reluctantly, he helped her get them in place.

"Where will you go?" he asked.

She shrugged. "It doesn't matter. Something will turn up."

"I can help."

She looked up at him with sad resignation. "You can't go against your own blood kin, Ed," she replied. "I'm the outsider here. And one way or another, I've already caused too much trouble. See you around, pal. Thanks for everything."

He sighed miserably. "Keep in touch, at least."

She smiled. "Certainly I'll do that. See you."

He watched her walk away with pure anguish. He wished he could make her stay, but even he wouldn't wish that on her. When Matt came home, he'd be out for blood. At least she'd be spared that confrontation.

Chapter 9

Leslie didn't have a lot to pack, only a few clothes and personal items, like the photograph of her father that she always carried with her. She'd bought a bus ticket to San Antonio, one of the places nosy reporters from Houston might not think to look for her. She could get a job as a typist and find another place to live. It wouldn't be so bad.

She thought about Matt, and how he must feel, now that he knew the whole truth, or at least, the reporter's version of it. She was sure that he and Carolyn would have plenty to gossip about on the way back home. Carolyn would broadcast the scandal all over town. Even if Leslie stopped working for Matt, she would never live down the gossip. Leaving was her only option.

Running away. Again.

Her hands went to a tiny napkin she'd brought home from the dance that she and Ed had attended with Matt and Carolyn. Matt had been doodling on it with his pen just before he'd pulled Leslie out of her seat and out onto the dance floor. It was a silly sentimental piece of nonsense to keep. On a rare occasion or two, Matt had been tender with her. She wanted to remember those times. It was good to have had a little glimpse of what love might have been like, so that life didn't turn her completely bitter.

She folded her coat over a chair and looked around to make sure she wasn't missing anything. She wouldn't have time to look in the morning. The bus would leave at 6:00 a.m., with or without her. She clumped around the apartment with forced cheer, thinking that at least she'd have no knowing, pitying smiles in San Antonio.

Ed looked up as Matt exploded into the office, stopping in his tracks when he reached Leslie's empty desk. He stood there, staring, as if he couldn't believe what he was seeing.

With a sigh, Ed got up and joined him in the outer office, steeling himself for the ordeal. Matt was obviously upset.

"It's all right," he told Matt. "She's already gone. She said she was sorry for the trouble she'd caused, and that…"

"Gone?" Matt looked horrified. His face was like white stone.

Ed frowned, hesitating. "She said it would spare you the trouble of firing her," he began uneasily.

Matt still hadn't managed a coherent sentence. He

ran his hand through his hair, disturbing its neat wave. He stuck his other hand into his pocket and went on staring at her desk as if he expected she might materialize out of thin air if he looked hard enough.

He turned to Ed. He stared at him, almost as if he didn't recognize him. "She's gone. Gone where?"

"She wouldn't tell me," he replied reluctantly.

Matt's eyes were black. He looked back at her desk and winced. He made a violent motion, pressed his lips together, and suddenly took a deep audible breath and with a furious scowl, he let out a barrage of nonstop curses that had even Ed gaping.

"...and I did *not* say she could leave!" he finished at the end.

Ed managed to meet those flashing eyes, but it wasn't easy. Braver men than he had run for cover when the boss lost his temper. "Now, Matt..."

"Don't you 'Now, Matt' me, dammit!" he raged. His fists were clenched at his sides and he looked as if he really wanted to hit something. Or someone. Ed took two steps backward.

Matt saw two of the secretaries standing frozen in the hall, as if they'd come running to find the source of the uproar and were now hoping against hope that it wouldn't notice them.

No such luck. "Get the hell back to work!" he shouted.

They actually ran.

Ed wanted to. "Matt," he tried again.

He was talking to thin air. Matt was down the hall and out the door before he could catch up. He did the only thing he could. He rushed back to his office to phone Leslie and warn her. He was so nervous that it took several tries and one wrong number to get her.

"He's on his way over there," Ed told her the minute she picked up the phone. "Get out."

"No."

"Leslie, I've never seen him like this," he pleaded. "You don't understand. He isn't himself."

"It's all right, Ed," she said calmly. "There's nothing more he can do to me."

"Leslie…!" he groaned.

The loud roar of an engine out front caught her attention. "Try not to worry," she told Ed, and put the receiver down on an even louder exclamation.

She got up, put her crutches in place and hobbled to open her door just as Matt started to knock on it. He paused there, his fist upraised, his eyes black in a face the color of rice.

She stood aside to let him in, with no sense of self-preservation left. She was as far down as she could get already.

He closed the door behind him with an ultracontrolled softness before he turned to look at her. She went back to her armchair and eased down into it, laying the crutches to one side. Her chin lifted and she just looked at him, resigned to more verbal abuse if not downright violence. She was already packed and almost beyond his reach. Let him do his worst.

Now that he was here, he didn't know what to do. He hadn't thought past finding her. He leaned back against the door and folded his arms over his chest.

She didn't flinch or avert her eyes. She stared right at him. "There was no need to come here," she said calmly. "You don't have to run me out of town. I already have my ticket. I'm leaving on the bus first thing in the morning." She lifted a hand. "Feel free to search if you think I've taken anything from the office."

He didn't respond. His chest rose and fell rhythmically, if a little heavily.

She smoothed her hand over the cast where it topped her kneecap. There was an itch and she couldn't get to it. What a mundane thing to think about, she told herself, when she was confronted with a homicidal man.

He was making her more nervous by the minute. She shifted in the chair, grimacing as the cast moved awkwardly and gave her a twinge of pain.

"Why are you here?" she asked impatiently, her eyes flashing at him through her lenses. "What else do you want, an apology…?"

"An apology? Dear God!"

It sounded like a plea for salvation. He moved, for the first time, going slowly across the room to the chair a few feet away from hers, next to the window. He eased himself down into it and crossed his long legs. He was still scowling, watching, waiting.

His eyes were appraising her now, not cutting into her or mocking her. They were dark and steady and turbulent.

Her eyes were dull and lackluster as she averted her face. Her grip on the arm of the chair was painful. "You know, don't you?"

"Yes."

She felt as if her whole body contracted. She watched a bird fly past the window and wished that she could fly away from her problems. "In a way, it's sort of a relief," she said wearily. "I'm so tired...of running."

His face tautened. His mouth made a thin line as he stared at her. "You'll never have to run again," he said flatly. "There isn't going to be any more harassment from that particular quarter."

She wasn't sure she was hearing right. Her face turned back to his. It was hard to meet those searching eyes, but she did. He looked pale, worn.

"Why aren't you gloating?" she asked harshly. "You were right about me all along, weren't you? I'm a little tramp who lures men in and teases them...!"

"Don't!" He actually flinched. He searched for words and couldn't manage to find anything to say to her. His guilt was killing him. His conscience had him on a particularly nasty rack. He looked at her and saw years of torment and self-contempt, and he wanted to hit something.

That expression was easily read in his dark eyes. She leaned her head back against the chair and closed her eyes on the hatred she saw there.

"Everybody had a different idea of why I did it," she said evenly. "One of the bigger tabloids even interviewed a couple of psychiatrists who said I was getting even with my mother for my childhood. Another said it was latent nymphomania..."

"Hell!"

She felt dirty. She couldn't look at him. "I thought I loved him," she said, as if even after all the years, she still couldn't believe it had happened. "I had no idea, none at all, what he was really like. He made fun of my body, he and his friends. They stretched me out like a human sacrifice and discussed…my…assets." Her voice broke. He clenched his hand on the arm of the chair.

Matt's expression, had she seen it, would have silenced her. As it was, she was staring blankly out the window.

"They decided Mike should go first," she said in a husky, strained tone. "And then they drew cards to see which of the other three would go next. I prayed to die. But I couldn't. Mike was laughing at the way I begged him not to do it. I struggled and he had the others hold me down while he…"

A sound came from Matt's tight throat that shocked her into looking at him. She'd never seen such horror in a man's eyes.

"My mother came in before he had time to—" she swallowed "—get started. She was so angry that she lost control entirely. She grabbed the pistol Mike kept in the table drawer by the front door and she shot him. The bullet went through him and into my leg," she whispered, sickened by the memory. "I saw his face when the bullet hit him in the chest from behind. I actually saw the life drain out of him." She closed her eyes. "She kept shooting until one of the men got the pistol away from her. They ran for their lives, and left us there, like that. A neighbor called an ambulance and the police. I remember that one of them got a blanket from the bedroom and wrapped me up in it. They were all…so kind," she choked, tears filling her eyes. "So kind!"

He put his face in his hands. He couldn't bear what he was hearing. He remembered her face in his office when he'd laughed at her. He groaned harshly.

"The tabloids made it look as if I'd invited what happened," she said huskily. "I don't know how a seventeen-year-old virgin can ask grown men to get high on drugs and treat her with no respect. I thought I loved Mike, but even so, I never did anything consciously to make him treat me that way."

Matt couldn't look at her. Not yet. "People high on drugs don't know what they're doing, as a rule," he said through his teeth.

"That's hard to believe," she said.

"It's the same thing as a man drinking too much alcohol and having a blackout," he said, finally lifting his head. He stared at her with dark, lifeless eyes. "Didn't I tell you once that secrets are dangerous?"

She nodded. She looked back out the window. "Mine was too sordid to share," she said bitterly. "I can't bear to be touched by men. By most men," she qualified. "Ed knew all about me, so he never approached me, that way. But you," she added quietly, "came at me like a bull in a pasture. You scared me to death. Aggression always reminds me of...of Mike."

He leaned forward with his head bowed. Even after what he'd learned in Houston already, he was unprepared for the full impact of what had been done to this vulnerable, fragile creature in front of him. He'd let hurt pride turn him into a predator. He'd approached her in ways that were guaranteed to bring back terrible memories of that incident in her past.

"I wish I'd known," he said heavily.

"I don't blame you," she said simply. "You couldn't have known."

His dark eyes came up glittering. "I could have," he

contradicted flatly. "It was right under my nose. The way you downplayed your figure, the way you backed off when I came too close, the way you...fainted—" he had to force the word out "—in my office when I pinned you to the wall." He looked away. "I didn't see it because I didn't want to. I was paying you back," he said on a bitter laugh, "for having the gall not to fall into my arms when I pursued you."

She'd never imagined that she could feel sorry for Matt Caldwell. But she did. He was a decent man. Surely it would be difficult for him to face the treatment he'd given her, now that he knew the truth.

She smoothed her hands over her arms. It wasn't cold in the room, but she was chilled.

"You've never talked about it, have you?" he asked after a minute.

"Only to Ed, right after it happened," she replied. "He's been the best friend in the world to me. When those people started talking about making a television movie of what had happened, I just panicked. They were all over Houston looking for me. Ed offered me a way out and I took it. I was so scared," she whispered. "I thought I'd be safe here."

His fists clenched. "Safe." He made a mockery of the very word.

He got to his feet and moved to the window, avoiding her curious gaze.

"That reporter," she began hesitantly. "He told you about it when he was here, didn't he?"

He didn't reply for a minute. "Yes," he said finally. "He had clippings of the story." She probably knew which ones, he thought miserably, of her being carried out on a stretcher with blood all over her. There was one of the dead man lying on the floor of the apartment, and one of her blond mother shocked and almost catatonic as policemen escorted her to the squad car.

"I didn't connect it when you told Ed you were going to Houston. I thought it was some cattle sale, just like you said," she remarked.

"The reporter ran, but he'd already said that he was working with some people in Hollywood trying to put together a television movie. He'd tried to talk to your mother, apparently, and after his visit, she had a heart attack. That didn't even slow him down. He tracked you here and had plans to interview you." He glanced at her. "He thought you'd be glad to cooperate for a percentage of the take."

She laughed hollowly.

"Yes, I know," he told her. "You're not mercenary. That's one of the few things I've learned about you since you've been here."

"At least you found one thing about me that you like," she told him.

His face closed up completely. "There are a lot of things I like about you, but I've had some pretty hard knocks from women in my life."

"Ed told me."

"It's funny," he said, but he didn't look amused. "I've never been able to come to terms with my mother's actions—until I met you. You've helped me a lot—and I've been acting like a bear with a thorn in its paw. I've mistreated you."

She searched his lean, hard face quietly. He was so

handsome. Her heart jumped every time she met his eyes. "Why did you treat me that way?" she asked.

He stuck his hand into his pocket. "I wanted you," he said flatly.

"Oh."

She wasn't looking at him, but he saw her fingers curl into the arm of the chair. "I know. You probably aren't capable of desire after what was done to you. Perhaps it's poetic justice that my money and position won't get me the one thing in the world I really want."

"I don't think I could sleep with someone," she agreed evenly. "Even the thought of it is...disgusting."

He could imagine that it was, and he cursed that man silently until he ran out of words.

"You liked kissing me."

She nodded, surprised. "Yes, I did."

"And being touched," he prompted, smiling gently at the memory of her reaction—astonishing now, considering her past.

She studied her lap. A button on her dress was loose. She'd have to stitch it. She lifted her eyes. "Yes," she said. "I enjoyed that, too, at first."

His face hardened as he remembered what he'd said to her then. He turned away, his back rigid. He'd made so damned many mistakes with this woman that he didn't know how he was going to make amends. There was probably no way to do it. But he could protect her from any more misery, and he was going to.

He rammed his hands into his pockets and turned. "I went to see that reporter in Houston. I can promise you that he won't be bothering you again, and there won't be any more talk of a motion picture. I went to see your mother, too," he added.

She hadn't expected that. She closed her eyes. She caught her lower lip in her teeth and bit it right through. The taste of blood steeled her as she waited for the explosion.

"Don't!"

She opened her eyes with a jerk. His face was dark and lined, like the downwardly slanted brows above his black eyes. She pulled a tissue from the box on the table beside her and dabbed at the blood on her lip. It was such a beautiful color, she thought irrelevantly.

"I didn't realize how hard this was going to be," he said, sitting down. His head bowed, he clasped his big hands between his splayed knees and stared at the floor. "There are a lot of things I want to tell you. I just can't find the right words."

She didn't speak. Her eyes were still on the blood-dotted tissue. She felt his dark eyes on her, searching, studying, assessing her.

"If I'd…known about your past…" he tried again.

Her head came up. Her eyes were as dead as stone. "You just didn't like me. It's all right. I didn't like you, either. And you couldn't have known. I came here to hide the past, not to talk about it. But I guess you were right about secrets. I'll have to find another place to go, that's all."

He cursed under his breath. "Don't go! You're safe in Jacobsville," he continued, his voice growing stronger and more confident as he spoke. "There won't be any more suspicious reporters, no more movie deals, no more persecution. I can make sure that nobody touches you as long as you're here. I can't…protect you anywhere else," he added impatiently.

Oh, that was just great, she thought furiously. Pity. Guilt. Shame. Now he was going to go to the opposite extreme. He was going to watch over her like a protective father wolf. Well, he could think again. She scooped up one of her crutches and slammed the tip on the floor. "I don't need protection from you or anybody else. I'm leaving on the morning bus. And as for you, Mr. Caldwell, you can get out of here and leave me alone!" she raged at him.

It was the first spark of resistance he'd seen in her since he arrived. The explosion lightened his mood. She wasn't acting like a victim anymore. That was real independence in her tone, in the whole look of her. She was healing already with the retelling of that painful episode in her life.

The hesitation in him was suddenly gone. So was the somber face. Both eyebrows went up and a faint light touched his black eyes. "Or what?"

She hesitated. "What do you mean, or what?"

"If I don't get out, what do you plan to do?" he asked pleasantly.

She thought about that for a minute. "Call Ed."

He glanced at his watch. "Karla's bringing him coffee about now. Wouldn't it be a shame to spoil his break?"

She moved restlessly in the chair, still holding on to the crutch.

He smiled slowly, for the first time since he'd arrived. "Nothing more to say? Have you run out of threats already?"

Her eyes narrowed with bad temper. She didn't know what to say, or what to do. This was completely unexpected.

He studied the look of her in the pretty blue-patterned housedress she was wearing, barefoot. She was pretty, too. "I like that dress. I like your hair that color, too."

She looked at him as if she feared for his sanity. Something suddenly occurred to her. "If you didn't come rushing over here to put me on the bus and see that I left town, why are you here?"

He nodded slowly. "I was wondering when you'd get around to that." He leaned forward, just as another car pulled up outside the house.

"Ed," she guessed.

He grimaced. "I guess he rushed over to save you," he said with resignation.

She glared at him. "He was worried about me."

He went toward the door. "He wasn't the only one," he muttered, almost to himself. He opened the door before Ed could knock. "She's all in one piece," he assured his cousin, standing aside to let him into the room.

Ed was worried, confused, and obviously puzzled when he saw that she wasn't crying. "Are you all right?" he asked her.

She nodded.

Ed looked at her and then at Matt, curious, but too polite to start asking questions.

"I assume that you're staying in town now?" Matt asked her a little stiffly. "You still have a job, if you want it. No pressure. It's your decision."

She wasn't sure what to do next. She didn't want to leave Jacobsville for another town of strange people.

"Stay," Ed said gently.

She forced a smile. "I guess I could," she began. "For a while."

Matt didn't let his relief show. In a way he was glad Ed had shown up to save him from what he was about to say to her.

"You won't regret it," Ed promised her, and she smiled at him warmly.

The smile set Matt off again. He was jealous, and furious that he *was* jealous. He ran a hand through his hair again and glowered with frustration at both of them. "Oh, hell, I'm going back to work," he said shortly. "When you people get through playing games on my time, you might go to the office and earn your damned paychecks!"

He went out the door still muttering to himself, slammed into the Jaguar, and roared away.

Ed and Leslie stared at each other.

"He went to see my mother," she told him.

"And?"

"He didn't say a lot, except…except that there won't be any more reporters asking questions."

"What about Carolyn?" he asked.

"He didn't say a word about her," she murmured, having just remembered that Ed said Carolyn had gone to Houston with him. She grimaced. "I guess she'll rush home and tell the whole town about me."

"I wouldn't like to see what Matt would do about it, if she did. If he asked you to stay, it's because he plans to protect you."

"I suppose he does, but it's a shock, considering the way he was before he went out of town. Honestly, I don't know what's going on. He's like a stranger!"

"I've never heard him actually apologize," he said. "But he usually finds ways to get his point across, without saying the words."

"Maybe that was what he was doing," she replied, thinking back over his odd behavior. "He doesn't want me to leave town."

"That seems to be the case." He smiled at her. "How about it? You've still got a job if you want it, and Matt's taken you off the endangered list. You're safe here. Want to stay?"

She thought about that for a minute, about Matt's odd statement that she was safe in Jacobsville and she wouldn't be hounded anymore. It was like a dream come true after six years of running and hiding. She nodded slowly. "Oh, yes," she said earnestly. "Yes, I want to stay!"

"Then I suggest you put on your shoes and grab a jacket, and I'll drive you back to work, while we still have jobs."

"I can't go to work like this," she protested.

"Why not?" he wanted to know.

"It isn't a proper dress to wear on the job," she said, rising.

He scowled. "Did Matt say that?"

"I'm not giving him the chance to," she said. "From now on, I'm going to be the soul of conservatism at work. He won't get any excuses to take potshots at me."

"If you say so," he said with a regretful thought for the pretty, feminine dress that he'd never seen her wear in public. So much for hoping that Matt might have coaxed her out of her repressive way of dressing. But it was early days yet.

Chapter 10

For the first few days after her return to work, Leslie was uneasy every time she saw Matt coming. She shared that apprehension with two of the other secretaries, one of whom actually ripped her skirt climbing over the fence around the flower garden near the front of the building in a desperate attempt to escape him.

The incident sent Leslie into gales of helpless laughter as she told Karla Smith about it. Matt came by her office just as they were discussing it and stood transfixed at a sound he'd never heard coming from Leslie since he'd known her. She looked up and saw him, and made a valiant attempt to stop laughing.

"What's so funny?" he asked pleasantly.

Karla choked and ran for the ladies' room, leaving Leslie to cope with the question.

"Did you say something to the secretaries the other day to upset them?" she asked him right out.

He shifted. "I may have said a word or two that I shouldn't have," was all he'd admit.

"Well, Daisy Joiner just plowed through a fence avoiding you, and half her petticoat's still…out…there!" She collapsed against her desk, tears rolling down her cheeks.

She was more animated than he'd ever seen her. It lifted his heart. Not that he was going to admit it.

He gave her a harsh mock glare and pulled a cigar case out of his shirt pocket. "Lily-livered cowards," he muttered as he took out a cigar, flicked off the end with a tool from his slacks pocket, and snapped open his lighter with a flair. "What we need around here are secretaries with guts!" he said loudly, and flicked the lighter with his thumb.

Two streams of water hit the flame at the same time from different directions.

"Oh, for God's sake!" Matt roared as giggling, scurrying feet retreated down the hall.

"What were you saying about secretaries with guts?" she asked with twinkling gray eyes.

He looked at his drenched lighter and his damp cigar, and threw the whole mess into the trash can by Leslie's desk. "I quit," he muttered.

Leslie couldn't help the twinkle in her eyes. "I believe that was the whole object of the thing," she pointed out, "to make you quit smoking?"

He grimaced. "I guess it was." He studied her intently. "You're settling back in nicely," he remarked. "Do you have everything you need?"

"Yes," she replied.

He hesitated, as if he wanted to say something else and couldn't decide what. His dark eyes swept over her face, as if he were comparing her dark hair and glasses to the blond camouflage she'd worn when she first came to work for him.

"I guess I look different," she said a little self-consciously, because the scrutiny made her nervous. His face gave nothing away.

He smiled gently. "I like it," he told her.

"Did you need to see Ed?" she asked, because he still hadn't said why he was in Ed's office.

He shrugged. "It's nothing urgent," he murmured. "I met with the planning and zoning committee last night. I thought he might like to know how I came out."

"I could buzz him."

He nodded, still smiling. "Why don't you do that?"

She did. Ed came out of his office at once, still uncertain about Matt's reactions.

"Got a minute?" Matt asked him.

"Sure. Come on in." Ed stood aside to let the taller man stride into his office. He glanced back toward Leslie with a puzzled, questioning expression. She only smiled.

He nodded and closed the door, leaving Leslie to go back to work. She couldn't quite figure out Matt's new attitude toward her. There was nothing predatory about him lately. Ever since his return from Houston and the explosive meeting at her apartment, he was friendly and polite, even a little affectionate, but he didn't come near her now. He seemed to have the idea that any physical contact upset her, so he was being Big Brother Matt instead.

She should have been grateful. After all, he'd said often enough that marriage wasn't in his vocabulary. An affair, obviously, was out of the question now that he knew her past. Presumably affection was the only thing he had to offer her. It was a little disappointing, because Leslie had learned in their one early encounter that Matt's touch was delightful. She wished that she could tell him how exciting it was to her. It had been the only tenderness she'd ever had from a man in any physical respect, and she was very curious about that part of relationships. Not with just anyone, of course.

Only with Matt.

Her hands stilled on the keyboard as she heard footsteps approaching. The door opened and Carolyn came in, svelte in a beige dress that made the most of her figure, her hair perfectly coiffed.

"They said he let you come back to work here. I couldn't believe it, after what that reporter told him," the older woman began hotly. She gave Leslie a haughty, contemptuous stare. "That disguise won't do you any good, you know," she added, pausing to dig in her purse. She drew out a worn page from an old tabloid and tossed it onto Leslie's desk. It was the photo they'd used of her on the stretcher, with the caption, Teenager, Lover, Shot By Jealous Mother In Love Triangle.

Leslie just sat and looked at it, thinking how the past never really went away. She sighed wistfully. She was never going to be free of it.

"Don't you have anything to say?" Carolyn taunted.

Leslie looked up at her. "My mother is in prison. My

life was destroyed. The man responsible for it all was a drug dealer." She searched Carolyn's cold eyes. "You can't imagine it, can you? You've always been wealthy, protected, safe. How could you understand the trauma of being a very innocent seventeen-year-old and having four grown men strip you naked in a drug-crazed frenzy and try to rape you in your own home?"

Amazingly Carolyn went pale. She hesitated, frowning. Her eyes went to the tabloid and she shifted uneasily. Her hand went out to retrieve the page just as the door to Ed's office opened and Matt came through it.

His face, when he saw Carolyn with the tearsheet in her hand, became dangerous.

Carolyn jerked it back, crumpled it, and threw it in the trash can. "You don't need to say anything," she said in a choked tone. "I'm not very proud of myself right now." She moved away from Leslie without looking at her. "I'm going to Europe for a few months. See you when I get back, Matt."

"You'd better hope you don't," he said in a voice like steel.

She made an awkward movement, but she didn't turn. She squared her shoulders and kept walking.

Matt paused beside the desk, retrieved the page and handed it to Ed. "Burn that," he said tautly.

"With pleasure," Ed replied. He gave Leslie a sympathetic glance before he went back into his office and closed the door.

"I thought she came to make trouble," she told Matt with evident surprise in her expression. Carolyn's abrupt about-face had puzzled her.

"She only knew what I mumbled the night I got

drunk," he said curtly. "I never meant to tell her the rest of it. She's not as bad as she seems," he added. "I've known her most of my life, and I like her. She got it into her head that we should get married and saw you as a rival. I straightened all that out. At least, I thought I had."

"Thanks."

"She'll come back a different woman," he continued. "I'm sure she'll apologize."

"It's not necessary," she said. "Nobody knew the true story. I was too afraid to tell it."

He stuck his hands into his pockets and studied her. His face was lined, his eyes had dark circles under them. He looked worn. "I would have spared you this if I could have," he gritted.

He seemed really upset about it. "You can't stop other people from thinking what they like. It's all right. I'll just have to get used to it."

"Like hell you will. The next person who comes in here with a damned tabloid page is going out right through the window!"

She smiled faintly. "Thank you. But it's not necessary. I can take care of myself."

"Judging by Carolyn's face, you did a fair job of it with her," he mused.

"I guess she's not really so bad." She glanced at him and away. "She was only jealous. It was silly. You never had designs on me."

There was a tense silence. "And what makes you think so?"

"I'm not in her league," she said simply. "She's beautiful and rich and comes from a good family."

He moved a step closer, watching her face lift. She didn't look apprehensive, so he moved again. "Not frightened?" he murmured.

"Of you?" She smiled gently. "Of course not."

He seemed surprised, curious, even puzzled.

"In fact, I like bears," she said with a deliberate grin.

That expression went right through him. He smiled. He beamed. Suddenly he caught the back of her chair with his hand and swiveled her around so that her face was within an inch of his.

"Sticks and stones, Miss Murry," he whispered softly, with a lazy grin, and brought his lips down very softly on hers.

She caught her breath.

His head lifted and his dark, quiet eyes met hers and held them while he tried to decide whether or not she was frightened. He saw the pulse throbbing at her neck and heard the faint unsteadiness of her breath. She was unsettled. But that wasn't fear. He knew enough about women to be sure of it.

He chuckled softly, and there was pure calculation in the way he studied her. "Any more smart remarks?" he taunted in a sensual whisper.

She hesitated. He wasn't aggressive or demanding or mocking. She searched his eyes, looking for clues to this new, odd behavior.

He traced her mouth with his forefinger. "Well?"

She smiled hesitantly. All her uncertainties were obvious, but she wasn't afraid of him. Her heart was going wild. But it wasn't with fear. And he knew it.

He bent and kissed her again with subdued tenderness.

"You taste like cigar smoke," she whispered impishly.

"I probably do, but I'm not giving up cigars completely, regardless of the water pistols," he whispered. "So you might as well get used to the taste of them."

She searched his dark eyes with quiet curiosity.

He put his thumb over her soft lips and smiled down at her. "I've been invited to a party at the Ballengers' next month. You'll be out of your cast by then. How about buying a pretty dress and coming with me?" He bent and brushed his lips over her forehead. "They're having a live Latin band. We can dance some more."

She wasn't hearing him. His lips were making her heart beat faster. She was smiling as she lifted her face to those soft kisses, like a flower reaching up to the sun. He realized that and smiled against her cheek.

"This isn't businesslike," she whispered.

He lifted his head and looked around. The office was empty and nobody was walking down the hall. He glanced back down at her with one lifted eyebrow.

She laughed shyly.

The teasing light in his eyes went into eclipse at the response that smile provoked in him. He framed her soft face in his big hands and bent again. This time the kiss wasn't light, or brief.

When she moaned, he drew back at once. His eyes were glittery with strong emotion. He let go of her face and stood up, looking down at her solemnly. He winced, as if he remembered previous encounters when he hadn't been careful with her, when he'd been deliberately cruel.

She read the guilt in his face and frowned. She was

totally unversed in the byplay between men and women, well past the years when those things were learned in a normal way.

"I didn't mean to do that," he said quietly. "I'm sorry."

"It's all right," she stammered.

He drew in a long, slow breath. "You have nothing to be afraid of now. I hope you know that."

"I'm not frightened," she replied.

His face hardened as he looked at her. One hand clenched in his pocket. The other clenched at his side. She happened to look down and she drew in her breath at the sight of it.

"You're hurt!" she exclaimed, reaching out to touch the abrasions that had crusted over, along with the swollen bruises that still remained there.

"I'll heal," he said curtly. "Maybe he will, too, eventually."

"He?" she queried.

"Yes. That yellow-backed reporter who came down here looking for you." His face tautened. "I took Houston apart looking for him. When I finally found him, I delivered him to his boss. There won't be any more problems from that direction, ever. In fact, he'll be writing obituaries for the rest of his miserable life."

"He could take you to court..."

"He's welcome, after my attorneys get through with him," he returned flatly. "He'll be answering charges until he's an old man. Considering the difference in our ages, I'll probably be dead by then." He paused to think about that. "I'll make sure the money's left in my estate to keep him in court until every penny runs out!"

he added after a minute. "He won't even be safe when I'm six feet under!"

She didn't know whether to laugh or cry. He was livid, almost vibrating with temper.

"But you know what hurts the most?" he added, looking down into her worried eyes. "What he did still wasn't as bad as what I did to you. I won't ever forgive myself for that. Not if I live to be a hundred."

That was surprising. She toyed with her keyboard and didn't look at him. "I thought…you might blame me, when you knew the whole story," she said.

"For what?" he asked huskily.

She moved her shoulders restlessly. "The papers said it was my fault, that I invited it."

"Dear God!" He knelt beside her and made her look at him. "Your mother told me the whole story," he said. "She cried like a baby when she got it all out." He paused, touching her face gently. "Know what she said? That she'd gladly spend the rest of her life where she is, if you could only forgive her for what she did to you."

She felt the tears overflowing. She started to wipe them, but he pulled her face to his and kissed them away so tenderly that they came in a veritable flood.

"No," he whispered. "You mustn't cry. It's all right. I won't let anything hurt you ever again. I promise."

But she couldn't stop. "Oh, Matt…!" she sobbed.

All his protective instincts bristled. "Come here to me," he said gently. He stood up and lifted her into his arms, cast and all, and carried her down the deserted hall to his office.

His secretary saw him coming and opened the door for him, grimacing at Leslie's red, wet face.

"Coffee or brandy?" she asked Matt.

"Coffee. Make it about thirty minutes, will you? And hold my calls."

"Yes, sir."

She closed the door and Matt sat down on the burgundy couch with Leslie in his lap, cradling her while she wept.

He tucked a handkerchief into her hand and rocked her in his arms, whispering to her until the sobs lessened.

"I'm going to replace the furniture in here," he murmured. "Maybe the paneling, too."

"Why?"

"It must hold some painful memories for you," he said. "I know it does for me."

His voice was bitter. She recalled fainting, and coming to on this very couch. She looked up at him without malice or accusation. Her eyes were red and swollen, and full of curiosity.

He traced her cheek with tender fingers and smiled at her. "You've had a rough time of it, haven't you?" he asked quietly. "Will it do any good to tell you that a man wouldn't normally treat a woman, especially an innocent woman, the way those animals treated you?"

"I know that," she replied. "It's just that the publicity made me out to be little more than a call girl. I'm not like that. But it's what people thought I was. So I ran, and ran, and hid...if it hadn't been for Ed and his father, and my friend Jessica, I don't know what I would have done. I don't have any family left."

"You have your mother," he assured her. "She'd like

to see you. If you're willing, I'll drive you up there, anytime you like."

She hesitated. "You do know that she's in prison for murder?" she asked.

"I know it."

"You're well-known here," she began.

"Oh, good Lord, are you trying to save me?" he asked with an exasperated sigh. "Woman, I don't give two hoots in hell for gossip. While they're talking about me, they're leaving some other person alone." He took the handkerchief and wiped her cheeks. "But for the record, most reporters keep out of my way." He pursed his lips. "I can guarantee there's one in Houston who'll run the next time he sees me coming."

It amazed her that he'd gone to that much trouble defending her. She lay looking at him with eyes like a cat's, wide and soft and curious.

They had an odd effect on him. He felt his body react to it and caught his breath. He started to move her before she realized that he was aroused.

The abrupt rejection startled her. All at once she was sitting beside him on the couch, looking stunned.

He got up quickly and moved away, turning his back to her. "How would you like some coffee?" he asked gruffly.

She shifted a little, staring at him with open curiosity. "I... I would, thank you."

He went to the intercom, not to the door, and told his secretary to bring it in. He kept his back to Leslie, and to the door, even when Edna came in with the coffee service and placed it on the low coffee table in front of the sofa.

"Thanks, Edna," he said.

"Sure thing, boss." She winked at Leslie and smiled reassuringly, closing the door quietly behind her.

Leslie poured coffee into the cups, glancing at him warily. "Don't you want your coffee?"

"Not just yet," he murmured, trying to cool down.

"It smells nice."

"Yes, it does, but I've already had a little too much stimulation for the moment, without adding caffeine to the problem."

She didn't understand. He felt her eyes on his stiff back and with a helpless laugh, he turned around. To his amazement, and his amusement, she didn't notice anything wrong with him.

He went back to the couch and sat down, shaking his head as he let her hand him a cupful of fresh coffee.

"Is something wrong?" she asked.

"Not a thing in this world, baby doll," he drawled. "Except that Edna just saved you from absolute ruin and you don't even know it."

Leslie stared into Matt's dancing eyes with obvious confusion.

"Never mind," he chuckled, sipping his coffee. "One day when we know each other better, I'll tell you all about it."

She sipped her coffee and smiled absently. "You're very different since you came back from Houston."

"I've had a bad knock." He put his cup down, but his eyes stayed on it. "I can't remember ever being grossly unfair to anyone before, much less an employee. It's hard for me, remembering some of the things I said and did to you." He grimaced, still not looking straight at her. "It hurt my pride that you'd let Ed get close, but you kept backing away from me. I never stopped to wonder why." He laughed hollowly. "I've had women throw themselves at me most of my adult life, even before I made my first million." He glanced at her. "But I couldn't get near you, except once, on the dance floor." His eyes narrowed. "And that night, when you let me touch you."

She remembered, too, the feel of his eyes and his hands and his mouth on her. Her breath caught audibly.

He winced. "It was the first time, wasn't it?"

She averted her eyes.

"I even managed to soil that one, beautiful memory." He looked down at his hands. "I've done so much damage, Leslie. I don't know how to start over, to begin again."

"Neither do I," she confessed. "What happened to me in Houston was a pretty bad experience, even if I'd been older and more mature when it happened. As it was, I gave up trying to go on dates afterward, because I connected anything physical with that one sordid incident. I couldn't bear it when men wanted to kiss me good-night. I backed away and they thought I was some sort of freak." Her eyes closed and she shuddered.

"Tell me about the doctor."

She hesitated. "He only knew what he'd been told, I guess. But he made me feel like trash." She wrapped both arms around her chest and leaned forward. "He cleaned the wound and bandaged my leg. He said that they could send me back to the hospital from jail for the rest."

Matt muttered something vicious.

"I didn't go to jail, of course, my mother did. The leg was horribly painful. I had no medical insurance and Jessica's parents were simple people, very poor. None of us could have afforded orthopedic surgery. I was able to see a doctor at the local clinic, and he put a cast on it, assuming that it had already been set properly. He didn't do X-rays because I couldn't afford any."

"You're lucky the damage could even be repaired," he said, his eyes downcast as he wondered at the bad luck she'd had not only with the trauma of the incident itself, but with its painful aftermath.

"I had a limp when it healed, but I walked fairly well." She sighed. "Then I fell off a horse." She shook her head.

"I wouldn't have had that happen for the world," he said, meeting her eyes. "I was furious, not just that you'd backed away from me, but that I'd caused you to hurt yourself. Then at the dance, it was even worse, when I realized that all those quick steps had caused you such pain."

"It was a good sort of pain," she told him, "because it led to corrective surgery. I'm really grateful about that."

"I'm sorry it came about in the way it did." He smiled at her new look. "Glasses suit you. They make your eyes look bigger."

"I always wore them until the reporter started trying to sell an idea for a television movie about what happened. I dyed my hair and got contacts, dressed like a dowager, did everything I could to change my appearance. But Jacobsville was my last chance. I thought if I could be found here, I could be tracked anywhere." She smoothed her skirt over the cast.

"You won't be bothered by that anymore," he said. "But I'd like to let my attorneys talk to your mother. I know," he said, when she lifted her head and gave him a worried look, "it would mean resurrecting a lot of unpleasant memories, but we might be able to get her sentence reduced or even get her a new trial. There were extenuating circumstances. Even a good public defender isn't as good as an experienced criminal lawyer."

"Did you ask her that?"

He nodded. "She wouldn't even discuss it. She said you'd had enough grief because of her."

She lowered her eyes back to her skirt. "Maybe we both have. But I hate it that she may spend the rest of her life in prison."

"So do I." He touched her hair. "She really is blond, isn't she?"

"Yes. My father had dark hair, like mine, and gray eyes, too. Hers are blue. I always wished mine were that color."

"I like your eyes just the way they are." He touched the wire rims of her frames. "Glasses and all."

"You don't have any problem seeing, do you?" she wondered.

He chuckled. "I have trouble seeing what's right under my nose, apparently."

"You're farsighted?" she asked, misunderstanding him.

He touched her soft mouth with his forefinger and the smile faded. "No. I mistake gold for tinsel."

His finger made her feel nervous. She drew back. His hand fell at once and he smiled at her surprise.

"No more aggression. I promise."

Her fascinated eyes met his. "Does that mean that you won't ever kiss me again?" she asked boldly.

"Oh, I will," he replied, delighted. He leaned forward. "But you'll have to do all the chasing from now on."

Chapter 11

Leslie searched his dark eyes slowly and then she began to smile. "Me, chase you?" she asked.

He pursed his lips. "Sure. Men get tired of the chase from time to time. I think I'd like having you pursue me."

Mental pictures of her in a suit and Matt in a dress dissolved her in mirth. But the reversed relationship made her feel warm inside, as if she wasn't completely encased in ice. The prospect of Matt in her arms was exhilarating, even with her past. "Okay, but I draw the line at taking you to football games," she added, trying to keep things casual between them, just for the time being.

He grinned back. "No problem. We can always watch them on TV." The light in her eyes made him light-headed. "Feeling better now?" he asked softly.

She nodded. "I guess you can get used to anything when you have to," she said philosophically.

"I could write you a book on that," he said bitterly, and she remembered his past—his young life marked with such sadness.

"I'm sure you could," she agreed.

He leaned forward with the coffee cup still in his hands. He had nice hands, she thought absently, lean and strong and beautifully shaped. She remembered their touch on her body with delight.

"We'll take this whole thing one step at a time," he said quietly. "There won't be any pressure, and I won't run roughshod over you. We'll go at your pace."

She was a little reluctant. That one step at a time could lead anywhere, and she didn't like the idea of taking chances. He wasn't a marrying man and she wasn't the type for affairs. She did wonder what he ultimately had in mind for them, but she wasn't confident enough of this new relationship to ask. It was nice to have him like this, gentle and concerned and caring. She hadn't had much tenderness in her life, and she was greedy for it.

He glanced suddenly at the thin gold watch on his wrist and grimaced. "I should have been in Fort Worth an hour ago for a meeting with some stock producers." He glanced at her ruefully. "Just look at what you do to me," he murmured. "I can't even think straight anymore."

She smiled gently. "Good for me."

He chuckled, finished his coffee and put down the cup. "Better late than never, I suppose." He leaned down and kissed her, very softly. His eyes held a new, warm light that made her feel funny all over. "Stay out of trouble while I'm gone."

Her eyebrows rose. "Oh, that's cute."

He nodded. "You never put a foot wrong, did you?"

"Only by being stupid and gullible."

His dark eyes went even darker. "What happened wasn't your fault. That's the first idea we have to correct."

"I was madly infatuated for the first time in my life," she said honestly. "I might have inadvertently given him the idea…"

He put his thumb against her soft lips. "Leslie, what sort of decent adult man would accept even blatant signals from a teenager?"

It was a good question. It made her see what had happened from a different perspective.

He gave her mouth a long scrutiny before he abruptly removed his thumb and ruffled her short dark hair playfully. "Think about that. You might also consider that people on drugs very often don't know what they're doing anyway. You were in the wrong place at the wrong time."

She readjusted her glasses as they slipped further on her nose. "I suppose so."

"I'll be in Fort Worth overnight, but maybe we can go out to dinner tomorrow night?" he asked speculatively.

She indicated the cast. "I can see me now, clumping around in a pretty dress."

He chuckled. "I don't mind if you don't."

She'd never been on a real date before, except nights out with Ed, who was more like a brother than a boyfriend. Her eyes brightened. "I'd love to go out with you, if you mean it."

"I mean it, all right."

"Then, yes."

He grinned at her. "Okay."

She couldn't look away from his dark, soft eyes. It felt like electricity flowing between them. It was exciting to share that sort of intimate look. She colored. He arched an eyebrow and gave her a wicked smile.

"Not now," he said in a deep, husky tone that made her blush even more, and turned toward the door.

He opened it. "Edna, I'll be back tomorrow," he told his secretary.

"Yes, sir."

He didn't look back. The outer door opened and closed. Leslie got up with an effort and moved to the office door. "Do you want me to clean up in here?" she asked Edna.

The older woman just smiled. "Heavens, no. You go on back to work, Miss Murry. How's that leg feeling?"

"Awkward," she said, glowering at it. "But it's going to be nice not to limp anymore," she added truthfully. "I'm very grateful to Mr. Caldwell for having it seen to."

"He's a good man," his secretary said with a smile. "And a good boss. He has moods, but most people do."

"Yes."

Leslie clumped her way back down the hall to her office. Ed came out when he heard her rustling paper and lifted both eyebrows. "Feeling better?" he asked.

She nodded. "I'm a watering pot lately. I don't know why."

"Nobody ever had a better reason," he ventured. He smiled gently. "Matt's not so bad, is he?"

She shook her head. "He's not what I thought he was at first."

"He'll grow on you," he said. He reached for a file on his desk, brought it out and perched himself on the edge of her desk. "I need you to answer these. Feel up to some dictation?"

She nodded. "You bet!"

Matt came back late the next morning and went straight to Leslie when he arrived at the office. "Call Karla Smith and ask if she'll substitute for you," he said abruptly. "You and I are going to take the afternoon off."

"We are?" she asked, pleasantly surprised. "What are we going to do?"

"Now there's a leading question," he said, chuckling. He pressed the intercom on her phone and told Ed he was swiping his secretary and then moved back while Leslie got Karla on the phone and asked her to come down to Ed's office.

It didn't take much time to arrange everything. Minutes later, she was seated beside Matt in the Jaguar flying down the highway just at the legal speed limit.

"Where are we going?" she asked excitedly.

He grinned, glancing sideways at the picture she made in that pretty blue-and-green swirl-patterned dress that left her arms bare. He liked her hair short and dark. He even liked her glasses.

"I've got a surprise for you," he said. "I hope you're going to like it," he added a little tautly.

"Don't tell me. You're taking me to see all the big snakes at the zoo," she said jokingly.

"Do you like snakes?" he asked unexpectedly.

"Not really. But that would be a surprise I wouldn't quite like," she added.

"No snakes."

"Good."

He slid into the passing lane and passed several other cars on the four-lane.

"This is the road to Houston," she said, noting a road sign.

"So it is."

She toyed with her seat belt. "Matt, I don't really like Houston."

"I know that." He glanced at her. "We're going to the prison to see your mother."

Her intake of breath was audible. Her hands clenched on her skirt.

He reached a lean hand over and gently pressed both of hers. "Remember what Ed says? Never back away from a problem," he said softly. "Always meet it head-on. You and your mother haven't seen each other in over five years. Don't you think it's time to lay rest to all the ghosts?"

She was uneasy and couldn't hide it. "The last time I saw her was in court, when the verdict was read. She wouldn't even look at me."

"She was ashamed, Leslie."

That was surprising. Her eyes met his under a frown. "Ashamed?"

"She wasn't taking huge amounts of drugs, but she was certainly addicted. She'd had something before she went back to the apartment and found you with her lover. The drugs disoriented her. She told me that she doesn't even remember how the pistol got into her hand, the next thing she knew, her lover was dead and you were bleeding on the floor. She barely remembers the police taking her away." His lips flattened. "What she does remember is coming back to her senses in jail and being told what she did. No, she didn't look at you during the trial or afterward. It wasn't that she blamed you. She blamed herself for being so gullible and letting herself be taken in by a smooth-talking, lying drug dealer who pretended to love her in return for a place to live."

She didn't like the memories. She and her mother had never been really close, but when she looked back, she remembered that she'd been standoffish and difficult, especially after the death of her father.

His hand contracted on both of hers. "I'm going to be right with you every step of the way," he said firmly. "Whatever happens, it won't make any difference to me. I only want to try to make things easier for you."

"She might not want to see me," she ventured.

"She wants to," he said grimly. "Very badly. She realizes that she might not have much time left."

She bit her lower lip. "I never realized she had heart trouble."

"She probably didn't, until she started consuming massive quantities of drugs. The human body can only take so much abuse until it starts rebelling." He glanced at her. "She's all right for now. She just has to take it easy. But I still think we can do something for her."

"A new trial would put a lot of stress on her."

"It would," he agreed. "But perhaps it isn't the sort of

stress that would be damaging. At the end of that road, God willing, she might get out on parole."

Leslie only nodded. The difficult part lay yet ahead of her; a reunion that she wasn't even sure she wanted. But Matt seemed determined to bring it about.

It was complicated to get into a prison, Leslie learned at once. There were all sorts of checkpoints and safety measures designed to protect visitors. Leslie shivered a little as they walked down the long hall to the room where visitors were allowed to see inmates. For her, the thought of losing her freedom was akin to fears of a lingering death. She wondered if it was that bad for her mother.

There was a long row of chairs at little cubicles, separated from the prisoners' side by thick glass. There was a small opening in the glass, which was covered with mesh wiring so that people could talk back and forth. Matt spoke to a guard and gestured Leslie toward one of the cubicles, settling her in the straight-backed chair there. Through the glass, she could see a closed door across the long room.

As she watched, aware of Matt's strong, warm hand on her shoulder, the door opened and a thin, drawn blond woman with very short hair was ushered into the room by a guard. She went forward to the cubicle where Leslie was sitting and lifted her eyes to the tense face through the glass. Her pale blue eyes were full of sadness and uncertainty. Her thin hands trembled.

"Hello, Leslie," she said slowly.

Leslie just sat there for a moment with her heart beating half to death. The thin, drawn woman with the heavily lined face and dull blue eyes was only a shadow of the mother she remembered. Those thin hands were so wasted that the blue veins on their backs stood out prominently.

Marie smiled with faint self-contempt. "I knew this would be a mistake," she said huskily. "I'm so sorry..." She started to get up.

"Wait," Leslie croaked. She grimaced. She didn't know what to say. The years had made this woman a stranger.

Matt moved behind her, both hands on her shoulders now, supporting her, giving her strength.

"Take your time," he said gently. "It's all right."

Marie gave a little start as she noticed that Matt was touching Leslie with some familiarity, and Leslie wasn't stiff or protesting. Her eyes connected with his dark ones and he smiled.

Marie smiled back hesitantly. It changed her lined, worn face and made her seem younger. She looked into her daughter's eyes and her own softened. "I like your boss," she said.

Leslie smiled back. "I like him, too," she confessed.

There was a hesitation. "I don't know where to start," she began huskily. "I've rehearsed it and rehearsed it and I simply can't find the words." Her pale eyes searched Leslie's face, as if she was trying to recall it from the past. She winced as she compared it with the terror-stricken face she'd seen that night so long ago. "I've made a lot of mistakes, Leslie. My biggest one was putting my own needs ahead of everybody else's. It was always what *I* wanted, what *I* needed. Even when I started doing drugs, all I thought about was what would make me happy." She shook her head. "Selfishness carries a high price tag. I'm so sorry that you had to pay such a high price for mine. I couldn't even bear to look at you at the trial, after the tabloids came out. I was so ashamed of what I'd subjected you to. I thought of you, all alone, trying to hold your head up with half the state knowing such intimate things about our lives..." She drew in a slow, unsteady breath and she seemed to slump. "I can't even ask you to forgive me. But I did want to see you, even if it's just this once, to tell you how much I regret it all."

The sight of her pinched face hurt Leslie, who hadn't realized her mother even felt remorse. There had been no communication between them. She knew now that Matt had been telling the truth about her mother's silence. Marie was too ashamed to face her, even now. It eased the wound a little. "I didn't know about the drugs," Leslie blurted out abruptly.

Her tone brought Marie's eyes up, and for the first time, there was hope in them. "I never used them around you," she said gently. "But it started a long time ago, about the time your father...died." The light in her eyes seemed to dim. "You blamed me for his death, and you were right. He couldn't live up to being what I wanted him to be. He couldn't give me the things I thought I deserved." She looked down at the table in front of her. "He was a good, kind man. I should have appreciated him. It wasn't until he died that I realized how much he meant to me. And it was too late." She laughed hollowly. "From then on, everything went downhill. I didn't care anymore, about myself or you, and I went onto harder drugs. That's how I met Mike. I guess you figured out that he was my supplier."

"Matt did," Leslie corrected.

Marie lifted her eyes to look at Matt, who was still standing behind Leslie. "Don't let them hurt her anymore," she pleaded gently. "Don't let that reporter make her run anymore. She's had enough."

"So have you," Leslie said unexpectedly, painfully touched by Marie's concern. "Matt says…that he thinks his attorneys might be able to get you a new trial."

Marie started. Her eyes lit up, and then abruptly shifted. "No!" she said gruffly. "I have to pay for what I did."

"Yes," Leslie said. "But what you did…" She hesitated. "What you did was out of shock and outrage, don't you see? It wasn't premeditated. I don't know much about the law, but I do know that intent is everything. You didn't plan to kill Mike."

The older woman's sad eyes met Leslie's through the glass. "That's generous of you, Leslie," she said quietly. "Very generous, considering the notoriety and grief I caused you."

"We've both paid a price," she agreed.

"You're wearing a cast," her mother said suddenly. "Why?"

"I fell off a horse," Leslie said and felt Matt's hands contract on her shoulders, as if he was remembering why. She reached up and smoothed her hand over one of his. "It was a lucky fall, because Matt got an orthopedic surgeon to operate on my leg and put it right."

"Do you know how her leg was hurt?" the other woman asked Matt with a sad little smile.

"Yes," he replied. His voice sounded strained. The tender, caressing action of Leslie's soft fingers on his hand was arousing him. It was the first time she'd touched him voluntarily, and his head was reeling.

"That's another thing I've had on my conscience for years," the smaller woman told her daughter. "I'm glad you had the operation."

"I'm sorry for the position you're in," Leslie said with genuine sympathy. "I would have come to see you years ago, but I thought... I thought you hated me," she added huskily, "for what happened to Mike."

"Oh, Leslie!" Marie put her face in her hands and her shoulders shook. She wept harshly, while her daughter sat staring at her uncomfortably. After a minute, she wiped the tears from her red, swollen eyes. "No, I didn't hate you! I never blamed you!" Marie said brokenly. "How could I hate you for something that was never your fault? I wasn't a good mother. I put you at risk the minute I started using drugs. I failed you terribly. By letting Mike move in, I set you up for what he and his friends did to you. My poor baby," she choked. "You were so very young, so innocent, and to have men treat you...that way—" She broke off. "That's why I couldn't ask you to come, why I couldn't write or phone. I thought you hated *me!*"

Leslie's fingers clenched around Matt's on her shoulder, drawing strength from his very presence. She knew she could never have faced this without him. "I didn't hate you," she said slowly. "I'm sorry we couldn't talk to each other, at the trial. I...did blame you for Dad," she confessed. "But I was so young when it happened, and you and I had never been particularly close. If we had…"

"You can't change what was," her mother said with a wistful smile. "But it's worth all this if you can forgive me." Her long fingers moved restlessly on the table. Her pained eyes met Leslie's. "It means everything if you can forgive me!"

Leslie felt a lump in her throat as she looked at her mother and realized the change in her. "Of course I can." She bit her lip. "Are you all right? Is your health all right?"

"I have a weak heart, probably damaged by all the drugs I took," Marie said without emphasis. "I take medicine for it, and I'm doing fine. I'll be all right, Leslie." She searched the younger woman's eyes intently. "I hope you're going to be all right, too, now that you aren't being stalked by that reporter anymore. Thank you for coming to see me."

"I'm glad I did," Leslie said, and meant it sincerely. "I'll write, and I'll come to see you when I can. Meanwhile, Matt's lawyers may be able to do something for you. Let them try."

There was a hesitation while the other woman exchanged a worried look with Matt.

Both his hands pressed on Leslie's shoulders. "I'll take care of her," he told Marie, and knew that she understood what he was saying. Nobody would bother Leslie again, as long as there was a breath in his body. He had power and he would use it on her daughter's behalf. She relaxed.

"All right, then," she replied. "Thank you for trying to help me, even if nothing comes of it."

Matt smiled at her. "Miracles happen every day," he said, and he was looking at Leslie's small hand caressing his.

"You hold on to him," the older woman told Leslie fervently. "If I'd had a man like that to care about me, I wouldn't be in this mess today."

Leslie flushed. Her mother spoke as if she had a chance of holding on to Matt, and that was absurd. He might feel guilt and sympathy, even regret, but her mother seemed to be mistaking his concern for love. It wasn't.

Matt leaned close to Leslie and spoke. "It's rather the other way around," Matt said surprisingly, and he didn't smile. "Women like Leslie don't grow on trees."

Marie smiled broadly. "No, they don't. She's very special. Take care of yourself, Leslie. I... I do love you, even if it doesn't seem like it."

Leslie's eyes stung with threatening tears. "I love you, too, Mama," she said in a gruff, uneasy tone. She could barely speak for the emotion she felt.

The other woman couldn't speak at all. Her eyes were bright and her smile trembled. She only nodded. After one long look at her daughter, she got up and went to the door.

Leslie sat there for a minute, watching until her mother was completely out of sight. Matt's big hands contracted on her shoulders.

"Let's go, sweetheart," he said gently, and pressed a handkerchief into her hands as he shepherded her out the door.

That tenderness in him was a lethal weapon, she thought. It was almost painful to experience, especially when she knew that it wasn't going to last. He was kind, and right now he was trying to make amends. But she'd better not go reading anything into his actions. She had to take one day at a time and just live for the present.

She was quiet all the way to the parking lot. Matt smoked a cigar on the way, one hand in his pocket, his eyes narrow and introspective as he strode along beside Leslie until they reached the car. He pushed a button on his electronic controller and the locks popped up.

"Thank you for bringing me here," Leslie said at the passenger door, her eyes full of gratitude as they lifted to his. "I'm really glad I came, even if I didn't want to at first."

He stayed her hand as she went to open the door and moved closer, so that she was standing between his long, muscular body and the door. His dark eyes searched hers intently.

His gaze fell to her soft mouth and the intensity of the look parted her lips. Her pulse raced like mad. Her reaction to his closeness had always been intense, but she could almost feel his mouth on her body as she looked up at him. It was frightening to feel such wanton impulses.

His eyes lifted and he saw that expression in her soft, dazed gray eyes. The muscles in his jaw moved and he seemed to be holding his breath.

Around them, the parking lot was deserted. There was nothing audible except the sound of traffic and the frantic throb of Leslie's pulse as she stared into Matt's dark, glittery eyes.

He moved a step closer, deliberately positioning his

body so that one long, powerful leg brushed between her good leg and the bulky cast on the other one.

"Matt?" she whispered shakily.

His eyes narrowed. His free hand went to her face and spread against her flushed cheek. His thumb nudged at her chin, lifting it. His leg moved against her thighs and she gasped.

There was arrogance not only in the way he touched her, but in the way he looked at her. She was completely vulnerable when he approached her like this, and he must surely know it, with his experience of women.

"So many women put on an act," he murmured conversationally. "They pretend to be standoffish, they tease, they provoke, they exaggerate their responses. With you, it's all genuine. I can look at you and see everything you're thinking. You don't try to hide it or explain it. It's all right there in the open."

Her lips parted. It was getting very hard to breathe. She didn't know what to say.

His head bent just a little, so that she could feel his breath on her mouth. "You can't imagine the pleasure it gives me to see you like this. I feel ten feet tall."

"Why?" she whispered unsteadily.

His mouth hovered over hers, lightly brushing, teasing. "Because every time I touch you, you offer yourself up like a virgin sacrifice. I remember the taste of your breasts in my mouth, the soft little cries that pulsed out of you when I pressed you down into the mattress under my body." He moved against her, slowly and deliberately, letting her feel his instant response. "I want to take your clothes off and ease inside your body on crisp, white sheets..." he whispered as his hard mouth went down roughly on her soft lips.

She made a husky little cry as she pictured what he was saying to her, pictured it, ached for it. Of all the outrageous, shocking things to say to a woman...!

Her nails bit into his arms as she lifted herself against his arousal and pushed up at his mouth to tempt it into violence. The sudden whip of passion was unexpected, overwhelming. She moaned brokenly and her legs trembled.

He groaned harshly. For a few seconds, his mouth devoured her own. He had to drag himself away from her, and when he did, his whole body seemed to vibrate. There was a flush high on his cheekbones, and his eyes glittered.

She loved the expression on his face. She loved the tremor of the arms propped on either side of her head. Her chin lifted and her eyes grew misty with pleasure.

"Do you like making me this way?" he asked gruffly.

"Yes," she said, something wild and impulsive rising in her like a quick tide. She looked at the pulse in his throat, the quick rhythmic movement of his shirt under the suit he was wearing. Her eyes dropped boldly down his body to the visible effect of passion on him.

His intake of breath was audible as he watched her eyes linger on him, there. His whole body shook convulsively, as if with a fever.

Her eyes went back to his. It was intimate, to look at him this way. She could feel his passion, taste it.

Her hands went to his chest and rested against his warm muscles through the shirt, feeling the soft cushion of hair under it. He wasn't trying to stop her, and she remembered what he'd said to her in his office, that she was going to have to do all the running. Well, why not? She had to find out sooner or later what the limits of her capability were. Now seemed as good a time as any, despite their surroundings. Shyly, involuntarily, her nervous hands slid down to his belt and hesitated.

His jaw clenched. He was helpless. Did she know? Her hands slowly moved over the belt and down barely an inch before they hesitated again. His heavy brows drew together in a ferocious scowl as he fought for control.

He seemed to turn to stone. There was not a trace of emotion on his lean, hard face, but his eyes were glittering wildly.

"Go ahead if you want to. But if you touch me there," he said in a choked, harsh tone, "I will back you into this car, push your skirt up, and take you right here in the parking lot without a second's hesitation. And I won't give a damn if the entire staff of the prison comes out to watch!"

Chapter 12

The terse threat brought Leslie to her senses. She went scarlet as her hands jerked back from his body.

"Oh, good Lord!" she said, horrified at what she'd been doing.

Matt closed his eyes and leaned his forehead against hers. It was damp with sweat and he shuddered with helpless reaction even as he laughed at her embarrassment.

She could barely get her own breath, and her body felt swollen all over. "I'm sorry, Matt, I don't know what got into me!"

The raging desire she'd kindled was getting the best of him. He'd wanted her for such a long time. He hadn't even thought of other women. "Leslie, I'm fairly vulnerable, and you're starting something both of us know you can't finish," he added huskily.

"I'm…not sure that I can't," she said, surprising both of them. She felt the damp warmth of his body close to hers and marveled at his vulnerability.

His eyes opened. He lifted his head slowly and looked down at her, his breath on her mouth. "If you have a single instinct for self-preservation left, you'd better get in the car, Leslie."

"Okay," she agreed breathlessly, her heart in her eyes as she looked at him with faint wonder.

She got in on the passenger side and fastened her seat belt. He came around to the driver's side and got into the car.

Her hands were curling in on the soft material of her purse and she looked everywhere except at him. She couldn't believe what she'd done.

"Don't make such heavy weather of it," he said gently. "I did say that you'd have to do the chasing, after all."

She cleared her throat. "I think I took it a little too literally."

He chuckled. The sound was deep and pleasant as the powerful car ate up the miles toward Jacobsville. "You have definite potential, Miss Murry," he mused, glancing at her with indulgent affection. "I think we're making progress."

She stared at her purse. "Slow progress."

"That's the best kind." He changed gears and passed a slow-moving old pickup truck. "I'll drop you by your house to change. We're going out on the town tonight, cast and all."

She smiled shyly. "I can't dance."

"There's plenty of time for dancing when you're back on your feet," he said firmly. "I'm going to take care of you from now on. No more risks."

He made her feel like treasure. She didn't realize she'd spoken aloud until she heard him chuckle.

"That's what you are," he said. "My treasure. I'm going to have a hard time sharing you even with other people." He glanced at her. "You're sure there's nothing between you and Ed?"

"Only friendship," she assured him.

"Good."

He turned on the radio and he looked more relaxed than she'd ever seen him. It was like a beginning. She had no idea where their relationship would go, but she was too weak to stop now.

They went out to eat, and Matt was the soul of courtesy. He opened doors for her, pulled out chairs for her, did all the little things that once denoted a gentleman and proved to her forcefully that he wasn't a completely modern man. She loved it. Old World courtesy was delicious.

They went to restaurants in Jacobsville and Victoria and Houston in the weeks that followed, and Matt even phoned her late at night, just to talk. He sent her flowers at the boardinghouse, prompting teasing remarks and secret smiles from other residents. He was Leslie's fellow, in the eyes of Jacobsville, and she began to feel as if her dreams might actually come true—except for the one problem that had never been addressed. How was she going to react when Matt finally made love to her completely? Would she be able to go through with intimacy like that, with her past?

It haunted her, because while Matt had been affectionate and kind and tender with her, it never went beyond soft, brief kisses in his car or at her door. He never attempted to take things to a deeper level, and she was too shy from their encounter at the prison parking lot to be so bold again.

The cast came off just before the Ballengers' party to which all of Jacobsville was invited. Leslie looked at her unnaturally pale leg with fascination as Lou Coltrain coaxed her into putting her weight on it for the first time without the supporting cast.

She did, worried that it wouldn't take her weight, while Matt stood grim-faced next to Lou and worried with her.

But when she felt the strength of the bone, she gasped. "It's all right!" she exclaimed. "Matt, look, I can stand on it!"

"Of course you can," Lou chuckled. "Dr. Santos is the best, the very best, in orthopedics."

"I'll be able to dance again," she said.

Matt moved forward and took her hand in his, lifting it to his mouth. "*We'll* be able to dance again," he corrected, holding her eyes with his.

Lou had to stifle amusement at the way they looked together, the tall dark rancher and the small brunette, like two halves of a whole. That would be some marriage, she thought privately, but she kept her thoughts to herself.

* * *

Later, Matt came to pick her up at her apartment. She was wearing the long silver dress with the spaghetti straps, and this time without a bra under it. She felt absolutely vampish with her contacts back in and her hair clean and shining. She'd gained a little weight in the past few weeks, and her figure was all she'd ever hoped it would be. Best of all, she could walk without limping.

"Nice," he murmured, smiling as they settled themselves into the car. "But we're not going to overdo things, are we?"

"Whatever you say, boss," she drawled.

He chuckled as he cranked the car. "That's a good start to the evening."

"I have something even better planned for later," she said demurely.

His heart jumped and his fingers jerked on the steering wheel. "Is that a threat or a promise?"

She glanced at him shyly. "That depends on you."

He didn't speak for a minute. "Leslie, you can only go so far with a man before things get out of hand," he began slowly. "You don't know much about relationships, because you haven't dated. I want you to understand how it is with me. I haven't touched another woman since I met you. That makes me more vulnerable than I would be normally." His eyes touched her profile and averted to the highway. "I can't make light love to you anymore," he said finally, his voice harsh. "The strain is more than I can bear."

Her breath caught. She smoothed at an imaginary spot on her gown. "You want us to…to go on like we are."

"I do not," he said gruffly. "But I'm not going to put any pressure on you. I meant what I said about letting you make the moves."

She turned the small purse over in her hands, watching the silver sequins on it glitter in the light. "You've been very patient."

"Because I was very careless of you in those first weeks we knew each other," he said flatly. "I'm trying to show you that sex isn't the basis of our relationship."

She smiled. "I knew that already," she replied. "You've taken wonderful care of me."

He shrugged. "Penance."

She grinned, because it wasn't. He'd shown her in a hundred nonverbal ways how he felt about her. Even the other women in the office had remarked on it.

He glanced at her. "No comment?"

"Oh, I'm sorry, I was just thinking about something."

"About what?" he asked conversationally.

She traced a sequin on the purse. "Can you teach me how to seduce you?"

The car went off the road and barely missed a ditch before he righted it, pulled onto the shoulder and flipped the key to shut off the engine.

He gaped at her. "What did you say?"

She looked up at him in the dimly lit interior where moonlight reflected into the car. "I want to seduce you."

"Maybe I have a fever," he murmured.

She smiled. She laughed. He made her feel as if she could do anything. Her whole body felt warm and uninhibited. She leaned back in her seat and moved sinuously in the seat, liking the way the silky fabric felt against her bare breasts. She felt reckless.

His gaze fell to the fabric against which her hard nipples were distinctly outlined. He watched her body move and knew that she was already aroused, which aroused him at once.

He leaned over, his mouth catching hers as his lean hand slipped under the fabric and moved lazily against her taut breasts.

She moaned and arched toward his fingers, pulling them back when he would have removed them. Her mouth opened under his as she gave in to the need to experience him in a new way, in a new intimacy.

"This is dangerous." He bit off the words against her mouth.

"It feels wonderful," she whispered back, pressing his hand to her soft skin. "I want to feel you like this. I want to touch you under your shirt…"

He hadn't realized how quickly he could get a tie and a shirt out of the way. He pulled her across the console and against him, watching her pert breasts bury themselves in the thick hair that covered his chest. He moved her deliberately against it and watched her eyes grow languid and misty as she experienced him.

His mouth opened hers in a sensual kiss that was as explicit as lovemaking. She felt his tongue, his lips, his teeth, and all the while, his chest moved lazily against her bare breasts. His hand went to the base of her spine and moved her upon the raging arousal she'd kindled. He groaned harshly, and she knew that he wouldn't draw back tonight. The strange thing, the wonderful thing, was that she wasn't afraid.

A minute later, he forced his head up and looked at her, lying yielding and breathless against him. He touched her breasts possessively before he lifted his eyes to search hers. "You aren't afraid of me like this," he said huskily.

She drew in a shaking breath. "No. I'm not."

His eyes narrowed as he persisted. "You want me."

She nodded. She touched his lips with fingers that trembled. "I want you very much. I like the way you feel when you want me," she whispered daringly, the surprise of it in her expression as she moved restlessly against him. "It excites me to feel it."

He groaned out loud and closed his eyes. "For God's sake, honey, don't say things like that to me!"

Her fingers moved down to his chest and pressed there. "Why not? I want to know if I can be intimate with you. I have to know," she said hesitantly. "I've never been able to want a man before. And I've never felt anything like this!" She looked up into his open, curious eyes. "Matt, can we…go somewhere?" she whispered.

"And make love?" he asked in a tone that suggested he thought she was unbalanced.

Her expression softened. "Yes."

He couldn't. His brain told him he couldn't. But his stupid body was screaming at him that he certainly could! "Leslie, sweetheart, it's too soon…"

"No, it isn't," she said huskily, tracing the hair on his chest with cool fingers. "I know you don't want anything permanent, and that's okay. But I…"

The matter-of-fact statement surprised him. "What do you mean, I don't want anything permanent?"

"I mean, you aren't a marrying man."

He looked puzzled. He smiled slowly. "Leslie, you're a virgin," he said softly.

"I know that's a drawback, but we all have to start somewhere. You can teach me how," she said stubbornly. "I can learn."

"No!" he said softly. "It's not that at all." His eyes seemed to flicker and then burn like black coals. "Leslie, I don't play around with virgins."

Her mind wasn't getting this at all. She felt dazed by her own desire. "You don't?"

"No, I don't," he said firmly.

"Well, if you'll cooperate, I won't be one for much longer," she pointed out. "So there goes your last argument, Matt." She pressed deliberately closer to him, as aware as he was that his body was amazingly capable.

He actually flushed. He pushed away from her and moved her back into her own seat firmly, pulling up the straps of her dress with hands that fumbled a little. He looked as if she'd hit him in the head with something hard.

Puzzled, she fiddled with her seat belt as he snapped his own into place.

He looked formidably upset. He started the car with subdued violence and put it in gear, his expression hard and stoic.

As the Jaguar shot forward, she slanted a glance at him. It puzzled her that he'd backed away from her. Surely he wasn't insulted by her offer? Or maybe he was.

"Are you offended?" she asked, suddenly self-conscious and embarrassed.

"Heavens, no!" he exclaimed.

"Okay." She let out a relieved sigh. She glanced at him. He wouldn't look at her. "Are you sure you aren't?"

He nodded.

She wrapped her arms around her chest and stared out the windshield at the darkened landscape, trying to decide why he was acting so strangely. He certainly wasn't the man she thought she knew. She'd been certain that he wanted her, too. Now she wasn't.

The Jaguar purred along and they rode in silence. He didn't speak or look at her. He seemed to be deep in thought and she wondered if she'd ruined their budding relationship for good with her wanton tendencies.

It wasn't until he turned the car down a dirt road a few miles from the ranch that she realized he wasn't going toward the Ballengers' home.

"Where are we?" she asked when he turned down an even narrower dirt road that led to a lake. Signposts pointed to various cabins, one of which had Caldwell on it. He pulled into the yard of a little wood cabin in the woods, facing the lake, and cut off the engine.

"This is where I come to get away from business," he told her bluntly. "I've never brought a woman here."

"You haven't?"

His eyes narrowed on her flushed face. "You said you wanted to find out if you could function intimately. All right. We have a place where we won't be disturbed, and I'm willing. More than willing. So there's no reason to be embarrassed," he said quietly. "I want you every bit as badly as you want me. I have something to use. There won't be any risk. But you have to be sure this is what you really want. Once I take your virginity, I can't give it back. There's only one first time."

She stared at him. Her whole body felt hot at the way he was looking at her. She remembered the feel of his mouth on her breasts and her lips parted hungrily. But it was more than just hunger. He knew it.

She lifted her face to his and brushed a breathless little kiss against his firm chin. "I wouldn't let any other man touch me," she said quietly. "And I think you know it."

"Yes. I know it." He knew something else, as well; he knew that it was going to be a beginning, not an affair or a one-night stand. He was going to be her first man, but she was going to be his last woman. She was all he wanted in the world.

He got out and led her up the steps on to the wide porch where there was a swing and three rocking chairs. He unlocked the door, ushered her inside and locked it again. Taking her hand in his, he led her to the bedroom in back. There was a huge king-size bed in the room. It was covered by a thick comforter in shades of beige and red.

For the first time since she'd been so brazen with him, reality hit her like a cold cloth. She stood just inside the doorway, her eyes riveted on that bed, as erotic pictures of Matt without clothing danced in her thoughts.

He turned to her, backing her up against the closed door. He sensed her nervousness, her sudden uncertainty.

"Are you afraid?" he asked somberly.

"I'm sorry, I guess I am," she said with a forced smile.

His lean hands framed her face and he bent and

kissed her eyelids. "This may be your first time. It isn't mine. By the time we end up on that bed, you'll be ready for me, and fear is the very last thing you're going to feel."

He bent to her mouth then and began to kiss her. The caresses were tender and slow, not arousing. If anything, they comforted. She felt her fear of him, of the unknown, melt away like ice in the hot sun. After a few seconds, she relaxed and gave in to his gentle ardor.

At first it was just pleasant. Then she felt him move closer and his body reacted at once to hers.

He caught his breath as he felt the sudden surge of pleasure.

Her hands smoothed up his hard thighs, savoring the muscular warmth of them while his mouth captured hers and took possession of it a little roughly, because she was intensifying the desire that was already consuming him.

His body began to move on her, slow and caressing, arousing and tantalizing. Her breasts felt heavy. Her nipples were taut, and the friction of the silky cloth against them intensified the sensations he was kindling in her body, the desire she was already feeling.

His knee edged between both her legs in the silky dress and the slow movement of his hips made her body clench.

His hands went between them, working deftly on the tiny straps of her dress while he kissed her. It wasn't until she felt the rough hair of his chest against her bare breasts that she realized both of them were uncovered from the waist up.

He drew away a little and looked down at her firm, pretty little breasts while he traced them with his fingers.

"I'd like to keep you under lock and key," he murmured gruffly. "My own pretty little treasure," he added as his head bent.

She watched his mouth take her, felt the pleasure of warm lips on her body. She liked the sight of his mouth over her nipple, that dark, wavy hair falling unruly onto his broad forehead while his heavy eyebrows met and his eyes closed under the delicious whip of passion. She held his head to her body, smoothing the hair at his nape, feeling it cool and clean under her fingers.

When he finally lifted his head, she was leaning back against the door for support. Her eyes were misty with desire, her body trembled faintly with the force of it. She looked at him hungrily, with all the barriers down at last. Other men might repulse her, but she wanted Matt. She loved the feel of his hands and his eyes and his mouth on her body. She wanted to lie under him and feel the delicious pressure of his body against and over and inside her own. She wanted it so badly that she moaned softly.

"No second thoughts?" he asked gently.

"Oh, no! No second thoughts, Matt," she whispered, adoring him with her eyes.

With a slow, secret smile, he began to divest her of the dress and the remaining piece of clothing, leaving her standing before him with her body unveiled, taut with passion.

She was shy, but his hands soon made a jumble of her embarrassment. She felt her body jerk rhythmically as he suckled her breasts. It was so sweet. It was paradise.

When he eased her down onto the huge bed, she lay back against the pillows, totally yielding, and watched his evening clothes come off little by little. He watched her while he undressed, laughing softly, a sensual predatory note in his deep voice. She moved helplessly on the coverlet, her entire being aflame with sensations she'd never known. She could barely wait. She felt as if she was throbbing all over, burning with some unknown fire that threatened to consume her, an ache that was almost painful.

Her eyes widened when the last piece of fabric came away from his powerful body and her breath caught.

He liked that expression. He turned away just for a minute, long enough to extricate a packet from his wallet. He sat down beside her, opened it, and taught her matter-of-factly what to do with it. She fumbled a little, her eyes incredibly wide and fascinated and a little frightened.

"I won't hurt you," he said gently, searching her eyes. "Women have been doing this for hundreds of thousands of years. You're going to like it, Leslie. I promise you are."

She lay back, watching him with wide gray eyes full of curiosity as he slid alongside her.

His dark head bent to her body and she lay under him like a creamy, blushing sacrifice, learning the different ways she responded to his touch. He laughed when she arched up and moaned. He liked the way she opened to him, the way her breath rasped when his mouth slid tenderly over her belly and the soft, inner skin of her thighs. He made a sensual meal of her there on the pretty, soft comforter, while the sound of rain came closer outside the window, the moonlit night clouding over as a storm moved above the cabin.

She hadn't known that physical pleasure could be so devastating. She watched him touch and taste her, with eyes equally fascinated and aroused by some of the things he did to her.

Her shocked exclamation pulled an amused laugh from him. "Am I shocking you? Don't you read books and watch movies?" he asked as he poised just above her.

"It isn't…the same," she choked, arching as his body began to tease hers, her long legs shifting eagerly out of his way as he moved down against her.

Her hands were clenched beside her head, and he watched her eyes dilate as his hips shifted tenderly and she felt him against her in a shattering new intimacy. She gasped, looking straight into his dark eyes. "I… never dreamed…!"

"No words on earth could describe how this feels," he murmured, his breath rasping as he hesitated and then moved down again, tenderly. "You're beautiful, Leslie. Your body is exquisite, soft and warm and enticing. I love the way your skin feels under my mouth." His breath caught as he moved closer and felt her body protest at the invasion. He paused to search over her flushed, drawn face. "I'm becoming your lover," he whispered huskily, drawing his body against hers sensuously to deepen his possession. "I'm going inside you. Now."

His face became rigid with control, solemn as he met her eyes and pushed again, harder, and watched her flinch. "I know. It's going to hurt a little, in spite of everything," he said softly. "But not for long. Do you still want me?"

"More than anything...in the world!" she choked, lifting her hips toward his in a sensual invitation. "It's all right." She swallowed. Impulsively she looked down and her mouth fell open. She couldn't have imagined watching, even a day before. "Matt...!" she gasped.

Her eyes came back up to his. His face looked as if every muscle in it was clenched. "It feels like my first time, too," he said a little roughly. His hands slid under her head, cradling it as he shifted slightly and then pushed once more.

Her pretty body lifted off the bed. It seemed to ripple as he moved intimately into closer contact. "I never thought...we could talk...while we did something so intimate," she whispered back, gasping when he moved again and pleasure shot through her. "Yes...oh, yes, please do...that!" she pleaded huskily, clutching at his shoulders.

"Here, like this?" he asked urgently, and moved again.

Her tiny cry was affirmation enough. He eased down on her, his eyes looking straight into hers as he began a rhythm that combined tension with exquisite pleasure and fleeting, burning pain.

His eyes dilated as he felt the barrier. He shivered. His body clenched. He'd never had an innocent woman. Leslie was totally out of his experience. He hadn't thought about how it would feel until now. Primitive thoughts claimed his mind, ancestral memories perhaps that spoke of an ancient age when this would have been a rite of passage.

She was feeling something very similar as her body yielded to the domination of his. The discomfort paled beside the feelings that were consuming her. Glimpses of unbelievable pleasure were mingling with the stinging pain. Past it, she knew, lay ecstasy.

He kissed her hungrily as his lean, fit body moved on her in the silence of the cabin. Suddenly rain pounded hard outside the curtained window, slamming into the roof, the ground, the trees. The wind howled around the corner. There was a storm in him, too, as he lay stretched tight with desire, trying to hold back long enough to let Leslie share what he knew he would feel.

"I've never been so hungry," he bit off against her mouth. His hands contracted under her head, tangling in her hair. His body shuddered. "I'm going to have to hurt you. I can't wait any longer. It's getting away from me. I have to have you...now!"

Her legs moved sensuously against his, loving the faint abrasion of the hair that covered his. "Yes!" she said huskily, her eyes full of wonder. "I want it. I want... it with you."

One lean hand went to her upper thigh. His lips flattened. He looked straight into her eyes as his hand suddenly pinned her hips and he thrust down fiercely.

She cried out, grimacing, writhing as she felt him deep in her body, past a stinging pain that engulfed her.

He stilled, holding her in place while he gave her body time to adjust, his eyes blazing with primitive triumph. His gaze reflected pride and pleasure and possession.

"Yes," he said roughly. "You're part of me and I'm part of you. Now you belong to me, completely."

Her eyes mirrored her shocked fascination. She moved a little and felt him move with her. She swallowed, and then swallowed again, her breath coming in soft jerks as she adjusted to her first intimacy. She loved him. The feel of him was pure delight. She was a woman. She could be a woman. The past was dying already and she was whole and sensuous and fully capable. Her smile was brilliant with joyful self-discovery.

She pulled his head down to hers and kissed him hungrily. The pain had receded and now she felt a new sensation as his hips moved. There were tiny little spasms of pleasure. Her breath came raggedly as she positioned herself to hold on to them. Her nails bit into the hard muscle of his upper arms.

His dark eyes were full of indulgent amusement as he felt her movements. She hesitated once, shy. "Don't stop," he whispered. "I'll do whatever you want me to do."

Her lips parted. It wasn't the answer she'd expected.

He bent and kissed her eyelids again, his breath growing more ragged by the minute. "Find a position that gives you what you need," he coaxed. "I won't take my pleasure until you've had yours."

"Oh, Matt," she moaned, unbearably touched by a generosity that she hadn't expected.

He laughed through his desire, kissing her face tenderly. "My own treasure," he whispered. "I wish I could make it last for hours. I want you to blush when you're sixty, remembering this first time. I want it to be perfect for you."

The pleasure was building. It was fierce now, and she was no longer in control of her own body. It lifted up to Matt's and demanded pleasure. She was totally at the mercy of her awakened passion, blind with the need for fulfillment. She became aware of a new sort of tension that was lifting her fiercely to meet every quick, downward motion of his lean hips, that stretched her under his powerful body, that made her pulse leap with delicious throbs of wild delight.

He watched her body move and ripple, watched the expression on her face, in her wide, blind eyes, and smiled. "Yes," he murmured to himself. "Now you understand, don't you? You can't fight it, or deny it, or control it..." He stopped abruptly.

"No! Please, don't...stop!" Her choked cry was followed by frantic, clinging hands that pulled at him.

He eased down again, watching as she shivered. "I'm not going to stop," he whispered softly. "Trust me. I only want to make it as good as it can be for you."

"It feels...wonderful," she said hoarsely. "Every time you move, it's like...like electric shocks of pleasure."

"And we've barely started, baby," he whispered. He shifted his hips, intensifying her cries. She was completely yielded to him, open to him, wanton. He'd never dreamed that it would be like this. His head began to spin with the delight his body was taking from hers.

She curled her long legs around his powerful ones and lifted herself, gasping when it brought a sharp stab of pleasure.

His hand swept down her body. His face hardened as he began to increase the pressure and the rhythm. She clung to him, her mouth in his throat, on his chest, his chin, wherever she could reach, while he gave in to his fierce hunger and threw away his control.

She'd never dreamed how it would be. She couldn't get close enough, or hold on tight enough. She felt him in every cell of her body. She was ardent, inciting him, matching his quick, hard movements, her back lifting to promote an even closer contact.

She whispered things to him, secret, erotic things that drove him to sensual urgency. She was moaning. She could hear her frantic voice pleading, hear the sound their movements made on the box springs, feel the power and heat of him as her body opened for him and clenched with tension that begged for release.

She whispered his name and then groaned it, and then repeated it in a mad, hoarse little sound until the little throbs of pleasure became one long, aching, endless spasm of ecstasy that made her blind and deaf under the fierce, demanding thrust of his body. She cried out and shivered in the grip of it, her voice throbbing like her body. She felt herself go off the edge of the world into space, into a red heat that washed over every cell in her body.

When she was able to think again, she felt his body shake violently, heard the harsh groan at her ear as he, too, found ecstasy.

He shuddered one last time and then his warm strong body relaxed and she felt it push hers deeper into the mattress. His mouth was at her throat, pressing hungrily. His lips moved all over her face, touching and lifting in a fever of tenderness.

Her dazed eyes opened and looked up into his. He was damp with sweat, as she was. His dark eyes smiled with incredible gentleness into hers.

She arched helplessly and moaned as the pleasure washed over her again.

"More?" he whispered, and his hips moved obligingly, so that the sweet stabs of delight came again and again and again.

She sobbed helplessly afterward, clinging to him as she lay against his relaxed body.

His hand smoothed over her damp hair. He seemed to understand her shattered response, as she didn't.

"I don't know why I'm bawling my head off," she choked, "when it was the closest to heaven I've ever been."

"There are half a dozen technical names for it," he murmured drowsily. "It's letdown blues. You go so high that it hurts to come down."

"I went high," she murmured with a smile. "I walked on the moon."

He chuckled. "So did I."

"Was…was it all right?" she asked suddenly.

He rolled her over on her back and looked down into her curious face. "You were the best lover I've ever had," he said, and he wasn't teasing. "And you will be, from now on, the only woman I ever have."

"Oh, that sounds serious," she murmured.

"Doesn't it, though?" His dark eyes went over her like an artist's brush committing beauty to canvas. He touched her soft breasts with a breathlessly tender caress. "I won't be able to stop, you know," he added conversationally.

"Stop?"

"This," he replied. "It's addictive. Now that I've had

you, I'll want you all the time. I'll go green every time any other man so much as looks at you."

It sounded as if he was trying to tell her something, and she couldn't decide what it was. She searched his dark eyes intently.

He smiled with indulgent affection. "Do you want the words?"

"Which words?" she whispered.

He brushed his lips over hers with incredible, breathless tenderness. "Marry me, Leslie."

Chapter 13

Her gasp was audible. It was more than she'd dared hope for when she came in here with him. He chuckled at her expression.

"Did you think I was going to ask you to come out to the ranch and live in sin with me?" he teased with twinkling eyes. His hand swept down over her body possessively. "This isn't enough. Not nearly enough."

She hesitated. "Are you sure that you want something, well, permanent?"

His eyes narrowed. "Leslie, if I'd been a little more reckless, you'd have something permanent. I wanted very badly to make you pregnant."

Her face brightened. "Did you, really? I thought about it, too, just at the end."

He smoothed back her hair and found himself fighting the temptation to start all over again with nothing between them.

"We'll have children," he promised her. "But first we'll build a life together, a secure life that they'll fall into very naturally."

She was fascinated by the expression on his face. It was only just dawning on her that he felt more than a fleeting desire for her body. He was talking about a life together, children together. She knew very little about true relationships, but she was learning all the time.

"Heavy thoughts?" he teased.

"Yes." She smoothed her fingers over his lean cheek.

"Care to share them?" he murmured.

"I was thinking how sweet it is to be loved," she whispered softly.

He lifted an eyebrow. "Physically loved?"

"Well, that, too," she replied.

He smiled quizzically. "Too?"

"You'd never have taken me to bed unless you loved me," she said simply, but with conviction. "You have these strange old-world hang-ups about innocence."

"Strange, my foot!"

She smiled up at him complacently. "Not that I don't like them," she assured him. The smile faded as she searched his dark eyes. "It was perfect. Just perfect. And I'm glad I waited for you. I love you, Matt."

His chest rose and fell heavily. "Even after the way I've treated you?"

"You didn't know the truth," she said. "And even if you were unfair at first, you made all sorts of restitution. I won't have a limp anymore," she added, wide-eyed. "And you gave me a good job and looked out for me…"

He bent and kissed her hungrily. "Don't try to make it sound better than it was. I've been an ogre with you. I'm only sorry that I can't go back and start over again."

"None of us can do that," she said. "But we have a second chance, both of us. That's something to be thankful for."

"From now on," he promised her solemnly, "everything is going to be just the way you want it. The past has been hard for me to overcome. I've distrusted women for so long, but with you I've been able to forget what my mother did. I'll cherish you as long as I live."

"And I'll cherish you," she replied quietly. "I thought I would never know what it was to be loved."

He frowned a little, drawing her palm to his lips. "I never thought I would, either. I was never in love before."

She sighed tenderly. "Neither was I. And I never dreamed it would be so sweet."

"I imagine it's going to get better year after year," he ventured, toying with her fingers.

Her free hand slid up into his dark hair. "Matt?"

"What?"

"Can we do that again?"

He pursed his lips. "Are you sure that you can?" he asked pointedly.

She shifted on the coverlet and grimaced with the movement. "Well, maybe not. Oh, dear."

He actually laughed, bending to wrap her up against him and kiss her with rough affection. "Come here, walking wounded. We'll have a nice nap and then we'll go home and make wedding plans." He smoothed down her wild hair. "We'll have a nice cozy wedding and a honeymoon anywhere you want to go."

"I don't mind if we don't go anywhere, as long as I'm with you," she said honestly.

He sighed. "My thoughts exactly." He glanced down at her. "You could have had a conventional wedding night, you know."

She smoothed her hand over his hair-roughened chest. "I didn't know that you'd want to marry me. But just the same, I had to know if I could function intimately with you. I wasn't sure, you see."

"I am," he said with a wicked grin.

She laughed heartily. "Yes, so am I, now, but it was important that I knew the truth before things went any further between us. I knew it was difficult for you to hold back, and I couldn't bear the thought of letting you go. Not that I expected you to want to marry me," she added ruefully.

"I wanted to marry you the first time I kissed you," he confessed. "Not to mention the first time I danced with you. It was magic."

"For me, too."

"But you had this strange aversion to me and I couldn't understand why. I was a beast to you. Even Ed said it wasn't like me to treat employees that badly. He read me the riot act and I let him."

"Ed's nice."

"He is. But I'm glad you weren't in love with him. At first, I couldn't be sure of the competition."

"Ed was a brotherly sort. He still is." She kissed his chest. "But I love you."

"I love you, too."

She laid her cheek against the place she'd kissed and closed her eyes. "If the lawyers can help my mother, maybe she'll be out for the first christening."

"At least for the second," he agreed, and smiled as his arms closed warm and protective around her, drawing her closer. It was the safest she'd ever been in her life, in those warm, strong arms in the darkness. The nightmares seemed to fade into the shadows of reality that they'd become. She would walk in the light, now, unafraid. The past was over, truly over. She knew that it would never torment her again.

Matt and Leslie were married in the local Presbyterian church, and the pews were full all the way to the back. Leslie thought that every single inhabitant of Jacobsville had shown up for the wedding, and she wasn't far wrong. Matt Caldwell had been the town's foremost bachelor for so long that curiosity brought people for miles around. All the Hart boys showed up, including the state attorney general, as well as the Ballengers, the Tremaynes, the Jacobs, the Coltrains, the Deverells, the Regans and the Burkes. The turnout read like the local social register.

Leslie wore a white designer gown with a long train and oceans of veiling and lace. The women in the office served as maids and matrons of honor, and Luke Craig acted as Matt's best man. There were flower girls and a concert pianist. The local press was invited, but no out of town reporters. Nobody wrote about Leslie's tragic past, either. It was a beautiful ceremony and the reception was uproarious.

Matt had pushed back her veil at the altar with the

look of a man who'd inherited heaven. He smiled as he bent to kiss her, and his eyes were soft with love, as were her own.

They held hands all through the noisy reception on the lawn at Matt's ranch, where barbecue was the order of the day.

Leslie had already changed clothes and was walking among the guests when she came upon Carolyn Engles unexpectedly.

The beautiful blonde came right up to her with a genuine smile and a present in her hands.

"I got this for you, in Paris," Carolyn said with visible hesitation and self-consciousness. "It's sort of a peace offering and an apology, all in one."

"You didn't have to do this," Leslie stammered.

"I did." She nodded toward the silver-wrapped present. "Open it."

Leslie pulled off the paper with helpless excitement, puzzled and touched by the other woman's gesture. She opened the velvet box inside and her breath caught. It was a beautiful little crystal swan, tiny and perfect.

"I thought it was a nice analogy," Carolyn murmured. "You've turned out to be a lovely swan, and nobody's going to hurt you when you go swimming around in the Jacobsville pond."

Impulsively Leslie hugged the older woman, who laughed nervously and actually blushed.

"I'm sorry for what I did that day," Carolyn said huskily. "Really sorry. I had no idea…"

"I don't hold grudges," Leslie said gently.

"I know that." She shrugged. "I was infatuated with Matt and he couldn't see me for dust. I went a little crazy, but I'm myself again now. I want you both to be very happy."

"I hope the same for you," Leslie said with a smile.

Matt saw them together and frowned. He came up beside Leslie and placed an arm around her protectively.

"Carolyn brought this to me from Paris," Leslie said excitedly, showing him the tiny thing. "Isn't it beautiful?"

Matt was obviously puzzled as he exchanged looks with Carolyn.

"I'm not as bad as you think I am," Carolyn told him. "I really do hope you'll be happy. Both of you."

Matt's eyes smiled. "Thank you."

Carolyn smiled back ruefully. "I told Leslie how sorry I was for the way I behaved. I really am, Matt."

"We all have periods of lunacy," Matt replied. "Otherwise, nobody in his right mind would ever get into the cattle business."

Carolyn laughed delightedly. "So they say. I have to go. I just wanted to bring Leslie the peace offering. You'll both be on my guest list for the charity ball, by the way."

"We'll come, and thank you," Matt returned.

Carolyn nodded, smiled and moved away toward where the guests' cars were parked.

Matt pulled his new wife closer. "Surprises are breaking out like measles."

"I noticed." She linked her arms around his neck and reached up to kiss him tenderly. "When everybody goes home, we can lock ourselves in the bedroom and play doctor."

He chuckled delightedly. "Can we, now? Who gets to go first?"

"Wait and see!"

He turned her back toward their guests with a grin that went from ear to ear. "Lucky me," he said, and he wasn't joking.

They woke the next morning in a tangle of arms and legs as the sun peered in through the gauzy curtains. Matt's ardor had been inexhaustible, and Leslie had discovered a whole new world of sensation.

She rolled over onto her back and stretched, uninhibited by her nudity. Matt propped himself on an elbow and looked at her with eyes full of love and possession.

"I never realized that marriage would have so many fringe benefits," she murmured. She stretched again. "I don't know if I have enough strength to walk after last night."

"If you don't, I'll carry you," he said with a loving smile. He reached over to kiss her lazily. "Come on, treasure. We'll have a nice shower and then we'll go and find some breakfast."

She kissed him back. "I love you."

"Same here."

"You aren't sorry you married me, are you?" she asked impulsively. "I mean, the past never really goes away. Someday some other reporter may dig it all back up again."

"It won't matter," he said. "Everybody's got a skeleton or two. And no, I'm not sorry I married you. It was the first sensible thing I've done in years. Not to mention," he added with a sensual touch of his mouth to her body, "the most pleasurable."

She laughed. "For me, too." Her arms pulled him down to her and she kissed him heartily.

Her mother did get a new trial, and her sentence was shortened. She went back to serve the rest of her time with a light heart, looking forward to the day when she could get to know her daughter all over again.

As for Leslie, she and Matt grew closer with every passing day and became known locally as "the lovebirds," because they were so rarely seen apart.

Matt's prediction about her mother's release came true, as well. Three years after the birth of their son, Leslie gave birth to a daughter who had Matt's dark hair and, he mused, a temper to match his own. He had to fight tears when the baby was placed in his arms. He loved his son, but he'd wanted a little girl who looked like his own treasure, Leslie. Now, he told her, his life was complete. She echoed that sentiment with all her heart. The past had truly been laid to rest. She and Matt had years of happiness ahead of them.

Most of Jacobsville showed up for the baby's christening, including a small blond woman who was enjoying her first days of freedom. Leslie's mother had pride of place in the front pew. Leslie looked from Matt to her mother, from their three-year-old son to the baby in her arms. Her gray eyes, when they lifted to Matt's soft, dark ones, were radiant with joy. Dreams came true, she thought. Dreams came true.

* * * * *

Visit her Author Profile page at Harlequin.com,
or brendajackson.net, for more titles!

HIDDEN PLEASURES

Brenda Jackson

To the love of my life, Gerald Jackson, Sr.
This year (2010) marks my fifteenth anniversary
as a published author and I want to thank
all of you for your support. To my readers
who have been with me since my first book,
this seventy-fifth book is especially for you.
To my good friend and classmate
Valeria Stirrup Jenkins of the Chloe Agency
Finishing and Modeling School in Memphis,
Tennessee, for her feedback on proper etiquette
and manners. Thanks for your help.
It was truly appreciated.

Hear thou, my son, and be wise,
and guide thine heart in the way.
—*Proverbs* 23:19

Chapter 1

"Holy crap!" Galen Steele muttered as he turned away from the bank of elevators and raced for the stairways of the Ritz-Carlton Hotel in Manhattan. A high school soccer team was checking out and filling all the elevators going down to the lobby. Galen could not be late for this wedding. His cousin Donovan would kill him if he were.

All the other groomsmen had left for the church a good thirty minutes ago, but he'd lagged behind when a woman he'd met at the bar last night had unexpectedly knocked on his hotel room door just when he was about to walk out. Not one to turn down a booty call, he'd thought he could make it quick. He had no idea Tina What's-Her-Name didn't believe in a quickie. A smile split his lips as he recalled how she'd made it worth his while.

And now he was late. He'd heard of weddings being held up for the bride or the groom, but never for a groomsman.

He vividly remembered Donovan's warning last night at the bachelor party. His cousin, who'd been engaged two months shy of a year, had made it clear that he'd waited long enough for his wedding day and he intended for it to go off without a hitch. And that meant he wanted all twenty of his groomsmen to be at the church on time. As he spoke, he'd looked directly at Galen and his five brothers—not so affectionately known as the "Bad News Steeles from Phoenix."

Hell, it wasn't Galen's fault that his father, Drew Steele, had actually gotten run out of Charlotte over thirty years ago by a bunch of women out for blood—namely his. Drew's reputation as a skirt chaser was legendary, and although the old man had finally settled down with one woman, his six sons had been cursed with his testosterone-driven genes. Galen, Tyson, Eli, Jonas, Mercury and Gannon didn't know how to say no to a willing woman. And if she wasn't willing, they had the seductive powers to not only get her in a willing mood, but to push her right over the top. Or let her stay on the bottom, depending upon her favorite position.

Galen glanced at his watch again as he reached the main floor. Hurrying toward the revolving doors, he prayed a taxi would be available. This was New York City, the Big Apple, and yellow cabs were supposed to be all over the place, right?

He smiled. One was pulling up as soon as he exited

the hotel and he ran toward it, thinking he might be on time to the wedding after all.

Not waiting to be assisted by a bellman, he opened the cab's door, slid in the seat and was about to direct the driver to the church when he felt a tap on his shoulder. He looked up and his gaze collided with a face he could only define as gut-grippingly beautiful. Eyes the color of caramel, naturally arched brows, a cute little nose and a pair of too-luscious lips.

The beauty he'd finally gotten out of his room less than ten minutes ago had nothing on this woman. It was like comparing apples to oranges. Both were good fruit, but one was sweeter.

He found his voice to speak. "Yes?"

"This is my cab."

He couldn't help but grin when he asked, "You own it?"

Her frown gave him a warning. It also gave him one hell of a hard-on. "No, I don't own it, but I called for it. It's here to take me to the airport. I have a flight to catch."

"And I have a wedding to attend and I'm late."

She crossed her arms over her chest, and the shapeliest pair of breasts he'd ever seen pressed tight against her blouse. The sight of them made his mouth water. "Sorry, but your lack of planning does not constitute an emergency on my part," she said in a haughty voice. "The proper thing for you to have done was to allow yourself ample time to reach your destination."

"Well, I didn't and as much as I've enjoyed chatting with you, I have to go." He regretted saying so, because he would love to spend more time with her.

She dropped her arms and arched her shoulders. Once again his attention was drawn to her breasts. "This is my cab!"

"It was your cab, lady, and I really do have to go." He turned his attention to the driver and said, "I need to get to the Dayspring Baptist Church in Harlem in less than twenty minutes."

The driver shook his head, reluctant to move. "I don't know, man," he said with a deep Jamaican accent. "I was called to take a lady to the airport."

Galen took out his wallet, pulled out a hundred-dollar bill and offered it to the guy. "I'm down to nineteen minutes now."

The man almost snatched the bill out of Galen's hand and shot the woman an apologetic look. "Sorry, miss, I have a large family to feed. I'll call in and have another cab sent for you."

Satisfied, Galen reached over to close the door, but the woman—the sinfully beautiful but very angry woman—was blocking the way. He tilted his head back and looked up at her. "Do you mind?"

"Yes, I do mind. You have to be the rudest man I've ever met. Someone needs to teach you some manners."

He smiled. "You're probably right, but not today. Some other time, perhaps."

She glared at him as she moved out of the way, but not before saying, "And for heaven's sake, will you please zip up your pants."

He glanced down. "Oops." He quickly slid up his zipper before closing the door.

The cab pulled away then and he couldn't resist glancing back through the window at the woman they'd left at the curb. She was not a happy camper. In fact she looked downright furious. And he should give a damn why? Because he *had* behaved like an ill-mannered brute, which was not his typical behavior, especially when it came to beautiful women. It was definitely not the impression he would want to leave with one. If he'd had the time he would have charmed her right out of her panties and bra. It was the Steele way.

Oh, well. You win some and you lose some. And he'd much preferred losing her than his behind, and there was no doubt in his mind that Donovan would kick that very part of his anatomy all over New York if he was late for his wedding.

"I now pronounce you man and wife. Donovan, you may kiss your bride."

Donovan Steele didn't waste time pulling his wife into his arms and giving her a kiss many probably thought was rather long. And if that wasn't bad enough, when he'd finally pulled his mouth from hers, he whispered, "I love you, sweetheart."

Natalie Ford Steele smiled up at her husband and said, "And I love you."

And then she was swept up into her husband's arms and carried out of the church.

Galen swallowed to keep from gagging as he watched the entire scene. Even though Natalie was a nice-looking woman, a real beauty, he'd still had a hard time believing that Donovan had decided to hang up his bachelor shoes and take a wife. Donovan's reputation as a womanizer was legendary; in fact, he'd been so infamous in Charlotte that there were some who thought he was one of Drew Steele's sons instead of a cousin. Galen figured Charlotte wouldn't be the same without a bachelor Steele to keep things lively. Maybe he ought to consider leaving Phoenix and moving east.

He kicked that idea out of his mind real quick. His older Steele cousins in Charlotte would probably give him a job in their Steele Manufacturing Company. He much preferred remaining in Phoenix doing what he loved, which some people thought was trivial.

And his father topped that list of critics. Drew Steele believed that a man was supposed to get up at seven o'clock, Monday through Friday, and work at some job until at least five. It had taken Drew a long time to buy into the Principles According to Galen Steele, which said that a man was supposed to work smarter, not harder. That was why at the age of thirty-four Galen was a multibillionaire and was still building an empire, while working less than twenty hours a week and having fun at what he did.

Fourteen years ago while attending the University of Phoenix, pursuing a degree in engineering, he and his two roommates decided to do something to make money, something different than what their friends were doing—like selling their blood or their sperm. So they began creating video games. After their games became a hit on campus, they formed a business and by the time they graduated from college two years later, they were millionaires. The three of them were still partners today.

Their business, the SID Corporation, was represented by three CEOs, Galen Steele, Eric Ingram and Wesley Duval. Their only employees were their art team. He, Eric and Wesley shared duties as game designers and programmers and leased a suite in an exclusive area of Phoenix's business district for appearances' sake and as a tax write-off. They preferred designing their games right in the garage of their homes. Simple. Easy. Shrewd.

He shook his head. He and his brothers had inherited the old man's penchant for women, but they'd been born to excel. Drew's expectations for his six sons had been high, and all of them had become successful in their own right.

Seeing the other groomsmen move forward, Galen brought his attention back to the ceremony in time to stay on cue and file out with the rest of the wedding party. He took the arm of his partner, Laurie, one of Natalie's friends from college. She was pretty—and she was also very much married.

Outside in the perfect June day, he couldn't help but chuckle as he checked out the faces of his brothers and a number of Donovan's still-single friends. They had stood up there and witnessed the entire ceremony and they looked as if they were in shock. Galen understood how they felt. There wasn't a woman alive who'd make him consider tying the knot. He got shivers just thinking about it.

"You barely made it."

Galen came out of his reverie to glance over at two of his brothers, Tyson and Gannon. "Doesn't matter, Tyson. I made it," he said, smiling. "With a minute to spare."

"Should we ask why you were almost late?" Gannon asked with a curious look on his face.

Galen chuckled. He was the oldest and at twenty-nine Gannon was the youngest. Galen knew he was his youngest brother's hero and because of that he tried walking a straight-and-narrow path. Doing the role-model thing wasn't always easy, especially when you were the offspring of the infamous Drew Steele. But on occasion Galen liked pulling his youngest brother's leg. Like now.

"I'll be glad to tell you why I was almost late," Galen said, leaning close to his brothers as if what he had to say was for their ears only.

"I got caught up in a foursome and lost track of the time," he lied. And just so they would know what he meant, he said, "It was me and three women in my hotel room. Get the picture?"

"No kidding?" Gannon said, easily impressed.

Tyson rolled his eyes. "Yes, he's full of it, Gannon. Don't believe a word he says. It might have been one woman, but it wasn't three."

Galen could only smile. There were only eleven months' difference in his and Tyson's ages. A lot of people thought they were twins, but they were as different as night and day. Dr. Tyson Steele tended to be too serious at times.

"Tell him the truth, Galen, or Gannon is going to go around believing you're superhuman or something," Tyson said.

"All right." He gave Gannon his serious look. "There were two women. I took care of one and the other one got away," Galen said, thinking of the woman whose cab he'd been forced to hijack. He could still see the anger on her gorgeous face, especially the fire that had lit a striking pair of eyes.

"Was she good-looking?" Gannon had to ask.

Galen lifted a brow. "Who?"

"The one who got away."

Galen couldn't help but smile. "She was more than good-looking. The woman was absolutely stunning."

"Damn, man. And you let her get away?" Gannon looked clearly disappointed.

"It was either that or get my behind kicked by Donovan if I was late for his wedding."

"Okay, everyone, let's go back inside the church for pictures," the wedding director said, interrupting their conversation. "Then we'll return to the Ritz-Carlton for the reception."

Galen's thoughts shifted back to the woman. The one who got away. Like he'd told Gannon, she was more than good-looking and for some reason he could not get her out of his mind.

And at that moment he thought he'd give just about anything to see her again.

Brittany Thrasher tucked a loose strand of hair behind her ear after bringing her car to a stop in front of her house. It was nice to be back home after attending that seminar in New York.

A few minutes later she was walking through her front door wheeling her luggage behind her. The first thing she planned to do was strip off her clothes in deference to the Tampa heat that flirted with the hundred-degree mark.

She looked at the stack of envelopes on the table and couldn't help but appreciate her neighbor and friend Jennifer Barren for coming over every day to get her

mail and water her plants. This was Brittany's busiest
travel time of the year. As CEO of her own business,
Etiquette Matters, she and her ten employees traveled all
over the country teaching the basics of proper etiquette
to businesses, schools and interested groups. Last week
her students consisted of a group of NFL players who'd
been invited to the White House for dinner.

Kicking off her shoes, she went to her bedroom and
her mind went to the man in New York, the one who'd
had the audacity to take her cab from right under her
nose. And with his pants unzipped. He hadn't seemed
the least bit embarrassed when she'd brought it to his
attention. The jerk.

She shook her head. Another thing she remembered
about him other than the open zipper was his eyes. He
had Smokey Robinson eyes, a mossy shade of green
that would have taken her breath away had she not been
so angry. The man had no manners, which was a real
turnoff. She would love to have him as a student for just
one day in Etiquette Matters. She would all but shove
good manners down his throat. In a gracious and con-
genial way, of course.

She flipped through the stack of envelopes, sorting
out the junk mail that needed to be trashed. One envelope in particular caught her attention. The handwrit-
ing on it was so elegant, she'd give just about anything
to have that kind of penmanship.

The envelope had no return address, but the postal
stamp indicated it had been sent from Phoenix. She
didn't know a soul in Phoenix and it was one of the
few places she'd never visited. Using her mail opener,

she opened the letter and her eyes connected to words that had her gaping in shock.

Ms. Thrasher,
I have reason to believe you are the daughter I gave up for adoption twenty-eight years ago.

Chapter 2

Six months later

"Will any of my sons ever marry?"

Galen refused to look up from reading the documents that were spread out on his desk. He didn't have to glance at Eden Tyson Steele to know she was on a roll. Ever since Donovan's wedding, his mother had been swept away by wishful thinking. She had witnessed the ceremony, heard the wedding music and seen how happy the bride and groom were. Since then she'd felt something was missing in her life, especially because Galen's kinfolk in Charlotte could now claim that all the North Carolina Steeles, both male and female, had gotten hitched.

He'd gotten a call earlier from Mercury warning him

that their mother was making house calls to each of her sons. Her message was consistent and pretty damn clear. She wanted daughters-in-law. She wasn't pushing for grandbabies yet, but the brothers figured that craving wouldn't be long. First she had to work on getting them married.

"Galen?"

He breathed out a deep sigh. There was no way he could ignore her question any longer. Besides, he figured that the sooner he gave her an answer, the quicker she would move on to the next son.

He glanced up and gazed into eyes identical to his and those of his five brothers. They might have Drew Steele's features and most of his genes, but their eyes belonged to Eden Steele all the way. And Drew would be the first to admit that it had been Eden's eyes that had captured his attention and then his heart. "Yes, Mom?"

"Will any of you ever marry?"

He fought back a smile because he knew for his mother this was not an amusing moment. She was as serious as a heart attack whenever she broached the subject of her sons' marital status.

Galen leaned back in his chair and gave her his direct attention, which he felt she deserved, even if she was asking him something he'd rather not address again. "I can't speak for everyone else, but my answer to your question is no. I don't ever plan to marry."

Her expression indicated his response had been one she hadn't wanted to hear. Again. "How can you say that, Galen?"

"Easily."

Seeing her agitation, he went on to say, "Look, Mom,

maybe saying I'll never marry is laying it on rather thick, so let's just say it's not in my immediate future. Dad was almost forty when the two of you married, and everyone had given up on the idea he'd ever settle down and stop chasing skirts. So maybe there's hope for me yet."

He couldn't help but smile. What he'd said sounded good and should hold her for a while, but with the scowl on her face, he wasn't so sure. His mother was a beautiful woman and he could see how Drew Steele had taken one look at her and decided she was the best thing since gingerbread. There was a ten-year difference in their ages and according to Drew, the former Eden Tyson, a fashion model whose face graced a number of magazines worldwide, had made him work hard for her hand. And when they'd married, Drew had known his womanizing days were over and that Eden would be the only woman for him for the rest of his life.

Galen doubted such a woman existed for him. He had yet to meet one who could knock him off his feet... unless it was to make him fall flat on his back in their bed. He enjoyed women. He enjoyed making love to them. He enjoyed whispering sweet nothings in their ears. There was not one out there he would sniff behind other than to relieve the ache behind his zipper. What could he say? He was one of Drew's boys.

Most people in Phoenix either knew or had heard about "those" Steele boys. While he was in high school, most mothers had tried keeping their daughters behind lock and key. It never worked. Chances were those he missed out on had fallen for the likes of Tyson, Eli,

Jonas, Mercury or Gannon. No female was safe from that lethal Steele charm.

That lethal Steele charm…

Too bad he hadn't had the time to lay it on that woman in New York. The same woman he couldn't get out of his mind. When they'd gotten back to the hotel for the reception, he'd actually glanced around for her, hoping that perhaps she'd change her mind about leaving. He'd even gone so far as to wish that perhaps she'd missed her flight and had to come back. No such luck. But just for him to hope that much bad luck on anyone proved what an impact the woman had made on his senses.

"You and your brothers are not your father, Galen."

"No, but we are his sons," he said, holding his mother's gaze. "Dad didn't marry until he found that special woman, so I'd say the same will hold true with the six of us."

"And I hope when she comes along, the six of you won't screw things up."

He chuckled. "Like Dad almost did?" Of course he'd heard the story about how their father had refused to accept his fate and ended up pushing Eden away. By the time he'd come to his senses, she had left the country to do a photo shoot somewhere in Paris. Panicked that he had lost her forever, he had tracked her down and asked her to marry him. To some the story might sound romantic, but to Galen it was a good display of common sense on his father's part. His mother was world-class.

"So, Mom, where's your next stop?" he asked, throwing out the hint that their little talk had come to a close.

She sighed in resignation and tossed back the hair

from her face. "I guess I'll drop by and see Tyson. This is his day off from the hospital."

Galen smiled. "You might want to call first. He probably has company." Usually any day off for Tyson meant a day spent in bed with some woman.

His mother made a face before waving her hand at his words. "Whatever," she said it in that I-don't-care-what-I-catch-him-doing voice.

He stood and came around his desk to give her a hug. "You do know that I love you and enjoy your visits, don't you, Mom?"

His mother sighed. "I won't give up hope on any of you, especially you because you're the oldest."

He lifted a brow and wondered what that was supposed to mean. She would have it easier marrying Gannon off than him. Galen had been out in the world the longest and still enjoyed sampling what was out there, whereas Gannon was just getting his feet wet. His mother would best grab him now before he discovered the true meaning of women.

"I'll make a deal with you, Mom," he decided to say, reaching out and gently squeezing her hand. "If I ever meet a woman who can hold my interest, you'll be the first to know."

Brittany sank into the chair opposite the man's desk. Luther Banyon was the attorney who'd sent her the recent letter, advising her that Gloria McIntyre, the woman who'd sent her that handwritten letter over six months ago, had died of ovarian cancer at the age of forty-four. That meant Gloria had only been sixteen when she'd given birth to Brittany.

Her tongue pressed against her sealed lips as she thought about how unfair it was to lose the mother she'd only just found. The letter from Ms. McIntyre had answered a lot of questions Brittany had always had. She'd known she had been given up at birth. That had been evident from her trek from foster home to foster home during her adolescent years.

There had been a time in her teens when she'd desired to find her birth mother, but after a while she'd gotten over it and had accepted things as they were. She'd moved on with her life, finishing high school at the top of her class and going on to college, then taking out a loan and opening Etiquette Matters.

"Now, Ms. Thrasher, we can begin."

Mr. Banyon pulled her out of her reverie. She had arrived in Phoenix a couple of hours ago, picked up a rental car and had come to his office straight from the airport.

"As stated in my letter, Gloria McIntyre died last month. I hadn't known she'd hired a private investigator to locate you until after she'd passed. That explains some things."

Brittany raised a brow. "What does it explain?"

"What she's been doing with her money for the past five years. When she died, her savings account was down to barely anything. And her home, although it has been paid off for years, was almost in foreclosure due to back taxes."

The man paused and said, "The doctor gave her five years to live and she used every day of those five years trying to find you. I'm so sorry her time ran out before the two of you could meet. She was a fine woman."

Brittany nodded. "Were you her attorney for long?"

"For over twenty years. She was married to Hugh McIntyre, but he died close to eight years ago. They never had any children. I guess it was after Hugh died that she decided she wanted to find you, the child she'd given away at sixteen."

Brittany didn't say anything. And then, "Mr. Banyon, your correspondence said she left a sealed letter for me."

"Yes, and she also left something else."

"What?"

"Her home. Though I must tell you that although it's been willed to you, there's a tax lien on it and it's due to be auctioned off tomorrow."

Brittany's chest tightened. "Tomorrow?"

"Yes. So if you want your mother's home, you arrived in the nick of time."

Brittany nodded. Yes, she wanted her mother's home because it was the key to who her mother was and why and how she'd made the decision that she had over twenty-eight years ago.

"And the items in the house?"

"Everything is still intact. However, house and contents are due to be auctioned. If someone else outbids you, you will have to negotiate with them and reach some sort of agreement or settlement as to the contents. All the city is concerned about is making sure the back taxes are recovered."

"I understand. Where will the auction take place tomorrow and what time?"

"I'll have my secretary provide you with all the information you need. Now if you will excuse me, I'll get that letter."

* * *

Brittany pulled in a deep breath at the same time she felt her heart soften. She'd known from the last letter that Gloria McIntyre wasn't one to say a lot, but what she did say had a profound impact. This letter was no different.

To my daughter, Brittany Thrasher, I leave my home and all my worldly goods and possessions. They aren't much, but they are mine to pass on to you with the love of a mother who always wanted the best for you.
Gloria McIntyre

"Are you all right, Ms. Thrasher?"

Brittany glanced up and met Mr. Banyon's concerned gaze. "Yes, I'm fine. Do you know how much the back taxes amount to?"

"Yes, we're looking at almost five years' worth," he said, browsing through a stack of papers. "Here we are. It comes to close to seventy thousand dollars."

Brittany blinked. "Seventy thousand dollars!"

Mr. Banyon nodded. "Yes. Although the house itself isn't all that large, it sits on a whole lot of land and it has its own private road."

Brittany swallowed deeply. Seventy thousand dollars was more than she'd expected to part with. But it really didn't matter. She'd manage it. The business had had a good year. Paying the back taxes to gain possession of her mother's house was something she had to do. Something she wanted to do.

Her mother.

The thought made her quiver inside. Her only regret was that they'd never met. She could only fantasize about the type of relationship they would have shared if there had been more time. Just the thought that the reason the taxes had gotten delinquent in the first place was because her mother had placed locating her as her top priority was almost overwhelming.

"Is there a way I can get inside the house?" she asked Mr. Banyon.

He shook his head. "Unfortunately, there is not. It's locked and the keys have become the property of the city of Phoenix. They will be given to whoever becomes the new owner tomorrow. Ms. McIntyre's home is a rather nice one, but I can't and won't try to speculate as to who else might be interested."

Nodding, she stood. "Well, I intend to do everything in my power to make sure I become the new owner tomorrow."

"I know that's what Ms. McIntyre would have wanted and I wish you the best."

A few moments later after leaving Mr. Banyon's office, Brittany punched Gloria McIntyre's address into the car's GPS system. The directions took her a few miles from the Phoenix city limits, to a beautiful area of sprawling valleys.

She turned off the main highway and entered a two-lane road lined by desert plants. When the GPS directed her down a long private road, she slowed her speed to take in the beauty of the area covered in sand and tumbleweeds. Although this was the first week of December, the sun was shining bright in the sky. When the private road rounded a curve at the end of the drive, she saw the house with a wrought-iron fence around its ten acres of land. With all the cacti and a backdrop of a valley almost in the backyard, the scene looked like a home on the range.

She stopped the car and a feeling of both joy and pain tightened her chest. This was the house her mother had lived in for over twenty years and was the house she had left to her.

Mr. Banyon was right. It was modestly sized but it sat on a lot of land. The windows were boarded up; otherwise, she would have been tempted to take a peek inside. Several large trees in the front yard provided shade.

Something about the house called out to her, mainly because she knew it was a gift from a woman whom she'd never met but with whom she had a connection nonetheless. A biological connection.

As she put her car in gear to drive away, she knew whatever it took, when she left the auction tomorrow, this house would be hers.

Chapter 3

Galen had never been one not to take advantage of golden opportunities. Plus, he'd discovered a fascination with the auction mart since the day he'd bid on his first old muscle car. Snagging another one cheap was what drew him to the newest Phoenix auction today.

In addition to the car auction going on, there were several other things up on the auction block. Foreclosed homes, jewelry, electronic equipment, music memorabilia and trading cards. None of those items interested him. All he wanted was that classic 1969 Chevelle he'd heard about. After which, he would return home and continue to work on Sniper, the video game SID planned to unveil at the Video Game Expo in Atlanta in the spring.

Right now the biggest thing on his, Eric's and Wesley's

minds was the success of Turbine Force, the game they had debuted earlier that year. Because of an extremely good marketing campaign—thanks to his brother Jonas's firm—at present Turbine Force was the number-one-selling video game this holiday season.

He slowed his pace when his cell phone went off and pulled it out of his back pocket. "Yes?"

"Where are you?"

Galen rolled his eyes. "If I wanted you to keep up with me, Eli, I would be tweeting on Twitter."

"Funny. So where are you?"

Galen glanced at his watch. The auction for the Chevelle was starting in twenty minutes and he needed to be in place. "I'm at the auction mart. That Chevelle I was telling you about goes on the block today. What's up?"

He engaged in all-about-nothing chitchat with his brother for all of five minutes. Eli was the attorney in the family and handled SID's business concerns.

After putting away his cell phone, Galen headed toward the auction area. Adrenaline rushed through his veins. There was no telling how many car enthusiasts would be there waiting to buy and—

"Brittany Thrasher! I can't believe it!"

"Nikki Cartwright! I can't believe it, either."

Galen couldn't believe it, either, when the two women held their little reunion right in the middle of the floor and blocked the aisle. Anyone trying to maneuver around them had to squeeze by the huge decorated Christmas tree standing front and center.

He was about to follow the crowd and walk around the two when something about one of the women caught his attention. He slowed his pace and stared. He knew the one in the business suit. She was the woman whose cab he'd hijacked in New York six months ago. He'd recognize her anywhere, although now she was smiling instead of frowning.

Hell, he'd had a mental snapshot of her since that day. There were some things a man couldn't forget and for him a gorgeous woman topped the list. At that moment a primitive instinct took hold of him and he drew in a deep breath, absorbed in the implication of what it meant. Whatever else, he was no fool. He knew the signs, fully understood the warning, but it was up to him if he wanted to heed them. Desire was a potent thing. Too much of it could get you into trouble.

He'd desired women before, hundreds of times. But there was something about this woman that was tempting him all the way to the bone.

He stepped out of the flow of the crowd and moved off to the side, feigning interest in the rack of brochures in front of him. As he pretended to read a brochure that listed over fifty Elvis items being auctioned, he listened to the women's conversation. Okay, eavesdropping was rude, but hadn't this same woman told him he needed to be taught manners?

He would consider it research. He wanted to know who she was and why was she here causing all sorts of crazy thoughts to go through his mind. He glanced over at her. She had tilted her head to the side while talking and he thought there was beauty in her neck, a gracefulness. And he liked the sound of her voice. Hell, he'd liked it that day in New York. He'd just been in too much of a rush to truly appreciate it at the time.

The last thing he wanted was to be seen, in case she

remembered him, more specifically his lack of manners. And he knew firsthand that some women had long memories. They also were driven to get even. Galen wasn't up for that today. To be honest, he was distracted. He had a project in his garage that needed his absolute attention, so technically he had no business being here. But he had to bid on that '69 Chevelle.

The Chevelle.

He glanced at his watch and moaned. The bidding had already begun and more than likely the entry doors had been closed. He had missed out on the opportunity to own the car he'd always wanted because of his attention to this woman. Now he'd be forced to do an off-bid for the car, which meant if others were interested, the bidding war could go on forever. He pulled in a disgusted breath. They said payback was a bitch. Was losing out on that Chevelle his payback for the grief he'd caused the woman six months ago? He wasn't ready to accept his punishment.

He wasn't ready to do anything but find out who she was and why their paths had crossed yet again. Not that he was complaining. He listened more closely to their conversation to try to find out as much as he could about her.

There was a reason he was drawn to her. A reason why such a cool, calm and reserved sort of guy like himself would love to cross the floor, interrupt their conversation and pull her into his arms and kiss her. To be quite honest, he wanted to do more than just kiss her.

He figured he was going through some sort of hormonal meltdown. Over the years he'd learned to deal with an overabundance of testosterone. But he was definitely having trouble doing so today.

After finding out who she was, he might decide to come out of hiding and make a move. They were not in New York, squabbling over a cab. She was in Phoenix, the Steele neck of the woods, and for her that could be a good thing or a bad thing.

Brittany couldn't help but smile as she stared at Nikki. It had been over twelve years since they'd seen each other. At fourteen they had been the best of friends and had remained that way until right before their sixteenth birthdays when Nikki's father, who'd been in the navy, had received orders to move his family from the Tampa Bay area to San Diego.

They had tried staying in touch, but in Brittany's junior year of high school, when Mrs. Dugan got sick, Brittany had been sent to another foster home. During that first year with the Surratts, she had been too busy getting adjusted to her new family and new school to stay in contact.

"You look the same," she couldn't help but say to Nikki. She still had her curly black hair and her energetic chocolate-brown eyes. She truly hadn't aged at all.

"And so do you," Nikki replied on a laugh. "Are we really twenty-eight already?"

Brittany chuckled. "Afraid so. So what are you doing in Phoenix?"

"I live here now. After I graduated from high school in San Diego I followed a group of friends to the university here. I got a job with a photography firm after I graduated and I've been here since."

"How are your parents?"

"They're fine and still living in San Diego. Dad's retired now and driving Mom nuts. My brother Paul got married and has two kids, so the folks are happy about that."

Brittany nodded. "Well, I'm still single. What about you?"

"Heck, yes. I'm building a career in freelance photography and not a career of heartache due to men. And that's all the single guys in this city will give you. Now tell me about you, and please don't say you've been living in Phoenix all this time and our paths never crossed."

Brittany smiled. "No, I just arrived in town yesterday. In fact this is my first visit to Phoenix." And because Nikki had been her best friend during that phase of her life when she'd wanted to know her mother, she couldn't help but say in an excited voice, "And I'm here because of my mother."

Nikki's face lit up like a huge beam of light, and the smile and excitement made her face glow. "You found her?"

"No, actually she found me." Then sadness eased into Brittany's eyes when she added, "But we didn't get a chance to meet before she died."

"Oh, Brit," Nikki said, giving her a huge hug. "I'm sorry. What happened?"

Brittany found herself telling Nikki the entire story and why she was in Phoenix and there at the auction.

"Well, I believe things will work out for you. There are so many foreclosures out there, you might not have much competition in the bidding. I wish you luck because I know how much getting that house means to you. It's your only link to your mother."

Brittany nodded. "I'll do anything to get it. I already got my loan approval letter, so the money is not a problem. I just hope things go smoothly."

Nikki smiled. "And they will. I'll keep my fingers crossed. Now tell me, are you still living in Tampa? And what do you do there?"

"I'm still in Tampa and I own Etiquette Matters, a mobile etiquette school. I and the ten people I employ travel all over the country and hold seminars and teach classes. Each of us is assigned a certain section of the country. Things are going great because a number of corporations have begun introducing business etiquette and protocol as part of their corporate image training."

"Wow, that sounds wonderful. So when can we get together? There is so much that we need to catch up on," Nikki said.

"What about dinner later? If everything works out— and I'm keeping positive that it will—I'll have reason to celebrate. And I plan on staying for a couple of weeks when I get the house. I want to move in and spend time there, knowing it was where my mother once lived."

Shivers of excitement raced up Brittany's spine when she added, "And what you said earlier is true. It is my one connection to my mother."

Galen waited until the women had exchanged contact information by way of business cards and hugged for what he hoped would be the last time before they finally headed in different directions.

The conversation between them had lasted a good

twenty minutes. They had been so busy chatting away, catching up on old times as well as the new, that they hadn't even noticed him standing less than ten feet from them in the same spot, eavesdropping the entire time. It had been time well spent, because he'd gotten a lot of information about her.

Her name was Brittany Thrasher. She was twenty-eight, she lived in Tampa and she owned some sort of etiquette school that taught proper protocol and manners. He shook his head. Go figure.

He also knew all about the house she would be bidding on and why she wanted it so badly. It was a house on a private road off Rushing Street. He knew the area.

Galen glanced at his watch and figured he would hang around after all and make sure he and Brittany Thrasher got reacquainted on more pleasant terms. It was time she saw that he wasn't such a bad guy. He'd just had an off day that time in New York. He would just throw on the Steele charm, talk her into taking him along when she went and took a tour of her new house. No telling where things would lead from there.

He was about to head in the direction she'd gone when another conversation caught his ears. This time between two men who were standing together talking.

"Are you sure the house off Rushing Street is going on the block today?" the short, stocky man asked his companion, a taller bald-headed guy.

"I'm positive. I verified it was listed in the program. If the rezoning of the area goes as planned—and I have no reason to believe that it won't with all the money we're pouring into the rezoning commissioner's election campaign—I figure that within a year, that property will be approved for commercial use."

The short, stocky man chuckled. "Good. Then we can tear the house down and use all that land to build another one of our hotels. We just need to make sure no one else outbids us for it."

Galen watched the men walk off. Evidently they wanted the same house Brittany would be bidding on. He shrugged, thinking it wasn't any of his business. That was the nature of an auction and there was no reason for him to get involved. Then he released a short laugh. Who in the hell was he fooling? Even when she had been in New York he'd made her his business. Time just hadn't lent itself for anything more than a confrontation between them.

He glanced at his watch before pulling his cell phone out of the back pocket of his jeans. The push of one button had his phone connected to Eli.

"What do you want, Galen?"

He smiled. Eli was the moody brother. Ready for chitchat one minute and a grouch the next. "I'm still here at the auction mart. I need you to fax me a loan approval letter with an open line of credit."

"What do you think I am, your banker?" his brother snapped.

"Just work miracles and do it and stop whining."

"Dammit, what's the fax number?"

"How the hell do I know? Just look it up." He quickly hung up the phone before Eli decided to get real ugly.

Galen made his way toward the auction area. Following the crowd, he wondered just when he'd begun rescuing damsels in distress. It was a disconcerting thought for a Steele, but in this case it was one he was looking forward to doing.

Chapter 4

Brittany got nervous as she glanced around the room. It was crowded, wall to wall. She knew there were fifteen homes being auctioned off today and she hoped none of these people were interested in the one she wanted. She would do as Nikki had suggested and think positive.

She smiled when she thought of how she'd run into her friend again after all these years. Although she'd had other friends, she'd never felt that special closeness with them that she'd felt with Nikki. And now they had agreed to do a better job of staying in touch and would start off rekindling their friendship by going out to dinner tonight. They had so much to catch up on.

She checked her watch. The auction would start in less than ten minutes and she was already nervous. This was the first time she'd ever attended an auction and hoped it wouldn't take long to get to her house.

Her house.

Already she was thinking of it as hers. She couldn't wait to go inside and look around. And she bet if she tried hard enough she would be able to feel her mother's presence. She shifted in her seat at the same time the hair on the back of her neck stood up. She scanned the room, wondering about the reason for her eerie feeling. But she didn't know anyone in the room, and no one here knew her.

The announcer at the front of the room hit his gavel on the table several times to get everyone's attention. She glanced down at the program and saw her house was listed as number eight. She pulled in a nervous breath when the auctioneer announced the auction had begun.

Galen was satisfied to sit in the back where he could see everything going on, and had a pretty good view of Brittany Thrasher. He also had a good view of those two guys who wanted her house. Of course he didn't plan to let them have it. Hopefully she had enough cash on hand to handle her own affairs, but in case she didn't, then unknowingly she had a guardian angel.

The thought of him being any woman's angel had him chuckling. He didn't do anything without an ulterior motive, and in her case he didn't have to dig deep to find out what it was. He wanted her in his bed. Or, if she preferred, her bed. It really didn't matter to him at this point.

He leaned back in his chair as he thought about all

the heat the two of them could and would generate. But he had a feeling that with Brittany Thrasher he would need to proceed with caution. There was something about her and this intense desire he was feeling whenever he looked at her that he just couldn't put his finger on. But he would.

"Now we will move on to house number eight," the auctioneer was saying, interrupting his thoughts. For now it was a good thing.

"Who would like to open the bid?"

Brittany's heart raced when the bidding had officially begun on her house. She had gone on the Internet last night and visited the Web site that outlined the most effective way to participate in an auction. Rule number one said you should not start off the bid. Instead you should scope out the bidders to see if and when you could enter the fray. The key was knowing how much money you had and working with that.

The minimum bid had been set and so far the bidding remained in what she considered a healthy range with only three people actually showing interest. The highest bid was now at thirty-five thousand with only two people left bidding. She decided to enter at forty-six thousand.

She kept her eyes straight ahead on the auctioneer and didn't bother looking back to see who the other bidders were. That was another rule. Keep your eyes on the prize and not your opponents.

"We have a bid of fifty-two thousand. Do I hear fifty-three?"

She lifted her hand. "Fifty-three."

"We have a fifty-three. What about fifty-five?"

"Fifty-five."

Brittany couldn't resist looking sideways and saw a short, stocky man had made the bid. A nervousness settled in the pit of her stomach at the thought that the man wanted *her* house.

"We've got fifty-five. Do I hear fifty-seven?"

She lifted her hand. "Fifty-seven."

"The lady's bid is fifty-seven. Do I hear a sixty?"

"Seventy."

Brittany gasped under her breath at the high jump. Her approval letter was for a hundred thousand. She'd figured since the taxes were less than that it would be sufficient. Now she practically squirmed in her seat.

"We have seventy. Do I hear a seventy-two?"

She raised her hand. "Seventy-two." There were only two people left bidding, and she wondered how far the man would go in his bids.

She couldn't help but turn at that moment and regard the man. He flashed a smile that didn't quite reach his eyes. He wanted her house and—

"We have seventy-two. Can we get a seventy-five?" the auctioneer interrupted her thoughts by asking.

"Seventy-five," the man quickly spoke up.

The room got silent and she knew why. They had reached the amount of the taxes that were due, but the auctioneer would continue until someone had placed the highest bid.

"We have seventy-five. Can we get eighty?"

Galen sighed, getting bored. The bidding for this particular house could go on all evening and he was ready for it to come to an end. It was obvious to everyone in the room that both of the two lone bidders wanted the house and would continue until someone conceded. He seriously doubted either would.

"We have eighty-six. Can we get an eighty-eight?" the auctioneer asked.

The short, stocky man raised his hand at eighty-eight.

"Can we get ninety?"

Brittany raised her hand. "Ninety." She had sent a text message to her banker for an updated approval letter asking for an increase but hadn't gotten a response. What if he was out of the office and hadn't gotten her request? She couldn't let anyone else get her house.

She glanced across the room at the man bidding against her. He appeared as determined as she was to keep bidding.

"We have ninety. Can we get ninety-two?"

"Two hundred thousand dollars."

Everyone in the room, including Brittany and the short, stocky man gasped. Even the auctioneer seemed surprised. Brittany closed her eyes feeling her only connection to her mother slipping away and a part of her couldn't believe it was happening.

"We have a bid of two hundred thousand dollars from the man in the back. Do we have two-ten?" No one said anything. Both Brittany and the short, stocky man were still speechless.

"Going once, going twice. Sold! The house has been sold to the man in the rear. And I suggest we all take a fifteen-minute break."

The people around her started getting up, but Brittany just sat there. She couldn't believe what had just happened. She had lost her mother's house. Her house.

She glanced over at the short, stocky man and he seemed just as disappointed as she felt. He nodded in her direction before he and the man he was with got up and walked out. The room was practically empty now with everyone taking advantage of the break. There was nothing left for her to do but leave. However, she couldn't help wondering the identity of the individual who had won her house. She really needed to get that person's name and if nothing else, hopefully she could negotiate with him to purchase her mother's belongings and—

"Fancy running into you again."

With so much weighing heavily on her mind, it took Brittany some effort to lift her head up to see who was talking to her. As soon as her gaze collided with the man's green eyes, she knew. Her mouth gaped open as she stared at him while he stood there smiling down at her.

"Wh-where did you come from?" she stuttered as she tried recovering from shock.

This was the same man who, even with all his less-than-desirable manners, had been able to creep into her dreams once or twice. She swallowed knowing it had been more often than that. And just thinking about those times sent a shiver through her. Fantasizing about him in her dreams was one thing, but actually seeing him again in the flesh was another.

What was he doing in Phoenix, and better yet, why did their paths have to cross again? Especially now?

"Where did I come from?" he asked, repeating her

question as if he'd found it amusing. "I came from my house this morning and don't worry I came by car and not by cab."

She glared at him. If he thought that line was amusing he was wrong. All it did was remind her of just how impolite he'd been that day. That's really what she should be remembering, not thinking about the way the smile touched his lips, or what a gorgeous pair of eyes he had, or why even now when she had just lost the one thing she'd ever wanted in life, that she could feel the charge in the air between them. The heat. She'd felt it that day in New York, too, even with all her anger.

She hadn't taken the time to analyze it until a few days later, in the privacy of her bedroom when every time she would close her eyes she would see him looking so extremely handsome and dressed in a tux. And his pants had been unzipped. A sensation stirred in her belly at the memory.

Automatically, her gaze lowered to his zipper and she was grateful he was more together this time. Boy, was he. He was wearing a pair of jeans and a white Western shirt and a pair of scuffed boots. He was holding a dark brown Stetson in his hand, and she appreciated that at least he didn't have it on his head. Someone evidently hadn't told a couple of the men who'd attended the auction that it was bad manners to wear a hat inside a building.

And he was tall. She had to actually tilt her head back to look at him. He was built and she particularly liked the way his jeans stretched tight across his thighs. His shoulders were broad beneath his tailored shirt. She could tell.

The sight of him could make a woman drool, and as she continued to study him she remembered how his eyes had captured her from the first. Although she hadn't wanted them to. Those gorgeous Smokey Robinson eyes. She'd thought that then and was thinking the same thing now.

"Small world, isn't it?"

His statement made her realize she was still sitting down. The shock of losing her house hadn't worn off. She slowly stood up and didn't miss the way the green-eyed gaze traveled over her when she did so. She rolled her eyes. She was a big girl and could handle lust for what it was. He was a man and, she presumed, a single man. At least he wasn't wearing a ring, not that it meant anything these days. Besides, no matter how good he looked she couldn't forget that he was the epitome of rude.

And she was quick to size him up. He was a man on the prowl. She'd met more than one in her day and had always managed to convince them to prowl someplace else, in some other woman's neck of the woods. She'd discovered long ago that the whole idea of sex was overrated. She certainly hadn't gotten anything out of it so far.

"So, what about you? Where did you come from?" he prompted.

She thought that perhaps they were standing too close. Had he taken a step closer and she hadn't noticed it? She glanced around. The room was completely empty except for them.

"Doesn't matter where I'm from because I'm on my

way back there." She glanced at her watch. "If you will excuse me, I need to find someone."

"Who?"

She tightened her lips to keep from saying it wasn't any of his business but decided not to. Besides, if he had been in the room during the bidding, there was a chance he might know the identity of the person who'd won her house.

"The man who placed the winning bid on the house I wanted. I really need to see him," she said.

"Okay."

When he didn't step back she moved around him. "Have a nice day," she said, throwing the words over her shoulder as she headed for the exit door.

"Where are you going? We haven't been introduced."

She stopped and turned to him. She refused to be rude even if he had a history of doing so. "I'm rather in a hurry. Like I said, I've got to find—"

"Me."

Brittany tilted her head slightly. "Excuse me?"

A slow, sinfully sensual smile touched his lips. "I said in that case you're looking for me. I'm Galen Steele and I'm the person who placed the winning bid on house number eight."

Brittany took a step back thinking that couldn't be possible. This man, this rude man, could not be the new owner of *her* house. Not a man on the prowl. The man whose high testosterone level spoke volumes, to the point where even she—a person who'd never enjoyed sex—could read it. She guessed you didn't have to enjoy the act to feel the effect. Case in point, the way her heart was thumping in her chest.

"You have *my* house?" she asked, taking a deep, steadying breath. She still didn't want to believe such a thing was possible.

He nodded. "Signed, sealed and delivered. But it could be yours. I'm definitely willing to negotiate, Ms....?"

"Thrasher. Brittany Thrasher." She brushed her fingers against her throat trying to keep up with him. "Are you saying that you might want to part with the house?"

He shrugged. "Why not? It serves me no purpose. I already have a house that I happen to like."

She threw up her hands in frustration, anger and total confusion. "Then why did you bid on it?"

He chuckled. "Because I saw how much you wanted it and I figured it would be a good bargaining tool."

Her brows furrowed in confusion. "A bargaining tool for what?"

"For when we make a deal. I'm going to make an offer that I hope you can't refuse."

She pulled in a deep breath. Did he think she wanted the house that bad that he could make a quick profit right here and now? Evidently that's just what he thought. And unfortunately, he was right. She wanted that house.

"How much?" she decided to cut to the chase and ask.

He lifted a brow. "How much?"

"Yes, how much do you want for it?"

"A week."

"Excuse me? I must have misunderstood you."

He smiled. "No, you didn't. I won't take money for the house, Ms. Thrasher, but I will take a week. Just one week of your time, on my terms, and the house is yours, free and clear."

For a stretch of more than a minute, the only sound in the room was their breathing, and then Brittany spoke and she tilted her head back and her gaze locked with his as she stared up at him. "Let me get this straight. You will turn over that house to me if I spend a week with you?"

He nodded slowly and the gaze holding hers didn't flinch or waver. It was steadfast and unmovable. "Yes, but on my terms, which includes living under my roof."

Galen watched as she crossed her arms over her chest, just like she'd done that day in New York, reminding him what a nice pair of breasts they were. Standing this close to her again was calling his attention to a number of things about her that he'd missed that day. Like how her bottom lip would start quivering when she was angry or how her eyes would darken from a caramel to a deep, rich chocolate when things weren't going her way. He wondered if that same transformation took place while she was in the bedroom making love.

Her eyes narrowed on him. "Mr. Steele, you've lost your mind. What you're proposing is preposterous."

"No, it's not. It's what I want and personally, I think it's a rather good deal considering what you'll be getting," he pointed out. "In the end you'll get what you want and I'll get what I want."

Fire leaped into her face and he actually got aroused watching it. He wondered if anyone ever told her how hot she looked when she was angry. "How can you even suggest such a thing? A decent man would never talk that way to a lady. How dare you."

He chuckled again. "Yes, how dare me."

"And why in the world would I want to live with you for a week? Give me one good reason."

He shrugged. "I'll do better than that. I'll give you two. First, you want that house, so that should be incentive enough. Because it's not, there's the issue of what you said that day in New York about someone teaching me some manners."

"Well, they should!"

"Then do it. I dare you. I dare you to stay with me for a week and teach me manners." He reached into his back pocket and pulled out his wallet. And then he handed her his business card.

"You have only forty-eight hours to make your decision to contact me. If I don't hear from you, then I will donate the house, the land and all its contents to charity. Goodbye, Ms. Thrasher."

Then he walked off and didn't look back.

Chapter 5

The maitre d' greeted Brittany with a smile. "Good evening and welcome to Malone's. May I help you?"

"Yes. I have dinner reservations with Nikki Cartwright."

"Ms. Cartwright has already been seated. Please follow me."

Brittany glanced around while the man led the way. Nikki had suggested that they meet here and Brittany was glad Nikki had when the man stopped at a table next to a window providing a majestic view of the Sonoran foothills.

Nikki beamed when she saw her and stood and gave her a hug. "Well, did you get your house?" she asked excitedly.

Brittany fought to hold back the tears that had been

threatening to fall since she'd left the auction mart. "No, I was outbid," she said as she took her seat.

"Oh, Brit, I'm so sorry. I know how much getting that house meant to you. Have you talked to the new owner to see if you can at least get your mother's belongings because the house was willed to you?"

Brittany shook her head in disgust. "The man and I talked about a lot of things, but we never got around to that. He was so busy telling me how I'd be able to get the house from him free and clear."

"Really? How?"

"I have to live with him for a week."

Nikki nearly choked as she sipped on her water. "What?"

"You heard me right. He offered to sign the house over to me if I'd agree to spend a week with him."

Nikki looked aghast. "Just who is this guy? Of all the nerve."

"His name is Galen Steele and I have—"

"Galen Steele?" Nikki sat straight up in her chair. "Are you sure?"

"Yes, I'm sure. He gave me his business card and I have forty-eight hours to get back to him with my decision."

Nikki shook her head. "I can't believe he actually approached you like that, a complete stranger."

"We're not exactly strangers," Brittany said and then went on to explain how they'd met over the cab. "Luckily, I was early for the airport and another cab was dispatched within minutes. But still, before he left I told him that someone should teach him some manners. So now he wants me to move in with him and do just that."

"To teach him manners?" Nikki asked.

Brittany gave her friend a straight look. "I wasn't born yesterday, Nikki. I'm sure a class on manners isn't all he's expecting."

Nikki nodded. "Knowing those Steeles, it's probably not."

She raised a brow. "Do you know him?"

"Not personally, but there aren't many single women in Phoenix who don't know of the Steeles. There are six of them. All handsome as sin with green eyes that can make your panties wet if they look at you long enough. The green eyes are from their mother's side of the family. She used to be a fashion model and was well-known in her day. I heard that even now she's still quite beautiful."

"And Galen has five brothers?"

"Yes, and all of them were born within a year of each other. Galen is the oldest. It seems their father was serious about keeping his wife pregnant. And in addition to being handsome, all those Steeles are very successful. The only one I've ever said more than two words to is Jonas. He owns a marketing firm and I've done free-lance photography work for him once or twice. Jonas is a pretty nice guy, but all those Steeles have one thing in common besides good looks, success and green eyes."

"What?" Brittany wanted to know.

"They are hard-core womanizers, all six of them, which is why women consider them the 'Bad News Steeles.' People claim they got their womanizing ways from their father. I heard he used to be something else before settling down and marrying Eden Tyson."

Nikki then leaned over the table. "With you owning an etiquette school, you'll be the perfect person to teach him manners. Are you going to take Galen Steele up on his offer?"

Brittany pushed a lock of hair out of her face. "Of course not! He doesn't even know what I do for a living."

Nikki chuckled. "There's a joke around town that a woman hasn't been bedded unless she's been bedded by a Steele. They're supposed to be just that good."

No man was that good, Brittany thought. At least none in her past had been worth the trouble. "Well, I plan on contacting him tomorrow. There has to be another way."

Nikki shrugged as a half smile eased across her lips. "I don't know. I understand when they see a woman they want, they go after her. Of course they drop her after a while, but there are a lot of women who would love to be in your shoes right now, including me. Not for Galen, mind you, but I've always had this thing for Jonas. He's a hottie."

Brittany stared across the table at her long-lost friend. "Let me get this straight. If given the chance you would accept his terms of an affair?"

"Of course," Nikki said without any thought. "I'm a career woman and I've pretty much given up the notion of finding Mr. Right because it seems they're already taken. What you have out there now are men like the Steeles, the Hard-Ons, the Idiots and the Dawgs. They are the men who want one thing and one thing only. I'm prepared for them because personally, I want only one thing myself. I no longer have any grandiose ideas of settling down, marrying a man who is my soul mate, having babies and living happily ever after. All it takes is for me to watch divorce court on television to know it doesn't work that way. At least not anymore and not for most people."

Brittany felt sad for her friend. When they were teenagers, Nikki had dreamed of a knight in shining armor.

"What about you?" Nikki interrupted her thoughts by asking. "I remember you weren't in a rush to ever marry. You wanted to see the world first. And," she added, lowering her voice, "you were sort of against men because of what that man tried to do to you that time."

Nikki's words suddenly yanked Brittany out of the present and pushed her right smack back into the past when she'd been thirteen and Mr. Ponder, a male friend of one of her foster parents, had tried forcing himself on her. He would have succeeded had she not bit him hard enough for him to let her go. It was the first time she'd run away from a foster home. After telling the policemen who'd found her what happened—or almost happened—the authorities had placed her in another foster home right away.

That move had been a blessing because that's when she'd met Nikki. Nikki's family had lived across the street from the Dugans. At first the trauma of what the man had tried doing left Brittany withdrawn, confused and alone. But all that changed when Nikki became her friend. At some point she'd felt comfortable enough with Nikki to share her secret.

"Brit, maybe I shouldn't have brought it up," she heard Nikki saying. "I'm sorry."

She met her friend's apologetic gaze. "No, I'm fine,

although I haven't thought of it in years. But now I'm wondering if that episode has anything to do with why…"

When her words faltered, Nikki raised a brow and asked, "Why what?"

Brittany glanced around to make sure no one was listening to their conversation, leaned over the table and whispered, "Why I don't enjoy sex like most women."

"It might and then again, it might not. Some men are just selfish in the bedroom. It's all about them and they could care less if you get your pleasures or not. You might have been involved with those types."

Nikki smiled and then continued. "What you need is a man who has the ability to tap into those hidden pleasures. And if that's true, based on what I've heard, a Steele is just the man who can do it. I know several women who had short-term affairs with them and their only regret was missing out on all that pleasure. They claim that when it comes to fulfilling a woman's fantasy, those 'Bad News Steeles' are top-notch."

Brittany waited while the waiter placed menus in front of them. When the man walked off, she said, "And what if I don't have any hidden pleasures for anyone to tap into?"

Nikki gave her a somber look. "If you don't enjoy sex at the hands of a Steele, then I would suggest you get some serious counseling. Although that pervert didn't succeed in doing anything, I can imagine it was a traumatic experience for you to go through at the time. You were only thirteen."

Yes, Brittany thought. She'd been only thirteen. Now she understood those looks Mr. Ponder used to give her and why she wasn't comfortable when she received those kind of looks now from men.

"Do you know what I think, Brit?"

Brittany glanced across the table at Nikki. It was hard to believe they hadn't seen each other in over twelve years. That special bond they'd always had seemed to just fall into place. Nikki had been there to help her through some rough times in her life and when Nikki had moved away, she had truly lost her best friend. There hadn't been anyone she could talk to, share her innermost fears and secrets with. She had felt truly alone.

"No, what do you think?" she asked.

"Of course it needs to be your decision, but in a way you can practically kill two birds with one stone. If you accept Galen Steele's offer, not only will you get your mother's house free and clear, but you'll also find out if your dislike of sex is something you need to explore professionally. But I have a feeling Galen Steele will unlock all the hidden pleasures locked away inside you. It takes a man with an experienced touch to do that, and I hear that's what Galen Steele has."

Brittany shook her head, not convinced the suggested approach was the right one. "I don't know, Nikki. The couple of guys I slept with before… I could only do it because I liked them, although I never fancied myself in love with them. I'm not sure I can have casual sex with anyone just for the sake of sex. Besides, I'm not all that certain I even like Galen Steele. Both times when our paths crossed he didn't impress me as someone with good manners."

Nikki threw her head back and laughed. "Manners

are the last thing you'll think about when the big 'O' strikes. And trust me, Brit, you won't be doing it just for the sake of doing it. You'll be doing it for pleasure, and there's plenty of pleasure out there waiting for you. I think you just need the right man and I'm totally convinced Galen Steele is that man. Think about it."

Brittany nodded. She certainly had strong motivation for doing so—her house was at stake. However, like she'd told Nikki, she wasn't sure if she could engage in casual sex and enjoy it. Then again, she'd done it a couple of times with guys she was involved with at the time and hadn't enjoyed it, either.

She picked up her menu and eyed her friend over the top. "All right. I'll think about it."

Eli Steele glared at the man sitting on the opposite side of his desk. He'd often wondered about his oldest brother's mental state and this was one of those times. "Let me get this straight, Galen. You rushed me to fax that damn loan approval letter to you yesterday so that you could bid on some house you really don't want? A house you are now signing over to some woman you really don't know?"

Galen nodded slowly. "Yes, that sounds about right to me. You have a problem with any of it?" Eli was son number three and there was barely a two-year difference in their ages. It amused Galen how their father had kept their mother barefoot and pregnant for six years straight. She'd given birth to a son each year. They'd grown up close, and they still were, but that didn't mean they wouldn't rattle each other's cages at times. He often wondered how his mother had handled living in a house filled with so much testosterone.

"No, I don't have a problem with it because it's your money," Eli said.

"And you're my attorney," he reminded him, which his brother seemed to forget sometimes. In addition to being the corporate attorney for SID, Eli was legal counsel for several other private companies and was doing quite well for himself. Which was probably why a couple of years ago, right before his thirtieth birthday, he'd bought the perfect building for his law practice in downtown Phoenix: the hub of business activities, and right in the heart of the valley. Prime real estate property if ever there was any.

Galen would be the first to admit the high-rise building was a beautiful piece of architecture and had been a wise investment for his brother to make. It was huge, spacious and upscale. Eli's firm took up the entire twentieth floor. The other floors were leased, which brought him in a nice profit each month. Another plus was the view from Eli's office window. He saw straight into a penthouse fitness center across the street, and Galen could just imagine his brother sitting behind his desk checking out the women.

"I'll have the papers ready for you to pick up later this evening," Eli told him.

"Go ahead and overnight the deeds to her because I won't be seeing her again."

He decided not to tell Eli about the outlandish proposition he'd made to the woman, probably because knowing Eli, he wouldn't consider it outlandish at all. And under normal circumstances, neither would he. But again, he knew how much that house meant to Brittany Thrasher so for once he'd given in to his soft spot and not his hard-on.

He smiled thinking there were women who wouldn't believe he had a soft spot, and very few could touch it like Brittany Thrasher had.

Chances were she was on her way back home to Florida. He'd have loved to be there to see her face when she received the papers giving her the house, property and land, free and clear.

"Do you have her address?"

Galen rolled his eyes. "Why would I have her address? I met her only twice."

"Yet you're giving her a property worth a lot of money?"

Leave it to Eli to try and make things difficult. His brother had a habit of rationalizing things too much. "No, the house was already hers. I've already explained that it was willed to her by her biological mother."

"Gotcha. You're such a nice guy, a real champion of good causes," Eli said sarcastically. And then he added, "It's hard to believe there won't be anything in this for you."

It was hard for Galen to believe that, too. He'd made her that outlandish proposal, but hadn't really expected her to go for it. Not with her being Miss Manners and all. She probably figured his offer was just another display of his ill-mannered and brutish side. But he couldn't help but wonder how things might have been if she had accepted his offer.

He could just imagine spending a week behind closed doors with her. She would teach him manners and he would teach her how to let her hair down, live for the moment. He would love to see those caramel-colored eyes turn chocolate-brown from something other than anger. A full-blown orgasm would do the trick.

"Is there anything else? You're just sitting here not saying anything."

Eli's words whipped Galen's mind back on track and he quickly stood. "No, that's about it. If possible I'd like the papers sent today, so she'll get them tomorrow. She might want to return to Phoenix and go through her mother's belongings."

A part of him was counting on her doing so and he intended to make it his business to be around when she did. Maybe all wasn't lost after all.

"Excuse me, Galen, but I have work to do. Now you're just standing there, staring into space and smiling."

Galen shook his head. To know Eli was to love him. He could be such a pain in the ass. "You're going to the folks' for dinner tomorrow night?" he decided to ask before he left.

"Of course. Who could be brave enough to miss it? If we don't show up for Mom's Thursday-night family dinner hour, there's no telling what will happen the next day. She might decide to come around snooping."

Galen knew that to be true. Mercury hadn't shown up one night last month and before he could wake up Friday morning, Eden Steele was on his doorstep. She'd told him that because son number five had missed such an important family activity, she was duty-bound to spend the whole day with him. Unfortunately, Mercury hadn't been alone when their mother had shown up. By the end of the day, after driving their mother around town—to do some mother-and-son bonding as she'd called it—Mercury hadn't been too happy.

"Then I will see you tomorrow night." He turned to leave and then stopped and said, "And by the way, I like your new administrative assistant. She has nice legs."

Eli grunted. "I wouldn't know. I haven't noticed."

Liar, Galen thought. He happened to know Eli was a leg man. Chances were he'd not only noticed, but he'd already been between those same legs. If he hadn't gotten that far already, there was no doubt in Galen's mind that Eli was finalizing his plans to get there.

Galen couldn't help chuckling as he walked out the door. He wasn't mad at Eli. That was the Steeles' way. And why did another part of him wish things had worked out differently between him and Brittany Thrasher? It would have been nice had she agreed to his proposal. Just as well that she hadn't, though, because he had plenty of work to do back at his garage. He needed to get his mind back on track and finish working on his latest video game project.

But when it came to a woman who looked like Brittany Thrasher, he would trade in a bunch of electronic parts for her real body parts any day.

Brittany sat staring at her cell phone and the business card she had placed beside it. She had a decision to make and doing so wasn't easy. She had enjoyed dinner with Nikki; it'd been like old times as they'd reminisced and caught up on each other's lives. They had agreed to do lunch before Brittany returned home…if she didn't take Galen Steele up on his offer.

Drawing in a deep breath, she reached for her phone and then quickly snatched her hand back. She was not ready to do anything just yet. She glanced over at the clock. Only sixteen hours had passed since Galen Steele had made his offer and he'd given her forty-eight. That meant she had thirty-two hours to go. Because she hadn't been sure what to expect with this trip to Phoenix, especially how long she would have to stay, she had purchased a one-way ticket. One of her employees was covering her etiquette training classes for the next couple of weeks, so she didn't have to worry about work, either.

She stood and decided that no matter how much she wanted her mother's home and the belongings inside it, she would not make any hasty decisions where Galen Steele was concerned. It was quite obvious the man wanted only one thing from her and it had nothing to do with teaching him manners like he claimed. Mind you, his manners could use some improving, but she wasn't that gullible to believe he wanted her to stay under his roof for seven days to perfect his pleases and thank-yous.

She lay across the bed and grabbed the remote to flick on the television. She was not a television person, but for lack of anything else to do for now, she would see if there was anything on the tube worth watching. She had thought of driving back out to her mother's house, but there would be no purpose served in doing that.

As she lay there looking at the television without actually seeing it, she couldn't help wondering about the pros and cons of staying with Galen for a week. He didn't come across as the type of man who would try and force a woman to do anything she didn't want to do. But still…

Would she have a guest bedroom, or did he assume she would be sharing his? And just what type of manners did he want to be taught? Most people knew the basic manners; they just didn't use them. And then there was the issue of her little problem… If she spent an entire week with him, would Galen cure her of her sexual hang-ups? Her low libido had never bothered her. Now she was beginning to wonder if it should have.

She pulled the pillow from under her head and then smothered her face with it. It swallowed up her groan. This was all Galen's fault. The man not only had her thinking, but he also had her feeling things she'd never felt before. Nikki would think that was a good sign.

She removed the pillow off her face, tossed it aside and stared up at the ceiling. She thought about the last serious relationship she'd been involved in with Gilford Turner. For an entire year he would arrive after church on Sunday like clockwork and stay until Tuesday. They never discussed marriage and that had been fine with her as much as it had been with him. His mother had been the only one bothered by their lack of motivation to get to the altar. For them, there had been no big rush.

She hadn't fooled herself into thinking that she was in love with him or vice versa. They liked each other and that was as far as it went. That's why when he'd dropped by one day during the week to announce he wouldn't be coming back, with a smile on her face she'd gathered up all of his belongings, placed them in a box and walked him to the door and wished him well. In the days, weeks and months that followed, she hadn't pined after him, nor had she missed his presence. She had carried on with her life and her Sundays through Tuesdays had once again become her own.

And as for the sex...

She could honestly say she hadn't missed any of it because there hadn't been anything inspiring about it.

A year after Gilford, she'd tried getting back into the dating thing again and it took less than a month to decide she hadn't wanted the hassles, the aggravation or the drama of getting to know another man. Most tried to be slick and only had one thing on their mind. Sex. At some point she realized she'd rather have a root canal than to contemplate having sex with a man.

Would Galen be different? She was attracted to him, that much was a given. And around him she'd felt a sexual interest that she hadn't felt toward a man before, which could be considered a plus. And for the first time in her life she could admit to dreaming about hot, sweaty sex. Galen himself had crept into her dreams during those times.

Indulging her nervous habit, she bit her bottom lip. She had decisions to make and for now she needed her full concentration. She turned off the TV. She had to think. Boy, did she have to think.

Chapter 6

His cell phone rang and Galen absently pressed the Bluetooth in his ear without taking his gaze off the sixty pieces of software components in front of him. It was the middle of the day and he was in his air-conditioned six-car garage working on what would be the brain of his next video game. He had worked on what he considered the senses last night.

"This is Galen."

"Mr. Steele, this is Brittany Thrasher."

He shifted his gaze to a copy of the FedEx receipt Eli had dropped off earlier. Because he'd been busy at the time, he had placed it on his desk. He wasn't surprised she was calling. Evidently she'd gotten the overnight package and was calling to thank him.

"Yes, Ms. Thrasher?"

"I was wondering if we could meet somewhere and talk."

He lifted a brow, surprised. "You're still in Phoenix?"

"Yes."

He put down the pliers he'd been holding. If she was still in Phoenix that meant she was unaware he'd signed the house over to her. "And what do you want to talk about?"

"Your proposal. I have some questions about it."

He drew in a deep, steadying breath as he tried to get his heart rate under control, while at the same time ignore the throbbing in his groin. Was she seriously contemplating taking him up on his offer? He definitely hadn't expected her to do so. The decent thing to do would be to come clean and tell her that he'd signed the house over to her, so there was no need for them to discuss the proposal. But he couldn't help being curious about her questions.

"What kind of questions?" he heard himself asking.

"First of all, I want to know where I'll be sleeping while I'm under your roof."

Several visual images flashed through his mind. Maybe now was not a good time to tell her that if he had his way, she wouldn't be doing much sleeping. "Where would you want to sleep?" he decided to ask her.

"In a guest bedroom."

He smiled, not surprised. "That could be arranged for the first couple of days." There was no reason to tell her that if that's where she slept, then that's where he would also be sleeping.

"And I know granting this request might be a little

difficult, especially for a man I'm teaching manners to, but I'd like you to promise to keep your hands to yourself."

He couldn't help but throw his head back and laugh. "When?"

"Excuse me?"

Oh, he wouldn't excuse her, not even a little bit. "I asked when am I supposed to keep my hands to myself?"

"At all times."

His smile widened. He hadn't done that since grade school when Cindy Miller had squealed to the teacher on him for kissing her neck. "Sorry, I can't make you that promise because I *do* intend to touch you," he said, deciding he might as well tell her the truth.

"Mr. Steele, this is only a coincidence but believe it or not, I teach manners for a living."

He chuckled. "You don't say."

"I do say. I own Etiquette Matters and I take my work seriously. If I decided to accept your proposal— and that's a big 'if'—my sole purpose would be to teach you manners."

"In that case, Ms. Thrasher, maybe the first thing on your list should be to teach me how to keep my hands off you." He leaned back in his chair, clearly enjoying this. He could imagine she was pretty damn annoyed with him about now.

"Is there any way we can renegotiate your offer?"

She had to be kidding. "No. I have something you want and you have something I want. You either come to live with me for a week or the house and its contents go to charity."

"You are being difficult, Mr. Steele."

He smiled. Now that she had surprised the hell out of him by showing an interest, she hadn't seen anything yet. "There's no reason for me to make it easy for you, Ms. Thrasher. I gave you my terms. You can either accept them or reject them. You have less than ten hours to decide."

He wished they were talking face-to-face. He figured her bottom lip was quivering in anger about now, and he would love to see, even better, he'd love to taste that anger.

"I'd like to make a counteroffer."

He shook his head. She didn't know when to give up. She was definitely persistent and he liked that about her because he was the same way. He didn't say anything for a while, deciding to let her statement hover between them for a minute. And then, "Because I consider myself a fair man, I'll let you do that. But we need to meet in person," he said. He rubbed his chin. "I can come to your hotel."

"I prefer we meet someplace else."

"If you insist. Let's meet at Regis. It's a coffee shop in downtown Phoenix, walking distance from your hotel."

"I never told you the name of my hotel."

He thought quick on his feet. "I didn't say that you did. I assume you're staying at one of the hotels downtown."

Not wanting to give her time to think about his slipup, he asked, "Are you not staying at a hotel downtown?"

She hesitated a quick minute before saying, "Yes, I am."

"Fine. I'll meet you at Regis in an hour. Goodbye." He then quickly ended the call before she could rethink it.

Brittany thought it was a beautiful day for walking. Besides, it gave her some extra time to think before actually meeting with Galen. Even though it was lunchtime and the sidewalk was crowded with people, she couldn't help being fascinated with downtown Phoenix.

Earlier that day she had gone on a tour of the state capitol and had checked out the Phoenix Art Museum. She had arrived in time to see a small play on the history of the state; however, she'd been so preoccupied with her thoughts that she hadn't really paid attention.

When she saw the sign for Regis up ahead, she began nibbling on her lips. Meeting with Galen Steele wouldn't be so bad if he wasn't so darn handsome. Her attraction to him had taken her by surprise, because no man ever captured her interest the way he had.

Annoyance seethed through her when she remembered that he was a man with only one thing on his agenda. It would be up to her to try and sway his mind about a few things. If he didn't go along with what she was going to suggest, what did she have to lose?

Her house, for starters.

That realization made her heart sink as she opened the door to the café. She only had to scan the place a few seconds before her gaze locked with his. In an instant she was drawn to the most captivating pair of green eyes anyone could possess. They would be her downfall if she wasn't careful. But how could a woman be careful around the likes of Galen? Just seeing him issued an invitation to take every risk and then some.

He stood when he saw her and she was impressed that he could display some manners when he wanted to. Only thing was, now that he was standing, her gaze shifted from his eyes to encompass all of him. He was wearing a pullover shirt and a pair of khakis. His stance was sexy as sin.

The sunlight pouring through the windows struck him at an angle that projected brilliant rays on his skin, which was the color of mahogany. And if that wasn't bad enough, his shoulders looked broader in that particular shirt.

She continued to hold his gaze as she released the door to step inside. This meeting was utterly ridiculous, really. His proposal had been absurd. And the thought that she was here to negotiate anything was absolutely crazy. What she should do was turn right around, open the door and leave. But she couldn't do that. This man stood between her and the one thing she wanted more than anything. A connection to her mother. He was the key. To be even more specific, he *had* the key.

She broke eye contact with him long enough to note that the café was packed but somehow he'd grabbed a table. Sighing deeply and with a tight smile plastered on her face, she moved toward him.

There would be nothing proper or graceful about the way he would take her the first time, Galen decided as he watched Brittany stroll in his direction. It didn't have to be in a bed. Any spot in his house would suffice. And they didn't have to be lying down. Taking her against a wall would be fine. He should be downright mortified with the direction of his thoughts. Definitely ashamed. But he wasn't.

He kept his gaze trained on her. She walked with confidence, grace and style. And the look on her face was that of a woman on a mission. A mission not to change the world, just his mind.

His eyes scanned her. She was wearing a denim skirt that hit below the knee and a modest blouse. Who did modest and below the knee these days? he wondered. Still, he had to admit that both items of clothing looked rather nice on her. The skirt did an awesome job of showing her curves, and the blouse emphasized the firmness of the breasts pressing against it. And those legs he'd admired yesterday were still looking pretty damn good today. He could imagine those legs wrapped around him after he got between them.

Was that sweat he was beginning to feel on his brow? No matter, the lustful thoughts running through his mind were exhilarating. Hot and potent at their best. But that was okay because at some point he intended to turn those thoughts into reality.

As she got closer he couldn't help noticing that she had a prissy look, too prim and proper. For some reason he felt that a bout of hot, heavy and sweaty sex would suit her. He wanted to see her perfectly done hair get mussed up a bit. He wanted to be the one to nibble on that bottom lip, and he wanted to be the one to make love to her without an ounce of finesse.

When she reached his table, she held out her hand to him. "Mr. Steele."

Such formality. She had to be kidding, he thought, just seconds before saying, "Ms. Thrasher." And then he took a step closer and lowered his mouth to hers.

Before Brittany could move, his mouth was there, dead center on hers. And when she parted her lips in shock, it gave him the opening he needed to slide his tongue inside her mouth.

For a split second she forgot how to breathe, especially when she felt Galen's tongue giving her mouth a quick sweep before he pulled back, ending the kiss. In less than a minute he had taken the term *short and sweet* to a whole other level.

A quick glance indicated a number of people had witnessed the kiss. She narrowed her gaze at him. "It is not good manners to kiss in a public place."

He smiled, evidently amused. "It's not?"

"No."

"Do you want to go outside and continue, then?"

"Of course not!"

"A pity," he said, pulling a chair out for her. He brushed his fingers on her arms while doing so and she shivered, wondering if the touch had been accidental or if he'd meant to do it. She glanced over at him and from the smile on his face she knew he'd meant to do it.

And this was the man who wanted her to stay under his roof for a week. If he was taking these kinds of liberties in public, she could just imagine what he'd do in private. There was something about him that made her unbalanced, shaky, and she had to wonder if she had completely lost her mind to even be here with him.

"People are staring at us," she said in a low voice.

He shrugged. "Let them stare. They probably think we're lovers who didn't get enough of each other last night. They're just jealous."

She wondered if he was always this quick with a comeback and if his mind continuously revolved around sex. If nothing else, she was picking up on some heated vibes just sitting across the table from him. She wondered if he felt them or if her senses were the only ones under siege.

"You wanted to make a counteroffer."

His words had cut into her thoughts and she looked into his green eyes. Good Lord, the man was handsome. "Yes, that's right," she said, almost stumbling over the words.

"Would you care for something to eat and drink before we get started on the negotiations?"

"Coffee, please." What she needed was something stronger, but coffee would have to do.

She watched him motion to the waitress who came over with the coffeepot in her hand and ready to pour. After the woman walked away, he gave Brittany a chance to add her sweetener and take a sip before asking, "So, what's your counteroffer?"

Brittany breathed in deeply, shifted in her seat and said, "That I teach you manners for a week but I live in the house."

Galen immediately knew what house she was referring to, but decided to ask anyway. "And which house is that?"

"The one you won at the auction two days ago."

"Why? Once you carry out the terms of my offer it

will be yours in a week to do whatever you want with it, so what's the hurry?"

"If I told you I doubt you'd understand."

"Try me."

"I'd rather not."

Galen knew that even if she had shared her reason, he would not have changed his plans. "I prefer that you stay at my place. In fact, I insist on it. However, I'd give you the key to go there whenever you want when you have some free time."

Genuine surprise touched her eyes. "You would?"

"Yes."

He thought her smile perfection and it almost made him feel like a heel for playing her this way, when all he had to do was tell her that as of ten o'clock yesterday morning, the house had become hers anyway. But for some reason he couldn't do that. He'd never expected her to consider such an outlandish offer and now that she had, he couldn't back down.

She took another sip of her coffee and he took a sip of his, wishing it was a sip of her instead. That quick taste he'd gotten of her when they'd kissed wasn't enough, especially because he knew there was more where that had come from. Locking lips again with her was not something he was willing to pass up. And then there was her perfume. The scent was as luscious as she looked.

"So, are you ready to give me your answer?" he asked, while trying not to sound overly eager.

She looked up at him. "No, not yet. I have to think this through to the end."

He could only think of one reason why she was drawing this out and the thought of it annoyed him. "Why? Do you have a boyfriend back home?"

"Of course not! If I did, I wouldn't be here contemplating your offer. Just what kind of woman do you think I am?"

One who put too much emphasis on manners, he thought but didn't say. She wanted to teach him manners, and he wanted to show her that there was a time and a place for manners, and there was a time and a place *not* for them. "I don't know. What kind of woman are you?" he responded.

He wondered how long he was going to last, sitting here engaging in idle chitchat with her when all he wanted to do was take her somewhere and feel her body pressed next to his and indulge once more in the taste of her mouth. He knew he needed to proceed with caution with her, but he was finding it hard to do so.

"I'm a woman who takes life seriously," she said, frowning over at him.

His gaze automatically went to her lower lip. Seeing it quiver sparked a low burn in his groin and had his erection pressing hard against his zipper. She was annoyed, angry and probably frustrated and her facial features were letting him know it and turning him on in the process. He figured now would not be a good time to ask when was the last time she'd gotten buck-naked and wild in the bedroom. He knew for a fact that that was a good way to release tension and stress.

"I'm a man who takes life seriously, as well," he said, and from the look on her face, he could tell she doubted his sincerity.

"So what kind of manners do you want me to teach

you?" she inquired before taking another sip of her coffee.

"What kinds are there?"

She took another sip of her coffee. "There are the basic manners about not putting your elbows on the table and what fork to use while eating. Then there are the business manners, party and entertainment etiquette, gift-giving etiquette, and the—"

"What about bedroom etiquette?"

He watched her lips tighten and enjoyed seeing that, too. Anything she did with her lips aroused him. He took a sip of his coffee and noted she hadn't responded to his question. Had he hit a sore spot with her or something? That possibility called for further investigation.

"Bedroom etiquette?" she finally asked.

A slow smile touched his lips. "Yes, you know, the dos and don'ts while a couple is in the bedroom making love. I'm curious as to what's proper and what's not. Surely there are some specific manners governing that sort of thing."

"I'm sure there are."

"But those are the manners that you don't teach?" he asked. He had her swimming in unfamiliar waters— and he was enjoying it. He was good at reading people and he could tell this topic of conversation had her somewhat flustered. Was she one of those women who thought a discussion of sex should only take place behind closed doors and not over coffee in a restaurant?

"Ms. Thrasher?" She had clamped her mouth shut and now he was forcing her to open it again.

"I've never done so before, Mr. Steele."

"Please call me Galen, and why not? Are you saying no one has ever approached you for such instruction?"

She held his gaze and lifted her chin. "That's exactly what I'm saying. You are the first."

Galen took another sip of his coffee. She was upset with him and her features showed it. In addition to the quivering of her bottom lip, her brows arched in a cute formation over her eyes and her nostrils seemed to flare. Why did seeing all of that make adrenaline flow through his veins? If that wasn't insane, he didn't know what was.

"In that case, I'd love to be your first student, Brittany. I can call you Brittany, can't I?"

"I prefer you not be my first anything, and yes, you can call me Brittany."

Brittany took another sip of her coffee. He had turned those green eyes on her and she felt trapped by them. If he was playing some sort of game with her, then he was winning. The man had her tied up in all kinds of knots.

"But I am your first in at least two things that I know of, Brittany. Has anyone ever hijacked a cab from you before me?"

"No."

"Has anyone ever made a proposition like the one I have?"

"No."

"Seems like we're on a roll. We might as well continue."

She much preferred they didn't. "Why would you want to learn bedroom etiquette?" she decided to ask, more out of curiosity than anything.

"I might decide to date a real lady one of these days,

and I wouldn't want to run her off with my less-than-desirable behavior behind closed doors. Right now I like to keep things simple, and simple for me is delivering pleasure beyond measure. In a rather naughty and raunchy, hot and sweaty sort of way. The women I'm into now enjoy it, but I need to know how far I can go."

Naughty and raunchy? Hot and sweaty? She swallowed tightly at the thought of that description given to sex. "I really wouldn't know."

His mere words were causing more havoc to her body than Gilford's touch ever did. She actually felt a heated sensation between her thighs that made her cross her legs.

"If you want me to teach you manners, Galen, I prefer sticking with those areas I'm familiar with," she said in a clipped tone.

He leaned back in his chair thinking he so liked ruffling her feathers. "Okay. And when will you let me know if you plan to teach me any manners at all? When will I know for certain that you've accepted my proposal?"

She placed her coffee cup aside. "You've given me forty-eight hours. If you don't hear from me within that time frame, then you'll know my decision."

He nodded slowly. "And if I hear from you?"

"Then we can go from there." She stood. "Thanks for the coffee. Goodbye, Galen."

He stood, as well. "Goodbye, Brittany, and I'll look forward to your phone call."

She turned and walked away, and he continued to stand there and stare at her, appreciating the sway of her hips with every step she took.

* * *

An hour or so later Brittany was pacing her hotel room. Every time she slowed her pace and closed her eyes for a moment, she could see Galen Steele's arrogant smile in her mind.

Of all the nerve for him to ask her about bedroom manners. As far as she was concerned, there wasn't such a thing. What a couple did behind closed doors was acceptable as long as they both agreed and were comfortable with it, even if it meant swinging butt-naked from a chandelier. Of course he'd only asked to rattle her, she was sure of it, and it didn't help matters that she didn't have a clue as to what he was talking about. She wouldn't know naughty and raunchy or hot and sweaty if they came up and bit her on the butt.

A tingle went up her spine at the thought of someone, namely Galen, doing that very thing—biting her on the butt. Why on earth would she think such a thing? She didn't have a sadistic bone in her body. When it came to sex, she'd always gone for the traditional. Could that be her problem?

There was definitely one way to find out. She sat on the edge of the bed to think about what was at stake here. First and foremost was ownership of her mother's home. The offer was out there. One week under Galen's roof and he would sign it over to her, free and clear. Of course she would make sure he put it in writing. And then there was the issue of her not liking sex. Nikki was convinced it was her sex partners and not the sex act itself that was to blame. Or it could very well be the incident that happened when she was thirteen that had turned her off sex completely.

If something was wrong with her, then she owed it to herself to find out and seek professional help if she needed it. After all, she was twenty-eight and most women her age were involved in healthy relationships with men.

At that moment something clicked inside her mind. A sign, perhaps? Was it a coincidence that the house her mother had left her was now tied to Galen Steele? Had fate brought them together if for no other reason than to fix a personal problem she'd tried ignoring? Was Galen, without his knowledge, being used as a tool to right a wrong?

Okay, that thought might be taking things too far, but then, what were the chances of her crossing paths in Phoenix with the same man she'd met six months ago in New York? And then, not only did their paths cross again, but he had something she wanted. Back in New York, she'd had something he wanted—a cab.

She threw her head back. Maybe she was putting way too much thought into this, trying to find excuses to validate what she needed to do. She would be the first to admit that Galen Steele was different from any man she'd ever met. What was there about his brashness and arrogance that pulled her to a different level? All the guys she'd ever dated had impeccable manners, she'd made sure of it. So why was she now drawn to a man whose manners left a lot to be desired?

She reached up and touched her lips with her fingertips, remembering the exact moment he'd kissed her. It had been short but thorough, and she had tasted his tongue. Sensations had jolted her the moment their tongues had touched. None of her former boyfriends were much into kissing. They thought it unnecessary foreplay. But she had a feeling Galen took as much time with a kiss as he did with the sex act itself.

Regardless, it was inappropriate for him to kiss her in a restaurant, and maybe that should be the first thing she covered with him—how he should behave out with a woman in public. It was quite obvious that he was used to doing whatever he wanted, whenever he wanted and wherever he wanted. Her instructions would definitely nip that in the bud.

She felt her heart race at the thought that she had a game plan. Regardless of what he figured he was getting, the only thing she would be delivering to Galen Steele was exactly what he'd asked for, what he definitely needed. A crash course in manners.

And before she could get cold feet, she picked up the phone off the nightstand.

Chapter 7

Galen very seldom went online for anything other than to check out the competition. But here he was surfing the Internet for information on Etiquette Matters.

A half hour later he couldn't help but smile. What he'd just read was pretty darn cool. In his opinion, Brittany Thrasher was a highly intelligent woman. With an idea she started in college—pretty similar to how he, Eric and Wesley had gotten started—she had created Etiquette Matters. And over the years it had become a very profitable business. According to her bio, she'd had a fascination with the use of proper etiquette and had been considered an Emily Post wannabe. She'd started off with a small column in her university's newspaper and later she gave private classes to young women who'd come from the wrong side of the tracks, had made it to college and were determined to improve their social standing by getting a firm grasp on manners, etiquette and protocol.

She'd found her niche and within a year of graduating she'd hired five people to assist her. Now there were ten in her employ and the business seemed to be doing well. There was always some company or organization that wanted to know the right way to do things. Last year she'd even included a department on international protocol.

She had a waiting list of parents wanting private lessons for their children. And the contract she had snagged with the NFL was definitely impressive. He didn't have to be reminded that she was a professional. The shocked look on her face when he'd kissed her in the café proved that. Any other woman would have been ready to take it to the next level then and there, and would have thought it was a feather in her cap to be kissed in public by a Steele.

But not Brittany Thrasher. She'd been concerned they'd behaved inappropriately. He'd never forget the look on her face when he'd brought up the idea of her teaching him bedroom manners. It didn't take much to make her blush whenever he discussed a couple being intimate, which made him wonder about her sexual experience.

He tapped his fingers on his desk, thinking his mother would probably like her because Eden Steele was big into all that etiquette sort of stuff. She thought the women he was drawn to didn't have any class. How would his mother react knowing he had the hots for a woman who not only had class but was a master at teaching it to others?

He glanced at the clock on the wall. She had only a couple of hours left to call and he honestly didn't think she would. If that kiss hadn't scared her off, then he was certain the discussion of bedroom manners definitely had. The only thing he could hope now was that once she got home and found the package she'd realize the proper thing to do would be to at least call and thank him for his generosity. And when she made that call he would be quick to suggest they get together when she returned to Phoenix to take ownership of the house. From there he'd move things forward.

A short while later, he had finished getting dressed for dinner at his parents' house when the phone rang. He quickly picked it up because he was expecting a call from Eric.

"Yes?"

"I will accept your offer, Galen."

It took him a full minute to find his voice. He truly hadn't expected her to accept. "I'm glad to hear that, Brittany." Surprised, as well.

"I'd appreciate it if you'd have your attorney draw up the papers."

He lifted a brow. "The papers?"

"Yes. I want it stated in writing just what I'm going to receive after the seven days."

He pulled in a deep breath. She was concerned with what she would be getting after the seven days and his mind was already focusing on what he'd be getting *during* those seven days. Horny bastard.

"No problem," he heard himself say. "I'll have my

attorney draw up the papers immediately." There was no doubt in his mind he would have to practically kick Eli in the rear end to do it. No matter. Whatever it took.

A part of him—that decent side—figured he should end this farce by telling her that she already owned the house, but something was keeping him from coming clean. Probably the thought of her in his bed.

"When can I come pick you up?" he asked. Already he was feeling aroused. He shook his head. When had he wanted a woman this much? She had him intoxicated. He wished like hell that he could sober up but he couldn't.

"I think tomorrow morning will be soon enough," she said. He felt his stomach tighten in disappointment.

"That will give me time to check out of the hotel and shop for a few items of clothes I'll need I hadn't planned to stay in town but a few days." Then she added, "You don't have to pick me up because I have a rental car and I prefer keeping it."

He clamped his mouth shut after coming close to saying he preferred she turn the car back in. After all, there might be a time when he wasn't available to chauffeur her and he'd never let a woman drive any of his cars. "That's fine. Here's my address."

"Hold on, let me grab a pen."

Moments later she was back on the phone and he rattled off his address to her. "If you need directions I can—"

"I don't need directions. The rental car has GPS."

"So I can expect you around noon tomorrow?" he asked, trying to keep the eagerness out of his voice.

"Yes."

"Good, I'll see you then," he said.

"All right, and don't forget to have the papers with you."

"I won't. Goodbye."

He hung up the phone and rubbed a hand down his face. One part of him felt like a total bastard. The other part of him still felt like a total bastard, but a very happy and excited one.

Eli glared at his brother on the other side of his desk. "Whatever you're involved in, Galen, Brittany Thrasher will end up screwing you."

Galen smiled. Hell, he hoped so.

"You're thinking with the wrong head," Eli went on to add, clearly on a roll. "And don't be surprised if that head gets smashed with all of this."

Ouch! Galen couldn't help flinching at that. Like their old man, Eli had a way with words, especially while reminding you there were consequences for the actions you took.

"Just prepare those papers, Eli. She wants them tomorrow."

Eli shook his head, still not ready to let it go. "This doesn't make sense. She thinks she has to spend a week with you for a house you've already given to her."

"When she finds that out she'll be surprised and happy, now won't she?"

Eli grunted and then said, "Yes, but your ass still might be grass. Women don't like men taking advantage of them."

Galen rolled his eyes. "And those words are actually coming out of your mouth? You, who have more notches on your bedpost than I do."

"Yes, but I got them honestly."

Galen shook his head. Now he'd heard everything. Instead of arguing with Eli, he moved away from his brother's desk and went to look out the window. The gym across the street had closed hours ago.

He and Eli had come straight from their parents' home where everyone had congregated for dinner. All six sons had been present and accounted for, grudgingly or otherwise. Over the years he and his brothers had figured their mother insisted on her Thursday-night dinners as a way to show her sons that although their father had once behaved like them when it came to women, after meeting her all that had come to an end. In other words, she was allowing them to see with their own eyes that a man who'd been known for his whorish ways could fall in love one day, marry and be true to one woman for the rest of his days. Like Drew Steele.

It didn't take long being in their parents' presence to see just how much in love they were. He and his brothers had always known from the time they were able to walk and talk that Drew adored his Eden. And after nearly thirty-five years of marriage nothing about that had changed.

But what his mother refused to understand was that in her sons' eyes, she was one in a million. The woman who'd brought Drew Steele to heel. She was in a class by herself and there wasn't another woman like her. But most important if there was, the Steele brothers weren't looking for her at the moment. They enjoyed their womanizing ways. There were benefits to not settling down with one woman, but Eden Steele refused to see that.

"Here."

Galen turned his head. Eli had prepared the paper and was holding it out to him.

He couldn't help but smile. "Thanks, man," he said, taking the paper and scanning it. The wording was simple and legal. All he had to do was sign it.

"Whoa, hey, you owe me big. And don't think you won't get billed. For after-hours services, too."

"Whatever."

"And I'm beginning to question your logic when it comes to women, Galen. Are you sure this woman doesn't mean anything to you?"

Galen lifted his head and glanced over at his brother. "Very funny. She's a woman. They all mean something to me."

Eli rolled his eyes. "I'm not talking about *all* women. I'm referring to this particular one. Brittany Thrasher. The one you signed over a house to. The same one whose name I've seen a lot over the past couple of days."

Galen was silent for a few moments and then he leveled with his brother. "Okay, she's different, Eli. I can't put my finger on why, but I need this week with her."

"To teach you manners?"

Galen smiled. When he'd spelled out the terms of the agreement to his brother, Eli had looked at him like he was crazy. Any son of the eloquent and sophisticated Eden Tyson Steele had impeccable manners. Whether he displayed them or not was something else.

"Manners and whatever else she wants to throw into the class sessions," Galen replied.

Eli rubbed his jaw. "Hmm, maybe I need a class in manners, as well."

Galen's eyes darkened. "Don't even think it. We've never shared before and we won't be doing it now. If you even make an attempt, *my* head won't be the one that will get smashed. Yours will. I'll personally see to it."

Eli laughed. "Sounds like someone has acquired a jealous streak."

"Think whatever you want. Just remember what I said."

A few minutes later, after leaving Eli's office, Galen got in his car and stretched his neck to work out the kinks. He did not have a jealous streak. If anything he had a protective streak. Who wouldn't after hearing the tear-jerking story Brittany had shared with that other woman? He knew the story, although he'd eavesdropped to hear it.

He knew what the house meant to her, her biological mother's last gift, and although he had a reputation when it came to women, he still had a heart. He could still be compassionate when it came to some things, thanks to having Eden for a mother. So for him to have signed the house over to Brittany made perfect sense. At least to his Eden Steele genes. On the other hand, pursuing Brittany for the purpose of sharing his bed was true to his father's genes.

Galen knew he and his brothers had been blessed to have their parents. Brittany had never known her mother, and the house was her only connection to the woman. Seeing her come so close to losing it had brought out protective instincts in him. It didn't matter that he never knew he'd possessed those protective instincts until now. If any of his brothers had been placed in the same position, they would have done the same thing...

Well, maybe not.

The important thing was that he was the oldest and he needed to set good examples for the others to follow. And he'd told Eli the truth. As much as he and his brothers joked around, when it came to certain things, they were dead serious.

Eli thought he was thinking with the wrong head.

Maybe he was. If so, he needed to know why Brittany Thrasher had such pull on not only that part of him but his common sense, as well. He needed to know why he'd thought about her all evening through dinner, and why he couldn't wait to see her tomorrow at his home.

The thought that she would be with him for an entire week filled him with an emotion he didn't understand, and he figured the only way to understand it was to be around her. Spend time with her.

Oddly enough, as much as he wished otherwise, his mind and body didn't transcend into a sex-only mindset when he thought about her. He chuckled as he put his car into gear and headed home. No wonder Eli was concerned about him. The bottom line was that he had invited Brittany to his home to be his lover. He knew it and she knew it.

Knowing it made an unfamiliar sensation settle deep within him, and for some reason he welcomed the feeling.

Brittany tilted her head back to gaze up at the house. The sprawling two-story Tuscan-style structure sat on a hill with the mountains for a backdrop and looked like something that would be showcased in a magazine for the rich and famous.

Although Nikki said all six of the Steeles were successful, Brittany didn't have a clue what Galen did for a living. It was quite obvious that whatever he did paid well.

She glanced around the house and figured it had to be sitting on at least four acres of land. Fittingly, the house had sort of an arrogant look about it. She could see Galen living here, making this place his castle, his home on the range, his haven against the outside world.

And he was bringing her here to it.

To spend a week with him. Although he claimed she was supposed to teach him manners, she knew what side of the bread was buttered. To get her mother's house she had to be his lover for seven days.

The thought of that had bothered her until she'd talked to Nikki again. They'd had breakfast that morning. "Remember you'll be there for therapeutic purposes," Nikki had said. "No matter why he thinks you're there, Brittany, you're going to use this week to find out some things about yourself. You need to know if there's more to your inability to enjoy sex than what you think."

With that belief firmly planted in her head, Brittany told herself she was on a mission. She needed to see if there were hidden pleasures in her life and if so, Galen was just the man to find them. She was well aware that he had a mission as well—getting her into his bed. Wouldn't he be surprised to discover it wouldn't be as hard as he'd thought? But like Nikki had said, it was only for therapeutic purposes.

She began walking up the walkway when suddenly the huge front door, which looked to be made of solid maple, was flung open. And there he stood, in his bare feet with a pair of jeans hanging low on his hips, and an unbuttoned shirt that showed a hairy, muscular chest and broad shoulders.

"You're early. I just got out of the shower," he said, leaning in the doorway.

She could tell. Certain parts of his skin still looked wet and he had that unshaven look. And as she continued walking toward him, that spark of attraction that had taken hold of her senses six months ago, amidst all her anger and frustration, was back. She'd never experienced anything like this before. Maybe Nikki was right with her hidden-pleasures theory.

He was watching her approach with those deadly green eyes pinned directly on her. He looked as good as good could get and was stirring something within her with every step she took.

"Yes, I'm early," she found her voice to say. "I didn't need to shop for as many items as I'd thought I needed." She felt butterflies in her stomach flapping around. She hadn't known until him that a man's presence could do that to a woman. The idea slid over her and for some reason she felt good about it. Maybe what she'd heard about his abilities was true. A part of her hoped so. She would hate living the rest of her life denying the part of her that was woman.

She came to a stop in front of him. A combination of soap and man plus the scent of cactus gave him a masculine aroma. She studied his face. There was a firm set to his jaw, and the smile on his lips, best described as predatory, only added to the activity going on in the pit of her stomach.

"Come on in. I'll get your things later," he said, stepping back to allow her entrance. "First, I want to show you around and then I want you to relax."

She glanced back at him. "Relax?"

"Yes, you're uptight. I can feel it."

Brittany didn't understand how he could feel anything, but he was right. She was uptight. Who wouldn't be under the circumstances? She had dated Samuel Harold a full six months before they'd slept together and Gilford even longer than that. And here she was, contemplating sharing Galen's bed when he was a virtual stranger. It didn't matter one iota that their paths had crossed six months ago. That time meant nothing and the words they'd spoken to each other had been cross ones.

"I promise not to bite."

A thought occurred to Brittany and she had to fight not to laugh out loud. But she couldn't stop her gasp when she stepped over the threshold and looked around his house. If she'd thought the outside was beautiful, the inside was downright gorgeous. The Venetian plaster ceiling along with the hardwood hickory and stone flooring looked extravagant in a rustic sort of way. And the design of the travertine stairway was an artistic dream come true.

He led her from the formal foyer into a huge living room with a fireplace. She glanced up. The Venetian ceiling in this room was dome shaped and the back wall was made of glass, a wall-to-wall window that provided a forever view of the majestic Black Mountains and the pristine northeast valley.

"There's a fireplace in all the bedrooms," he was saying. "And a view of the Black Mountains can be seen from every room."

He glanced over at her when he said, "But my bedroom gives the best view of all."

Brittany kept looking around, refusing to acknowledge what he'd said. Had he added that tidbit for a reason? She followed while he gave her a tour of the downstairs, which included a spacious kitchen with granite countertops and stainless-steel appliances, a wine cellar, a huge family room, three guest bedrooms, three bathrooms and an office.

Brittany was impressed with his furniture as well as how orderly everything was. She followed him up the stairs and tried not to concentrate on what a nice backside he had in his jeans. As soon as she reached the landing, she let out a sigh. A huge floor-to-ceiling window in the hallway afforded a panorama of the mountains. The view was breathtaking and one you captured as soon as your feet touched the landing.

She could only stand there and stare out.

"I know the feeling," Galen said, smiling. "Sometimes in the evenings I stand in this very spot and watch the sun go down. The rugged terrain makes you appreciate not only the land but the entire earth."

He gestured to a telescope that was mounted in front of one of the windows. "Normally on a clear day you can see up to ten miles with the naked eye, but I use that when I want to see farther than that. I've seen a number of bobcats, mule deer, coyotes and fox. It's quite interesting to observe them in their habitat."

"I can just imagine," she said. Back home she'd seen plenty of sunsets over the Gulf of Mexico. It, too, had taken her breath away. But the only wildlife she'd seen were the ones at Busch Gardens.

She turned her attention away from the view and back to Galen. She hadn't known he was standing so close and tried to avoid looking into the depths of his green eyes by lowering her gaze to his chest. That wasn't a good thing because his shirt was open and all she could see was a sculpted hairy chest. Neither Samuel nor Gilford had hair on their chests and she wondered how it would feel for her breasts to come in contact with it. Or better yet, how it would be to peel off his shirt and then trail her lips down his chest, all the way to where the hair line flowed below the waist of his jeans.

Heat stained her cheeks and she snatched her gaze back to his face, not believing she'd thought of such things. She nervously licked her lips and couldn't help noticing how his eyes followed the movement of her tongue. The way he was looking at her mouth reminded her of their kiss yesterday. It had been short, but it had left a lasting impression on her.

"So what else is up here?" she asked after feeling a tightness in her chest.

He leaned down and placed his mouth near her ear to whisper, "Right now I couldn't care less about what's up here except me and you."

She figured had she been capable of speech he might not have made his next move. But she hadn't been able to talk with the warmth of his breath close on her skin. And when she tilted her head to look up at him, he took that opportunity to swoop his mouth down on hers.

This kiss was a lot different from the one yesterday. She still detected a sense of hunger, but it was as if he'd decided he had no reason to rush. They didn't have an audience and she was not going anywhere. It didn't take long for her to realize that he wasn't just kissing her. He was consuming her, every inch of her mouth and then some.

He angled his mouth in a way that provided deeper penetration and swirled his tongue with hers. And then her tongue started doing something it had never done before: it began mating with a man's. Her world started to spin and she felt grateful when he wrapped his arms around her and brought her body closer to his. Through her blouse her nipples pressed against the cushion of his hairy chest, and just the thought of the contact had her moaning deep in her throat.

Before she realized what he was doing, he had backed her against a wall while his lips and tongue continued to engage hers in a deep, hungry kiss that threatened to push her over the edge of madness. She wrapped her arms around his neck, kissing him back while blood roared like crazy through her veins.

She would be the first to admit she was experiencing some of those hidden pleasures Nikki had warned her about. They were coming out of hiding and she seemed incapable of concealing them again. Whether she liked it or not, she couldn't deny how Galen was making her feel. She stirred with an emotion she had never felt before. Passion. And she knew he was pushing her toward pleasure that only he could deliver.

But it was pleasure she wasn't quite ready for.

She broke off the kiss and pulled in a deep breath. He leaned over and kissed the corners of her mouth. "Is there a reason you stopped it?" he whispered against her moist lips. And it was then that she noticed his hand was underneath her skirt, actually on her thigh and squeezing it. How had it gotten there without her knowing it?

"Is there a reason you started it?" she countered. The man made seduction a work of art.

He lifted his head and smiled. Those green eyes were sexy as sin, totally irresistible. "Yes, there is a reason. I got a sample of you yesterday and I liked the way you taste and couldn't wait to kiss you again." His voice was so husky and deep, goose bumps were beginning to form on her arms.

"Do you always say what you think?"

He flashed an arrogant smile. "I always say what I feel. No need holding anything back."

She doubted he could do that even if he tried. He had the ability to render a woman mindless, make every cell and molecule in her body suddenly feel wicked. It would have been so easy to let him take her right here. Get it all over and done. But a part of her knew her experience with him would not be like the others. There would be no "over and done." He would take her slowly and deliberately. She would feel things she'd never felt before. Be driven to want to do things she'd never done before. And heaven help her, she wanted the experience. Yet at the same time she needed more from him. She needed to know more about him.

"You can let go of my thigh now, Galen."

"You sure?"

"Positive."

He let go and took a step back, and her traitorous thigh was tingling in protest from the loss of his touch. "Come on, let me show you the rest of the house. And just in case you're wondering about that kiss, the answer is no, I didn't get enough."

He led the way and she followed thinking, neither had she.

Chapter 8

Galen kept walking, very much aware of Brittany beside him. He had expected her to ask for the legal papers of their agreement before she entered his home, but she hadn't.

And she hadn't seemed bothered by the impromptu kiss. He could tell she had enjoyed it as much as he had. A part of him wished she hadn't stopped things. No telling what they might be doing now if she hadn't. He could imagine them getting downright naughty and raunchy, hot and sweaty, and tearing off each other's clothes, doing it against the wall and then moving right to the floor.

"How long have you lived here?"

He glanced over at her the exact moment she was pushing a lock of hair out of her face. The brightness of the sun coming in through the window was making her squint, but he thought at that moment she had to be the most beautiful woman he'd ever seen. In a way he found that hard to believe because he'd been involved with a number of gorgeous women in his lifetime. He still found it rather strange that Brittany Thrasher hit him on such a visceral level.

"I've lived here for four years," he replied. "Although my partners and I have a suite downtown, it's only for window dressing to make our business appear legit. Few would imagine we do most of our work out of our garages."

She glanced over at him. "What kind of work do you do?"

"I design video games."

"Video games?"

He turned to her, studied her features to decipher what she was thinking. His occupation got mixed reactions from people. Those who didn't know about the millions he made annually considered his occupation frivolous, certainly not a career a man of thirty-four could take seriously. Of course no one in his family agreed with that assessment, especially because they knew the vast amount of his wealth as well as the hard work it took to create and design a successful video game.

"Yes," he finally said. "That's what I do for a living."

He'd noticed that a smile would first start in her eyes and then extend to her lips before spreading over her entire face. Understandably, he hadn't seen that side of her in New York and hadn't really seen much of it here, except for when he'd witnessed that little reunion with her friend at the auction mart. Now he was seeing it again and the transformation sent his pulse throbbing.

She lifted a brow. "So, are you any good?"

He couldn't help but throw his head back and laugh. This woman was something else. He really liked her spunk once she stopped being angry and uptight.

"Well, are you?"

He shook his head as he finished off a chuckle. "There aren't too many things I'm not good at, Brittany."

She frowned. "It's not nice being conceited, Galen."

A smile touched his lips. "Bad manners?"

He could tell she was fighting hard not to return his smile when she replied, "The worst."

Their gazes tangled and he had to admit he was enjoying the moment. "I guess that's something I need to work on."

"I suggest that you do. Now back to the video games. Are there any out there that have your name attached to them?"

He started walking again and she fell in line beside him. There was something comforting about having her here with him. "There are a few. You ever heard of Time Capsule?"

"Yes."

"What about Wild Card?"

"Yes, I've heard of that one, too."

"And what about Turbine Force?"

"Of course." She stopped walking and turned to him. "Are all those yours?"

"All those are SID's, a corporation that I own along

with two college friends. All three of us can claim success of the company."

"See there," she said as a huge smile touched her face. "You're a fast learner. You could have been conceited and taken all the credit for the success of your company, but you didn't. You shared the spotlight. You remembered your manners. I'm proud of you for doing so."

Galen shook his head. For the first time in a long time a woman had left him speechless.

So instead of saying anything, he began walking again while wondering for the first time what he had gotten himself into.

Brittany couldn't help but notice that Galen had suddenly gotten quiet on her. Just as well because she needed to think a minute. One thing she'd learned over the years was to respect another's need for a quiet moment. So while Galen seemed to be indulging in his, she glanced around, thoroughly pulled in by the appeal of his home.

It had a charm about it that spoke volumes. Whether Galen realized it, his house revealed a lot about his personality. A segment of it at least. She doubted very few, except those close to him, knew the real Galen Steele.

She'd never considered herself an outdoorsy person, but evidently Galen was. Most of the paintings on his wall indicated his appreciation for nature, in that they captured the natural beauty of the outdoors. And then she couldn't get over the view outside the window they were walking by. It literally took her breath away. In Tampa she was mostly surrounded by water, but here in the desert, she was surrounded by mountains. Mountains out of which Galen had mapped his space. One he was comfortable with. One that was totally him.

He stopped when they came to another room and she did likewise. When he stood back she stepped inside. It was another bedroom and Brittany thought it just as nicely furnished as the others she'd seen so far.

She glanced over at him. "You have a lot of house for only one person."

"I like my space."

She'd figured as much and wondered if he was giving her a hint. But then she dismissed the idea when she recalled that her being here was his idea. She had offered to stay at the other house, but he'd turned her down.

Moments later after showing her three other guest bedrooms, several spacious bathrooms and an upstairs library stacked with numerous books and video games, they walked down a hall that jutted into a wing that was basically a separate extension of the house.

Galen glanced over at her and said, "In addition to my space I also like my privacy. I have five brothers and once in a while we get together and play video games until dawn. When I want to retire for the night I prefer not hearing their excitement from winning or their strong, colorful expletives from losing. They tend to be rather rowdy."

"You and your brothers are close."

"Yes, although we pretend not to be at times. Tends to be more fun that way and with us, there's never a boring moment, trust me. Our parents are our rock. They have a strong marriage, a solid one. And I think what I admire about them most of all is that they're best friends."

"That's impressive."

Galen nodded. He'd always thought so, and he knew his brothers had, as well. But to hear an outsider confirm it pretty much validated their feelings. He hadn't asked her anything about her family and he couldn't help wondering if she found that odd. No odder than her not asking for those papers when she had insisted on them just last night. He couldn't help speculating why.

He pulled in a deep breath wondering if she knew how good she smelled. He guessed it didn't matter, because he did. He covertly studied her profile and wondered why he was even bothering when he was used to openly checking out any woman he was interested in. Any woman he wanted. But he wanted to watch her when she wasn't aware she was being watched.

It didn't take long to decide the side of her looked just as nice as the front. Her nose seemed rather short, but her full lips made up for it, and when you tacked on a sexy-looking chin, what you got, in his opinion, were nearly flawless features.

His gaze returned to her lips and lingered, and he remembered the feel of them pressed against his while he took her mouth in a kiss that even now had him aching. He was so engrossed in her lips that it took him a moment to realize they were moving and she was asking him a question.

"Excuse me?" he asked.

She met his gaze and there was an inquiring look in them when she repeated her question. "Does this door lead to your bedroom?"

He then noticed they had reached his bedroom door. "Yes, this is my private haven, but I give you permission to enter it at any time."

She gave him a weak smile. "Do you?"

"Yes." He wanted to reach out and touch her, to see if this moment was real. Had he really just given her something he'd never granted another woman—the right to invade his space whenever she wanted to? That was so totally unlike him.

He opened the double doors and then stepped aside. He wanted to see her reaction. He smiled when she glanced around, totally in awe of his bedroom. It had a masculine overtone while at the same time captured so much of the outdoors with the one solid wall of glass that showcased the beautiful mountain scenery. And then there was his see-through ceiling where he could wake up any time of night and look up at the stars.

He followed her gaze up after seeing the look of astonishment on her face. At that moment he could imagine her sharing his bed beneath those same stars. He would love making love to her one night while lightning flashed in the sky or the rain poured down. He had seen such a ceiling in his travel to Paris one year and knew he had to have one for his own. When he had the house built, this ceiling was the first design he made sure was in the plans.

"This is truly awesome, Galen. I've never seen anything like it before. I bet sleeping in here is an adventure."

He could only smile at that assumption. "Yes, you can say that."

He then watched as she crossed the room to take a

closer examination of his bed. His bedspread was white, not the usual color a man would choose, and he hadn't. His mother had. In fact after buying the house, he had gone skiing one week to come back and discover she had decorated his bedroom.

It had taken a while for the white coverlet to grow on him and those days when it didn't, he would swap it out with a black one he kept in one of the closets. This morning while making the bed he'd decided to go with the white, thinking it would make a better impression. He propped against his bedroom door wondering when he started caring about making an impression on a woman.

He looked at her and knew it had been since meeting her. His first impression hadn't gone over so well, so now he was trying to win her over. That was even more so unlike him.

There was a momentary silence as she turned around slowly, taking it all in, the furnishings and the view outside the window. She then turned to him and said, "This room is simply beautiful."

"I'm glad you like it. This is where you will sleep every night while you're here."

She stared at him. "Why do you want me in here?"

Without taking his eyes off her he moved away from the door. There was no way he would tell her that the thought of having her in his bed was an arousing one, even if he wasn't in that bed with her. "Do I really have to go into details as to why I want you in here, Brittany?"

She broke eye contact and looked out the window. She returned her gaze to his and said, "No."

"Good. Now if you'll excuse me, I'll go bring in your luggage."

Chapter 9

Brittany stepped back from the dresser after placing the last of her unpacked items into the drawers. She glanced around the bedroom, still amazed at what she saw. She'd honestly never seen anything like it. Even the furniture was massive, as if specially made for a giant. On one side of the bed was a foot step to use when getting into the bed because it was so high off the floor.

She glanced up and saw the sky in all its brilliant blue. Galen had shown her the switch to use when she wanted a sliding shade to block the view, but she couldn't imagine not wanting to lie in bed and stare up into the sky.

He had delivered her luggage to her and without saying anything—other than telling her about the switch and indicating the top two drawers for her use—he'd left her to her own devices.

She figured he was having one of his quiet moments or he was one of those moody people who preferred being left alone when they had a lot on their minds. But because he was the one who insisted that she come live with him for a week, she assumed he wouldn't mind the company. She headed downstairs.

She didn't have to go far to find him. He was in the kitchen. At some point he had buttoned his shirt, but his jeans were still riding low on his hips and he was once again barefoot. He looked both sexy and domesticated standing at his kitchen sink.

"When can I go check out the house?" she asked.

It was easy to see from his expression that he hadn't known she'd been standing there and he waited a moment before he replied. "I'm ready when you are, but I'd think you'd want this."

He picked up a legal-size envelope from the table and handed it to her. "It's the papers you demanded yesterday."

She took the envelope from him and pulled out the legal document and read it silently. Everything was as it should be. She placed it back inside the envelope and glanced over at him. He had returned to the sink. "Your brother is your attorney?"

"Among other things. Usually a pain in my rear, mostly. But I can say the same thing about the others, as well. Being the oldest isn't all that it's cracked up to be."

He glanced at his watch and said, "I guess now is as good a time as any to check out that house. We can stop somewhere on the way back and grab lunch."

She smiled. "All right. I'll just go upstairs and get my purse."

Galen watched as she hurried toward the stairs. He knew why that house meant so much to her, but she didn't know that he knew, and for some reason he wanted her to feel comfortable in telling him herself. He drew in a deep breath thinking he'd much prefer staying here and getting something going with her, but he knew the best thing to do was to get them out of the house for a while. Just the thought that she would be sleeping in his bed, whether he was in it with her or not, had his heart beating something crazy in his chest.

He'd been close to the breaking point when he returned with her luggage and found her standing there, still checking out his bed. There had been something about the overwhelming look in her eyes that touched him in a way he'd never been touched before.

And that wasn't good.

"So tell me about your brothers, Galen."

Galen briefly glanced across the seat of the car to meet her inquiring gaze. After she indicated that she preferred they take the rental car, he suggested that he drive. He'd promised himself never to let another female behind the wheel while he rode shotgun after an angry Jennifer Bailey had taken the Sky Harbor Expressway at over one hundred miles an hour—all because he refused to make her his steady girl. He didn't care that he'd been a senior in high school at the time. Some things you didn't forget.

He tilted his Stetson back from his eyes. "Why do you want to know about them?"

"Because there seems to be so much unity among you, even though the six of you might disagree sometimes. I lived in a foster home while growing up and although there were a number of us, unity didn't exist. It seemed everyone had their own separate agenda."

"And what was yours?"

She hesitated a moment before answering. "Survival, mostly. And hoping the people who were my foster parents would want to keep me. I hated moving from place to place, making new friends, attending different schools. There was no stability."

Anger flashed within Galen at the thought that she'd never grown up with real parents, siblings or a home to call her own. Now more than ever he was grateful he'd made the decision to turn her mother's home over to her. Still, he wanted her to talk to him. Tell him why the house meant so much to her.

"Is that why you wanted that house so much?" he prompted. "Did you live there at one time as a foster child? Did you—"

"No," Brittany said, interrupting his questions. "That's not the reason."

She paused, then said, "I wanted the house because it was willed to me by someone I've never met. My birth mother. She gave me up for adoption when I was born. Only thing is, I never got adopted. Most of the people who took me in did so for the extra income. I have to say I was treated decently the majority of the time, so I won't complain."

She paused for a moment before continuing. "Six months ago…in fact, it was the same day I saw you and returned from New York. When I got home, I discovered I'd gotten a letter from a woman informing me that she believed I was the daughter she'd given up for adoption twenty-eight years ago, and that I would be hearing from her again soon with arrangements for us to meet if I wanted to do so. There was no return address and that's all the letter said. I anxiously waited, and last week I received a letter from an attorney letting me know that my mother had passed away and had left her house to me."

She paused again. He'd come to a traffic light and glanced over at her. She was staring straight ahead. "It was only when I got here and met with her attorney that I found out about the back taxes on the house. Her taxes got delinquent because she used the money to hire a private investigator to find me. She had been diagnosed with cancer and was given five years to live. She found me, but we didn't get the chance to meet face-to-face."

She drew in a deep breath and glanced over and met his gaze. "So now you know the reason I want that house."

Yes, he knew, Galen thought. He'd known all along. At least the part he'd overheard when he should not have been listening. He was silent for a long moment and was grateful when the traffic light changed and the car moved forward. He needed to concentrate on his driving and not on the woman sitting beside him. She was doing strange things to his emotions and Galen wasn't so sure he could stop them.

Brittany swallowed hard and her heart beat furiously in her chest when Galen brought the car to a stop in front of the house that used to be her mother's home.

She couldn't move, so she just sat there and gazed at it through the windshield. The first thing she noted was that the windows were no longer boarded up.

She glanced over at him. Her brow furrowed. "You've been here already?"

"No. Once I got your call yesterday afternoon I contacted someone to come take the boards off the windows. This is my first time seeing it."

She nodded. He'd said from the first that the only reason he'd bid on the house was because she'd wanted it. Galen Steele had proven that he definitely had an ulterior motive for owning this home now.

"Ready to go in?" he asked.

Her throat closed and she could barely get out her response. "Yes."

By the time she had unbuckled her seat belt, he had already gotten out of the car and walked around to open the car door for her. She was discovering that Galen used good manners and could be the perfect gentleman when it suited him.

They didn't say anything as they headed down the walkway. The moment she stepped onto the porch she saw up close what she hadn't seen from a distance. The house could use a paint job and the screen door needed to be repaired. She couldn't help wondering if these repairs, too, had taken a backseat to hiring a private investigator to find her.

Brittany paused for a moment to take in the enormity of what she was feeling, the emotions deep within her that had risen to the surface. Would she find answers to all the questions she had? Would she ever know why she'd been given away? Who was her father? Had he even known about her?

"You okay?"

She glanced up at Galen. She might have been mistaken, but was that concern in the depths of his green eyes? "Yes, I'm fine. Thanks for asking."

He reached into his pocket and pulled out a single key. "Here, the house is yours."

She raised a haughty brow. Did he assume because she was here at the house today that she would be in his bed tonight? "Jumping the gun, aren't you?"

He gave her an arrogant smile as he removed his Stetson. "No, I don't think so. Come on, let's go inside."

For a moment Galen stood back and watched as Brittany entered what had been her mother's home. He then followed her inside, closed the door behind them and glanced around. The interior looked a lot bigger than the exterior but everything inside, from the Early American–style furniture to the heavily draped windows, had a sense of home.

His gaze moved over to Brittany. She was no longer standing in the middle of the floor but had moved over to a vintage-looking desk and was looking at a picture in the frame. Deciding not to stare, he glanced around again.

It was evident that although the outside showed signs of deterioration and neglect, the interior did not. Everything looked well cared-for and maintained, even the hardwood floors. It was clear that the person who lived here believed in being clean and neat. The place gave off a feeling that its owner had merely stepped out a minute and would be returning momentarily.

"Nice place," he said to Brittany, mainly to get her talking again. She'd gone too quiet on him and continued to stare at that picture frame. Was it a picture of the woman who had been her mother?

When she didn't acknowledge his remark, he knew she had effectively tuned him out, although not intentionally because her manners wouldn't allow such a thing. Emotions had taken over her, and he wasn't used to dealing with emotional women. Usually that was when he would cut and run like hell. But he wouldn't be going anywhere today. He felt as if he had a vested interest in this woman, which really didn't make much sense. All he wanted was to get her in his bed so she could soothe the ache in his pants. What he didn't understand, and what he was trying like hell to figure out, was his insane fascination with her.

And at the moment he didn't like her wandering around this place sinking deeper and deeper into a maudlin state of depression he refused to accept for her. He'd rather have her mad than sad. But right now he wanted her talking.

She glanced over at him and the look in her eyes was like a kick in the gut. It was as if he felt her pain. She hadn't known the owner of the house, nor would she recognize her if they'd passed in the street. But none of that mattered. The woman who used to live here had been her mother. The woman who'd given birth to her.

The woman who, for some reason, had given her away.

He waited for her to say something. The look in her

eyes said she was ready. He wasn't Dr. Phil by any means, but he figured she needed to express her feelings, get them out in the open.

"I think I look like her," she said, holding the picture out for him to see.

He moved away from the door, crossed the room and took the picture frame she offered. He studied the image of the woman standing beside a tall man. She looked younger than Galen had expected, which meant she'd had Brittany at an early age. Probably a teen pregnancy. "Yes, you do favor her," he said honestly. "I wonder how old she was when she gave birth to you."

"Sixteen. According to her attorney she died at forty-four."

He nodded as he handed the picture frame back to her. "You want to check out the other rooms?"

"Sure."

She walked slowly and he did likewise beside her. The kitchen was nice and the bay window provided a view of a lot of the land. It seemed to go on for miles. And the view of the mountains was just as impressive as the one from his place. No wonder those men at the auction mart wanted to demolish the house and build a hotel on the land.

He walked around the kitchen to the table. Just like the rest of the house, the table and chairs were Early American and fit perfectly in their setting.

Brittany then moved to the window and was looking out at the mountains and all the land. He decided to keep her talking.

"Do you know if she had any other relatives?"

She turned around. "According to her attorney, Mr.

Banyon, she didn't. She and her husband never had any children. I'm not even certain he knew about me."

She moved away from the window and placed her hands on her hips and his gaze was immediately drawn to that area of her body. He liked how she looked in that skirt and figured he'd probably like her even better without it. Without a single stitch on her body. Okay, he would admit he was an ass, without a lick of manners. Here she was mourning the loss of her mother and his mind was in the bedroom.

"I guess we need to see the rest of the place," she said, lacking enthusiasm and reclaiming his attention. When she crossed the room to pass by him he got a whiff of her. Her scent had nearly driven him crazy on the drive over and it was playing havoc with his senses again.

There were two bathrooms, both of which he'd consider remodeling if the house was his. But it wasn't. He recalled her reaction when he'd handed her the key and told her the house was hers. Of course he'd meant it because legally it was. But the look she'd given him told a different story. She'd no doubt figured he'd given it to her because of the terms of their agreement. She was so far from right it wasn't funny.

"Thanks for having those boards removed, Galen. The view from every window is fabulous."

The midday sun was pouring through the windows of every bedroom they passed and seemed to hit her at every angle. There was just something about a beautiful woman. Now they stood in the master bedroom. It was a little larger than the other bedrooms and it did have its own bath. Brittany was standing next to the bed. The king-size and oversize furniture seemed to take up most of the space, making it tight to walk around much. Just as well. It wouldn't take much to tumble her onto that bed about now. It looked so inviting and she looked so damn enticing.

"Do you know what your mother did for a living?" he cleared his throat and asked, deciding to stay where he was standing in the doorway.

She looked over at him. "Mr. Banyon said she'd been a librarian within the public school system for years."

He nodded. "That doesn't surprise me. She was probably prim and proper just like you."

She tilted her head and met his gaze. "You think I'm prim and proper?"

"Yes. Don't you?"

She frowned. "No. I just believe a person should display good manners."

He glanced around and then looked back at her. "And I'm sure you're going to think I have atrocious manners when I say that I feel we've been here long enough and that I'm ready to go."

"But we just got here. You could leave me for a while and return for me later."

He could but he wouldn't. He wanted her with him, if that didn't sound crazy. It wasn't that he didn't have anything to do. He had Sniper to work on. But right now the only thing he wanted to work on was her. Tomorrow he'd probably feel differently and would give her a chance to come over here by herself to go through her mother's stuff. But today he couldn't handle her sadness any longer.

"That's not our agreement, Brittany. I brought you

here so you can check out the place and we've done that. It's past time for lunch. Do you have a taste for anything in particular?"

He could tell from the expression on her face that she hadn't liked being reminded about their agreement. "No, wherever you decide is fine."

He was glad she wasn't pouting or pitching a fit because they were leaving. There had been enough gloom for one day, and he wanted to take her someplace to put a smile on her face.

Chapter 10

An hour later they had returned to Galen's home and Brittany was rubbing her stomach. "I can't believe I ate that much. It's all your fault."

Galen chuckled. "It was my fault that you made a pig of yourself?"

"That's not a nice thing to say."

He rolled his eyes. "Okay, Miss Manners, it might not be nice but it's true."

She dropped down on his sofa. "Maybe next time you'll think twice before taking me to an all-you-can-eat place that serves barbecued ribs that fall off the bone."

He shrugged. "Then I'm not a good man," he said as if the thought didn't bother him in the least. "Earlier you schooled my manners on being conceited. Do you have any other lessons for today?"

"There are a couple I'd like to interject."

He took the armchair across from her. "Go ahead."

He was sitting right in her line of vision and a part of her wished he wasn't. Her reaction to him today wasn't good. She had handled it pretty well at her mother's house, because her mind had been filled with so many other things. But at the restaurant, she had been filled with images of him. So much so that her nipples pressing against her blouse had throbbed through most of the meal. And now there were these nerve endings inside her that seemed pricked, painfully stretched, whenever those laser green eyes lit on her.

He was leaning back in the chair, his legs crossed at the knees in a manly pose. His thighs were taut and his abs sturdy, masculine and ripped beneath his shirt. She felt a tingling in her fingers. They itched to reach out and touch his bare skin. She'd bet his flesh would be warm. How would it taste? Heat drenched her face. She'd never thought of putting her mouth on a man before.

She cleared her throat and forced her attention back to business. "Your cell phone," she said.

He lifted a brow. "What about it?"

"You answered it in the restaurant."

A smile touched his lips. "I answer it wherever it rings. That's why they call it a mobile phone. It's a phone on the go."

She rolled her eyes. "Proper etiquette dictates that you should turn your cell phone off in a restaurant just like you would do at church." From the look on his face she got the distinct impression that he didn't turn his phone off in church, either. Or maybe the look meant he didn't go to church.

"And if I miss a call?"

"You'll know it and you can call the person back once you leave the restaurant. Was it someone you couldn't call back later?" In a way she didn't want to know. What if it was a woman he was interested in?

"It was Mercury being nosy."

"Mercury?"

"My brother."

She nodded and tucked her legs beneath her on the sofa. She noticed his gaze followed her every movement. "You have a brother named Mercury?" she asked.

"Yes, and before you ask, the answer is no, he wasn't named after the planet or that Roman god. He was named for Mercury Morris. Ever heard of him?"

"Of course. I'm from Florida. He was a running back for the Miami Dolphins in the seventies, during the time they were unstoppable, undefeated one season."

She watched him smile and wanted to roll her eyes. Did men think they were the only ones who knew anything about football?

"My father was a huge Dolphins fan while growing up," he said. "He still is. In fact, he got drafted right out of college to play for them, but a knee injury kept that from happening before the start of what should have been his first season."

"How sad."

"Yes, it was for him at the time." He paused a moment and then said, "Okay, I get the 'no cell phone in the restaurant' rule. What's the other?"

She shifted in her seat when his gaze drifted down to

her breasts and she wondered if he'd noticed her hardened nipples through her blouse. "The other is toothpicks. I didn't see you use them and I'm glad for that, but several others in the restaurant did. You don't stick a toothpick in your mouth after finishing a meal."

"We had ribs."

"That makes it worse," she said.

"But they're on the table."

"I noticed. Usually there're at the cash register on your way out. There's nothing nice about a person using a toothpick to pick their teeth at a restaurant, especially when others are still eating. You should take the toothpick and use it in the privacy of your own home."

He leaned forward in his seat. "And you know all this stuff, how?"

She smiled. "I studied it in college. I got a degree in history, but I took every course offered on etiquette and even saved my money for Emily Post Finishing School a couple of summers."

He nodded and stood up, and her gaze traveled the length of him. He was tall, well over six foot, muscular and his body was honed to perfection. He had an abdomen with a six-pack if ever there was one. She was so enraptured by him that she barely heard him say, "So I read on the Internet."

She raised a brow. "You looked me up on the Internet?"

He smiled. "Of course. You said you had a business and I wanted to check it out to make sure you were legit. I was impressed. So now I know for sure that you know what you're talking about."

He glanced at his watch. "I have some things to do

in my garage. You can decide on dinner when I return in a few hours," he said as he was about to move away.

"Wait," she said. "Is that it? That's the manners lesson for today?"

His gaze then swept over her and she felt the heat emanating from the dark orbs wherever they touched. A sardonic smile then touched his lips when he said, "Yes, but there's always tonight. You can get prepared for whatever manners you want to go over with me then."

She lifted her chin. "That sounds like a proposition."

She saw irritation flash in the depths of his green eyes. "The proposition was made days ago. You accepted and as a result you're here under my roof. Mine for seven days to do as I please. And nothing will please me more than to have you naked in my bed beneath me every night while I breathe in your scent and make love to you until we both reach one hell of an orgasm."

She gasped at his words and she suddenly felt breathless. Her knees weakened and she was glad she was already sitting down or she would have fallen flat on her face. An image of her naked in bed beneath him flashed through her mind, and she was filled with a wanting she'd never known before.

His voice had deepened to a husky tone and he'd spoken promises he intended to deliver. He evidently didn't believe in holding back on anything, even words that a true gentleman wouldn't say, words that put her out of her comfort zone. She'd never dealt with a man like him before. He not only stated what he wanted, but he was letting her know he intended to have things his way.

And maybe that's exactly what she needed.

A man who was arrogant, sure of himself, a pure

alpha male through and through. One who had manners when they counted and refused to display them when they didn't. She fought the inclination to cross the room and kiss him, which at that moment seemed the most natural thing in the world for her to do. Her, of all people. A woman who before meeting him would never have considered doing such a thing.

But Galen Steele had a way of pulling something out of her, and like Nikki, she was now convinced if there were hidden pleasures lurking somewhere beneath her surface, she would know about it before she left his home seven days from now.

She slowly stood up and placed her hands on her hips, tilted her head back and gave him what she hoped was one hell of a haughty look. With a man like him, a woman needed to be able to hold her own. "Talk is cheap, Galen. We'll see later how well you are on delivering."

She inwardly smiled. The effect of her words was priceless. Although he tried to keep his emotions in check, she read the look of startled surprise in his eyes. He hadn't expected her to goad him.

Brittany pulled in a deep breath when he began walking toward her, but she refused to step back or move away, although her heart was beating a wild rhythm in her chest. He didn't need to know her hands were trembling on her hips and heat had gathered at the juncture of her legs.

"You're right, Brittany, talk is cheap," he said when he came to a stop in front of her. The sound of his deep, husky voice made those already-hardened nipples get even harder.

"But I won't be doing much talking and neither will you. I believe in action."

She swallowed. "Do you?"

"Very much so. And just so you know, I want you. I wanted you in New York and I definitely want you now. And I'll give you fair warning. Tonight is taste-you night. I want the taste of you in my mouth, all over my tongue and embedded in my taste buds when I wake up in the morning."

Brittany's stomach clenched. This man of Steele was making her hot merely with his words. He hadn't touched her yet. And now he would taste her? Just the thought was filling her with more desire and longing than she'd ever felt before. She suddenly became fully aware of something that was new and exciting to her. Carnal greed.

She swallowed. "Like I said. Talk is cheap."

He smiled in a hungry way. "And like I said, I'm a man of action."

Then he leaned in and captured her mouth, not giving her a chance to stifle the moan that immediately rose in her throat. His arms wrapped around her, and his hands stroked her back at the same time his tongue stroked every inch of her mouth.

She had long ago decided his kisses were unique, full of passion and capable of inciting lust. But she was also discovering that each time they kissed, she encountered a different effect. This kiss was tapping into her emotions and she was fighting like hell to keep them under tight control where he was concerned. This was all a game to him. Not for her. For her, it was about finding herself in more ways than one. Discovering her past and making headway into her future.

He deepened the kiss and she felt his hands move downward to cup her backside and pull her more fully against him. She groaned again when she felt his hard erection press into her at a place that was already tingling with longing. Unfamiliar sensations were floating around in her stomach and she was drenched even more in potent desire.

And then he suddenly broke off the kiss and took a step back. She watched him lick his lips as if he'd enjoyed kissing her and then he thrust his hands into his jeans pockets, looked at her and asked, "Did I make my point?"

Oh, he'd made it, all right, but she'd never admit it to him. "Kind of."

She quickly scooted around him. "I think you should get to work now. I plan on setting up my laptop and answering a few e-mails. And then I plan to work on tomorrow's manners lesson for you." She headed toward the stairs.

"Brittany?"

She stopped and turned around. "Yes?"

A smile touched both corners of his mouth. "I like you." His face lit up as if the thought of it was a revelation to him or something.

She rolled her eyes. "Should I be thrilled?"

He gave her an arrogant chuckle. "The thrill will come later."

She turned back toward the stairs and damn if she wasn't looking forward to her first orgasm ever.

Chapter 11

Galen shut off the lamp on his worktable. Surprisingly, he had gotten a lot done once he'd been able to put Brittany to the back of his mind.

He liked her.

He had told her that earlier and had meant it. There were no dull moments with her around. Just when he thought he had her figured out, she would do or say something to throw him off base, literally stun him. His Miss Manners was becoming a puzzle he needed to put together, but there were so many pieces, he wouldn't know where to start. One thing was for certain, she was definitely keeping him on his toes.

Just like he had plans to keep her on her back starting tonight.

He smiled at the thought and leaned back in his

chair as he recalled their meal at the restaurant earlier today. There was nothing like a buffet that included mouthwatering ribs and the best corn bread you'd ever want to taste. Jennie's Soul Food drew a lot of truckers, businesspeople and just plain everyday folks. Brittany hadn't been bothered by the mixture of clientele. The last woman he'd taken there had complained all through dinner, saying she'd felt out of place. That had been their first and their last date. He hadn't looked her up afterward, not even for a booty call. Personally, he didn't like women who whined or who felt they had a reason to complain about everything. Brittany was definitely not that type of woman.

He glanced at his watch. It was six already, which meant he'd been holed up in his garage for at least four solid hours. He'd still managed to get a lot done while anticipating tonight's events. He wondered if Brittany had taken his advice and was prepared. Probably not. He had pretty much spelled things out to her earlier. Laid them on the table, so to speak. Given her the real deal. If there had been any doubt in her mind just what his proposal had been about, now she knew. But he was certain she'd known all along that her being here was not just about teaching him manners. Oh, he was enjoying her little tidbits and would certainly keep them in mind, but manners weren't all he intended for them to cover over the next seven days.

He wondered where he would be taking her for dinner. Wherever they went he wanted to make sure she again ate well because she would definitely need her strength for later.

Galen stood to stretch his body and immediately felt

his erection kick in. He was hard. He was ready. And it was time to find his woman. *His woman?* Okay, it had been an unwitting slip. He didn't think of any woman as his. But in a way Brittany was his—at least for the next seven days. After she left, his life would get back to normal. He was sure of it.

It was a romantic setting straight out of a movie. Brittany drew in a deep breath as she glanced around the bedroom. She'd taken all the advice the Internet had to offer. After checking e-mails from her staff, she'd searched several Web sites on what to do for a romantic night. Then she'd put the bedroom together.

She had every reason to believe Galen would deliver tonight and if he did, it would be her first orgasm ever. She wanted more than just the bells and whistles; she wanted drums and several trombones, as well. She would have a lot to celebrate after twenty-eight years, and she just hoped and prayed things came through for her. The thought that she was emotionally damaged from her teenage trauma was a lot for her to take in.

She glanced at the clock on the nightstand and wondered how much longer Galen would be working in his garage. A couple of times she had started to go find him, but figured he might not appreciate the interruption. Besides, she'd needed to prepare for tonight.

Deciding she wouldn't be kept a prisoner, she had scribbled him a note and given him her cell-phone number so he would know how to reach her. And she'd taken off to shop for everything she needed for tonight. Because he hadn't tried reaching her, chances were he hadn't known she'd left.

In addition to purchasing scented candles, she'd also bought a bottle of wine and a dozen red roses whose petals she'd strewn over the bed. Then there was the racy new outfit guaranteed to escalate her seduction.

She felt a deep surge of nervousness as she glanced down at herself. Talk about being bold. She'd never owned a pair of stilettos until now. And red of all colors. She had paid good money for them, although she figured she wouldn't get much use out of them after tonight. According to the online article, men wanted sex frequently and they liked seeing their women looking sexy—preferably naked and wearing stilettos.

Brittany had decided she could go with the stilettos, but she would definitely not be naked. Instead she'd purchased the short red dress she'd seen in one of the stores' window. Like the shoes, it was a first for her. She had the legs to wear a hemline halfway up her thighs, but she worried that if she were to bend over in this dress, Galen wouldn't miss seeing much. Including her new red lace panties.

She drew an unsteady breath, wondering if perhaps she'd gone a little too far. But then she had to remind herself there was a reason for her madness. Not only had she gotten her mother's home out of the deal, but she would also find out tonight whether she was frigid.

She shuddered at the use of that word but knew she had to call it what it was or could possibly be. According to the research she'd done on the Internet today, that word described any woman who didn't have a sex drive. She fit into that category.

However, she believed all that would change tonight. Already she felt a deep attraction to Galen and he had been able to get her juices flowing, literally. But the last thing she wanted was for him to question why she was so eager to become intimate with him now after she'd resisted his offer initially. He didn't need to know that in addition to wanting her mother's home she had a hidden motive for accepting his offer. A secret she'd shared only with Nikki and one she would take to the grave with her.

In addition to turning his bedroom into a seduction scene, she'd made a pit stop at the grocery store after discovering his pantry bare. Another rule of manners he'd broken. She wasn't Rachael Ray by any means, but she didn't do so badly in the kitchen. And just in case the sex thing with her was a total flop, at least she'd have the meal as a consolation prize.

Her ears perked up when she heard the sound of a door closing and figured it was Galen coming out of the garage. She nervously nibbled on her bottom lip knowing at any moment he would be coming up the stairs for her. She knew what happened after that would determine her fate.

Whatever it took—even if it was every ounce of resolve she had—she would get through it. No matter the outcome.

Galen sniffed the air the moment he closed the door from the garage. He had to be at the right house, but couldn't remember the last time he'd encountered the smell of food cooking.

He walked into his kitchen and glanced around. He'd been living here for four years, and this was probably the first time his stove had earned its keep. And the only thing his refrigerator had been good for was to chill his beer because he ate out one hundred percent of the time. Getting a home-cooked meal at his parents' place was one of the reasons he actually looked forward to Thursday nights.

He glanced over at his table. It was set for two with elegant china, silverware and glasses. He then glanced back at the stove and saw all stainless-steel pots. He could only assume all this kitchenware belonged to him. Was it a house-warming gift from his mother when he'd first moved in? Now that he thought about it, he was sure of it.

Whatever was in those pots sure smelled good and he couldn't wait to get into it. But then he frowned. If for one minute Brittany assumed a home-cooked dinner would replace the sex they were to have later, then she had another thought coming. He could get a meal from just about anywhere.

Galen turned toward the stairs, bracing himself for what he figured would be opposition to keeping her side of their agreement. She had been the one who'd tossed the "talk is cheap" challenge out there, and he was so looking forward to hearing her give one hell of an orgasmic scream. He could just imagine his hard body intimately connected to her soft one, her arms wrapped around his neck or her hands gripping his shoulders. All that mattered was getting inside her, thrusting in and out. His penis, which had gotten hard from the moment he'd finished working that day, seemed to have taken on a life of its own. If he didn't know better he'd suspect it had Brittany's name written all over it.

He'd never been this hard up for a woman. Each step

he took up the stairs, closer to her, made his erection surge in anticipation. The lust that had been eating at him, nipping at his heels, from the first time he'd set eyes on her had overtaken his senses, was devouring his control and intoxicating his mind.

Galen wasn't sure what he would do if he'd discovered Brittany had reneged. He didn't expect her to be already naked waiting for him in his bed, but he didn't expect for her to come kicking and screaming, either.

He moved toward the hall that led to his bedroom, not sure what he would find. It wouldn't surprise him if he found her sitting with her laptop still working on her e-mails. He knew there hadn't been any food in the house, which meant she had gone to the grocery store at some point. No doubt she wasn't happy about doing that.

He placed one foot in front of the other thinking this had to be the longest walk of his life, mainly because what awaited him on the other side could make or break him. He should never have allowed any woman to sink her claws into him this deep. But he'd been a goner the first time she'd frowned at him when he'd hijacked her cab. And he hadn't been right in the head since.

When he stood in front of the closed double doors to his bedroom, his eyebrows furled. Was that music he was hearing? He reached out to open the doors and then quickly remembered his manners. Although it was his room, for the next seven days they would be sharing it and he had to afford Brittany the courtesy of knocking before entering. Pulling in a deep breath, he tapped his knuckles on the door.

"Come in."

He lifted a brow. Was he imagining things or had

he heard a tremble in her voice? Taking another deep breath, he opened the doors. What he saw made him blink and mutter in a shocked tone, "Holy crap."

Chapter 12

Galen was convinced his heart had stopped beating, his lungs had seized and his penis had doubled in size. He had to literally shake himself just to get his body back to working order.

Brittany stood there with a sexy smile on her gorgeous face, and the "come get whatever you want" invitation he saw in her eyes suddenly made him feel like Adam in the Garden of Eden. Only thing missing was the apple.

"It took you long enough to get up here, Galen."

He swallowed. If she hadn't said his name he would have wondered if she was talking to him. Was she saying she'd been waiting for him to make an appearance? What the heck was going on and why did he feel he had gotten caught in some sort of trap?

In his peripheral vision he saw that his room had been transformed into a setting he hadn't ever seen before. Candles, imparting the scent of vanilla, glowed all around the room, soft music was playing and red rose petals were sprinkled over his bed, giving the room an overall romantic effect. He'd never thought he had a romantic bone in his body—until now.

But what caught his attention and held it more than anything was Brittany herself. How in the hell had she known that a woman in stilettos was his weakness, especially if she had legs like hers? And if that wasn't bad enough, the stilettos were red.

It was her dress, however, that had his erection throbbing, his tongue feeling thick in his throat. Where in the hell had she gotten something like that from? It was red to match the shoes and it was short. The fabric crisscrossed at the top and tantalized at the bottom with its flirty hem that barely covered her thighs. What was she trying to do? Kill him?

That thought, quite seriously, sent all kinds of questions flying through his mind. But all it took was a whiff of whatever perfume she was wearing to lay them to rest unanswered. His main consideration was getting her out of that dress.

"So how did work go today?"

He blinked, realizing she had spoken, and then what she was asking. While heat drummed through him, he figured that he needed to move his tongue to answer. "I finished my goal for today. Just one or two more pieces to work on this week and I'll be ready."

None of what he said was making any real sense. His mouth was saying words that his body didn't comprehend. Finish what? Ready for whom? His mouth was merely responding to her inquiry when the rest of him wanted to respond in another way. Forget the small talk.

"I didn't know you were waiting for me," he said, moving toward her, deciding to dispense with preliminaries and anything keeping him from her. Manners be damned.

"Yes," she said. "You probably didn't notice, but I left for a while to do some shopping. Because I'd found your pantry bare, I also stopped by the grocery store to pick up a few things to prepare for dinner. Rule number four is to never invite someone to your home as an overnight guest without plans to feed them."

"I was going to take you out," he defended.

"For breakfast, lunch and dinner?"

"Yes."

"Don't you ever cook for yourself?"

"No."

"That can get kind of pricey," she pointed out.

"I can afford it," he said, coming to a stop in front of her. "Is this dress real?"

"Touch it and see," she challenged.

"I think I will."

Galen smiled and for one heart-stopping moment, Brittany suddenly realized he wouldn't stop at touching the dress. He reached out and his hands slowly made their way down the front of her dress, tracing his fingers across the soft material. But as expected, his hands didn't stop there.

They slid over the softness of her shapely figure, as if molding her in a way that made her breath choppy. When he took a step closer and cupped her buttocks, rubbing his hands over their firm curve, she fought back the moan from deep within her throat.

"What is this about, Brittany? Why are you all of a sudden handing yourself to me on a silver platter?" His voice was husky as his hands continued to roam.

She stared into the depths of his green eyes. "You ask too many questions," she said in a voice that trembled even to her own ears. He was standing close. His body was pressed into hers. She could feel the outline of his erection through his jeans. His eyes were trained on her face, causing goose bumps to appear on her arms and stirring a hunger within her. A hunger that was all new to her.

Deciding it was time to be bold and take things to the next level, she wrapped her arms around his neck and molded her body to his. She felt her already-short dress rise up in the process. Air fanned her butt as she pressed her hardened nipples into his solid chest. Instinctively, she shifted her body, causing her hips to move against his rock-hard thighs and his very aroused penis.

The thought that he wanted her filled her head with an excitement she'd never felt before. It made her bolder. Made her want things she'd never desired before. Made her want to do things she'd never done before.

She decided not to fight anything tonight, to just roll with the flow. Let loose. Be something she'd never been before—one of those sexually needy chicks. And with that thought in mind, she stood on tiptoes and offered her mouth to him.

He took it, and the thrust of his tongue between her lips made her quiver. At the same time that his mouth ravaged her, his hands took advantage of her raised dress and began caressing her backside and then slipping under her lacy panties to touch her bare skin.

He continued to kiss her in a way that made her moan and spread heat through all parts of her body. The juncture of her thighs tingled. Nothing she and any other man had done in the bedroom could equate to this. A mere kiss. Never had she gotten fired up to this degree. Or to any measure, to be honest. She hated admitting she used to pretend in the bedroom. Actually she'd gotten pretty good at faking it. But there was nothing bogus going on here.

Their lips clung and she wasn't aware until now a mouth could actually make love to her. It was as if he was determined to know her taste, emerge himself in her scent. He seemed content just to stand there, feel her body wherever he liked and explore her mouth. And she was pretty much content to let him. They had kissed before, but never like this. Never with this much hunger, greed and intensity.

He suddenly broke off the kiss and the sound of his breathing—rapid successions of quick, hard breaths—matched her own. He met her gaze and held it and she noticed his lips were wet from devouring her.

"You do know this dress is coming off, don't you?" he asked in a deep, throaty voice.

"And what if I said it was glued to my body?" she teased.

He smiled. "Then I would have to prove that it wasn't. Stitch by stitch. Inch by inch." And he began doing just that as his hands slowly moved over her body, tugging the dress off her shoulders and down her hips.

She heard his sharp intake of breath when he saw

her red lace bra. And with a flick of his wrist he undid the front clasp and let the bra fall, setting free her twin mounds. His mouth immediately set upon them, drawing a nipple into the contours of his mouth to begin sucking.

Brittany grabbed hold of his shoulders when she felt weak in the knees. She hadn't known her breasts were so sensitive. Hadn't known they could ache for a man's mouth, until now. He had moved his mouth to the other breast, and quickly he had latched onto the other nipple, sucking profusely, and causing her stomach to tighten with every pull.

Holding her nipple hostage, he tilted his head to gaze up at her and she saw a flicker in the depths of his eyes as his hands remained clenched around the curves of her buttocks.

He lifted his head, touched his lips to her neck when he whispered, "Remember I told you it was 'taste you' night." And without waiting to see if she recalled it or not, he dropped to his knees in front of her. "I want the taste of you in my mouth. We're going to see just how cheap talk is, baby."

Brittany tried to ignore his term of endearment when she lifted her heels to step out of the dress that had tangled around her feet. He tossed it aside and glanced up at her wearing nothing but red lace panties and red stilettos.

"Damn, you look sexy. And tasty," he said, leaning forward, his hot breath right there at the crotch of her panties. He reached out and slowly began easing them down her legs and over her shoes to toss them aside.

He leaned back on his haunches. She was standing in

front of him naked except for her high heels. When she made a move to take them off, he said, "Leave them on."

She looked at him questioningly, but only for a minute. His hands had slid up the backs of her thighs, while his face had moved close to her stomach. He was licking the flesh around her belly button. The feel of his tongue on her stomach sent unfamiliar sensations through her, flooding all parts of her. And then, in a simultaneous invasion, his hands cupped her backside at the same time his mouth lowered to her womanly folds. He slid his tongue between them, and Brittany let out a deep whimper.

Never had any man tasted her there. But he wasn't just tasting her. He was devouring her. She grabbed hold of his shoulders as his mouth seemed intent to make a meal of her. She deliberately rolled her hips against his mouth, instinctively pushed forward as blood rushed to her head, making her dizzy.

His hands held her buttocks, determined to keep her pressed to his mouth as his tongue filled her, sent widespread shivers through her. She continued to whimper as he ravaged her womanhood, openmouthed and thrusting deep, as far as his tongue could go.

This was what other women had experienced. Why they kept wanting more. Why they'd looked at her like she was crazy when she seemed oblivious to what an orgasm was about. Now she was finding out firsthand. She felt it building, right at the juncture of her thighs, under the onslaught of Galen's mouth and tongue.

The throbbing between her legs intensified until it was downright unbearable, and then suddenly her entire body ignited in one hell of an explosion and she cried out his name and catapulted in a free fall. This was pleasure. One of those hidden pleasures that Nikki had warned her about. The intensity of it held her captured within its grip.

How had she gone twenty-eight years without experiencing this? The cells in her body felt pulverized and she succumbed to every novel feeling, soared higher than she'd ever thought possible.

When she thought she would crumble to the floor, he pulled his mouth away, stood and swept her off her feet into his arms. He moved up the steps to the bed and placed her on it, right on those rose petals and among the scented candles. And then he moved back, stared at her stretched across his bed. Naked, except for her shoes.

At the questioning look in her eyes, he said, "Keep them on. It's my fantasy."

And then she watched as he began removing his clothes.

Chapter 13

Galen unbuttoned his shirt thinking there was no woman he wanted to make love to more than the one stretched out on his bed, naked except for those sexy red high heels he dreamed about.

He'd asked her to keep them on because he'd never made love to a woman with her shoes on, and because the ones she was wearing looked so damn hot on her. Too hot to take off. He'd seen women in sexy heels a number of times and had always gotten one hell of a boner. But seeing Brittany in them was messing not only with his body but also with his mind.

He couldn't take his gaze off her. She was lying on her side facing him and her breasts were full, firm and high and the nipples he had sucked on earlier looked ready for him to feast on again. And then there were the dark curls between her legs, looking as luscious as anything he'd ever seen. He was getting harder just looking at that part of her. Using his mouth, he had made her come. And before the night touched the stroke of midnight, she would come plenty more times.

As he tossed his shirt aside he tried to come to terms with what was going on with him where she was concerned. Why was she so embedded under his skin that he was intent on screwing her out of it?

He swallowed hard at the thought of that tactic backfiring on him and instead of screwing her out of it, he might just bury her deeper into it. But for some reason that possibility didn't bother him. He breathed in deeply, feeling antsy, unreasonably horny. Maybe he ought to slow things down a bit.

For what purpose? his mind snapped back and asked. She was in a giving mood tonight, so he'd best just take what she was offering.

His erection had thickened and lengthened, and like a divining rod, it was aimed straight toward her, namely the juncture of her legs. He removed the rest of his clothes and when he stood naked in front of her, he let out a deep growl when her scent reached him. And from her scent, he knew she wanted him as much as he wanted her.

But something was nagging his mind, making him wonder why she was being so generous tonight. She had known when she'd accepted his offer that it would come down to this. Still, she hadn't been happy about it. Why had she done a one-eighty?

"Manners rule number five, Galen. Never keep a lady waiting."

Her words made his heart pound and his pulse race. And as he moved toward the bed he knew that she *was* a lady. The sexiest lady he'd ever met. "There's a good reason for this delay, sweetheart," he said, moving to the bench at the foot of the bed. "A must-do." He lifted the top and pulled out a condom packet and proceeded to sheath himself.

He knew she was watching his every move. When he finished, he braced one knee on the bed, held out his hand and said, "Come here, baby."

He thought her movement was as graceful as a swan, and she looked sexier than any woman had a right to be. When she reached him and placed her hand in his, he leaned toward her and began placing kisses up the side of her neck while whispering how much he wanted her.

He then began trailing kisses along the curve of her shoulders, liking the taste of her skin there just as much as he had the area between her thighs. The sweet taste of her womanly essence was still on his tongue and would stay there for some time. And then he kissed her deeply as they tumbled backward onto the bed together.

It was then that Galen pulled back and stared deep into her eyes. "I need to know," he whispered. "I need to know that tonight isn't a fluke and tomorrow you'll regret everything that takes place in this bedroom. And even worse, that you won't share yourself with me the next six days."

He outlined her lips with the tip of his finger. "Tell me that won't happen, Brittany."

Brittany stared deep into Galen's intense eyes and at that moment she doubted she could deny him anything. Not this man who'd less than twenty minutes ago given her the experience of her first orgasm. And for that she was exceedingly grateful. The last thing she would have tomorrow was regrets. Nor did she want to deny herself this pleasure for the next six days. She was a late bloomer where sex was concerned, but tonight she'd become a woman finding out how to lose herself in the heat of passion and pleasure.

"Tell me, Brittany."

She swallowed. A part of her silently warned she was getting in too deep. She should take tonight and be done with it. Anything beyond this could lead to some serious trouble. What if he discovered it had been more than the lure of her mother's house that brought her to his bed? That it had also been her quest to find out more about herself. Her need to know if she could enjoy an amorous relationship with a man.

He'd proven she could. Should she take that knowledge and run? Be through with it? Let him know there wouldn't be any more sensual interludes between them and all he would be getting from her over the next six days were lessons in manners? She knew she wasn't capable of running anywhere. Now that he'd revealed all her hidden pleasures, she wanted to spend as much time as she could and explore those pleasures with him.

"There won't be any regrets tomorrow, Galen," she said in a soft voice. "And I'm committed to keeping my end of our agreement, so there will be more nights like this one."

He frowned and she wondered why he was doing so. Hadn't she just stated what he'd wanted to hear? They both had their own ulterior motives for sharing this week. He'd been right when he'd said that he had something she wanted and she had something he wanted.

But what happened after the seven days?

A shiver ran through her, although the answer to that question was simple. He went his way and she went hers. She would have her mother's home and he'd get his week of sexual enjoyment. What more could either of them expect?

She tilted her head and studied Galen, wondering the reason for the heavy silence. "That's what you want, isn't it?"

"Of course."

Still, she continued to look at him, wondering if she was missing something. She shook off the possibility that she was. Before she could dwell on it any more, he lowered his mouth and captured hers again.

Galen, she decided, was a perfectionist when it came to kissing. Some of the things he did with his tongue should be outlawed. Even now he was sucking gently on hers, while his hands were touching her everywhere, squeezing her breasts, teasing the hardened tips of her nipples. And then he lowered his hand between her legs and inserted a finger into her.

She pulled her mouth back and drew in a deep breath before burying her face in the warmth of his hairy chest. He smelled good. He smelled of man. And his intimate touch was driving her sensuously insane. When his free hand moved to caress the slope of her back she lifted her head from his chest and met his intense gaze.

"Make love to me, Galen."

She whispered the words not caring that her request probably lacked manners. The protocol was changing, and women were bold enough to ask something like that. Still, such an audacious request sounded strange coming from a female. However, at the moment the only thing she cared about was the deep ache in her stomach that had been there for a while and had become unbearable the moment he'd removed his pants to reveal the thatch of dark curly hair at his groin. There was just something about seeing him exposed and the thickness of his erection that had heat radiating to her lower limbs. She wanted him in a way she'd never truly wanted a man. With Galen she could be herself. She could be the woman she'd never been.

She wanted him. He wanted her. And for now that was all that mattered.

"Be careful what you ask for, sweetheart," he whispered as he gathered her close to the warmth and solid hardness of his body. She felt his arousal pressed against her belly and was compelled to reach down and grip his manhood in her hand.

She remembered touching Gilford once and the harsh words he'd said when she did. He'd reminded her that she was a lady who was above doing such things. Instead of being turned off by her actions, it was evident Galen had no such problem with her touching him, if the sound of his heavy breathing and deep guttural groans were any indication. Empowered by his response, she began stroking him, liking the feel of the thick veins that outlined the shaft of his penis, and the warmth that emitted from the tip of it.

"Damn, Brittany," he growled. "You're about to make me lose my manners."

She smiled thinking he just had. A true gentleman

would never swear in front of a lady. Instead of pointing that out to him, she decided to inflict her own brand of punishment by sinking her teeth into his shoulder and then licking the bruise with her tongue.

"Payback, Brittany."

He shifted their positions and she found herself flat on her back with him looming over her, sliding in place between her open legs and red stilettos. And she knew whatever patience he'd been holding in check had gotten tossed to the wind. She glanced up at the see-through ceiling. It had gotten dark and there were stars in the sky adding to the romantic effect she'd created.

That effect stirred everything within her and when she felt his manhood at the entrance of her mound, nudging her womanly folds apart trying to seek admittance, streaks of anticipation flooded her.

Then she felt him, the heat of him sliding inside her wet channel, stretching her, taking her, preparing to mate with her. Her muscles clenched him, gripped him, needing something only he could give. She knew she had to relax, stop being greedy, but this was all new to her and she wanted it all.

He remained still when he was inside her to the hilt and then he glanced down at her and whispered, "Wrap those legs and high heels around my waist. I want to feel you. I want to feel them. I'm about to do the very thing to you that those shoes stand for."

And he did.

He began moving in and out of her, and the throbbing between her legs intensified with each stroke. She did just as he suggested and wrapped her legs around him, stilettos and all.

He lifted her hips to receive him deeper and she could actually feel blood rushing through her veins. And then in a surprise move he lowered his head and captured a nipple in his mouth and began sucking while his body rode her hard. She bit her lips against a moan and then gave up and screamed out his name when a mass of sensations ripped through her.

She pressed closer to him, tightened her legs around him as he continued to pound into her. Heat burst into flames and she tightened her grip on him when he bucked several times with whiplash speed. They held nothing back. They shared passion, pleasure and possession. Tonight he was hers and she was his. He kept thrusting inside her until he had nothing left to give, and then finally he moaned her name and collapsed on top of her.

When his breathing returned to normal, he shifted his weight off her. She cuddled closer to him as if that was where she belonged.

He laid a hand across her thigh as he met her gaze, breathing in deeply and then saying, "That was simply amazing. Incredible." He then reached down to remove her shoes and tossed them across the room.

She lay there, completely sated, as she tried to catch her breath. She totally agreed with him. She wondered what he would think if he knew tonight was the first time she'd made love and considered it a pleasurable experience.

He wrapped his arms around her and pulled her closer. "Let's sleep a while. Dinner will keep until later. Besides, I doubt either of us has the strength to get out of this bed right now."

He was right, she thought, laying her head on his chest and giving in to her body's exhaustion. She felt drained, yet at the same time flagrantly and passionately pleasured. She moved her head to look at him, and when she did their eyes locked. He had been looking at her. At that moment something passed between them. Just what, she wasn't sure.

Sensations rippled through her all over again and she knew at that instant that Galen Steele was every woman's fantasy.

He was certainly hers.

Chapter 14

Brittany woke up the next morning, shifted her body and stared up into the sky. She could even see birds flying overhead through the bedroom ceiling. Amazing. She closed her eyes thinking nothing was as amazing as making love with Galen last night.

She had lost count of her orgasms. After they'd taken a nap and awakened to make love again, they had slipped into their clothes and gone downstairs to eat, totally famished.

Galen told her more than once how much he enjoyed her spaghetti, which she'd served with a salad and garlic bread. He had even asked for seconds. Then he had helped with the cleanup. The next thing she knew, she was swept into his arms and taken back upstairs where he'd made love to her again several more times.

She'd come close to telling him what last night had meant to her and how her better judgment had warned her against the indulgence. But Galen was a man used to sleeping with women who know the score, and although she wasn't a virgin, her experience left a lot to be desired. In the end, she kept the secret.

She shifted in bed and wished she'd stayed put when her muscles ached. The intensity of Galen's lovemaking last night had made her sore, which would no doubt slow her down a bit today. At least until she took a hot, relaxing bath. Then she would go over to her house. After yesterday she finally allowed herself to label the house as hers, especially after Galen had given her the key.

She wondered where he'd gone. Although today was Saturday, he was probably downstairs working in his garage. She had yet to see that part of his house and knew he considered it his private domain where he allowed his creativity to flow. She smiled thinking his creativity had done a pretty good job flowing right here in this bedroom last night.

Easing out of bed, she went into the bathroom. If Galen intended to work all day today, then she could very well revisit her house. If he thought she would be at his beck and call, then he had another think coming.

Galen's heart began racing when he heard Brittany moving around upstairs. Although he'd been tempted to wake her early this morning to make love again, he'd figured she needed her rest, especially because he'd kept her up most of the night.

He probably should feel like an oversexed, greedy ass, but he was too damn satisfied, far too content, to find fault in his behavior last night. Besides, he knew although Brittany might not have expected to go as many rounds with him, she'd enjoyed each and every one of them. Her screams were still ringing in his ears.

Something about her screams, though, hadn't been right. Not that he thought she'd been faking them, mind you, but he'd made love to enough women to recognize the tenor of a scream. Listening to Brittany's, one would get the impression she'd never screamed during a climax before. It could very well be that she assumed screaming displayed reproachful behavior, definitely a lack of manners. But still, lack of manners or not, some things couldn't be held back. And letting go while gripped within the throes of passion was one of them.

He moved away from the sink to open the refrigerator and again was taken aback by the sight of the items inside. Milk, eggs, cheese, fruit... The meal Brittany prepared last night had been off the charts. But he hoped she didn't assume she had to cook, because he'd made it clear he had no problems with their eating out. And then there was dinner at his parents' home on Thursday night and—

Holy crap! Brittany would still be here on Thursday night. According to the terms of their agreement that Eli had drawn up, she wouldn't be leaving his place until next Saturday morning. There was no way he would take her to his parents' place for dinner. He didn't want anyone getting the wrong impression, and knowing his mother, she would. It was not the norm for women to hang around his place on a frequent basis. Although several had spent the night, he didn't waste time helping them to the door bright and early the next morning. And it went without saying that he'd never taken a woman to his parents' dinners.

"Good morning."

He hadn't heard Brittany come down the stairs. But then why would he have been listening for her? Talk about irregular behavior…

He drew in a deep breath, closed the refrigerator door and turned around. The moment he did so, a fine sheen of perspiration touched his brow. Some women looked better than others in the morning and he quickly decided she fit in that category. She had taken a shower, which was probably the reason she looked so fresh in her top and jeans. But a shower hadn't put the glow on her face. He had posted enough notches on his bedpost to know only a night of earth-shattering sex could do that to a woman. He inwardly flinched at the thought of her being a notch on anyone's bedpost, including his.

"Good morning, Brittany." There was no need to ask if she'd gotten a good night's sleep because thanks to him she hadn't.

Instead he asked, "Where would you like to go for breakfast?" He had showered and shaved earlier and was ready to go. And getting out of the house wasn't such a bad idea; then he wouldn't have thoughts running through his head of taking her back upstairs.

"I can prepare something for us. Won't take but a minute. At least, if that's all right with you because it's your kitchen."

Yes, it was his kitchen, and as far as he was concerned, everything in it was his, including her. He then heaved a sigh, wondering how his mind could think such a thing. There was no woman alive that was his.

He borrowed them for the time it took to get his pleasure and then he returned them to where they'd come
from. It would be easy to tell Brittany she could go upstairs and pack, and that starting today she could stay
at her mother's place, but for some reason he couldn't
fix his mouth to say those words.

Instead he said, "I don't have a problem with it. I just
don't want you to assume I expect it of you."

He watched in fascination when her lower lip started
to quiver. Call him sick but he had missed seeing that,
although he knew she was vexed with him for some
reason. "Trust me, Galen. I know your expectations
where I'm concerned."

"Do you?"

"Yes."

A sudden smile touched his lips. "In that case…" He
moved toward her. As soon as he reached her, he picked
her up off her feet and placed her on his kitchen counter
and moved between her jeans-clad legs. Already he
missed seeing her in those sexy high heels.

"What do you think you're doing, Galen?" she asked,
staring at him with a frown on her face.

That elicited a laugh from him. "I bet you won't ask
me that in a couple of minutes." He then swooped his
mouth down to hers.

Brittany wondered why after a night like last night,
they were at odds with each other this morning. And
why did it take this, another Galen Steele mind-blowing
kiss, to put things in perspective?

Instead of thinking about the answers to those questions, she decided to concentrate on the kiss instead.

Might as well, because it would have snatched her focus anyway. Heat always sizzled between them whenever their lips locked and this morning was no exception.

His hands reached up to cup both sides of her face, making her feel the intensity of him making love to her mouth. And that was exactly what he was doing. His tongue was ravaging her, leaving no part of her mouth unscathed.

His mouth continued to move against hers with a hunger she felt all the way to her toes, and she couldn't resist returning the kiss with equal fervor. All she could think about was how last night this same mouth and this very naughty tongue feasted at her breasts and between her thighs, driving her over the brink of madness and lapping her into orgasm after orgasm. Neither could she forget his powerful thrusts into her, over and over, in and out, making her scream more times than she could count. It was a wonder her throat wasn't raw this morning.

He pulled back, breaking off the kiss, and she stared into his face, saw that arrogant smile on his moist lips and she swallowed hard. It was either that or grab his shirt and make him kiss her again.

"Now, you were asking?"

She blinked. *She'd asked him something?* Oh, yeah, she'd asked what he thought he was doing. He'd given her an answer in a tongue-tangling way. Brittany considered saying they should take this to the bedroom but decided not to. Instead she said, "Breakfast. What are we going to do about breakfast? This is Saturday, so I'm sure most breakfast places are crowded and it's after nine already."

He nodded and she noticed his gaze was glued to her lips. "So what do you suggest?"

"I suggest I prepare something. Afterward I'm sure you have your day planned."

"I had thought about putting in more time on Sniper today."

"And I plan to go over to my mother's place for a while."

He lifted her off the counter and placed her back on her feet. "It's no longer your mother's place. It's yours. I gave you the key yesterday and she willed the house to you, so you might want to start thinking of yourself as the owner."

She rubbed her arms where his hands had touched. "I know," she said smiling faintly up at him. "But no one has ever given me anything before." And that had been the truth. Even during the Christmas holidays when she'd received presents from her foster parents, she'd known the gifts had been donated by charity.

He took a step toward her and reached out and traced the curve of her mouth with his thumb. "But all that's changed now, hasn't it?"

He was standing close, so close she could feel his erection through his jeans pressing against her. She couldn't stop the stab of sexual sensations that spiked through her veins.

His question made her realize that yes, it had changed. Her mother may have given her away when she was born, but before Gloria McIntyre had left this earth she had found her and had tried making things right. Not that they had been wrong. A part of her had always figured her mother had been a teenager who'd wanted the best for her. She'd had no way of knowing that what she'd wanted for her daughter and what her daughter eventually got were two different things. But then maybe she did know once she'd gotten the investigator's report.

"Do you need my help?"

She gave Galen a reluctant smile. What she needed was for him to leave the kitchen so she could concentrate. "No, I can handle things. Why don't you go to the garage and start working," she suggested. "I'll call you when I'm done."

"And you're sure you don't need my help?"

"I'm positive."

"All right. And you don't have to come to the garage looking for me. I'll be back up in fifteen minutes or so. I'll lay out my supplies and come back."

He turned to leave, then, catching Brittany off guard, he pulled her against him and covered her lips in a kiss that sent her pulse racing. When he released her, he whispered against her moist lips, "I like you." And then he moved toward the door that led to his garage.

"Tell me about your brothers, Galen."

Galen glanced across the table. When he had returned from the garage, it had been just in time to see Brittany place the pancakes she'd prepared on a platter. Then there were the eggs, bacon and orange juice. Everything he would normally get at Flynn's Breakfast Café where he ate most mornings. But he would be the first to say the meal Brittany had prepared could hold its own against Flynn's any day.

He lifted a brow. "My brothers?"

"Yes."

She had asked about his brothers before, a couple of times, and he'd always avoided her question. His family was his family, and most people living in Phoenix knew the Steele brothers. Most women he'd dated didn't ask about his brothers, because Tyson, Eli, Jonas, Mercury and Gannon had managed to carve out reputations around the city on their own. He had to remember Brittany wasn't from Phoenix, though, which could be a good thing. She wouldn't know about the Steele brothers' reputation. She had no idea some women considered them the "Bad News Steeles." Nor would she know they liked women in their beds, but had no plans to keep them in their lives.

"I mentioned I'm the oldest," he started off by saying. "After me there's Tyson. There's only an eleven-month difference in our ages. At thirty-three he's the doctor in the family, a heart surgeon and a damn good one."

He took a sip of his coffee, thinking it tasted just as good as any he purchased from Starbucks. "After Tyson there's Eli. As you already know, he's the attorney in the family. He's thirty-two. Then there's Jonas, who's thirty-one. Jonas owns a marketing firm and has some top names as clients. After Jonas there's Mercury at thirty. He's an ex-NFL player turned sports agent. And last but not least is Gannon, the youngest at twenty-nine, but he's definitely not the smallest. He took over the day-to-day operations of my father's trucking company and even gets behind a rig himself every once in a while."

He leaned back in his chair. "So there you have it, the Phoenix Steeles."

She smiled and lifted a brow. "There's more?"

He chuckled. "Yes, mostly living in North Carolina. Have you ever heard of the Steele Manufacturing Company?"

"Yes."

"That's those Steeles."

"You're close to them, as well?"

"Of course, they're family."

"Of course."

He looked down into his coffee cup as he recalled that Brittany did not have a family, and he remembered what she'd said about never feeling a part of any of her foster families. He wished he could have changed that for her.

"So tell me about Galen Steele."

He glanced up thinking he'd rather not. But he would, because talking was a lot safer—he wouldn't be tempted to take her upstairs and communicate in a different way. "What do you want to know?"

"Anything. Everything."

He couldn't help but smile at the thought of that. Either could get the both of them in trouble. "I like sex." He thought the blush on her face was cute. Just as cute as the quivering of her lips when she got angry.

"I know that already. What else do you like?" she asked.

"You. I like you," he said honestly, even though he knew such an admission would rattle her.

He watched her bite her lip. "Yes, I think you've said that already, too," she said. "What else do you like besides sex and me?"

"I like auto racing. The Steele Manufacturing Company sponsors a car for NASCAR, so I travel to the races quite a bit."

She nodded. "When our paths crossed in New York, you were there for a wedding, right?"

He chuckled. She'd made it seem like it had been a casual meeting when it had been anything but. He'd swiped her cab. "Yes, my cousin Donovan. There wasn't supposed to be a wedding."

She lifted a brow. "There wasn't?"

"No, because Donovan wasn't ever supposed to marry. He was supposed to be a bachelor for life."

"Is that what he'd said?"

"Yes. Always."

Galen stared back into his cup of coffee, which was almost empty. Donovan used to say it and was quite serious about it, but a woman had come along and changed his mind. Galen was certain that he would never let that happen to him, and to this day he didn't understand how it happened to Donovan. His cousin had had everything going for him. Any woman he wanted. And then Natalie came along and whammo, he'd fallen in love and the next thing everyone knew, he was talking marriage.

Deciding they'd sat at the table and chitchatted long enough, he stood to clear his plate. "You sure you don't need me to help do anything over at your place?"

"Yes, I'm positive. Today I plan to go through her things and see what I need to pack up and what I want to keep."

"You don't have to do everything in one day, you know."

"Yes, I know. But I want to get it done."

"Well, call me if you change your mind and need my help," he said, taking his plate and cup to the sink.

"You have your own work to do."

Galen was about to say that he didn't care how much work he had to do; if she needed him, he wanted her to call. She came first. But he quickly clamped his mouth shut, wondering why on earth he'd think something like that. No woman came before his work...except his mother and most of the time that couldn't be helped. His father had basically spoiled Eden. She'd been the only female in a houseful of males and she'd been treated like a queen. Unfortunately, she hadn't pulled off her crown yet.

"Just call me if you decide you need me. And don't wash the dishes. Just put everything in the sink. You cooked breakfast, so I'll clean up on my next break."

Growing frustrated over what seemed to be his mounting fascination with her—memories of their night together weren't helping matters—he said, "I'll see you later." And then he left the kitchen.

Chapter 15

Brittany moved around her mother's home. In a way she was glad Galen hadn't come with her this time. She needed space from him to think. For some reason he'd appeared guarded this morning. Although he'd kissed her when he'd sat her up on the counter, from then on he seemed cool. Not cold but cool. She hoped he wasn't thinking she wanted something beyond this week because she didn't. All she wanted was full ownership of this house, fair and square, and then she would decide what she would do with it.

She moved toward her mother's room and pulled out several drawers. There were more pictures of Gloria McIntyre and a man Brittany could only assume was her mother's husband. They seemed like a close pair.

Brittany had decided if she didn't find anything to

give her a clue as to why her mother had decided to look for her all these years, then she would go talk to the private investigator she'd hired. Maybe the man could shed light on a few things.

She pulled out another drawer, thinking like the others she would find more pictures, and was surprised to find a journal. Her heart rate increased as she pulled out the journal and closed the drawer. It was thick and she could tell it contained many entries.

Moving quickly to her mother's bed, Brittany kicked off her shoes before lying down on the bed. One of the first things she'd done when she arrived this morning was strip the bed and put on fresh linen. The washer and dryer were going and she intended to have the sheets back in the linen closet before she left. It was still early yet, not quite four o'clock. More than likely Galen was working and hadn't noticed the time.

The first entry she came to was written eighteen years ago on January tenth. Brittany's tenth birthday.

I tried to bring up the subject of the baby I gave away, my beautiful little girl, but Hugh doesn't want to talk about it. He'd said he could handle it when I first told him about her last year, but now I'm not sure I did the right thing.

Brittany quickly sat up. Her mother had told her husband about her? Quickly she scanned ahead to another entry, recorded on her thirteenth birthday.

Today my daughter becomes a teenager. I hope the family that adopted her loves her as much as I do. It was so hard for me to give her up, but I wasn't given a choice. I couldn't abort her like Mom and Dad wanted. Especially after Britton drowned. She was to be our baby. Britton and I had so many plans, and when he died he left me all alone.

Brittany's heart jumped. Her father's name had been Britton and he'd drowned. A knot formed in her throat when she kept reading.

I cried for days and Mom and Dad refused to speak to me for months, but I wouldn't back down about the abortion. They finally sent me away to Phoenix to live with Uncle Milton and Aunt Pauline. I agreed to give my baby up for adoption since everyone said she would go to a couple who wanted a baby but couldn't have one. They would love and cherish my baby like I would have done. When I met with the people at the adoption agency a month before my due date, I thought they were nice, and they said I could even name the baby. I decided to name him Britton if he was a boy and Brittany if she was a girl. She was a girl so I named her Brittany. I got to hold her for only a little while and I thought she looked like Britton. She was a beautiful little girl with a head full of curly black hair. I noticed two of her fingers were crooked and her feet were turned in but the nurse said they would eventually straighten out. Happy Birthday, Brittany, wherever you are. I hope you're happy.

Brittany wiped a tear from her eye. She hadn't been happy. While her mother assumed she was somewhere being loved and cherished by some nice couple on her thirteenth birthday, it had been just weeks after that when Mr. Ponder had tried to molest her. And those fingers never changed, and as a child she had to wear heavy metal braces that fit into her shoes until her bones straightened out. Both birth defects made her a flawed baby nobody wanted to adopt.

Brittany looked down at her hand. All her fingers were straight now because one of the first things she'd done after making a profit at Etiquette Matters was to have surgery on her fingers.

She drew in a deep breath and continued reading. Seconds turned into minutes and minutes into hours. The entries came to an end and Brittany was so full of her mother's love that she couldn't stop the tears that poured from her eyes. All those years when she thought nobody loved her, nobody cared, here in this house located thousands of miles from where she lived in Florida, Gloria McIntyre had loved her. She had made an entry in memory of her on every birthday she'd had.

Brittany couldn't do anything but drop back down on the bed and cry her eyes out. She understood why her mother had given her up thinking she would get a better life, but still...

"Brittany? What's wrong?"

Brittany snatched her head up and through the tears she saw Galen. Where had he come from? She pulled herself up and by then he was there, pulling her into his arms, and she went willingly, circling her arms around his neck.

"What is it, Brittany?" he asked, his voice soft and filled with concern as he sat down on the edge of the bed with her in his arms.

And then the words came pouring out and she knew to him they probably made no sense and ran all together. "My mother loved me. My father's name was Britton and he drowned when he was eighteen, leaving my sixteen-year-old mother pregnant with me. My grandparents wanted her to get an abortion but she wouldn't, so they sent her here to live with her uncle and aunt. The people at the adoption agency let her name me after my father, and promised to give me to a nice couple who would love and cherish me. But nobody wanted me because two of my fingers were crooked and I had to wear those metal leg braces until my bones straightened out. And then when she thought I was doing fine on my thirteenth birthday, that was the year Mr. Ponder tried to molest me, which is why I've never liked sex. And I paid a plastic surgeon to fix my fingers. She wanted to find me but had to wait until her husband died and then she died before I could meet her."

There, she'd said it all and then she cried even more. And Galen just held her.

It wasn't supposed to be this way, Galen thought as he stared into space while holding the woman in his arms. She wasn't supposed to wiggle her way into his heart so easily. Now he fully understood what had happened to Donovan.

He glanced down at Brittany. The sound of her crying tore at his heart. But he was letting her get it all out—all the pain, heartache, heartbreak, loneliness, the feeling of belonging to no one. And as she cried he gently rubbed her back, held her in his arms and whispered over and over again that everything would be okay.

He doubted when it was over she would remember even half the stuff she'd told him just now, but he would never forget it. She thought she'd never liked sex? A part of him inwardly smiled knowing she'd certainly enjoyed it last night. Was that what last night had been about? Testing the waters to see if perhaps, considering all the sexual chemistry between them, she could possibly enjoy it with him?

And what was all that about her fingers and legs? Was that why she hadn't gotten adopted as a baby? Most people wanted newborns instead of an older child, and for her not to have gotten adopted meant that someone thought something was wrong with her. So, she'd had a couple of crooked fingers and weak legs, big damn deal. Was that a good reason not to take a baby into your home and love it? And he would love to be in the same room as this Ponder guy about now. He'd put both his feet up the man's rear end.

Pulling in a deep breath, he continued to rock her and kept whispering that everything would be okay.

Earlier that afternoon he'd begun getting concerned when she hadn't returned, and when she hadn't answered her cell phone, concern turned to worry. A first for him over a woman.

All he could think was that she was alone in a house on a secluded road. He'd driven like a maniac to get here. And now that he was here with her, there was no need to question why his heart was filled with so much love for her.

Damn.

And with that realization he could only shake his head. No need to ask how it happened, where it happened or when it happened. Those logistics really didn't matter. All that mattered was that he had fallen hopelessly in love with Brittany Thrasher. Especially when it had been just yesterday he'd assured himself his fascination with her was bound to wear off. Today he realized he had no intentions of letting her go. Ever.

When she finally pulled her face from his chest and tried wiping away any traces of tears, he asked softly, "Where's your cell phone, sweetheart? I tried calling you a hundred times."

She didn't look up at him, pretending interest in the buttons of his shirt. She was probably trying to recall just how much she'd told him. No doubt she figured she'd given him too much information.

"It's in my purse on top of the washing machine. I guess I didn't hear it ring."

"Okay, we'll grab it on our way out." He then swept her into his arms. At her gasp of surprise he looked down at her and said, "And before you ask, I'm taking you home."

She really didn't have a clue just how much he meant it.

"You are mine," a raspy voice whispered as Brittany felt her clothes being removed from her body. She couldn't stay awake. She felt so sleepy.

She recalled Galen bringing her back here and leaving her car at her mother's place. The drive over here was a blur, but she did remember him carrying her into the house and then up the stairs to his bedroom.

She had the faintest memory of him giving her a glass of wine to drink, but only because the sweet taste of fermented grape was still on her tongue. And now Galen was whispering to her, letting her know he was removing her clothes and getting her ready for bed. That only made her want to cry even more because no one had ever really taken care of her. But tonight he was.

"Hold up your arms, Brittany, so I can slip the T-shirt on you."

Like a child, she did what she was told, because all she wanted to do was sleep. And she shivered when she felt the cotton material sliding over her head and past her shoulders to hardly cover her thighs.

Through barely opened eyes, she watched as he tossed the covers back and then, reaching his hand out to her, she took it and slid beneath the covers. When he tucked her in, a tear fell from her eye. No one had ever tucked her into bed before.

"You're going to read me a story?" she asked, trying to tease but barely getting the words out. She had a feeling she'd taken too many sips of wine.

"Do you want me to?" he asked, and she felt his callused fingertips brush across her cheek. So gentle.

"Yes, but nothing sad."

She felt the bed dip and knew he'd slid in bed beside her, fully clothed, to gather her into his arms. She inhaled his scent and took comfort in his nearness.

"This story has a happy ending," he whispered close to her ear.

"All right."

"There once was a man name Drew, who had so many women he didn't know what to do. And he thought he was happy until one day he saw this girl named Eden, and figured he would make her another one of his women. But he soon realized Eden was special. She couldn't be like his other women. Because this girl had done something the others couldn't do. She had captured his heart. And then he and Eden got married and lived happily ever after."

She snuggled closer to him and his warmth. "Hmm, nice." And then she drifted off to sleep.

Chapter 16

Brittany opened her eyes and stared up at the gray clouds in the sky. It was supposed to rain today, wasn't it? She closed her eyes, not sure what day it was. Sunday, she believed.

Parts of yesterday floated through her memory. She remembered going to her house and washing the bed linens and then finding her mother's journal.

She opened her eyes. The journal. She recalled reading the journal and the parts that had made her cry. And she remembered Galen showing up and holding her while she cried and bringing her back here.

Brittany threw back the covers and glanced down at herself. She was wearing one of his T-shirts. The details of last night were sketchy, but she did recall him undressing her and tucking her into bed. He'd even told her some story, although she couldn't exactly remember it. Hopefully, it would all come back later.

She eased out of bed and stretched. She needed to shower, put on some clothes and go apologize to Galen for her actions yesterday. It was not good manners for a woman to get all emotional on a man.

As she headed toward the bathroom, she promised herself that she would make it up to him.

"So, Galen, where's your houseguest?"

Galen stared across the table at Jonas. This brother had asked the very question the other four were wondering but hadn't the nerve to inquire about. Galen was no fool. He'd known the moment he had opened the door to them that they had visited for a reason. He couldn't recall the last time they'd dropped by bringing him breakfast.

"Brittany's upstairs," he said as he continued eating.

"Nice name," Gannon interjected.

Galen nodded. "She's a nice girl."

"Classify nice."

That had come from Tyson. Eli, he noticed, wasn't saying anything. He was just looking, listening and eating. "She's not anyone I'd typically mess around with."

"Then why are you?" Mercury asked.

Galen smiled. "Because I like her." He thought about what he'd just said and decided these five men deserved his honesty, even though what he was about to say would stun them. "In fact, I'm in love with her."

Their reaction was comical at best. Only Eli had managed to keep a straight face—one of those "I told you so" expressions. The others looked shocked.

"What do you mean you love her? The way Drew

loves Eden or the way Colfax loves Velvet?" Mercury asked.

Everyone was familiar with Mercury's friend Jaye Colfax. He claimed he was in love with Velvet Spencer; however, he wasn't in love with the woman, just the sex because it was off the chain.

"It's like Drew and Eden."

That confession was like a missile going off in his kitchen, and with it came a blast. Colorful expletives were discharged in different languages because he and all of his brothers spoke several foreign languages. In fact, maybe that was a good thing considering Brittany was upstairs. He hadn't heard her moving around, but that didn't mean she hadn't awakened. The last thing she needed to hear was the Steele brothers discussing her.

"Let's speak German," Galen suggested.

English or German, what his brothers were saying was scorching his ears. He was being called everything but a child of God. Now he knew how Donovan felt, because Galen had been one of the first to read his cousin the riot act, as if falling in love was something he could have avoided.

When he felt they'd pretty much gotten everything off their chests, and probably every filthy word they could think of out of their mouths, he stood and said in German, "Okay, you've all had your say, now get over it."

It wasn't just what he said, but the tone he used that made his kitchen suddenly get quiet. Five pairs of green eyes stared at him. And then he said, "What happens to me has no bearing on the five of you."

He knew it was a lie even as he said it. Eden Tyson

Steele wouldn't see it that way. She would think one down and five more to go.

"And you truly love her? This woman you met…less than a week ago?" Jonas asked, looking at him like he ought to have his head examined.

"We didn't just meet. I met her in New York six months ago."

"Hey, wait a minute," Gannon said, as if something had just clicked inside his head. "Is she the one who got away?"

Galen couldn't help but smile. Gannon had a tendency to remember everything. "Yes, she's the one, which is why I don't plan on letting her get away again"

"So when is the wedding?" Jonas asked. "If I'm going to be in a wedding, I need to know when. My schedule is pretty crazy for the next few months."

Galen shrugged. "Don't know because she hasn't a clue how I feel. And chances are she might not return the feelings."

His brothers looked aghast at such a possibility. After all, Galen was a Steele and all women loved the Steeles. "So you're going to have to work on her? Convince her you're worthy of her affections?" Tyson asked, as if the thought of Galen doing such a thing was downright shameful.

"Yes, and I intend to win her over."

"And if you don't?"

An assured and confident smile touched his lips. "I will."

Brittany was halfway down the stairs when she heard the sound of male voices…and they were speaking in a different language. German, she believed, but wasn't sure. The only other language she spoke was Spanish. Why would they be doing such a thing? She stopped walking, wondering if she should interrupt.

She shrugged. A few days ago when she'd asked about meeting his brothers, Galen had said they'd come around sooner or later, when word got out about her. They were here, so evidently word was out and she might as well get it over with and make an appearance.

She walked into the kitchen. "Good morning."

The room went silent and six pairs of eyes turned to her. Her gaze immediately latched onto Galen's as the other men just stared at her. The one thing she did notice was that they appeared to be sextuplets. All six had the same height and build and those Smokey Robinson eyes. And all were handsome as sin.

Galen walked over to her and she felt a semblance of relief because his brothers just continued to eye her up and down. She was glad she looked pretty decent in her knit top and skirt.

"Okay, guys, I want you to meet Brittany Thrasher," Galen said, wrapping one arm around her waist. "Brittany, from left to right, that's Tyson, Eli, Jonas, Mercury and Gannon."

She smiled warmly, then said, "Nice meeting all of you."

But the men didn't reply. They just continued to gawk. "It's not polite to stare."

Simultaneously, their faces broke into smiles and Brittany knew Nikki's warnings about these brothers were true. They were Phoenix's most eligible bachelors, heartbreakers to the core. Even the one standing close by her side.

"Sorry. Please forgive our manners," the one introduced as Tyson said. "Your beauty has left us speechless."

Yeah, right, she thought to herself. This one, Dr. Tyson Steele, was the epitome of suave and sophisticated, exuding an aura of self-assurance and confidence. Instead of saying what she really thought about his compliment, though, she decided to accept it graciously. "Thank you."

"My brothers brought breakfast. Please join us," Galen invited.

She shook her head. "That's okay. I didn't mean to interrupt."

"And you didn't," Eli said. "Please join us. We insist."

Her gaze lit on the man who looked like he could easily grace the cover of *GQ*. In fact they all did, including Galen. She allowed herself a moment to size up the brothers the same way they were doing with her. They were probably trying to figure things out between her and their brother. Evidently, Galen hadn't told them much and now they probably wanted to pump information out of her.

She'd never had siblings, so she didn't know how they operated collectively. But she had a feeling those Steeles were rather unique when it came to looking out for each other. She wondered if they saw her as a threat to Galen for some reason.

Deciding to go along with the invitation, she said, "Thanks. I'd love to join you for breakfast."

She glanced up at Galen. His arms were still around

her waist, but he had an odd look on his face. Had he expected her to turn down his invitation? Sometimes she could read him and sometimes she could not.

This was one of those times.

Galen leaned back in his chair watching Brittany. She conversed and joked easily with his brothers and they had definitely warmed up to her. Over breakfast she had told them about her business and in kind, they told her about theirs. That unfortunately extended their stay. He was about to suggest they think about leaving when Jonas remembered their golf game at noon, and the five reluctantly left.

"I like your brothers," Brittany said when Galen returned after walking them to the door with strict orders not to come back anytime soon.

"They're okay." He had sat there and watched her interactions with his siblings, thinking of just how well she would fit in with his family. His parents would adore her; especially his mother. Brittany said she'd never had a family before; well, she had one now. His brothers didn't take to people easily. They were usually guarded and reserved. But they had taken to her.

"Did you sleep well last night?" he asked, walking over to her.

He saw the blush that stained her cheeks when she said, "Yes. I didn't mean to be so much trouble. I see you got me ready for bed and tucked me in."

And I told you a story you probably don't remember, he thought. "You weren't any trouble. I didn't mind taking care of you."

"But you shouldn't have had to. That wasn't part of our agreement, Galen."

Damn the agreement, he wanted to say. Instead he said, "So what are your plans today? We left your car at the house. Do you want to go back and get it now or do you want to wait until later?"

"I'll wait until later, if you don't mind. Do you usually work on your video games on Sunday, as well?"

"It depends on what I have to do to it. Sniper is relatively finished except for a few components. Would you like to see it?"

He could tell by her expression she was surprised he'd asked. "Can I?"

"Sure. Come on."

She followed him to the door that led to his garage. He opened it and then held it for her to precede him through it and down the steps. "Is this a garage or a dungeon?" she threw over her shoulder to ask.

He laughed as he closed the door and followed her downstairs. "In a way it's both. My house is built on a high peak, but the driveway is on a slope, which means you have to drive down to the garage. It's a six-car garage."

"You have that many cars?"

He chuckled. "Not yet, but I'm working on it. I collect vintage cars, specifically muscle cars," he said when they reached the bottom.

She glanced over at him. "What's a muscle car?"

"It's a high-performance automobile that was manufactured in the late sixties and early seventies. I own three now and I'm always looking to add more to my collection."

She glanced around. "This is a huge area and I've never seen a garage floor that's tiled, and with such nice stone pavers."

He smiled. "Thanks. Come on. I'll show you my cars and then I'll let you watch me work with Sniper."

Brittany followed Galen and admired the vintage cars he had in his collection. They were beautiful, all three of them—a 1967 Camaro, a 1969 GTO and a 1968 Road Runner. They went along with his everyday cars, the late-model SUV, Corvette and Mercedes sedan.

"Where did you get your interest in muscle cars?" she asked, admiring the sleek design and craftsmanship of each vehicle. She didn't know a lot about cars, but she could tell these were in great shape. A collector's dream.

"My father. He has his own collection," he explained as he led her over to his work area.

She couldn't believe how spacious his work space was, and how neat and organized. She could see why he preferred working in his garage instead of an off-site office or warehouse. Everything was at his fingertips here.

He offered her the seat next to his and then proceeded to explain how the video game would work and what he needed to do to get it ready for the Video Game Expo in the spring. She could hear the excitement in his voice when he told her about it. She was touched that he was sharing his work with her. He hadn't invited her in here before and she wondered why he was doing so now. Still, it felt good knowing he had allowed her into his private space.

Brittany scooted her chair closer as he talked her through the assembly of one of the components of the game. Everything was being designed on a huge computer screen in front of him. She was amazed at how much graphic art expertise went into the creation of a game, as well as the game engine. The more she watched, the more she admired his skill, proficiency and imagination.

She glanced over at him. His face was set with determination and concentration. But he was her focal point as she studied him, scanned his features with the intensity of a woman who wanted a man.

She liked watching his hands move and remembered those same hands moving over her as his fingertips caressed the curve of her breasts, cupped her backside or slid between her thighs. A rush of heat hit her in the chest as her body responded to the memories. She let out a slow breath.

"Getting bored?" he asked, glancing over at her.

"No, not at all. I enjoy looking at you work." And I enjoy looking at you.

She watched him save whatever program he'd been working on and then turn to her. Galen had a way of looking at her that left her breathless, made her hot. Made the area between her legs tingle.

"You ever make out in the backseat of a car?"

She clamped her mouth shut to keep it from dropping open. Was she really supposed to answer that? Evidently, because he seemed to be waiting on her response. "No."

"You want to try it?" There was that arrogant smile on his face. The one she both loved and detested.

"Before you answer, let me tell you how it will work," he said, leaning closer so that his heated breath came into contact with her skin. "The backseat of the car will be the ending point. We will actually start here in my work space. I want to take you all over it."

His words sent a surge of anticipation through her. Adrenaline pumped through her bloodstream; visual imagery danced in her head. "I'll start off by licking you all over and then going inside you so deep, you won't know where your body ends and mine begins."

He reached out and with the tip of his finger he caressed her arm. She could feel the goose bumps forming there. "And after we make love over in this area a few times..."

A few times? Mercy.

"Then we'll move to the cars. You can take your pick."

Boy, was he generous. In more ways than one. His fingers had moved from her arm and had dropped to her thigh and were now slowly sliding beneath her skirt. One spot he touched made her quiver inside. And she was convinced her panties were getting wet.

"So, Brittany Thrasher, what do you say?"

She couldn't say anything. She wasn't capable of speech. As an intense ache spread all over her body, she reached up and wrapped her arms around his neck. She decided to let her actions show him what she couldn't put into words.

Chapter 17

Galen didn't have a problem with Brittany taking the initiative with this kiss after he'd planted a few sensuous seeds in her mind. He would use any tactic he thought would work. He was determined to bind her to him and they might as well start here, because they did enjoy making love.

And today he intended for there to be plenty of foreplay. When it was all said and done, Brittany would know without a doubt that she was his. Permanently and irrevocably.

While her tongue tangled with his, she began kneading the muscles in his shoulders, heating his blood to flash point. He pulled her out of her chair and into his lap, scooting his own chair back from the table so that her body was practically draped over his.

And then he took over the kiss and decided to seduce her Galen Steele–style. The exploration of her mouth was intense and he intended for his tongue to leave a mark wherever it went. He was on the verge of getting intoxicated just with a kiss and a touch. Then he slid his fingers into her womanly folds, and her groan sent spirals of intense longing right to his crotch, making his erection press hard against the zipper of his jeans.

With her in his arms he stood and stripped her naked in record time, for desire consumed him in a way it never had before. When he was done with hers, he removed his own clothes and noticed her staring down at his erection.

"You want it, Brittany?"

She glanced up at him. "Yes, I want it."

"Then take it."

He didn't have to say the words twice. She eased down in front of him.

"I've never done this before," she said, looking up at him, "but I want so much to do it for you."

He smiled down at her. "Practice makes perfect."

"And if you don't like it?"

"I'm going to like it. Trust me."

She held his gaze for a moment and then said in a soft voice, "I do trust you, Galen."

And then she dipped her head and took him into the warmth of her mouth. Every part of his body, every cell and molecule, quivered in response. Her hand gripped him while her mouth drove him crazy. Using her tongue she covered every inch of him, from the tip all the way to the base.

He reached out and tightened his hand in her hair and

let out a deep guttural groan. Had she actually thought he wouldn't like this? How could he not like the feel of her hot tongue gliding over him, and then pulling him inside the sweet recesses of her mouth? When he felt a deep throbbing about to erupt, he quickly pulled her up and swept her into his arms and placed her on his work desk, spreading her legs in the process.

He sheathed himself with a condom and made good his threat to lick her all over. With erotic caresses his tongue covered every inch of her, intent on giving her the pleasures she thought she could never enjoy. And he didn't let up until he had her on the verge of a climax. But then he didn't really let up; he delved in deeper, using his tongue to deliver powerful strokes. She moaned and writhed beneath his mouth.

And then she screamed, shuddered uncontrollably and clutched the sides of his head as the intense sensations erupted inside her. Sensations Galen felt in his mouth. He hadn't been prepared for a woman like her. He hadn't been prepared to fall in love with her.

But he had.

When he pulled his mouth away while licking his lips, he leaned forward and whispered in her ear, "Now we make out in my car."

Galen knew for the rest of the day he would continue to assault her mind with desire and fill her body with pleasure. He couldn't imagine ever being inside any other woman but her for the rest of his days.

And as he picked her up into his arms and carried her toward his 1969 GTO, he knew that sex between them would never be enough. But he intended to make it a good start.

* * *

Brittany stepped out of the shower and caught her reflection in the vanity mirror and couldn't help but smile. For someone who'd started out the week with hidden pleasures, Galen had done a pretty good job of uncovering them.

Her smile slowly faded when she remembered they had only two more days and then their week together would end. She thought of her mother's home as hers, and had even gone so far as to order repairs to those areas that needed it. And she would be interviewing a painter later today after having lunch with Nikki.

She would leave Saturday morning to fly back to Tampa with plans to return to Phoenix in a week's time. She had finished reading all of her mother's entries in the journal and continued to feel the love her mother had for her. She'd thought about expanding the house and using it to open a home base for Etiquette Matters. She had discussed the idea with Galen, who thought it was a good one.

The only problem she saw—and it was her problem—was how she would handle it when she returned to Phoenix and ran into him with another woman. She knew they didn't have any hold on each other; they weren't even dating. Their agreement was for her to live with him for a week and she was only two days short of fulfilling her terms. But she knew leaving here would be the hardest thing she'd ever had to do.

Because she'd fallen in love with him.

Every time he touched her, made love to her, she fell deeper and deeper in love with him. Emotions washed over her and they were emotions she had no right to feel

where Galen Steele was concerned. He hadn't made
any promises, hadn't alluded to the possibility that he
felt anything for her. To a man like him, sex was sex.
When their affair ended, his affair with another woman
would begin. Her heart ached at the thought, but she
knew it to be true. She had fallen in love with him, but
he hadn't fallen in love with her.

She pulled in a deep breath. That was the story of her
life. None of the couples wanting to adopt a child had
found her worthy, either. But deep down she believed
she had a lot to offer a man. That man just wasn't Galen.

She lifted her chin as she proceeded to rub lotion on
her body. As far as she was concerned it was his loss
and not hers.

"Have you told Brittany how you feel?"

Galen glanced up at Eli. He had stopped by his
brother's office to sign papers for SID. "No, I haven't
told her."

One of Eli's brows rose. "What the hell are you waiting for?"

Galen leaned back in his chair, thinking Eli's question was a good one. The only excuse he could come
up with was that the last few days with Brittany had
been perfect and he hadn't wanted to do anything to
mess them up. He had no idea how she would react to
such an admission on his part, especially because she
seemed content with how things were now.

In the mornings she was over at her place taking care
of her mother's belongings while he worked on perfect-
ing Sniper. Then in the afternoon she would arrive home
and they'd spend time together. One afternoon they'd

gone hiking, another time they'd shared his hot tub, and still another day he'd given her lessons on how to properly use a bow and arrow. He enjoyed having her in his space and spending time with her.

And at night he enjoyed sleeping with her. Making love to her under the moon or the stars overhead. She was so responsive that they had to be the most intense lovemaking sessions of his life. Even the breathless aftermath made him shiver inside just thinking about it.

He also enjoyed waking up with her wrapped in his arms every morning, and making love to her before either of them started their day. And they would talk. She trusted him enough to share her secret with him about Mr. Ponder and why making love to Galen had been a crucial step to overcoming her inability to enjoy sex.

He was well aware that Brittany assumed that in two days she would be leaving, walking out of his life, and he hadn't a clue how to break it to her that that was not how things were going to be.

"Galen?"

He glanced up to find Eli staring at him. "What?"

"When are you going to tell Brittany how you feel about her? Doesn't she leave in a couple of days?"

"Yes, but she'll be back."

"Back to Phoenix but not to your place. She thinks when she leaves here Saturday morning what's between the two of you will be over."

Galen pulled in a deep breath, not surprised Eli knew as much as he did. Brittany had sought him out to handle a couple of legal issues regarding her house. She was trying to get the area rezoned to open the headquarters for Etiquette Matters.

"Nothing between us will be over. I love her," Galen said.

"Then maybe you ought to tell her that. She needs to know she's worthy of being loved."

Galen ran his hand down his face. Over the last few days, even though he'd warned them to stay away, his brothers had revisited anyway and had grown attached to Brittany. They were now her champions and wanted to make sure he would do the right thing by her, although he'd told them from day one what his feelings had been.

"She's never been part of a family and I want so much for her to feel a part of ours."

"Then tomorrow night will be perfect. Thursday-night dinner at Mom's."

Galen's head jerked up. Damn, why hadn't he thought of that? Eli was right. Galen had never brought a woman home to meet his mother before. None of them had. She would have to know the importance of that, wouldn't she? And if she didn't, he would explain things to her.

"That's a good idea."

Eli grinned. "Thank you."

Galen eyed his brother suspiciously. "And just what's in it for you?"

Eli's features broke into a serious expression when he said, "Your happiness."

Galen held his brother's gaze and then nodded. He and his brothers might have inherited Drew's horny genes, but they'd also inherited Eden's caring genes, as well.

"Okay, there's no way after tomorrow night Brittany won't know how I feel."

Once Galen had left his brother's office and slid behind the steering wheel of his car, he pulled out his cell phone and punched in a few numbers.

A feminine voice picked up on the second ring. "Hello."

"Mom, this is Galen. And I'm keeping my promise that you'd be one of the first to know." He couldn't help but smile. His brothers had been the first to know, but there was no reason to tell Eden Steele that.

"Know what?"

"There's a woman I'm interested in." He shook his head and decided to go for broke. "I'm in love with her and I'd like to bring her to dinner tomorrow night."

Chapter 18

Brittany checked her lipstick again before putting the small mirror back in her purse. She then glanced over at Galen as he drove to his parents' home for dinner. "Are you sure I look okay?"

Without taking his eyes off the road, he said, "You look great. I love that outfit, by the way."

She smiled. "Thanks. Nikki and I went shopping yesterday and I bought it then." She had introduced him to Nikki a few days ago. She had been helping her with packing up her mother's things. She felt so very blessed having her best friend back in her life.

"So this is a weekly event for you and your brothers with your parents?" she asked.

"Yes. Just for our family. No outsiders."

Brittany frowned. Then why had she gotten invited?

She shrugged. Evidently Galen felt he would lack manners if he were to not include his houseguest. She felt bad knowing the only reason she'd been invited was because he'd felt compelled to bring her.

"What time do you fly out Saturday morning to return to Tampa?" he asked her.

"Eight." She couldn't help wondering if the reason he was asking was because he was eager for her to leave. Her heart ached at the thought.

"Well, here we are."

Brittany glanced through the window and saw the huge house whose exterior was beautifully decorated for the holidays. It was twice the size of Galen's home. "And this is the house you lived in as a child?" she couldn't help asking.

"Yes. We moved in here when I was in the first grade. My parents knew they wanted a lot of children and went ahead and purchased a house that could accommodate a large family."

Brittany nodded, thinking that made perfect sense.

Galen brought the car to a stop among several others and she said, "Looks like your brothers are here already."

"Yes, it looks that way."

She felt relieved. Over the last few days she'd gotten to know Galen's brothers and truly liked them. She wouldn't feel so out of place with them around. She could just imagine what Galen's mother was going to think when she walked in with him.

"Ready?" Galen asked, glancing over at her.

She released a deep breath and said, "Yes, I'm ready."

* * *

Brittany took a sip of her wine thinking it odd that Galen's parents hadn't asked how they met or how long they'd known each other. It seemed the moment she and Galen had walked in and all eyes turned to them, she'd felt a strange sort of connection to his mother. It was as if beneath all her outer beauty was a heart of gold. Someone beautiful on the inside as well as the outside. And Eden Tyson Steele was beautiful. She didn't look as if she should be the mother of six sons. The woman didn't look a day over forty, if that. And it was plain to see her husband simply adored her.

It was also plain to see that although Galen and his brothers had their mother's eyes, the rest of their features belonged to Drew Steele. The man was tall, dark and definitely handsome, and Brittany could just imagine him being a devilish rogue in his day, capturing the hearts of many women but giving his heart to only one.

She'd asked Galen how his parents had met and he'd said his father owned a trucking company and was doing a run one night from Phoenix to California, filling in for a sick driver, when he came across Eden, who'd stowed away in the back of his truck at a truck stop, in an attempt to get away from an overbearing agent.

The moment Brittany had walked in with Galen, Eden had given her a smile that Brittany felt was truly genuine and the woman seemed pleased that Galen had brought her to dinner with him. Galen's father was kind as well, and it was quite obvious that he loved and respected his sons and was proud of the men they'd become.

Brittany had never been around such a close-knit family.

"You okay?"

She glanced up at Galen and smiled. "Yes, I'm fine."

He'd rarely left her side and when and if he had, one or all of his brothers had been right there. Except for the time his mother asked if she wanted to see how she had personally decorated the courtyard for the holidays.

Brittany had figured the woman had wanted to get her alone to grill her about her life and discovered that had not been the case. They had talked about fashion, movies and things women talk about when they get together. Brittany found herself talking comfortably, and had told Eden about the home she'd inherited from her birth mother. She had found it so easy to talk to Galen's mother and a part of her wished things were different between her and Galen. Eden would be the type of mother-in-law any woman would want to have. But she knew she would never be hers because she and Galen didn't have that sort of relationship. For some strange reason, though, Brittany had a feeling his family thought otherwise.

"So what do you think of my parents?" he leaned close and asked her.

"I think you are blessed to have them. They are super."

"Yes, they are," he agreed. "And what do you think of my mother's courtyard?"

Brittany grinned. "If I wasn't in the holiday spirit before arriving here, I would definitely be now."

Galen threw his head back and laughed, and Brittany couldn't help herself when she joined in with him.

His mother's courtyard looked like a Christmas won-
derland. Beautiful as well as festive.

"Christmas is her favorite holiday," he said, placing
an arm around her shoulders and bringing her closer
to his side.

She lifted her glass to her lips and smiled before taking a sip of her wine. "I can tell."

It didn't take a rocket scientist to see his parents were
taken with Brittany, Galen thought. From the moment
she walked into their home, Drew and Eden had begun
treating her like the daughter they'd never had. Galen
could tell that at first Brittany was overwhelmed, didn't
know what to make of such an overflow of love and
kindness, but then he figured she assumed that's just
the way his parents were.

Not really.

He would be the first to admit his parents were good
people, but even he had noticed how solicitous they
were toward her. And his brothers were no exception.
They flocked around her like the caring brothers they
would become once they married. He had thought of
that word a lot lately and he knew he truly wanted to
marry Brittany. He couldn't imagine his life without her.

They needed to talk, he knew, and he'd start that
conversation in earnest when they returned to his place.
Now he crossed the room to where Brittany stood talking to his parents and brothers.

"Time to go, sweetheart," he said softly.

She smiled over at him. "All right." She then turned
to his parents. "Thanks so much for having me here
tonight."

Eden beamed. "And we look forward to you coming back." She then shifted her gaze to her oldest son. "You will bring her back, Galen, won't you?"

Galen grinned. "Yes, whenever she's in town. If I come, she'll be with me."

"Wonderful!"

Galen noticed on the way back home that Brittany seemed awfully quiet. He knew for sure something was bothering her when they arrived back at his place and he saw her lips quivering. She was mad about something. What? He found out the moment he closed the door behind them.

"How could you do that, Galen?" she asked angrily. "How could you let your parents assume I meant something to you and I'd be back to have dinner with them again when you don't want me? Do you know how that made me feel?"

Yes, Galen thought, leaning back against the door. He knew precisely how she felt. She had gone through life assuming no one wanted her. In her eyes, she had been the flawed baby no one wanted to adopt. Not worthy of anyone's love. Well, he had news for her and he might as well set her straight right now and not while making love to her later tonight as he'd planned.

He moved away from the door and crossed the distance separating them. When he came to a stop in front of her, he saw the tears she was trying hard to hold back and promised himself that he would never let her shed a single tear for thinking no one wanted her.

"It should have made you feel loved, Brittany, because you are. My parents treated you the way they did tonight because they knew what you evidently don't.

Granted, I've never said the words, but I'd thought my actions spoke loud and clear. I love you."

He could tell she didn't get it for a moment because she just stood there and stared at him. And then she spoke. "What did you say?"

He had no trouble repeating it. "I said I love you. I love you so much I ache. I believe I fell in love with you that day in New York when you saw me at my worst. And when I saw you again here in Phoenix, I knew I would do whatever it took to have you with me, even concocting a plan to bid on the house you wanted just so you'd stay a week here with me. Of course I didn't think you would go for it, but I wanted you to have the house anyway. In fact, when you get back to Tampa you'll have the packet Eli sent giving you the house free and clear *before* you decided to take my offer."

Brittany blinked. "But, if that was the case, then why did you still make me think I had to stay here for a week?"

He gave her an arrogant smile. "Because I wanted you in my bed. I'm a Steele."

She just stood there and stared at him for a long moment and then a smile trembled on her lips. "Your conceit is showing again," she pointed out.

"Sorry."

"I'm not. I love you just the way you are. And I do love you, Galen. I was so afraid you couldn't love me."

Another smile touched his lips, this one filled with care, concern and sincerity. "You are an easy person to love, Brittany. If there is any way I could redo your childhood, I would. But I think you're the person that you are because of it and the challenges you had to face," he said, reaching out and caressing her cheek with his thumb.

"But for the rest of your days, I will make up for all the love you didn't get. I will love you and honor you."

"Oh, Galen." Tears she couldn't hold back streamed down her face.

It was then that Galen swept her off her feet and into his arms to carry her up the stairs. "I told my brothers how I felt about you that day they met you and advised my parents yesterday. Tonight they treated you just as they should have—as a person who will soon become an official member of our family."

He looked down at her and paused on the stair. "Will you marry me?"

Brittany smiled up at him. "Yes! Yes, I will marry you."

Galen grinned as he continued walking up the stairs to his bedroom. "Just so you'll know, I'm having your ring specially designed by Zion."

Brittany's mouth dropped open. "I'm getting a ring by Zion?"

Galen threw his head back and laughed when he placed her on the bed. "Yes." He knew any jewelry by Zion was the rave because Zion was the First Lady's personal jeweler.

She beamed. "I feel special."

"Always keep that thought, because you are."

Galen glanced down at the woman he had placed on his bed. His soul mate. The woman he would love forever. The thought nearly overwhelmed him. "And just so you'll know, I've cleared my work schedule. I'm going with you back to Tampa."

Surprise lit her face. "You are?"

"Yes. I don't intend to let you out of my sight." He dipped his knee on the bed. "Now come here." When she lifted a brow, he added, "Please."

Brittany chuckled as she moved toward Galen and when he wrapped her in his arms and kissed her, she felt completely loved by the one man who had discovered all her hidden pleasures. "How could things be this way for us this soon?"

He understood her question and had a good reason for what probably seemed like madness. "My mother has always warned her sons that we're like our father in a lot of ways," he said. "We're known to be skirt chasers until we meet the one woman who will claim our hearts. You are that woman for me, Brittany. I realized just how empty my life has been until this week while you were here with me. I love you."

She fought back tears in her eyes when she said, "And I love you, too."

And then Galen kissed her and she knew a lot of people would think their affair had been rather short, but she knew it had been just like it was meant to be. Now they would embark upon a life together filled with romance and passion.

Epilogue

Four months later

Galen glanced around the room at all the Steeles in attendance. The last time they'd all gotten together had been at Donovan's wedding in New York. Now they'd all assembled here in Phoenix to watch the first of Drew's boys take the plunge. And very happily, he might add.

Nikki had been Brittany's bridesmaid and his father had been his best man. They'd wanted it simple and decided to have a wedding on the grounds of the home Brittany's mother had left her. Brittany felt her mother's presence there and wanted to start their life off surrounded by love.

"So, what were the nasty things you said to me when

I told you I was getting married?" his cousin Donovan said, pulling him out of his reverie.

Galen smiled. "Okay, that was before I knew better. Before I understood the power of love." He glanced over to where Brittany stood with his mother and his heart expanded twice the size.

"You have a beautiful bride and I wish the two of you happiness always."

"Thanks, Donovan."

Deciding his mother had taken up enough of his wife's time, Galen crossed the room and when Brittany glanced up and saw him, she smiled. She had been a beautiful bride and looked absolutely radiant. And when he opened his arms, she stepped into his embrace. They would be leaving later that day to fly to London where they would catch a ship for a twelve-day Mediterranean cruise.

"I love you, Mrs. Steele," he whispered, holding her tight in his arms.

She smiled up at him. "And I love you."

Over his shoulder he saw his mother eyeing his brothers, who seemed oblivious of her perusal. Galen knew exactly how their mother's mind worked. She was thinking, "One down, five to go."

His brothers would deal with Eden Steele as they saw fit. Galen knew he would have his hands full with the beautiful, sexy woman in his arms. She would continue to teach him manners and he intended to make sure her pleasures were never hidden again.

"Are you ready for your wedding gift now, Galen?"

He arched a brow. "I have another one?" A couple of days ago she had given him a new digital camera. And she'd given him a book on manners. He had given her a gold bracelet with the inscription "Galen's Lady." And he'd given her a toy yellow cab to replace the one he'd taken from her that day in New York.

"Yes, you have another one. I'm not going to blind-fold you but you must promise to close your eyes and keep them closed until I say you can open them."

"All right."

He closed his eyes and felt himself being led no telling where, and after a few minutes, Brittany instructed, "You can open them now, Galen."

He did and sucked in a quick breath when he saw the car he'd wanted, the 1969 Chevelle, parked only a few feet away from where he stood. He couldn't believe it. It looked beautiful, but then when he glanced over at Brittany, he knew she was the most beautiful thing in his life.

"But how?" he asked, barely able to get the words out past his excitement.

She smiled. "After you confessed to eavesdropping on my and Nikki's conversation that day, I felt bad that you missed out on the chance to bid for this car because of me, so I gave your brothers the job of locating it for me. Luckily, they did. I hope you like it."

"Oh, sweetheart, I love it, but not as much as I love you." He pulled her into his arms intent on showing her how much. He took her mouth in a lingering kiss, not caring if his brothers or any of the other wedding guests could see them.

She was his and he was hers. Forever.

* * * * *

HARLEQUIN
PLUS

Try the best multimedia
subscription service for romance
readers like you!

Read, Watch and Play.

Experience the easiest way to get
the romance content you crave.

Start your **FREE TRIAL** at
<u>www.harlequinplus.com/freetrial</u>.